the distant land of my father

Bo Caldwell has published short stories in numerous literary magazines. Her non-fiction writing includes a long-running series of personal essays in the *Washington Post Magazine*. Born in 1955 in Oklahoma City, she is a former Stegner Fellow in creative writing at Stanford University, and now lives in Northern California with her husband, novelist Ron Hansen, and her two children. This is her first novel.

the distant land of my father

:: bo caldwell ::

WILLIAM HEINEMANN : LONDON

First published in the United Kingdom in 2002 by William Heinemann

3 5 7 9 10 8 6 4 2

William Heinemann
The Random House Group Limited
20 Vauxhall Bridge Road, London SW1V 2SA

Random House Australia (Pty) Limited
20 Alfred Street, Milsons Point, Sydney,
New South Wales 2061, Australia

Random House New Zealand Limited
18 Poland Road, Glenfield,
Auckland 10, New Zealand

Random House (Pty) Limited
Endulini, 5a Jubilee Road
Parktown 2193, South Africa

The Random House Group Limited Reg. No. 954009

www.randomhouse.co.uk

A CIP catalogue record for this book is available
from the British Library

Papers used by Random House are natural, recyclable products made from
wood grown in sustainable forests. The manufacturing processes conform to the
environmental regulations of the country of origin

Designed by Benjamin Shaykin
Composition by Candace Creasy,
Blue Friday Type & Graphics
Typeset in Wessex and Trade Gothic

ISBN 0 434 01003 0 (hb)
ISBN 0 434 00888 5 (tpb)

Printed and bound in Great Britain by
Clays Ltd, St Ives plc

AUTHOR'S NOTE

With a few exceptions, this book uses the Wade-Giles system for spelling Chinese terms and places. This is the system that was used by foreigners living in Shanghai during the time the story takes place. Wade-Giles was in use from the nineteenth century until 1958, when the People's Republic of China introduced a new system of romanization called Pinyin, which was then adopted by the United Nations as the standard form for spelling Chinese words in 1977. I am grateful to Professor Xiaobin Jian of the College of William and Mary for his generous help with the spelling of Chinese phrases in these pages.

I'm also very grateful to Heather Washam, who encouraged me day after day, chapter after chapter, and to my husband, Ron Hansen, who read and reread, giving me hope and inspiration and support of every kind with every reading.

For my mother, Hester,
and in memory of my father, John

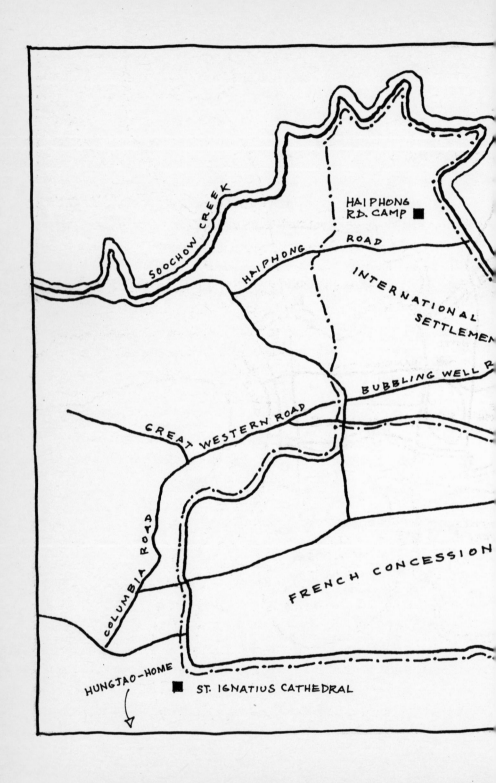

SOOCHOW CREEK

HAIPHONG
RD. CAMP ■

HAIPHONG   ROAD

INTERNATIONAL

SETTLEMEN

BUBBLING WELL R

GREAT WESTERN ROAD

COLUMBIA ROAD

FRENCH CONCESSION

HUNGJAO-HOME ■ ST. IGNATIUS CATHEDRAL

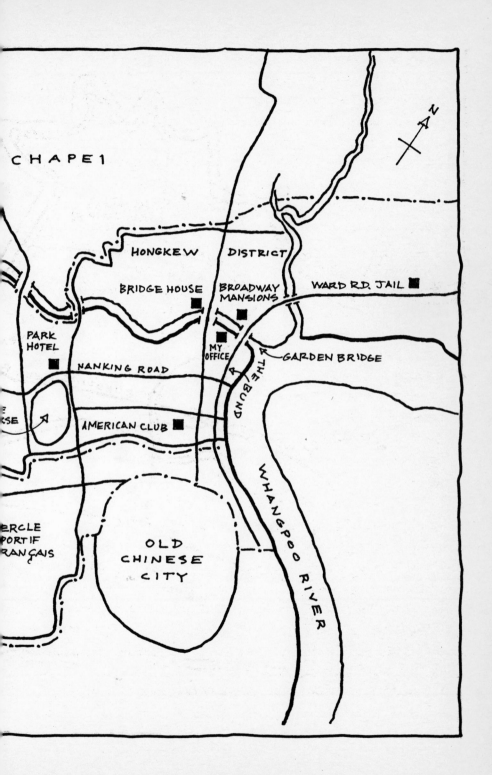

prologue

MY FATHER WAS A MILLIONAIRE in Shanghai in the 1930s. Polo ponies, a Sikh chauffeur, a villa on eight acres in Hungjao, in the western part of the city. Nights out with my mother at the Cercle Sportif Français, the Venus Café, the Cathay Hotel, the Del Monte— these were the details of his life. He was also an insurance salesman and a smuggler, an importer-exporter and a prisoner, a borrower and a spender, leading, much of the time, a charmed life, always seeming to play the odds and for a long time coming out on top. On the day he was born, in the province of Shantung, neighbors presented my missionary grandparents, the only Americans for miles, with noodles in great abundance and one hundred chicken eggs, in honor of their son's birth.

In May of 1961 when he died of cardiac arrest, the task of sorting and dispensing with his by-then modest belongings was left to me. My mother had died six years earlier and I was, as his will stated, his only issue. A week after his death I spent the day cleaning out the small room he had rented in an old Victorian rooming house on

Bunker Hill in downtown Los Angeles. I had almost finished when
I saw, high on a shelf, a wooden fruit crate that I hadn't noticed until
then. I stood on a chair and tried to pull it down. It was heavy, and
I had to work to lift it from the shelf. I carried it carefully to the
single bed in the corner of the room and sat down to see what it was.

It was for me; that part was clear immediately. On top of everything was an envelope with my name on it in my father's careful
script. I opened the envelope and took out a letter, typed on his old
manual typewriter, and for a moment I thought, *I can't do this. It's
going to hurt too much.* But the fact that it was from him made it feel
almost as though he was there with me, and I took a deep breath and
began to read.

March 20, 1959

My dear Anna,

*I don't know when you will read this. I say "when" instead
of "if" because I am hopeful that you will read it someday–
I just don't know when. I have just come from your house,
where I asked you to do me the difficult favor of reading my
will. As I told you, I have no large estate to leave you. I am
simply trying, at this late stage of my life, to do things right,
which is also the reason you have never seen where I live.
I'm too proud, as I'm sure you will understand why when you
eventually do come here, but I won't worry about that for now.*

*You are holding much of my life in your hands: journals
that I kept during my years in Shanghai, along with a few
books that describe Shanghai as it was when I lived there.
From the vantage point of the present, there is not much about
that part of my life that I am proud of. But I am, in a strange
way, proud of having these journals. I knew when I wrote them
that they were for you, one of the rare incidents of foresight in
my life, and one for which I am grateful.*

I know you, Anna—you're wondering why. Why would I tell you this now, and why wouldn't I talk about it with you face to face? The answer, plain and simple, is that it was just too hard. I could never have explained everything that happened, and I didn't want my time with you muddied with my failings. So I am depending on these journals to explain what happened so long ago in that place that I loved.

I'll start with this: I have made more mistakes in my life than I can number, and I cannot begin to count their cost. I've squandered more money than people make in several lifetimes. I've betrayed people I loved, and I've lied and been negligent and careless. I will not enumerate the particular ways in which I hurt your mother. They are too private, and one of my few good qualities is that I have never been one to display my wounds. I will tell you that I have come to see that your mother was light and map and destination for me. Losing her is the regret of my life.

But I have done one thing that cancels out all of those huge errors: I have left the world with you. You are my one accomplishment, my one asset, my estate and my bequest, worth far more than all of the millions I lost so long ago. And I guess that's the reason for all these pages: they're my attempt to explain, in the hope that you will understand why I did what I did.

In Shanghai, when your mother and I first arrived, there was a woman at the Cercle Sportif Français that I have never forgotten. The vocalist in the nightclub was singing "Body and Soul," and I thought it was the right song for this woman. She was sitting alone. No one spoke to her, no one waved to her, no one seemed to know her. She wore an emerald green cheongsam, and her earrings and high heels matched. She sipped a glass of crème de menthe, and she even held a green cigarette. I was awestruck. The next night, your mother and I were at the Del Monte and there she was again, still alone, only this time *in red. A few nights after that I saw her at the Tower Restaurant on the roof of the Cathay Hotel. That night she was in blue.*

When I looked at that woman, I thought, She is what Shanghai means. It's a place where you can be anything you choose. Reinvent yourself every day, if you want, a thousand times, if you want. Anything can happen here. I had never felt like a man with many choices, but at that time in Shanghai, anything seemed possible.

I have just finished reading through all of this. It has been difficult to go over the past, after so many years. There is much that I have worked hard to forget, and recalling some of it is painful. But I want you to know of it. Do what you will with these pages after you have read them. They were written with love, for you, Anna, my only child.

Attached to the letter was a hand-drawn map of Shanghai, and I read the places my father had marked: *My office, Broadway Mansions, The Bund, St. Ignatius Cathedral, Hungjao–Home.* I put the letter and map aside and looked inside the box, where I found several account-ing ledgers, the kind I remembered my father using for business when I was a child. They were black with the word LEDGER in red letters on the front cover, and their covers were worn smooth, their once-sharp corners softened. Underneath them were some books: *All About Shanghai–A Standard Guidebook*, published in 1934; histories of the city; and memoirs by people who had lived there when my father did. And I knew what my father was doing: he was, once again, teaching me about Shanghai, something he'd done in my childhood. Only this time he was telling me about himself as well.

I flipped through one of the ledgers and read some lines at ran-dom: *At the start, it wasn't so bad. You wore your armband, you did as you were told, and the Japanese didn't bother you so long as you kept to your-self.* I flipped forward a few more pages and read of a place called

Haiphong Road, and of Bridge House and Fletcher's tree and a year spent alone. I flipped further and saw Ward Road Jail, interrogations and questionings, demands for a confession. And I saw that I held the missing stories of my father's life.

In the months that followed, I read and reread my father's journals. I read the books as well, and others like them that I found at the Pasadena Main Library. For nearly a year, I read about Shanghai as though it could save me. And it probably did, in a way. Thinking about the city my father loved eased the huge ache that his death had caused. And as I read and imagined and began to understand, scenes from my childhood played before me like long-forgotten photographs, and I found myself in the distant land of my father.

dust

SHANGHAI, JUNE 1937, the air hot and muggy. My father stood on the verandah of our home, a villa on Hungjao Road in the western suburbs outside of the International Settlement. His back was to me as he looked out at the expanse of lawn that to me, at six, seemed vast as an ocean. He faced east, toward the Bund and the Whangpoo River, and I thought I smelled the river's familiar sharpness, a grimy mix of factory smoke and seaweed and fish, though the Whangpoo was some ten miles away.

It was dusk, a word that I understood as "dust," which made sense to me, one of those few words whose meaning matched its sound. That was how the world seemed at that hour: slightly dusty, softened and dimly covered in some eerie talc, the sharp edges chalk-picture blurry. My father had played polo that afternoon and still wore his riding clothes, off-white jodhpurs and a jersey shirt, the color so creamy it appeared liquid, and black leather boots that I wanted to touch to see if they were real. They seemed somehow conjured up. He, too, seemed conjured up, in that dim light. He leaned on the verandah wall, his drink next to him, a tumbler that held Four Roses, golden, the color of caramel, and it was as though the Scotch softened everything: the night, the stone wall, the leaves of the plane trees just beyond, the sharp edges of the crystal tumbler, my father himself.

My father stood very still, gazing out at a city that he loved. To me, it was simply home, no more, no less. But as I stood in the doorway, watching him, waiting for him to feel my presence, I felt certain inside that I was in exactly the right place: this house, this doorway, this night, this father. I wore a white cotton nightgown that had been sewn by hand. I was clean, just out of the bath, my long brown hair a cool wet trail down my back. Chu Shih, our cook, had given me long-life noodles and jasmine tea for dinner, then helped me get ready for bed so that I could say good night to my parents before they went out.

I heard my mother's voice then, and I turned from the doorway before my father saw me. She was descending the long curved staircase, and she wore a wine-colored silk dress with a border of pearls sewn into the neckline. My mother's name was Genevieve, and it suited her: she was elegant and graceful, and was always known only by her full name, with one exception: to my father she was Eve, and when he said her name, he did so intimately. Our last name, Schoene—pronounced "show-en"—meant beautiful or handsome in German, and I thought it suited both of my parents. When I was afraid, I would repeat their names to myself, and the sound of those names lulled me and made me feel safe: Joseph and Genevieve Schoene.

My mother smiled at me, and I suddenly wanted her not to go out. I wanted her close, though there was no reason to be anxious. This was just an ordinary night. My parents went out most evenings. I learned only later, when my mother and I had moved to the United States, the startling fact that parents usually stayed at home with their children in the evenings.

My mother did not share my father's passion for Shanghai, but rather held the city at arm's length. It was an entity she did not want to know better, and she was every bit as diffident toward it as my father was affectionate. He knew every part of the city, while my mother knew only what she had to. She seemed to regard it as a temporary post, not a home, and she used what she called her landmark system. In each neighborhood, she chose a starting point, and she always started from that place, regardless of where she had to end up. In the French Concession it was the Cercle Sportif Français, a nightclub she liked on Route Cardinal Mercier. In the International Settlement it was the Sun Sun Department Store at the corner of Tibet and Nanking Road. On the Bund it was the brass lions in front of the Hongkong and Shanghai Bank. Her plan seemed to work; my mother was never lost. I understood her system, for I had a landmark of my own, a place I always started from to get wherever I was going, a reference point for everything I did. It was my father.

My father was, from my careful observations of him, a person who solved problems. When I was five, I accidentally swallowed a Reese's cinnamon drop whole, and I began to choke. My father stood only a few feet away; we were at the home of his friend Will Marsh, and he was just saying good night. He glanced at me, looked back at his friend, looked at me again, and said, "Excuse me." Then he simply picked me up by my ankles, held me upside down, and laughed when the cinnamon drop popped out of my mouth. For a long time, his ability to fix whatever was wrong was a given of my childhood.

There were other givens as well. My mother's elegance, her patient manner, her propriety and composure. She taught me never to say I was full after a meal, but only that I had "had a sufficiency." Her beauty was a given. I knew even as a young child that she was beautiful, not the way children *think* their mothers are—I knew she was, from the way men stared when she entered the room, the way other women regarded her, the intensity with which my father watched her. For a long time, her beautiful long hair was a given, always worn in a chignon at the nape of her neck. It seemed somehow private, the most intimate part of her, as though it held secrets she would never divulge. Her intense yet somehow odd devotion to my father was also a given. She was like his moon: she circled only him, yet always at a distance.

On that summer evening, when my mother reached the bottom of the stairs, she glanced around her as though getting her bearings. It was a familiar gesture; she was looking for my father, and it was what she always did first when she entered a room or a house or a garden. Now she glanced about and, not seeing him, looked at me.

"He's outside," I said simply.

She nodded, then leaned toward me, smoothing the wet strands of my bangs off my forehead. "You're warm, Anna."

"Can I see your hair?" I asked.

She stooped so that she was closer to my height. She did this gracefully, a small miracle in her long, fitted dress. She smelled like Chanel No. 5, and just under it, a trace of lilac from her bath. She turned so that I could see her back, and her hair was the way it always was, bound at the nape of her neck. I leaned close to see what she was using to hold it there. On the carved mahogany dresser in her room was a Venetian leather jewelry box that held in its crimson velvet lining more than a dozen fasteners and combs made of ivory, tortoiseshell, silver, jade. Tonight she wore my favorites: two intricately carved ivory needles that intersected and held her hair perfectly in place.

We heard my father's footsteps then. My mother looked up, about to stand, and I asked the question that was always in my mind but which I had never voiced. "Do you love him more, or me?"

She did not hesitate. "I love you both," she said simply. And then she rose, smoothed her skirt, and went outside to join him.

They left a short time later, after my father had showered and shaved and dressed in a dinner coat. He whistled "Moonglow" as he came downstairs, and I knew he was in good spirits. My mother stood at the large window in the kitchen, sipping a glass of sherry, waiting for him. He came into the room and smiled at her. And then he saw me, sitting at the table, drawing.

"*You*," he said, and he headed toward me and seemed as large as the huge brass lions that guarded the entrance of the Hongkong and Shanghai Bank. "And now for *you*." And in two strides he reached me and lifted me from my chair and held me so high that I felt the closeness of the ceiling just above my head. I breathed in his scent of Old Spice and Four Roses and Philippine cigars, and I was certain that my father was strong enough to hold up the world. His hands were warm and firm and huge around my rib cage, and I wanted him to never put me down.

But he did, of course, and my sides stayed warm from his grip as he roughly kissed my cheek and held the door for my mother and headed into the still night, whistling again. I heard the sound of car doors as my parents slid into the backseat of the Packard, which waited for them outside, then the crunch of gravel as Mei Wah, my father's Sikh chauffeur, walked to the front of the car, and then the sound of his door. And then I heard the even hum of the Packard's engine, a sound I came to dread, as it eased toward the street.

I went out on the verandah. My father's glass was still on the wall, empty except for its strong scent of Scotch. I watched the car slowly make its way toward the street, its red taillights bright. When it reached the end of the driveway and left the gravel to meet the road, it blew out a small cloud of dirt, like a kiss, and I took a deep breath and felt the fine dust of my father's presence, familiar, another given, filling the cracks and covering the surface of my life.

shanghai

WHEN I WAS A CHILD, my father handed Shanghai down to me as though it were my inheritance, a family treasure meant only for me. He took pains to teach me about the city, and there was an urgency in that teaching that said, *Listen, Anna, this is important, remember it.* He said he admired its aliveness, its possibilities, its spirit. I understood that he wanted me to love Shanghai too, and so I listened and I tried to see what he saw, and I remembered what I was taught, but not because I cared about Shanghai. Because I loved my father and wanted to please him.

My father differed from most of Shanghai's foreign residents at that time, British and Europeans and Americans–Shanghailanders, they were called–who lived in the city for decades and took from it without hesitation. My father looked down on them, and although he was wealthy, we lived more simply than most of the foreigners my parents knew. We had only a few servants, and from the time I was five and able to dress myself and put myself to bed, our cook was the closest thing to an amah, or nanny, for me, an unusual situation and one that my mother had protested at first. But my father won her over, and by the time I was six, Chu Shih and Mei Wah were the only servants who lived with us. These things seemed to make my father feel that he was right in chastising the more ostentatious foreigners, who, he said, were houseguests without any manners, intruders who'd simply taken over their host's home. Their appropriation was made easier because of extraterritoriality and the fact that at that time Shanghai was really three cities: the International Settlement, the French Concession, and the Chinese city. Foreigners in the Settlement and Concession were subject not to China's laws, but to the laws of their home countries, which made them feel right at home on Chinese soil.

But for my father, China was home. He was born in the north, in Tsao Chou Fu in the province of Shantung, to Nazarene missionary parents. He grew up there and did not come to the United States until he was sixteen, when his parents were on furlough. When they returned to China two years later, he stayed in the United States and went to Vanderbilt University, where he met my mother at a frater-nity mixer. He approached her because she was the most beautiful girl there; my mother said she liked him because he had nerve and was far more straightforward than the other boys. When he gradu-ated in 1931 and married my mother a few weeks later, it seemed only natural to him to go home to China. He had, after all, lived there for far more years than he'd lived in the United States. And although my mother was doubtful—she was a Californian, eager to remain one, and Vanderbilt had been more than far enough from home—my father convinced her. It would only be for a few years, he said, of course they wouldn't spend their whole *lives* in China. She finally said yes, despite the objections of her parents, particularly her mother, who did not trust my father's easy charm. But my mother simply said it wouldn't be for long, and in the end, there was nothing her parents could do.

My missionary grandparents had returned to Shantung province and started a village clinic there. A small cure was worth a hundred hours of preaching, my grandfather said, and although neither of my father's parents had extensive medical training, they were able to provide basic care. They taught hygiene, and they cleaned cuts and boils. They treated skin diseases, blood poisoning, and eye afflictions. They gave cholera inoculations and tetanus shots to newborns to prevent lockjaw, and santonin for worms. They baptized infants dying of smallpox, and they instructed the sick in the teachings of Christ.

It was my father's hope to help his parents in their work, and to start by going to Peking to study medicine at the Rockefeller Institute. He and my mother left for China in March of 1932, sailing from San Francisco to Shanghai on the NYK Line's *Chichibu Maru*. From there my father planned to travel north to Peking, but when they arrived in Shanghai, they were told that Peking was unsafe. The Japanese had recently occupied it, and nothing was certain. Well, they'd wait until it *was* safe, my father said, and he took the first job he could find in Shanghai, as an automobile claims adjuster for American Asiatic Underwriters, starting at one hundred dollars a week.

And then his life changed: six months after his arrival in Shanghai, he received word that his father had died of diphtheria. A month later, his mother died of the same disease. My father was devastated, and despite my mother's attempts at encouragement, he gave up his plans for medical training.

He turned instead to business; he had to do something while he and my mother decided what to do next. After six months with American Asiatic Underwriters he became a claims adjuster for foreign companies, and soon after that he started importing Dodge cars and trucks, which was easy because he knew all the car dealers, thanks to the auto claims business. Before long, something he'd never expected happened: he began to make money. With his success, he stopped thinking about going to Peking. My mother suggested that they just go home—*her* home, she meant, Los Angeles—where my father could start his own business. He had enough money now. But he wouldn't consider it. There was far too much opportunity to pass up. Why would anyone leave now? *This* was home, at least for now.

My father was a good businessman, and he had some things working in his favor that others lacked. For one, because he'd been raised in China, he was fluent in Mandarin, unusual for a foreigner. On hearing him speak for the first time, Chinese were struck by his command of the language, and from the time I was small, he made sure I knew a little as well. *Ai* was love, *fuch'in* was father, *much'in* mother, and *nüerh* was daughter—me. *Lai pa!*, come here, he'd call to me, and when my mother came in from a day of shopping, the chauffeur's arms loaded with boxes, he'd say, *T'iênhsia!*, everything under the sky! The word *coolie* was from *k'uli*, bitter strength, a definition I understood when I saw how hard coolies worked. When my father smoothly handed a bill to his barber after a haircut, or to a waiter for bringing him a newspaper, he'd lean close to me and whisper, *Cumshaw*, a Shanghai word whose literal meaning was "grateful thanks" but had come to mean simply "tip." And later, as we clinked glasses over a lunch of long-life noodles at Sun Ya's, my father's glass filled with Chefoo beer, mine with jasmine flower tea, he'd watch me, waiting for me to remember, until I said, *Kanpei*, bottoms up!

He didn't stop with the meanings of the words. When he knew them, he taught me their origins as well, a part of his thoroughness. Shanghai meant "on the sea" and was an early name for the city, from the time, centuries ago, when it was only a fishing village. And while Shanghai wasn't exactly on the sea—it was some fifty-four miles from the Pacific, my father pointed out—there was plenty of water. The Whangpoo River, a tributary to the Yangtze, flowed along the eastern side of the city, and Soochow Creek ran from west to east along the north, then met the Whangpoo.

That was where the Bund started. It was Shanghai's major thoroughfare, a wide boulevard that ran along the waterfront. While geographically it was on the east side of the city, it was really the city's heart, for it was everything to Shanghai: main street, waterfront, downtown, business and financial district, promenade. On the east side was the muddy Whangpoo River, winding its way toward the Yangtze, twelve miles away. Shanghai was a trading port, and the Whangpoo was a traffic jam of every kind of vessel. There were foreign warships and cruisers that my father named as we walked along the river—the HMS *Cumberland*, the USS *Augusta*, the Japanese *Idzumo*—and cargo ships and passenger liners from all over the world: the Messageries Maritimes Line, the Cathay American Line, the Nippon Yusen Kaisha Line, Britain's *Empress of Asia*. Next to them were sloops and freighters, barges and ferries, and finally the smaller ones, the ones I liked, sampans and junks that looked like water spiders from the shore.

Beside the river was a promenade that was more European than Chinese. Facing it were the offices of all of the large *hongs*, the Western trading firms and banks. That was what people first saw when they reached Shanghai: facades made of granite and stone, a clock tower, a green dome, marble columns, and a pair of huge bronze lions that told you Shanghai was a place to be reckoned with.

:: :: ::

On a Saturday morning in July 1937, my father came to my room early and woke me with a whisper. "Your mother needs her sleep," he said softly. "Get up and get dressed and come downstairs. It's time to go."

I nodded, and as I got up, I knew from the warm, still air in my room that the day was already hot. Chu Shih had told me that Chinese weather forecasts were based on the cycles of the moon, and this time of July was called *tashu*, great heat. It exhausted my mother.

Every other year we'd escaped it by taking a steamer up to the port of Tsingtao, *green island*, on Kiaochow Bay, to the north of Shanghai. We'd stay in a cottage there, a place my mother said she loved because the white sandy beaches reminded her of Southern California, and because the place was a relief from the flatness and humidity of Shanghai. But that year she refused to leave the city. "Things are a little uncertain," was all she said, and when I'd asked my father what she meant, he said, "That's just how it is," which meant he didn't want to talk about it.

I put on a summer dress and white socks, then slid my feet into shoes that had damp insides and rims of mold in the toes, normal for summer in Shanghai. I hurried downstairs, knowing what the day would hold and happy with the prospect of it. My father and I were going to the Bund, which was exactly what we did every Saturday, always early, and always by ourselves.

He was waiting for me in the kitchen, drumming his fingers on the butcher board and staring out the south window at the Chinese elm he'd planted the week before. His father had taught him about growing things when he was a child, and although it was unusual in Shanghai to find a wealthy businessman digging around in the garden, my father did so constantly, planting and replanting, pruning and examining, caring for elm trees and magnolias and Chinese junipers as though they were his wards. There were plane trees with mottled trunks whose bark I liked to peel when no one was looking, Hankow willows that bent in the breeze like gentle ghosts, a blackwood acacia, angel's tears narcissus with their small white flowers, and—my father's favorite—yellow and coral and pink cathedral roses that bloomed recklessly and, my mother said, far too long, all the way through September.

When I walked into the kitchen, he turned from the window. "That elm's roots aren't taking hold," he said, the same thing he'd said the night before. He handed me his idea of breakfast—a handful of sugared lotus seeds and a boiled Chefoo pear to eat in the car—then he swooped me up and carried me outside.

Mei Wah was my father's age and had been his chauffeur for years. He drove us the five miles to downtown Shanghai in my father's Packard, which smelled of Mei Wah's patchouli and Egyptian cigarettes, a scent that I loved because it was mysterious and familiar at the same time. We headed east across the city along Bubbling Well Road to where it turned into Nanking Road, then north along the Bund. We crossed Soochow Creek on the Garden Bridge, the last bridge before the creek met the Whangpoo. And then Mei Wah pulled over, and my father and I got out.

"In front of the Park Hotel at two," my father said.

Mei Wah nodded, then pulled away from the bridge.

My father and I walked the short distance to the Broadway Mansions, a redbrick apartment building with staggered terraces that looked like giant steps. We took the elevator up and got out on the top floor, the Foreign Correspondents Club, where my father nodded to some American journalists he knew. One of them winked at me as though we shared a secret, and I smiled, then followed my father out to the terrace that overlooked the Bund, so that we could find out what I knew.

We stepped outside into heat so thick it wasn't like air. It had rained the day before, and everything felt wet. My father seemed not to notice. Sixteen storeys below, the Bund was spread out like a gift, and he looked at it as though it were something of great beauty. I stared, too; it seemed as if we could see the whole world from where we stood. I spotted the huge magnolia tree in the Public Gardens, tiny from here, and the bandstand where people had picnics in the summer before listening to the Municipal Orchestra on Saturday evenings. A little further down were the silkworm mulberry trees that grew next to the iron benches set along the river's edge.

Finally my father spoke. "How many buildings do you think you can name, Anna?" he asked. "More than last week?"

I nodded. My back was damp and the thin linen of my dress stuck to my skin, but I tried not to notice it. This was important, and I wanted high marks. The buildings along the Bund stared back at me as though they, too, were waiting for me to start, a dare. Finally I took a breath and pointed to the first buildings on the other side of the Garden Bridge. "The British Consulate," I began, and I looked down at its huge gates and expansive lawn, all of it guarded by Sikhs in red turbans. "And then the Russian Consulate." Words I knew but didn't understand.

My father nodded. "That's a start," he said, his voice restrained.

"Then the trading firms and banks," I said cautiously. "The NYK Line, then the Banque . . ." I paused, trying to remember how to say the word.

"De l'Indochine," my father said quietly. "Go on."

"Then the Glenn Line," I said, "and Jardine Matheson." I took a breath, my confidence gaining slightly. "Then Yangtze Insurance, the Yokohama Specie Bank, and the Bank of China."

"And then?" My father shook a cigarette from the package of Lucky Strikes that was in the pocket of his seersucker coat. He lit it slowly, waiting for me to continue.

"And then, at Nanking Road, the Cathay." I stared down at one of the busiest corners in Shanghai, the intersection of the Bund and Nanking Road, marked by the green pyramid tower of the Cathay Hotel, twenty storeys tall. My father had taken me there, and I remembered a place as lovely as a dream: rose drapes, crystal lights, a dance floor so polished it looked wet, paintings of dragons on the ceiling.

My father rested his hand on my head and smoothed my hair. "That's good, Anna," he said, "you're learning," and I savored both his affection and his approval, more valuable and certainly more rare. "Listen and I'll tell you the rest."

And then he continued down the Bund as I tried to pay attention so that I could do better next week. "Across from the Cathay is the Palace Hotel, where your mother likes to eat lunch and go to the tea dances. Then the Chartered Bank of India, America, and China; the North China Daily News; the Russo-Chinese Bank; the Bank of Communications; the Customs House, with Big Ching on top."

He paused and I whispered, "Big Ching," for luck. It was thought that Big Ching brought all of Shanghai good luck. There had been fewer fires since the clock was built, which the Chinese said was because of the chimes. The god of fire confused them with fire alarms, and concluded that Shanghai had enough fires without his sending more.

My father continued. "Next there's the Hongkong and Shanghai Bank, Anna. That's the largest bank in the Far East. You see it?" I nodded and gazed at white pillars and a green dome and huge bronze doors, then at the two bronze lions that stood guard at the entrance. One lion roared, the other rested. They, too, brought good luck, if you rubbed their noses.

"And then," he said, "when you cross Canton Road, you're almost at the end. There's the Union Building, the Shanghai Club, and the McBain Building."

I nodded and stared at the six columns in front of the Shanghai Club. I knew it was famous for its bar, the longest in the world, over one hundred feet. But my father had told me something that I found more impressive.

"They iron the newspapers there," I said softly.

My father laughed. "*Hao tê-hên*," he said, very good. "We'll celebrate." And this time he didn't smooth my hair, he mussed it, a stronger show of affection, and I felt my face grow hot.

We took the lift back down and went out into the heat and across the Garden Bridge on foot. At the start of the Bund were the Public Gardens, and I took my father's hand as we neared the magnolia trees.

The crows that nested in them were known for their meanness, and I felt certain that they particularly disliked small girls.

On the Bund, everything was so busy and crowded and loud that I thought we must be in the center of the world. On our left were the jetties, where coolies unloaded barges and ships and cranes hovered overhead. In the street, trams rattled past us and cars fought for space while rickshaws wove around them. The coolies who pulled them never looked up, and their long black queues of hair looked like braided whips on the bare skin of their backs. On the sidewalks were hawkers, some of them offering to polish my father's shoes, others holding things out for sale, things like fountain pens, Chinese slippers, cold drinks, pomelos, and small green bananas that you would never eat without washing and maybe boiling. And there were the beggars, all ages, all of them missing something—a few teeth, a leg, an arm, an eye, a nose. They hunched in doorways, they crouched along the curb, they stood in the street, ahead of us, behind us, next to us, in our steps, everywhere, all of them demanding *cumshaw*, at least a few dragon coppers.

My father and I walked without speaking. I held his hand tightly and concentrated on staying close. He was alert and appreciative, taking everything in as though it were his. The air smelled of garlic and bean curd frying in peanut oil, of smoke and the Whangpoo and of too many people. Cars honked, coolies called for people to make way, turbaned Sikhs directing traffic yelled and blew high-pitched whistles that hurt my ears. It seemed as if everyone was talking. Chinese compradores, employees of the foreign firms, argued in hurried Mandarin. Two Frenchmen chatted alongside us, and behind us, English cotton merchants with bowler hats and walking sticks talked business. Next to us a mother scolded her children in a language I didn't know.

At the Customs House, my father stopped to watch a passenger liner that had just docked, the streamers that clung to its sides already damp from the humidity. "More griffins," he muttered. "Bunch of four-minute tourists," his name for travelers who stopped in Shanghai for only a few days. A small band on the ship's bow played as passengers talked and laughed and made their way down the gangplank. It was easy to spot those new to Shanghai. My father said you smelled Shanghai before you saw it, and as we watched, a woman in a dark suit winced when she first took in the Whangpoo's stench of fish and garbage and smoke from the ships' coal burners and the cotton mills and power company. She leaned on the railing as though she might faint. But then she glanced up and saw the Bund, and her expression changed from distaste to wonder, and for a moment she just stared.

My father gestured toward her and laughed softly. "You see, Anna? She likes it here already. That's just what happened to me."

:: :: ::

The businessmen my father knew in Shanghai were men who were doing exactly what they'd set out to do. Bankers and stockbrokers and cotton merchants, journalists and insurance agents, they'd been sent to Shanghai by their firms at home, large companies like Standard Oil, Dutch Royal Shell, Texaco, Eastman Kodak, British American Tobacco. Shanghai was simply a post for them, where they had a job to do. Eventually they'd go back home.

There was none of that purposefulness in my father's choice of business. He was an importer-exporter because that was just what he'd wound up doing. He approached his business as though it were a competitive sport rather than a career, and he was always looking for ways to pull ahead. He worked for himself from an office at 133 Yuen Ming Yuen Road, a small street that ran parallel to the Bund one block behind it, near Shanghai's financial section on Szechuan Road. That Saturday, as every Saturday, his office was our next stop so that he could look at his mail and, as he said, put the week right.

The office was a small, sparsely furnished room with not much more than the necessities: a huge carved blackwood desk, a chair, a file cabinet. A watercolor of the Public Gardens, a gift from my mother, hung on the wall next to the window. On his desk were things I was not allowed to touch—the green fountain pen that his father had given him and the small wooden box that held his chop, or seal, which he used with his signature on important documents. Though the chop was forbidden to me, I knew it well from watching my father use it. Inside its box were two compartments. The larger one held the chop itself, a block of pale marble that was three inches tall, a half inch square. On one end was a small carved elephant; at the other end, carved on the bottom, was my father's seal, the Chinese character for the name Schoene. The smaller compartment held a neat square of bright red ink, its consistency that of thick paste.

While my father worked, I sat on the floor and ran my fingers over the intricate carvings on the desk, scenes of willow trees and pagodas, coolies pulling rickshaws or carrying sedan chairs that held beautiful women and wise men. The office smelled of the Philippine cigars my father smoked, a smell that I loved, and I was happy to be in a place that was only his. I played by myself for what felt like a long time, perhaps half an hour or so, and then I grew restless. I went and stood next to him, wanting him to be finished. He glanced at me, then kept writing. "What is it?" he asked.

I shrugged.

He glanced around the room as though wondering where I'd come from. Then he said, "I know." He stood and took a globe from a high shelf in the corner and set it down on the floor next to the desk. He yanked open the stubborn bottom drawer of his desk and rummaged through stale papers and dog-eared folders and curled magazines, and under his breath he said, "Thought I'd stuck it down here. Ha! I did," and he took a pad of newsprint and dropped it next to the globe, where it made a loud smack on the wooden floor. Then he opened another drawer and took out a bottle of India ink. As I watched, he filled his green fountain pen with the blue-black ink.

"You can draw maps," he said when he'd finished, "and learn about the world."

I looked at the globe, then back at him, and I saw the beginning of impatience in his expression.

He tapped the newsprint pad. "Look at China. See if you can get to know the coastline a little bit. You start up here, with Port Arthur, then around and down to Wei Hai Wei, where Dr. McLain and his wife go every summer. You go along the Yellow Sea, past Tsingtao, and further south to Shanghai, then down to Fuzhou, you see? The coastline gets a little more uneven, with smaller turns and bends, and then you go all the way to Ghangzhou." He looked at me. "It's your home, Anna. You should know where you live, don't you see?"

I nodded, not really convinced, but interested in the thick ink and the possibilities in the newsprint and fountain pen, off-limits until now. My father handed me the pen, then turned his attention back to his work.

I sat down on the floor and looked closely at the dark blue vastness of China on the globe. I stared at the coastline for a moment, not convinced that I could draw anything that resembled it. But that was what my father had asked, and so I would try.

I put the pen down and stared at the globe for a moment. I found Shanghai, the only word on the globe I knew, and I stared hard at the words near it, trying to will them to make sense. That summer I had started to learn to read. Not officially—I wouldn't start school until September—but just picking up whatever words my father thought important. I knew "Shanghai." I knew "Hungjao," where we lived. I knew my name, and my parents' names, and "Mei Wah" and "Chu Shih." And I knew "China."

But I wanted more. I wanted to read everything, everywhere we went, so that I wouldn't have to ask questions all the time. I wanted to read the names of the buildings along the Bund so I wouldn't have to memorize them. I wanted to read the names of the streets, the names of the stores, what they sold, how much it cost. If I could only learn to read, I thought, I would be almost an adult, only smaller and without money.

But none of the words on the globe presented themselves to me. All I saw were combinations of letters that looked jumbled up. Finally I stood and carried the globe to my father and set it on his desk.

"What are all these names?" I asked.

My father was reading about yesterday's polo matches in the *North China Daily News*. He puffed evenly on his cigar while his finger moved down the column of newsprint as he searched for the names of friends. He glanced at me. "What's that?"

I pointed to China on the globe and said, "These names. Are they other cities? What are they?"

My father glanced at his newspaper, and I saw his reluctance to turn from it. But I knew he would. Asking about China always got his attention.

"Some are cities," he said finally, "and some are provinces. I'll show you, Anna, it's a good question." He pulled his chair closer to his desk and examined the globe. "Now these"—he pointed to the names spelled in large capital letters—"these are the names of the provinces, you see?" He touched each one lightly. "Szechuan, Kiangse, Hunan, Shantung, Fokien, Kwangse, Yunan, Tibet."

I found myself nodding in surprised recognition. I *knew* those names. I couldn't read them, but I knew them, and had since I was four, when my father had taught them to me. They were the names of Shanghai's streets, the ones that ran the same way as the Bund. "Those are our streets," I said suddenly.

My father nodded. "Yep. And these"—he touched the globe again, pointing to names in smaller letters—"are China's major cities. Nanking, Hong Kong, Peking, Ningpo, Tientsin, Kukiang, Hankow, Foochow, Canton."

I was rewarded again. They, too, were familiar—they were the streets that ran crossways to the Bund. I looked at my father. "Everything's named after us," I said. "The whole country's named after Shanghai, because we're so important." I had a moment of doubt. "Isn't that right?"

My father started to smile. "No, Anna," he said, and he laughed softly. "*We're* named after *them*, but that's all right." He traced the fat black line that was China's border with his finger. "It's only natural, you thinking that, because you know Shanghai."

I felt my face grow hot. I hated being wrong, and I tried to hide my embarrassment by staring harder at the globe. I saw a small island off the coast of China and thought it must be a province my father hadn't named. I put two fingers on it and covered it completely.

"What's that?" I asked.

"Japan," he said.

I was confused. "Where's the rest of it? All that's here is this little part." I tapped the globe lightly. "See?"

He laughed grimly. "There isn't any more. That's the whole thing, right there under your nose." He frowned. "What made you think there was more?"

"There has to be, or else how could they think of taking us over? We're so big, and they're so small."

He smiled, pleased at my choice of words: taking *us* over. "Well, you've got something there. But nobody's taking anybody over, not us or them. It's just a lot of talk. And some fighting here and there. But look at us"—and as he gestured around him, I tried to understand whether he meant his office, Shanghai, China, Americans, or simply him and me, which was what I hoped—"nobody can touch us here."

"Here?" I looked around me, trying to judge the safety of my father's small office.

"In the Settlement," he laughed. "We're safe as can be. Japan can do what it wants, and we'll still be right here, where we belong. We're on top of the world."

I nodded. My father's confidence in extraterritoriality—*extrality* was the shorter, affectionate term—was familiar, and even though I didn't understand exactly what extrality was, I understood that my father believed in it no matter what and that it somehow kept us safe.

My father turned from the globe and folded his newspaper, then opened a manila folder on his desk and turned his attention to it in a way that told me our conversation was over, at least for the moment. I picked up the globe and set it carefully on the floor, then went back to my map, trying to fill in more of China.

When I'd tired of drawing, I looked around the office for something else to do. There was a small closet in the corner, a place I'd never explored. I glanced at my father and saw that he was engrossed in his accounting ledger, and I walked quietly to the closet and opened the door. Inside I found a winter coat I didn't recognize and an old sweater and an umbrella propped against the wall. But toward the back of the closet, on the floor, I saw something else. I guessed it was a coat or sweater that had fallen off its hanger, and I crawled inside to retrieve it. When I did, I found a sort of wide belt made of thick black canvas, far too heavy for a piece of clothing. I dragged it to the front of the closet, sure I'd found forgotten treasure. I struggled to lift it, then struggled to stand with it, and I carried it to my father's desk.

"Look what I found," I said softly, pleased and curious, sure that my father would be grateful.

When I had set the treasure down, I thought I'd put it squarely on the desk. But I hadn't. As soon as I let go, it fell to the floor with a solid thud that made me jump and caused my father to swear and push his chair back from his desk.

At our feet were unfamiliar foreign bills, more money than I'd ever seen, all of it spread around us like someone had thrown it at us. For a horrible moment, my father said nothing, but I could feel his anger. Then he said, "These are yen. Japanese money. What do you say we tidy it up?"

I nodded. I didn't know exactly what I'd done, but I knew it was wrong, and I knelt next to my father and together we began to pick everything up and neaten the bills into fat stacks. Except for the hushed sound of our movements, the room was silent.

Finally I asked what I knew he didn't want to answer. "Why do you have these?"

He didn't speak at first, and I knew he was trying to be patient. Then suddenly he smiled. "I'm an arbitrageur, Anna. Part of my business."

"What's that?"

"It's someone who buys and sells money." He motioned to the pile of money at his feet, like something from a fairy tale. "You see? I'm my own bank." He continued fitting the bills back into the money belt, and when he'd finished, he laid it carefully on his desk. Then he looked at me and saw that I held one more bill. I was staring at it with longing. I recognized the number 100 on it. I thought it must be a huge amount of money, and suddenly I wanted it intensely in that way that children yearn for things that don't always make sense.

My father reached into his pocket and held out three Chinese yuan, worth about a dollar. "Here's how it works. I give you a few yuan, and you give me the yen. You see?"

I stared at the yuan in his palm. On the face of the coins, Dr. Sun Yat Sen stared back at me as though he, too, were trying to win me over.

"A trade, all right? Just a simple business deal between the two of us, the yen for the yuan. And then we can walk home along Nanking Road and you can do some shopping. Like your mother." He smiled again.

I nodded, picturing trinkets I'd admired on Nanking Road that were suddenly and unexpectedly within reach: a carved ivory elephant, a set of eight tiny pottery horses, a hand-painted fan. And then I made the swap, yen for yuan.

My father picked up his money belt and carried it to his safe in the back of the office. "This is where it should have been in the first place," he said. I thought this was his fault, not mine, but the reprimand sounded as though it were meant for me. His back was to me, and as he knelt and began to turn the knob on the lock, I saw one last yen note that we hadn't picked up. It was under his desk, right at the corner. I stared at it for a moment and started to tell him to wait, there was another one, but no words came. Instead, I stooped down and picked it up, then unbuckled my shoe.

My father glanced back at me. "What's the matter?"

"A pebble in my shoe," I said. It was the first time I had ever lied to him, and I felt a wink of surprise inside. It had been so easy.

He turned away again while I took off my shoe, shook it to get rid of the pebble I'd made up, and put the shoe back on. Then I folded the yen and hurriedly slipped it under my foot. I considered it "squeeze," the Shanghai word for bribe. I'd decided that everyone else got squeeze, I might as well, too.

When my father had shut the safe, he turned to me. "Well," he said, too cheerfully. "That was something, wasn't it?"

I nodded, expecting a scolding.

But he surprised me. "What would you say to lunch at Jimmy's?" he asked.

I stared hard, knowing that we were making some kind of deal. "Jimmy's?" I asked cautiously.

He nodded, watching me closely. "Yep. Just say the word."

"I'd like that," I said, working hard at restraint. "Very much," I added, to be on the safe side.

He smiled but still looked shaken. "Then Jimmy's it is."

Lunch with my father on Saturday could be anything. It might be food from street vendors that my mother never allowed—fried noodles with shrimp or bits of ham or chicken, grilled shrimp and sausage, sweet almond broth, or *chiaotzû*, steamed dumplings filled with minced pork and cabbage and ginger. It could be a stop at a sukiyaki shop, or coolie food, a plain dish of steamed vegetables and rice. But I'd never been to Jimmy's, where my father ate most days.

When we got there, my father took my hand and led me to a wooden table in the center of the room, *his* table, I guessed, since he usually had a favorite place, wherever we went. We sat down and he glanced around for the waiter while I stared hard at everything around me.

The place was crowded with English and American and European businessmen, some with their Chinese compradores. Saturday wasn't a day off in Shanghai; most men worked at least in the morning, and the loudness of the lunchtime conversation was startling. But I noticed it for only a moment, because I was amazed by what I saw. I'd never been anyplace like it, a place that was completely foreign to me for the simple reason that it was so American. Our wooden table was covered with a blue-and-white checked tablecloth and paper napkins, and in the middle of the table were French's mustard, A.1. sauce, Worcestershire sauce, Heinz 57 ketchup, and a sugar pourer. I smelled hamburgers cooking and corned beef hash and chili and barbecued chicken all at once, the smells so different from noodles and vendor food on the street that it alone was worth the trip. I thought it was the most wonderful place I'd ever been.

A waiter handed my father a menu and he read what he thought I might like. When he finished and I said nothing, he laughed softly, for he realized I was overwhelmed. He ordered barbecued chicken for both of us, a lemonade for me, a Clover beer for him, and he told me I was in for a treat.

We'd just been served our food when we were joined by Will Marsh, a friend of my father's who worked for the American Consulate in Shanghai. He was at our house often, and was my favorite of my parents' friends because he always acted more like he was my friend, too. That day at Jimmy's, he smiled at me and held out his hand, and I gripped his hand the way my father had taught me—"no cold fish, now, all right, Anna? A good strong grip is how you do it"—and I looked Will Marsh in the eye and smiled at him, and I saw the pleasure and approval that my apparent confidence brought to my father.

Will sat down across from us. I didn't know if my father was handsome—he mostly just looked like my father—but I knew Will Marsh was. He looked like a movie star, confident and friendly and tall and strong, with thick dark hair and brown eyes, and I was always a little in awe of him.

"Tell me what's new in the land of Hungjao, those great western suburbs, home of the wealthy taipans," he said, and he smiled.

I licked barbecue sauce from my finger and blinked tears from my eyes. I had a paper cut, and the sauce stung sharply. But I thought about home, and I tried to come up with something interesting, something adult. The yen came to mind, and I looked at my father, who seemed to read my thoughts and frown. "We planted a new Chinese elm," I offered.

Will feigned amazement. "No kidding. Another addition to that Public Garden you call a backyard?"

I smiled, pleased for my father. "It's beautiful," I said, "but noisy."

Will leaned forward. "How so?"

"The cicadas," I said.

My father nodded. "They seem to consider us home. A whole city of them."

Will shrugged. "That's easy enough. You need a batch of cicada killers."

I smiled at his teasing, picturing soldiers armed with nets, but he was serious. "No, they're digger wasps, and they kill those noise-making cicadas, then use them for building up their nests. That's what you need, all right."

I frowned at the idea of importing wasps. Will gave my father a sidelong glance and said in an offhand way that I associated with adults, "But you can't blame those cicadas for moving in with you out there. That's quite a spot. Sounds to me like the Schoenes will be there for a hundred years, give or take. *They're* not leaving Shanghai."

I took this as more teasing, but when I looked at my father, he wasn't laughing.

"You're right about that," he said simply. His voice was flat, his mouth a straight line.

"Still? Even with Thursday?" Will turned his full attention to my father, and I understood that the conversation had turned adult, and that I was no longer part of it.

My father shrugged. "A skirmish is supposed to make me pack my bags and walk away from my business? I don't think so."

Will glanced around the crowded restaurant, and when he looked at my father again, his eyes were intent. "You're nuts, you know that? Everything's changed, and you're a fool if you don't admit it. Shanghai's not going to bounce back this time. There's a lot more at stake here."

My father finished his chicken, then stared at his plate, checking, I knew, to see if he'd missed anything. He always cleaned his plate and picked bones clean. Then he glanced at me, trying to gauge how much of the conversation I understood, which wasn't much, though he had tried to explain things to me. The day before, he had told me that a war might be starting, but that it was far, far away, and that it wouldn't affect us. He said there would be a lot of talk about it, but I wasn't to worry because we were safe and sound. Nothing would change.

On July 7, just a few days before, there had been a skirmish that became known as the Marco Polo Bridge Incident. It didn't sound like much at first, just another border incident, people said. The Marco Polo Bridge was an arched stone footbridge in the village of Lukouchiao, twenty miles west of Peking. The bridge stretched nearly two hundred and fifty yards across the Yungting River, with three hundred marble lions set along either side of the bridge. Reports about exactly what had happened were confused and contradictory, but the gist of it seemed to be that Japanese soldiers had crossed the bridge, then refused to budge, forcing Chinese militia to fire on them and giving the Japanese a pretext for invasion.

Will leaned closer to my father. "I'm telling you, Shanghai isn't going to stay peaceful. That may mean a lot of trouble for us, or it may just mean inconvenience, but either way, we're about to become onlookers of a war. With box seats, no less."

My father laughed in a way that sounded good-natured but that made me nervous because I heard the disagreement in his tone. "But don't you see? Onlookers, you said, that's exactly it. No matter what, we're just privy to a family squabble, all from a very comfortable guest room called the International Settlement. We mind our manners, we don't favor one side over the other, we politely look the other way when it gets nasty. This is between the Chinese and the Japanese. It's not our concern." He took a long drink of beer. "And by the way, the Japanese will never make it this far south. That's a long way. A few units in Peking are no reason to leave. It just won't happen, not on the scale some of these guys are talking about anyway." He looked at me then, and I must have looked worried, or at least puzzled, because he winked and added, "I won't let it."

Will said only, "You're an optimist."

My father laughed. "Wrong. I'm a businessman. And I don't make money by leaving my place of business."

Will said, "In that case, you're a fool. Or else you've got a good reason to stay."

My father gave Will a careful look. "Now, that's a funny thing to say."

Will shrugged. "I'm just talking about your business, Joe. What did you think I meant?"

My father's face reddened.

Will went on. "Because I just can't figure out what else it would be, what else could keep you here, and I just wonder. What kind of hold does this place have over a guy like you?"

My father shifted in his seat. "It's got no hold," he said, "and I still say it won't happen. It's a lot of talk is what it is, people overreacting. I'm dealing with the Japanese, I'll keep dealing with them, and any high-minded somebody who doesn't is throwing money away. I'll sell them whatever I can—newsprint, oil, insurance, Dodge trucks, for crying out loud—just as long as I'm not breaking any rules. What are you saying, that I'm supposed to shut down and stop making money because a few shots were fired on a bridge?" He shook his head. "The Communists are the ones to worry about, *they're* the danger here. Bunch of bandits. The Japanese are just guys like us, out to make a buck."

"Or a yen," I said suddenly. Will laughed. My father silenced me with a look.

Will took a box of Craven A cigarettes from his shirt pocket, shook one out and lit it. And then our table was silent for a long moment.

"You want an answer?" my father said finally.

Will nodded. "As your friend, yeah, I'd like an answer. What keeps Joseph Schoene in Shanghai?"

My father lit a cigarette, then inhaled deeply and held the smoke in as though it were the answer, then exhaled slowly toward the ceiling, nodding. "Business," he said flatly. "My business and none of yours." And he stood to leave.

He was quiet as we walked down Nanking Road, and I worried that he knew what I'd done. The folded yen made a wrinkle under the thinness of my cotton sock, a rough spot that was like an accusation, and I had to fight the urge to blurt out my secret and make amends. But I wasn't worried enough to confess. The yen felt like a treasure, and I wasn't going to give it up. If my father noticed my worry, he didn't let on, and I was glad of his inattention, a first. After a while, I stopped thinking about it so much and gave in to the distractions of Nanking Road.

Nanking Road was Shanghai's biggest shopping street. My father said it was the biggest shopping street in China, a claim I never doubted. The whole street felt like a festival, with shop banners of scarlet and gold and white hanging like oversized streamers, a place where the storefront windows held anything you could name: hand-sewn silk underwear, Japanese wedding kimonos, electric razors, newspapers from all over the world, cashmere sweaters, porcelain, pottery, jeweled opium pipes, pianos. The first few blocks were mostly Western offices and stores—Kelly & Walsh, the American Book Shop, Whiteway & Laidlaw, the American Drug Company, the Chocolate Shop. My father had learned to fox-trot and tango and peabody at the Arthur Murray Dance Studio—a concession to my mother, who loved to dance—and earlier that week he'd taken me to see *The Gold Diggers of 1937* at the Grand Theater.

But after a mile or so, the street became Chinese. One shop sold only chopsticks, another silk umbrellas, another lamps and lanterns, and another only walking sticks carved from wood, or bamboo, or rattan, or willow. My mother bought silk at Lao Kai Fook, the colors so deep they looked like wet paint. When she'd chosen one, a clerk in a long gray gown would nick the fabric with round-handled scissors, then rip it straight across, the sound like that of paper tearing. The Chinese department stores were there, always crowded and noisy. Wing On was famous for its linens and tablecloths and sheets, but there was also Sun Sun & Sincere, where you could buy anything from anyplace—French perfume, Scotch whiskey, German cameras, English leather, Chinese pajamas and slippers and silks.

That day my father let me wander in the shops, an indulgence since he himself wasn't much of a shopper. The only time I knew of him shopping had been the year before, when the English department store Lane Crawford had closed. They'd had a huge liquidation sale, and my father became their best, if unlikeliest, customer, going every day as though shopping that sale were his employment. He picked out tailored serge suits, wool sport coats and trousers, cashmere sweaters, shirts and Jaeger underwear and silk ties by the dozen, leather loafers and wing tips. On the first day, when he came to the counter with an armload of clothing, he talked a clerk in the men's department into letting him use one of the huge drawers behind the counter for his stash, and every day, as the prices went down, he added to it. When he finally brought everything home after settling up and loading the trunk of the Packard with his purchases, my mother had laughed as Mei Wah brought in box after box. "Now, *that's* shopping," she'd said, and my father had turned to her and said seriously, "No, it's business."

It was a few minutes before two when we reached Tibet Road, where Nanking Road became Bubbling Well Road. We were to meet Mei Wah where we always met him, in front of the Park Hotel, the tallest building in the East, taller than any of the buildings on the Bund. The Park was across from the Race Course and the Public Recreation Ground, a huge park with a swimming pool, a golf course, a baseball field, tennis courts, and probably more, though I didn't know what.

The Park was a little more than a mile from the Bund, a long walk for me, and I was dragging. My father asked me to hurry up—Mei Wah would be waiting for us, he said—and I tried to. When we got to the corner and my father looked at his watch, he said we were a few minutes early, and there was no sign of Mei Wah.

"Have a seat, Anna. It won't be long. You can watch the birds." My father nodded toward a stone bench under a willow tree a few feet away, and I sat down in the shade gratefully, glad to be out of the sun. The bird men were out—that was what I called them, mostly old men who owned pet birds and liked to air them in the early morning and afternoon in the summer and spring. But I was too tired to take much notice of them.

I held a small wooden box in my hand. Inside was my one purchase, a tiny elephant carved out of ivory. It reminded me of the elephant on my father's chop. Mei Wah had told me that in India elephants were good luck, especially if the trunk was raised, as this one's was. Now the elephant was wrapped in cotton wool and packed in a small box, which I held carefully.

I'd decided on the elephant at lunch. My father's tone of voice and the accusatory look on Will Marsh's face had given the day the frayed-edge feeling of worry. I didn't like arguments, and as I sat on the bench, I concentrated on home as a way to make the worried feeling go away. I imagined the coolness of our house. I knew that when we got there, my father would pour himself some Scotch and go out to the verandah. I knew he would not want to talk, that he would want to be alone. I knew that my mother would have bathed. She would be wearing the deep blue silk kimono that my father had brought her from Osaka last year, and her hair would be swept up on top of her head instead of coiled at the base of her neck, her only concession to the heat. She would smell of lavender and Cashmere Bouquet, the only soap she used, and she would be sitting in the study, reading *Life* or *The Saturday Evening Post*, and listening to *Let's Dance*, an NBC Network program that the American radio station in Shanghai carried. She liked the Latin music. I would sit with her on the cool leather sofa and show her my treasure, and tell her about our day.

None of those things happened.

A car turned onto Bubbling Well Road at the corner. The sun made it hard to see, and I stood, thinking it was Mei Wah. My father was several feet away from me, right on the corner so that he was in plain sight, and he squinted at the car and shaded his eyes, then looked at his watch.

The car came closer, and I saw that it wasn't my father's dark green Packard. It was a black sedan, solid and imposing and modern looking, and it slowed as it neared us. Then it stopped at our corner. My linen dress was limp and I tried to smooth the wrinkles out, thinking these must be friends of my father's and that I would be introduced and expected to shake hands and be polite. But when the back door opened, my father's expression changed from annoyance to surprise.

Two Chinese in dark blue trousers and tunics jumped from the car and stood on either side of my father. They spoke to him in Cantonese, their southern accents harsh, their words unrecognizable to me. My father tried to pull away, and he strained to look at me and said, "Run, find Mei Wah!" I didn't want to leave him and I started to move toward him, but one of the men glared at me. His skin was terrible, so pockmarked that he looked diseased, and I backed away from him and watched, terrified, as he hit my father on the back of the head with the butt of a pistol, grimacing as though he were the one being assaulted. My father slumped and was shoved into the backseat of the car, and the two men pushed in after him, one sitting on either side. The door was pulled shut and the car drove away, the sound of its tires on the road a raw scratchy sound that tightened my throat and hurt my eyes.

I stood there, my heart thumping wildly in my too-small chest. I looked around Bubbling Well Road, expecting my father to reappear behind me or beside me or across the street, and I saw that people had stopped walking and were staring at me, as though they, too, were waiting for whatever was next. I was embarrassed. They seemed to think it was my turn now, that I was supposed to bring him back.

"He's gone," I whispered, hoping that those were the magic words.

Only seconds had passed, but the world felt different and I was suddenly cold. Then another car turned the corner, and I stepped back and leaned against the wall of the apartment building, feeling its cool roughness on my back through my dress. This time it was our car, and I let my breath out when I saw the long green hood and the bright white of Mei Wah's turban. I wiped my hands on my dress and tried to see the humor in the trick my father had played on me, setting all that up, and I hoped I'd be able to laugh with him.

The Packard jerked to a stop in front of me and Mei Wah got out of the driver's seat. "Come," he said, and he took hold of my shoulders and pushed me roughly into the backseat. And then he was at the wheel and the car lurched into the street. He looked at me in the rearview mirror as we sped down Bubbling Well Road, and he shook his head.

"Where is he?" I asked, for the backseat was empty except for me. No father. No magic. No trick.

"Very bad," was all Mei Wah said. "Very bad indeed."

acrobats and vinegar

WE DROVE ALONG STREETS I KNEW, but nothing felt familiar. We crossed Chengtu Road and passed the American Women's Club, where my mother often met friends for lunch. We crossed Yates Road with its lingerie shops, and we reached the apartment buildings where my parents' friends lived—the Uptown, the West Gardens, Tiny Mansions, the Medhurst. But that day I could name none of them. At Avenue Haig I stared hard at the centuries-old cemetery and the Bubbling Well Temple and the Bubbling Well itself, all sources of good luck, I believed, simply because they were old and Chinese. I wanted Mei Wah to stop so that I could touch the water in the well, or leave something for Kwan Yin, the Goddess of Mercy, for it was said that she heard the cry of the world. But having anything to do with the Chinese gods was something my mother strictly forbade, so I said nothing.

Mei Wah sped by everything. We left the International Settlement through the Great Western Road exit, and Bubbling Well Road became Great Western Road. We turned onto Columbia Road and passed sprawling estates with latticed windows, Western homes made of sturdy brick, Spanish and Mediterranean villas with red-tiled roofs. We passed south-facing gardens that offered glimpses of tulip trees and lily magnolias and lion's head camellias behind garden walls that were topped with barbed wire and shards of broken glass, and I knew that we were home.

Mei Wah turned the sharp corner of our driveway and barely stopped the car before he jumped from the front seat. He jerked my door open and lifted me from the backseat, then carried me quickly into the house. I held him tightly and his beard rubbed against my cheek as he ran.

He passed through the kitchen in a few strides, calling for Chu Shih, and when he rounded the corner and reached the cook's bedroom, he rapped on the door and didn't wait for an answer before he pushed it open and laid me on the bed. He said something to Chu Shih in rushed Chinese that I didn't understand, and Chu Shih said, "*Shei?*" Who?

Mei Wah answered only, "*Pu chihtao,*" I don't know, his voice gruff and angry. Then he hurried out and I was left in the dim light and quiet heat.

I had started to cry by then, wanting to follow Mei Wah and find my mother, partly for comfort, but also because I wanted to hear whatever it was that Mei Wah told her right now, which I knew would be the real story, and more than they would tell me later. But Chu Shih turned and started mixing something on the electric burner he kept in the corner of his room, his large back to me. When I sat up, he made a clucking sound and patted the air next to him as though it were a bed. "*Pu tung,*" stay put, he said, and I lay back on his bed.

He was making something to soothe me. Every Saturday he went to the Old Native City's Chinese pharmacies, where he bought things he believed in, medicines and herbs and fairy-tale ingredients that possessed healing powers, things with names like toothed-bur clover and coltsfoot, shepherd's purse and Chinese angelica, names that were too strange and wonderful to be made up. It was Chu Shih who seemed made up, a kind and magical giant. He was from the north and was huge, over six feet tall and more than two hundred pounds. He was never afraid, and when he entered the room, he always looked as though he was sure you'd be glad to see him. I never knew his age, but he seemed old and strong and wise.

I lay on his bed and watched as he worked in silence, leaning over the cramped corner where he'd set up his private kitchen, his short blue cotton jacket the size of one of my coats, his black trousers immense as tablecloths. Finally he turned and came toward me with a steaming cup, the porcelain so thin that the rim was translucent.

I sat up and took a deep breath. I was still crying, mostly the crying that comes at the end of fatigue and fear. Chu Shih cleaned my face with a cool, damp linen towel that smelled of lemon and cucumber. Then he looked at me for a long moment, his eyes sad, his expression worried, and he whispered a word I didn't know. I shook my head. He tried another; no again. We always spoke in bits and pieces, our own blend of English and Mandarin, a language that worked fine in our day-to-day lives. But it was clear that we didn't have words for what had just happened.

He thought for a moment and stared hard at me, as though he was playing a game and was searching for a clue. And then he said, "*Hsiao t'ou,*" thief.

"*Hsiao t'ou,*" I repeated. I knew the word, but not what he was saying.

Chu Shih nodded back at me. "*Hsiao t'ou,*" he said more urgently, and then he added, "*Hsiao t'ou* take your father." He smoothed my hair awkwardly, something he'd never done before, and I thought he must have seen my father do it.

I let my breath out, the only sound in the room. He was telling me that my father had been kidnapped.

Chu Shih handed me the cup, and I sipped the tea, the same tea he'd made for me when I fell from the second branch of the Chinese magnolia in the backyard the year before and broke my arm. I tasted ginseng and rose oil, licorice and saffron. It was warm and sweet and smelled vaguely floral, and I drank it without hesitating. Chu Shih had cured me of stomachaches and toothaches and tiredness and fever, and I knew enough to do what he said.

When I finished the tea, I lay down again and stared at the few soft stripes of afternoon light that managed to make their way through the wooden blinds. Chu Shih was back at his burner, fooling with the teapot and putting things away, but I knew he was only trying to look busy while I was, he hoped, falling asleep.

"My mother," I started, but Chu Shih shook his head.

"She will come," he said. "Later."

I reached into my pocket and found the small cardboard box, my purchase from the afternoon, which seemed like at least a day ago. I opened it and took out the elephant, and held him up to the light. He looked brave, I thought. There was no telling what a beast as brave as he could do. I touched his trunk and put him on the table so that I would not harm him by holding him too tight. And then I fell asleep.

:: :: ::

When I woke, the strips of light were gone, and the room had the dimness of the last minutes of day. Though I didn't feel hot, I was damp from sweat and my chest felt tight, as though something were binding me. I started to sit up and saw, on the blackwood table next to Chu Shih's bed, the teacup, filled again. I picked it up carefully, my hands shaking, and drank the lukewarm tea.

I heard Chu Shih sounds in the kitchen, the soft scraping and padding of his cotton shoes on the quarry tile floor, the sound of a wooden spoon on a ceramic bowl, the sharp sound of slicing on the butcher block, and I got up from the bed and went to find him.

The kitchen smelled of ginger and scallions and garlic. Chu Shih stood at the sink. When I came in and stood next to him, he set a piece of sesame bread in front of me, and I realized I was starved.

He was making *chiaotzû*, steamed dumplings. I watched as he dropped minced ginger into a metal bowl and combined it with what would be the filling for the dumplings: ground pork, shredded cabbage, green onions, eggs to hold everything together. He shook in soy sauce and sesame oil, salt and pepper, half a cup of oolong tea that he'd steeped hard and strong, especially for this, and the smell got better and stronger, so that all I wanted was to eat one *now*. Last was a dash of sherry, which he added to most of what he cooked, a trick my mother had taught him, like adding coffee to chocolate to make the taste stronger.

"I can help?" I asked.

He nodded toward the huge maple worktable in the middle of the room. "*Tso*," sit, he said, and though he was stern, I understood that he wanted me to stay.

I sat down on one of the worn stools and Chu Shih dropped a handful of flour onto the table in front of me, where it made a small *poof!*, then settled. I smoothed it into a circle, the table cool and hard and solid against my palm, then I rubbed flour between my hands as though it were talc. Chu Shih sat down next to me and floured more of the table, then took a ball of dough from a ceramic bowl and began to flatten it, first with his huge hands, then with the rolling pin, back and forth, back and forth, his motions even and controlled. When the dough was rolled almost as thin as paper, he turned a teacup upside down and began cutting out circles with the rim, his wrist making quick, sharp turns. Then he slid the circles—the skins, we called them—toward me, one by one. I picked each one up and held it carefully in my palm while I put a forkful of the filling in the middle. Then—this was the hard part—I folded the circle into a half circle, and pinched the edges together hard, the way you would the edge of a pie crust, turning the half circle into a crescent as I worked. When I finished, I set the fat moon-shaped dumpling on a metal tray in the middle of the table and started another.

We worked that way in silence. A few times I thought I heard steps in the rest of the house and I looked at the door, waiting for someone to enter, but no one did, and each time Chu Shih nodded sharply at the *chiaotzû* I was making, telling me to pay attention to what I was doing.

I understood that we were waiting. It was common knowledge, even for a child: after someone had been kidnapped, you waited until you heard what to do next, and then you waited until the person you loved was finally home. That was how it worked. I knew about kidnapping the way I knew about beggars. It was part of life, so much so that I was never allowed to go anywhere alone. I had heard stories since I was small. The stories that frightened me most were about young girls who were taken by troupes of acrobats and forced to drink vinegar to soften their bones and make their spines more supple so that they would be better performers. Or girls who were taken to brothels, which I took to be a mispronunciation of "brothers," and I wondered what had made the brothers so evil that they would kidnap their own sisters. I was taught to be wary of all of the everyday strangers around us: hotel boys, theater ushers, waiters, flower girls, newspaper sellers, coolies, *mafu*, carriage men. No one was trustworthy; anyone could be a *fahsiong*, a trafficker, literally "father-brother," someone who was cunning and ruthless and patient, who might abduct a female and sell her. A woman was called a *t'iaotsû*, or item, a girl was a *shiht'ou*, or stone, and once she'd been taken, her abductors would hide her in a bakery or barbershop or who knew where until she could be sold and forced to "sell her smiles," another phrase I took literally.

At the time my father was kidnapped, the most common victims were wealthy businessmen like him, men who were blindfolded and carried off in broad daylight. Kidnappings were reported almost every day in the *North China Daily News*. I heard my mother relay those stories to my father when she thought I was out of earshot, stories that fascinated me as much as they frightened me. A broker from the Shanghai Stock Exchange was taken while buying stamps, the owner of the Buick agency on Nanking Road was whisked away while leaving the Empire Theater. The kidnappers could be anyone: members of the Red Gang or Green Gang, who could be told apart by how they held their cigarettes; or outlaws; or political extremists like the Blue Shirts, who were ultra-loyal to Chiang Kai-shek and threatened anyone who dealt with the Japanese or the Communists. Many of the city's affluent businessmen simply took the threat in stride and hired bodyguards, menacing White Russians or bulky Chinese boys from the country, a practice my father viewed as showy and unnecessary, nothing more than a way to get "great face." He depended solely on Mei Wah, a strategy that, until now, had worked just fine.

And so, as Chu Shih and I made *chiaotzû* after *chiaotzû*, I kept my questions to myself. When we'd finished and he got out the huge bamboo steamer and let me arrange the first batch of dumplings on spread-out cabbage leaves to cook, a first, I saw that I was being comforted, and the fear inside me rose like dough.

:: :: ::

Chu Shih and I ate our fill at the kitchen table, and still the rest of the house stayed quiet. Though it wasn't typhoon season, there was a strong hot wind outside that made the house rattle, and each time it did, Chu Shih looked anxiously at the door, then at the windows, and each time he smiled nervously when he saw me notice his anxiety. The sky outside grew black. When I stared hard at the windows, watching for some sign of my father, I no longer saw the magnolia and the plane trees and the willows, but only the reflection of my own worried face in the dark glass.

That was when my mother came for me: just when it was night.

She came into the kitchen without a sound, and I jumped when she touched my shoulder and spoke my name. Her face was pale, and there were circles under her eyes. I reached for her as though I'd never expected to see her again.

"Anna," she said, and she loosened my hold on her and knelt next to me, so that we were at the same level. Her fingers shook as she set a pink and gold package of Ruby Queen cigarettes on the table. When she pushed my hair off my face and pressed her palms against my cheeks, her hands were cold. She smelled of Chanel No. 5, the scent so strong it was like something you could touch, which made me start to cry because it seemed so everyday, and the night was so wrong.

"Are you all right?" she asked, and although I thought I was, her question made me cry more. My mother looked truly confused. She turned to Chu Shih and said, "She's been like this all day? You should have come—"

"No, no," Chu Shih said, "just now. Not all day." He shook his head and looked grieved, as if he had been the cause of my tears.

I caught my breath and ordered myself to calm down. I was, I told myself, my father's daughter, which meant I had a certain standard to meet. There was no reason to act like this; I certainly wouldn't have fallen apart if he had been in the room. I took another breath. "I was afraid."

My mother nodded. "I know," she said. "Let's go upstairs and you can tell me what happened." She stood and smoothed her skirt, and I started to follow her out of the kitchen. She stopped at the door and turned to Chu Shih.

"You've checked the doors?"

"*Shih*," yes.

"The windows?"

"*Shih*."

"Well, then," my mother said, "we'll be fine. We'll all be fine." And she took my hand.

When we reached my room, my mother sat on my bed, her legs crossed, her back straight. Despite her composure, in that instant I thought she might cry and I stared at her hard, willing her not to. She coughed, covering her mouth with a white handkerchief, and licked her lips. Then she patted the space next to her and forced a smile. I sat down beside her.

"Are you all right?" she asked. She looked evenly into my eyes, concerned.

"Yes," I said. "Chu Shih gave me tea."

She nodded. "That's good. You needed to rest."

"Where is he?" I asked. I felt as though we'd been talking for hours, avoiding that question.

My mother brushed my hair from my face. She took a deep breath and exhaled unevenly. "I don't know exactly," she started, "that's part of the problem. We don't know exactly who's abducted him. It could be any number of—"

She stopped and looked at me. "Let me start again," she said, and she told me about calling Will Marsh and getting the money that the men had demanded, and arranging for Will to see that it was delivered. She said she was sure that my father would be returned the next day, or the day after that at the latest. Everyone knew, she said, that people who were kidnapped were well cared for, and released once the kidnappers had their ransom.

It all sounded like a business arrangement, and though I listened hard, it made no sense and had nothing to do with my father being hit with a gun and pushed into a car and taken away. My mother's anxious tone did not reassure me.

"Where is he?" I asked again.

She took another breath. "I told you. I don't know. I just know he'll be home soon. I've done all I can do."

"Why did they take him?"

My mother smiled grimly and looked away from me. "Hard to say," she answered. "That's something else I don't know." She stared at her skirt. "Your father," she said, and her voice caught and she cleared her throat. "Your father is somewhat unpredictable. And he's very"— she paused—"complicated. He has strong ideas and people don't always agree with those ideas, and he does what he wants, whether people like it or not. And sometimes it gets him into trouble." She looked at me and said, "Can you understand that?"

I nodded, and she attempted a smile. Then she closed her eyes and smoothed the delicate skin under her eyes with her fingers. "I'm so tired," she murmured, and for a moment I was stumped. My mother was never tired, and I was suddenly concerned that maybe things were even worse than I'd thought.

"Are you all right?" I asked.

She opened her eyes and seemed to think for a moment. "Yes," she said, "I'm all right." She leaned close and kissed my forehead, then stood up. "Get your shoes off, Anna, and we'll get you ready for bed."

My shoes. I stood, remembering my father's office as though it were last year, forgotten till this instant, and I backed away from her as though she'd asked the unthinkable. "No," I said suddenly, and then, thinking I was being rude, I added, "No, thank you."

She laughed. "What's the matter with you? Come, take off your shoes and dress and put your nightgown on. It's late."

I shook my head and took a few more steps back.

"Stop it, Anna," she said, more firmly now. "Don't be difficult. We're tired and upset. Just put your nightgown on and get into bed and you'll fall asleep, and things will be better in the morning. You'll see."

But I didn't see. I didn't see how things could be fine, or how she could be so calm, or how my father could possibly be all right, or how the criminals who had taken him would ever return him with everyone acting so casually. And I certainly didn't see how taking my shoes off and letting my mother find the yen I had kept would help.

"I want to keep my shoes on," I said, and I hoped a reason would come to me.

"Don't be silly," she said.

"I'm not. I'm just not taking my shoes off. I might have to get up in the night."

"That's ridiculous," she said. There was an edge to her voice, and when she stood, she looked at me so matter-of-factly that I almost lost my nerve and gave in.

"I'm not taking them off," I said again, mostly to myself. "And I won't go to sleep if you take them off of me."

She took a deep breath and stared at me hard. I stared back and told myself that I was as strong as she was, just not as big. Finally she said, "You're not yourself, but I'm far too exhausted to argue with you. Let's just hope you're reasonable in the morning." She turned to my bed and pulled back the sheets. "Fine. In you go."

I had not moved. "You have to promise," I said.

"What?" The thinness of her voice let me know that her patience was all but gone.

"That you won't take them off while I'm asleep."

She did not hesitate. "Of course I will. Children don't sleep in their shoes. Period. Now get into bed and go to sleep." She looked at me and softened. I was terrified of this stance I'd invented, and it must have showed. "Anna, please. Everything will be all right in the morning. You'll see."

I nodded and got into my bed in my clothes and tried not to wince as my dirty shoes slid between the whiteness of clean cotton sheets. I thought of all the dirt and grime I'd seen all day, and I felt as though I'd brought it all home with me.

"I'll tell you what," she said. "Let me go and change out of these clothes and I'll sit with you until you're asleep. And I won't take your shoes off unless you tell me it's all right. Deal?"

I nodded.

She turned and walked out of my room and I watched her until she turned the hallway corner to go to her bedroom.

I sat up and pushed the covers off and pulled off my shoe, took the yen out, and squeezed my foot back into my shoe. The yen note was limp and damp. I unfolded it and tried to smooth it against the sheet, then held it up and examined it, wishing that it could tell me something I didn't know. Then I went to the window, pushed it open, and unlatched the screen. I leaned out enough to reach the loose tile, the second one on the right. I refolded the yen and pulled up the tile enough to slip the yen underneath it, then pulled it up again to make sure I could reach the yen later. I could. I latched the screen, closed the window, and got back into my bed, my heart pounding as though I'd committed a crime.

A door opened and closed down the hall and I heard the softness of my mother's steps. She came down the hallway and into my room, wearing a white satin robe that I knew was soft as water.

"I brought you something," she said. "Maybe it will help." She handed me a postcard. The back was filled with a neat black handwriting that was far too complicated for me to decipher.

"No," she said, and she turned the postcard over. "The other side."

The front was a photograph of a city of lights. It was twilight, and behind the city were dark blue cut-out mountains that looked so close, they might have been right behind the houses. In the lower corner it said something that I tried to sound out.

"The city of angles," I read.

My mother laughed gently. "No, Anna, the City of *Angels*. It's Los Angeles, in California. My mother sent the picture, and it's where I grew up. I was thinking we might take a trip there sometime."

I looked at her uneasily. "A trip?"

She shrugged. "A vacation," she said. "Just for a while."

I nodded and looked back at the postcard and stared hard at the lines and intersections of all those streets, everything so straight and precise. It *looked* like a city of angles.

"The City of Angels," I said, and I turned to my mother. "Is it nice?"

She was quiet for a minute. Then she said, "Yes. And it's safe."

I nodded. That day I understood, for the first time, the appeal of "safe."

"Why don't you put it under your pillow and I'll tell you all about it tomorrow?"

I nodded and turned my pillow over so that the cool side would be against my cheek, then I slipped the postcard under it. My mother stood and turned out the light, then sat down on the edge of my bed and tucked the sheet around me. The light from the hall was behind her, and it was easy to believe that she was from a city of angels. She seemed like one herself, and I felt ashamed. I was grimy all over, outside from a long, terrible day, and inside from lying to both of my parents, first one, then the other, and doing so with ease. I was glad I couldn't see her face.

"It was awful," I whispered.

She leaned close and kissed my forehead. "I know," she said. "I'm sorry." We were quiet then, and for a moment I wanted to tell her everything—about the yen and about Jimmy's and about my father's mood that day—and to ask her for a bath and a clean nightgown and a better way to go to sleep.

But I said nothing. I was too tired and too ashamed and too afraid. My mother seemed to be waiting, to be expecting something, but she didn't ask. She just stayed close, patting my back and rubbing the spot that always hurt when I was tired, the spot that only she knew how to find.

the battle of shanghai

IN THE MORNING, I went with my mother to Mass at the Cathedral of St. Ignatius in Siccawei, in the southwest part of the city. Mei Wah drove us there with the car doors locked and the windows rolled up tight, and his hard expression and no-nonsense driving made it clear that he did not like us going out. But I could not remember a Sunday when my mother had missed Mass, and when she strode into the kitchen and called for Mei Wah, she had let it be known that no exceptions were going to be made that day. The two of us were going to Mass, as usual. My father never went; faith was my mother's domain, a foreign country to him.

Inside the church, I followed my mother to our pew and stood next to her and listened as Father Jacquinot spoke words that were like a door opening to a place I loved though I did not completely understand. *"In nomine Patris, et Filii, et Spiritus Sancti,"* he said, and I made the sign of the cross and tried to keep my thoughts on the Father and the Son. But over and over again, I thought of my father and I began to pray, not using the prayers my mother had taught me when I was small, but saying what I felt, pleading for my father's safety, the only thing I wanted just then. And although I wasn't completely sure that what I was doing really counted as prayer, I felt that God didn't mind, that He even welcomed my worried thoughts. It was the first time I had ever prayed so directly and so plainly and with such urgency. While I listened to the Mass, and heard and sang the *Kyrie*, and the *Gloria*, and the *Credo*, the *Sanctus* and the *Agnus Dei*, and tried to think about those words, I prayed a second litany in my heart: *Bring him home, keep him safe, bring him home, keep him safe.*

Mei Wah was waiting outside when we came out of the cathedral into the summer heat. He glowered at us and at anyone who came too close to us, and then he drove us home in angry silence.

At home, Chu Shih had made round wheat cakes stuffed with lamb and hard-boiled eggs that had been steeped in tea soy sauce, things we usually had only on holidays or picnics, attempts to cheer us. I picked at my food as though it were a penance. My mother said it looked wonderful and barely ate a thing, then went to the den and sat staring at the *Shanghai Times*, pretending to read. The day before she had done as she'd been instructed. With Will Marsh's help, she'd gotten together the money the kidnappers had demanded and sent it via their messenger, who had appeared at our door three hours after my father had been taken. She had not considered calling the Municipal Police—the families of kidnap victims never did, there was too much at stake. Now she was waiting, which was all she could do.

All through that day and evening, my mother acted as though my father would reappear any minute. But he didn't, not that day or the next, or the one after that. My mother grew more anxious each day. She ran to the phone every time it rang, and to the window every time a car went by. She looked up from the newspaper at every breeze, and when she heard Chu Shih in the kitchen, and when a dog barked in the distance. She appeared tired and frail, and her hands shook as she sipped rosemary mint tea, Chu Shih's cure for nerves.

Home felt like a rickety place that week. Because my mother was easily startled, I was reprimanded every time I made a sound. I wasn't allowed in the garden, a place where I'd always had free rein— it wasn't safe, my mother said. After the first two days, I just stayed in my room, where I tried to draw maps of Shanghai, wondering where in this vast city my father might be. And I wondered if I had some- how caused the badness. He had been kidnapped on the day I stole the yen, a secret that was too awful to tell.

:: :: ::

On Saturday, a week after the kidnapping, Will Marsh telephoned in the middle of the afternoon to tell my mother he'd received a phone call. My father would be dropped off on the corner of Bubbling Well Road where he'd been taken, and could be collected in an hour. Will said he would be there waiting, and that he would bring my father home.

Everything was all right, I thought. Chu Shih had told me over and over again that my father would be fine, and I thought that when Will Marsh brought my father home, he would be the same as before. When Will Marsh's brown Austin pulled into our driveway and I fol- lowed my mother to the front door, I expected to run to my father, to be picked up and swung in the air, to welcome him home just as I always did when he came home from a business trip.

But at the front door, my mother held me back from running to the car, and my first glimpse of my father told me why. As he got out of the car, he looked and moved like an old man, and I realized I would have knocked him down. My mother walked to him and held him to her gently, and I heard her whisper, "You'll be all right," words that sounded good, except for the worry in her face. Then she turned to me. "He's home, Anna, and everything's all right. You see?"

I didn't see at all. What I saw was that my father looked horrible and as though he were in pain. His rumpled seersucker suit coat hung on him, and though he smiled at me, he seemed not to see me. I'd expected to be kissed and smiled at, to be comforted and reassured and made to feel safe again. But as I walked to him, I didn't know what to do, he was so changed.

When I reached him, he said nothing. He simply knelt so that he was my height, and then he held me to him tightly and I let myself be crushed by his wiry embrace. I could feel him shaking.

In the evening, when he had showered and put on clean clothes, he had a dinner of noodles and tea. I stayed near him but out of sight, waiting for him to feel better. Finally, after he had eaten, I found him sitting on the pearwood bench by the large window that faced the garden. I sat down next to him without asking if he wanted me there, and when he looked at me and tried a smile, I took his hand and just held it for a moment, pretending that I knew how to comfort him. My mother had wanted him to go to St. Marie's Hospital on Route Père Robert in the French Concession so that his physician, Dr. McLain, could just take a quick look at him. But my father wouldn't consider it. So there we were, on a warm Saturday evening at home, staring out at willows and magnolias and the blackwood acacia.

The evening was eerie. There were no cars on the streets, and the only sound was the cicadas. I thought of Will Marsh's suggestion of cicada killers, and the idea made me shudder. Everything seemed alive in the garden: the plane tree in the corner moved slightly in the press of hot breath that passed for a breeze, and the huge magnolia in the center of the lawn nodded back, as though in private conversation. The willows and poplars along the back wall swayed like graceful women. I focused on the flower beds and said their names under my breath, names my father had taught me, practicing in case he should ask: poet's narcissus, orchids, cathedral roses, the waterlily tulips he'd ordered from a catalog and planted as bulbs the day they arrived. I looked at the stone bench in the corner, under the plane tree whose leafy branches seemed like a kingdom all their own, and I wondered if any lizards were still out. It was the best place to catch them. And you could turn over the flat rocks that bordered the flower beds and find spiders and millipedes with red undersides and red dots on their legs, the ones that amazed me and frightened me at the same time.

I was waiting for my father to speak, and finally he did. "We're going to have to get rid of that acacia," he said quietly, and he pointed to it below us. Its dark green leaves seemed somehow secretive in the dim light. "It was a mistake. In the right place it's pretty well behaved, but down there, in all that confinement, it's a troublemaker. The roots are too aggressive."

I nodded as though he'd said just what I was thinking.

"It's a bad actor," he added.

I nodded again. It was a phrase he used often for a plant or tree that did not do well where it was planted. We were quiet for a moment, and then, although I was afraid, I asked my question. "Who were they?"

My father glanced at me, and I thought I saw some of his old look, an expression that was canny and knowing and appreciating the attention. He also looked exhausted and I immediately wondered if asking was a mistake.

"They were Japanese," he said simply, as though that explained everything.

"But you're friends with the Japanese," I said. "You said that day at Jimmy's. You buy and sell, you get them what they want—" I stopped when I saw him wince.

"They want me to do more," he said in a low voice. "They want me to collaborate." He looked at me to see if I understood and I shook my head, wishing for once he didn't have to explain. "To help them," he said.

"Help them what?"

He laughed grimly. "That's the question," he said.

"Are you going to do that?"

He shook his head, started to say something, stopped. He seemed unable to answer the question, so I made a suggestion.

"It's complicated," I offered, remembering my mother's words from the week before.

My father closed his eyes and nodded. "Yes," he said, "it is."

That night was the only time I heard him speak of his kidnapping or the Japanese or their request for collaboration. He did not explain the faint lacerations on his wrists, reddish lines that looked like the smaller rivers on the globe in his office, or the bluish bruise below his eye, or the slight limp he had. The subject of his kidnapping was off-limits, and if I tried to venture anywhere near it in conversation, a look from my mother silenced me.

My parents set about acting as though nothing had happened. They went out again, though not every night. They had friends in for cocktails and dinner, and on the surface the only thing that was different was the way Will Marsh gave me a hug and looked at me carefully and asked me how everything was whenever he came over. In the mornings, my father went to his office, and though we didn't go to the Bund the next few Saturdays, he said it was because of the heat. I should stay inside where it was cool, he said.

:: :: ::

Over the next few weeks, my parents' conversations with each other and with friends became more and more centered on the war that my father had said would not happen and would not matter. My father tracked it as though it were a weather system that he hoped would pass over us, and he recorded its progress in the accounting ledger he'd begun using as a journal. On the twenty-eighth of July, 1937, Peking fell to the Japanese, and in the days that followed, the Japanese army headed south, one long file going by way of the Nankow Pass and Shansi Province, the other heading toward Nanking via the railway from Tientsin. On the seventh of August, the Chinese National

Defense Council declared a War of Resistance against Japan, and Chinese commanders were ordered to prepare to drive Japanese troops from Shanghai. The next evening, when my father went into the den and switched on his new Stewart Warner radio, he heard the news on XQHB instead of the usual tango program, and on XMHA instead of the soap operas, and he told my mother that the city felt like war. That same day, the International Settlement authorities declared a state of martial law, and from that time on, my father was never far from his radio when he was home.

On an evening in early August, things grew more serious. A Japanese commander and his aide drove to the Hungjao airfield, which the Chinese military was using as a base. When they got there, a Chinese sentry forbade them to proceed. They ignored his commands and both were shot, as was the Chinese sentry. The bodies of the Japanese were found on the side of the road, mutilated. Japan demanded an apology and the withdrawal of Chinese troops thirty miles from the city. Those demands went unmet, and two days later, when my father was walking near his office, he saw the Japanese flagship *Idzumo* on the Whangpoo next to the Japanese Consulate, accompanied by some twenty warships. The next day, August 12, Chiang's best military divisions arrived in Shanghai from Nanking and established themselves in Chapei, the Chinese area on the north side of Soochow Creek, and Kiangwan, further north still. The day after that, Friday the thirteenth, the Shanghai Volunteer Corps was called up. Orders for Volunteers to report for duty were broadcast constantly on the radio, and displayed on theater screens all over the city.

And then China made a demand of her own, the withdrawal of Japanese troops by four o'clock the next afternoon. This was something new, an unprecedented firmness from the Chinese and a welcome change. The Chinese military was at last taking a stand, backed by the recent addition of modern bombers and ten two-thousand-pound bombs to Chiang's air force.

On that Friday afternoon, my mother had planned to take me to Whiteway & Laidlaw on Nanking Road for new school shoes. As Mei Wah drove us into town, I sat in the backseat of the car and tried to picture my feet in saddle shoes, which seemed so grown up that I was having a hard time imagining them. I was so focused on my feet that it was only when my mother groaned that I looked out the window to see what was wrong.

The city had been transformed, and I looked out on streets that should have been familiar but had become nightmarish. We passed barbed-wire barricades and sandbag shelters, and foreign soldiers stood on every corner. Chinese crowded the streets and sidewalks and doorways, their possessions in wheelbarrows or carts or just strapped onto their backs. They were refugees, my mother said, people who'd left Chapei and Hongkew to the north of Soochow Creek to make their way across the Garden Bridge because they were afraid to stay where they were.

My mother immediately gave up on buying shoes. The wind was blowing and the red warning light on the top of the Customs House was blinking, signaling a typhoon. She told Mei Wah to just turn around and take us back home. On our way, we passed the Great World, a six-storey amusement hall on the corner of Avenue Edouard VII and Tibet Road in the French Concession. I remembered its shooting galleries, hall of mirrors, Ferris wheels, Chinese classic dramas, magicians and fireworks and acrobats, but a few days earlier, it had been converted into a refugee center, as had theaters and schools around the city. It was mealtime as we passed. I looked out at a line of people that seemed endless, all of them waiting for a bowl of rice.

When we got home, my father met us at the door. It was only four o'clock, and it was unusual for him to be home so early. His expression was grim, his mouth a straight line. When my mother got out of the car, he said only, "It's Chapei." Then he looked at me and said, "You might as well see this," and he took my hand and led me up the outside stairs to the verandah, then to the north side of the house, where he put his hands on my shoulders and faced me toward Chapei across Soochow Creek.

The sky was a Halloween orange, darker than sunset and tinged with black, with low clouds that were blacker still. The air smelled of smoke, and there was a sound I'd never heard before. The closest thing was thunder, but this was faster and staccato sharp, an aggressive rapping that I wanted to stop.

"It's started," my father said. "That's the sound of shelling. Things won't be the same for a while now."

We watched in silence as it grew dark. By dusk the whole sky over Chapei was black smoke, and when we finally went inside, I stayed close to my parents out of fear, as though no place was safe. In the den, my father switched on the radio, and its miniature cathedral shape made me think of Mass. *Keep us safe*, I thought. My parents were listening to the news: the first shots had been fired at Yokohama Bridge, on the northern border of the International Settlement, leading to an exchange of fire between the outposts of the two militaries. Across the Whangpoo at Pootung, Japanese marines were disembarking from their cruisers under covering fire from gunboats.

The next morning, the clouds over Chapei were still black. The sound of shelling had become a backdrop that seemed to be everywhere and to come from all directions. It made my head hurt. There were other sounds, too, which my father said was cannon fire and the playback of shelling from ships, and firing from the gunboats in the Whangpoo, all of it making the French doors that opened onto the verandah shudder.

My parents had been invited to a wedding reception that afternoon. The bride was the daughter of my father's first employer in Shanghai, a man who ran the Asiatic American Underwriters, and there was to be a garden reception at the Cercle Sportif in the French Concession. It was clear that my mother had no wish to go, but it was equally clear that my father had no intention of staying home. He'd been at home more than usual that week, acquiescing to my mother's nervousness. By Saturday he was feeling cooped up and he made a deal with my mother: they would go to the reception, but only for a short time, just to make an appearance. And they would take me with them, so that my mother wouldn't worry.

We left at two. My father wanted something from his office, and he told Mei Wah to drive to the Bund before going to the French Concession. But as we neared the city, the roads became packed with people. Mei Wah inched his way through the crowds and it took almost half an hour to reach Yuen Ming Yuen Road, where my father hurried into his office while my mother and Mei Wah and I waited in the car, the motor running. My mother tried to play "I spy" with me, but she couldn't stay interested, and we had to keep starting over.

We heard planes overhead, and although I'd heard the sound earlier in the day when Chinese Northrups had flown low over the Settlement, the noise was more frightening now because it was so much closer. I leaned forward and saw the planes through the front windshield. My mother's expression became more anxious and she glanced at my father's office but said nothing. Then the shelling grew louder, and the planes nearer still, and I heard Mei Wah curse under his breath. My mother looked around frantically, as though trapped, and she spoke in Mandarin to Mei Wah, who only shrugged in answer.

And then a terrible sound shook the whole car, an explosion louder than anything I'd ever heard or imagined. My father hurried out a moment later, threw himself into the front seat, and told Mei Wah to get away from the Bund as quickly as possible.

But nothing was quick that afternoon. Downtown was packed and steaming, and our car barely moved. I looked behind us at the Garden Bridge and saw the stream of refugees still coming from across Soochow Creek. There was no end to them. When we neared the intersection of Nanking Road, my mother gasped and my father barked at Mei Wah again and I stared hard. I could not understand what I was seeing.

Nothing was identifiable. The front of the Cathay was gone, completely shattered, and the roof and walls of the Palace Hotel had been destroyed as well. The street was full of craters and littered with glass and metal and plaster, and everything was covered by smoke. The whole place was strewn with something I couldn't name, and there were people running everywhere—Municipal Police, Volunteers, the fire brigade, the Chinese Red Cross. There was a terrible smell of something burning, which I thought must be the cars on fire, the tires maybe.

And then I looked harder at one of the cars, and I saw that there had been a person inside. The corpse was black and burned, and I understood that there had been people in all of the burning cars around us, and I knew without knowing that what I smelled was burning flesh. I stared harder at the debris, unable to look away, and I saw bodies everywhere, some whole, some in parts. A man in a white flannel suit lay in the crosswalk, minus his head. The bloody body of a child was a few feet away. Torsos. Arms. Legs. Heads, hands, feet, as though someone had thrown an armful of broken dolls from a window high above.

My mother began to weep; my father said nothing. I sat very still, staring, mute.

There was a second explosion then, from the direction of the French Concession. My mother screamed and held me close, but there was no need. I was clinging to her as tightly as I could. I felt her breath catch, and she said, "Oh, Joseph, please," as though he somehow had the power to save us.

We made our way through the city streets to the French Concession. On Race Course Road, a few blocks from the Great World, I finally looked outside again and saw something dark running in the gutters. It was too dark to be water and it was not quite mud.

I remembered my father showing me a dye factory once, a place where he'd had to appraise some equipment, and I thought another bomb must have hit the factory. My mother was staring outside, too, and I started to say, "Look, it's paint," because I couldn't remember the word *dye*. But my mother choked and curled over and I understood that I was seeing blood.

And then we reached the Great World.

Through gray smoke, I saw a street full of bodies, even more than at Nanking Road, many of them torn into pieces. A Chinese police-man who had been directing traffic hung from his crow's nest. The body of a man in a tuxedo lay below in the street, and near him was a pretty Chinese woman in a blue cheongsam, her legs blown off, her right arm torn. On the curb, just outside the car window, was a woman's charred hand, the manicured nails painted bright red, a gold wedding ring on the finger, and near it was a baby's foot in a pink bootie. The air was filled with cries and moans and screams, and blood was everywhere.

Cars waiting for the traffic light to turn green, their passengers trapped inside them, were completely burned. The French police had just arrived, and their hands and arms were already bloody from sort-ing the living from the dead. The smell was hideous. My mother took off her wrap and held it to my face to lessen the stench, but it did no good, and I was sick on the floor of the car.

We were within two miles of the Cercle Sportif, much closer to the wedding than to home. My father told Mei Wah to take us there so that he could find out what had happened. It would, he thought, be safe.

Mei Wah drove down Tibet Road to Avenue Joffre, then down Route Père Robert to Route Cardinal Mercier. When we turned into the driveway of the Cercle Sportif, the day became even stranger. Here, everything was orderly and elegant. Chauffeurs wearing clean white gloves watched over long rows of parked cars. Mei Wah opened

our doors and my mother and I slowly got out of the car and followed
my father across the lawn.

Inside the club, there were hundreds of guests, Chinese, European, British, and American. The women wore brightly colored
dresses of silk and brocade and satin and lace. The Western men were
in tuxedos, the Chinese men in long gowns made of dark blue silk.
Paper lanterns hung everywhere, their soft light making the ballroom seem fragile and enchanted. I hardly moved. I was afraid that
if I moved too quickly, everything might disappear.

A waiter offered my parents champagne, and there were nougats
and Perugina chocolates that I usually coveted. A sixteen-course
Chinese dinner was just being served, and a Chinese woman in a pale
gold cheongsam commented to my father that the wine was warmed
just enough. I watched my father stumble in conversation with her
about the groom and his family and how she knew them until he
finally asked, "Do you know what's happened?"

She frowned. "There is a rumor of trouble near the Bund," she
said. "It doesn't sound like much to worry about."

My father opened his mouth as if to speak. Then he closed it and
just looked around him for a moment. He looked at my mother, who
seemed barely able to stand. "I can't stay here," he said. She nodded
and he picked me up and the three of us went to the car.

The roads had become even more crowded with refugees and
cars. I thought the world was made of smoke now. It was all I could
see over the Bund, and it was all I could smell. My father sat in the
front seat and fooled with the Motorola radio, trying to hear the news,
but everything was static. He finally snapped it off and slumped
back in his seat. "We'll find out soon enough," he said. "I suppose we
can wait."

Finally, an hour later, we were home. My mother took me upstairs
while my father went into the den to turn on the radio. Some time
later, he came to my room to tell my mother what he'd learned. It had

all been an accident: Chinese pilots trying to hit the Japanese *Idzumo* had dropped four two-thousand-pound bombs over the city. Two had fallen into the Whangpoo, raising a huge wall of water that had washed across the Bund and over any cars unlucky enough to be there just then. The third had fallen through the roof of the Palace Hotel, and the fourth had landed in front of the entrance to the Cathay. Hundreds of people had died instantly; hundreds more were wounded.

And then, my father continued, fifteen minutes after those first bombs, a disabled Chinese plane had accidentally dropped two more bombs over the Great World. The first had detonated the second, and another thousand people had been killed, mostly Chinese refugees. The news reports were calling that a record: the largest number of people killed by a single bomb in the history of aerial warfare.

:: :: ::

Late that Saturday night, long after my mother had put me to bed, my father came to my room, something he did often at the end of his evening. He would sit on the edge of my bed and pat my back and hum. I usually pretended I was sleeping. I was afraid that if he thought he'd woken me, he would leave so that I would go back to sleep.

That night he sat down and let his breath out, a long, tired sound.

"I have to give you something," I said suddenly, my voice startling him. I crawled out of bed and went to the window. I could feel him watching me as I pushed the screen open and found the yen, which felt cool and damp. I closed my fingers over it and wished for courage. I walked back to him, took his hand, and placed the yen in his open palm, then closed his fingers over it. I climbed back into bed and said, "Now you can look."

He opened his hand and held the yen up to the dim light that came in through the window. Then he looked at me.

"Where did this come from?"

"I took it that day. In your office."

He looked confused. "Any reason?"

"I just wanted it," I said. "But then everything bad started happening. Maybe"—my voice caught with guilt—"maybe that's why. Because I took it." I took a breath. "*Teh-nung*," I started, and I tried again. "*Teh-nung vachee*," I'm sorry.

He started to smile but stopped when he looked at me. "No," he said. "Some things happened because of some mistakes I made. Not you. Nothing that's happened has been your fault, Anna. It's just"—he faltered—"it's a bad time."

I took a breath and willed myself to believe him. "What's going to happen next?"

My father looked toward the hallway. "Your mother's afraid," he said, and he paused and looked at me carefully. "She wants to go home. To *her* home."

I nodded.

"You know that?"

I nodded again and hoped he would say more. "Sort of."

"To Los Angeles," he said.

"The City of Angels," I prompted, glad that I had it right for him.

He smiled gently. "Yep," he said. "That's about it. That's the deal, I suppose. The City of Angels."

"Are we going to do that?"

He shook his head. "I don't know," he said. "Shanghai's our home, right? What would we do anyplace else?"

I shrugged.

"We'll have to see," and he stood and slipped the yen into his pocket. "Everything's all right, Anna. You know that, don't you?"

I forced a smile, and he patted the pocket that held the yen and whispered, "*Hsiehhsieh*," thank you. Then he leaned close and kissed my forehead as though we'd made a pact.

We had, in a way, and when he turned and left my room, I hurt inside, but I also felt proud of myself. I had managed to do what I'd wanted most: I had managed not to cry, and when he told me that everything was all right, I had pretended to believe him.

the wounded

THERE WAS HEAVY RAIN AND WIND that Saturday night and all day Sunday, too, as though this was the way weather was now. The sounds of the storm were constant: the rain dripped evenly from the tile roof onto the pebbled path below my room, the wind shoved the poplars roughly against the window screens. But it wasn't just the weather. Everything seemed different. I was allowed to stay up later, and no one bothered about what I ate. Chu Shih rarely left the kitchen. He sat at the table whistling softly through his teeth while he read *Shên Pao*, Shanghai's leading daily Chinese newspaper, or *Damei wanbao*, the Chinese edition of the American *Shanghai Evening Post and Mercury*. Or he cleaned, scrubbing the kitchen counters, the pots and pans, the floor, as though if things were just clean enough, our lives would return to normal. He refused to leave the kitchen except to sleep, and when he heard my mother's footsteps, he watched the door intently, waiting to see what news she would have, or what she might need. He seemed to think that anything could happen.

My father turned on the radio in the den whenever he was within earshot, and my mother snapped it off as soon as he was out of range. She said there was more than enough evidence of the Battle of Shanghai around us without having to hear about it all day. I thought she was right. The sky was dark and filled with smoke that made my eyes sting, and when the wind blew, it brought the fumes of the Japanese funeral pyres from across Soochow Creek. The pounding of the guns of the Japanese warships moored in the Whangpoo shelling the city and of the bombs and anti-aircraft guns over Chapei was there all the time. The terrifying *boom!* when I stood with my father that Friday night on the verandah soon became routine, a dull thud in the background that frightened me only when I remembered what it was.

On Sunday night there was a knock at our front door just after my mother had turned out my lights and left my room. It was after ten, late for visitors, and Jeannie, my father's German shepherd, barked loudly. I lay in my bed on sheets that were damp from the humidity, and I listened hard to my father's muted voice from downstairs as he told Jeannie to hush. I heard the door open, and then I heard him say something else, and I heard alarm in his voice. He called for my mother, who said, "What is it, Joe?" and I glimpsed her hurrying along the upstairs hallway, tying the sash of her white satin robe. When she reached the entryway, I heard her say, "Oh, no," almost as though she'd been hurt, and then she said, "Mac, what's happened to you?"

I got out of bed and tiptoed to my doorway. From there I could just see the top of the front door and a neat triangle of the entry, where Dr. McLain, our neighbor and my father's friend and physician, stood staring at my parents as if in disbelief. He was filthy. His dark hair was unwashed and in disarray, and his suit was rumpled and dirty. My mother hurried toward the kitchen, calling for Chu Shih, while my father led Dr. McLain into the living room. I crept onto the landing at the top of the stairs and leaned against the staircase railing, holding it tight to keep myself still. I leaned back when I heard my mother's footsteps coming from the kitchen. She carried a tray that held a bottle of Scotch and three glasses. A linen towel was draped over her arm.

Dr. McLain sat on the edge of the leather ottoman near the doorway. I saw my mother lean toward him and I saw him take a glass of Scotch and the towel she offered, which he used to wipe his face. Then my mother sat down where I couldn't see her. I guessed she and my father were sitting on the divan.

Dr. McLain sat forward and held his head in his hands, and even from my perch some distance away, I could see that he was exhausted. My father asked a question I couldn't hear, and Dr. McLain shook his head, then he sat up straighter, his arms braced at his sides, as though holding himself up. He took a breath and he began to talk.

"It was unbelievable," he started. "You've no idea, no concept . . ." He paused, as if he was waiting for someone to finish his sentence.

"Go on," my father said quietly, not with encouragement, but with a grim okay-let's-hear-it tone in his voice. I inched down two more stairs, though I risked being caught, and I leaned forward so that I could hear.

Dr. McLain said he had been at home when the bombs had dropped yesterday afternoon, the day that was already being called Bloody Saturday. He had driven to St. Marie's Hospital as soon as he'd understood what had happened, not waiting to be called, just knowing he would be needed.

"At the hospital, the Sisters told the survivors to wait wherever there was space," he said. "They filled up the hallways, the men's outpatient ward, the reception areas, even the courtyard. All the time we worked, they were screaming, but not just from pain. They were screaming for attention. They understood that we weren't going to waste any time on the ones we thought wouldn't make it. They were the ones we just—" Dr. McLain coughed, and there was a long pause.

When he continued, his voice was anguished. "They were the ones that we injected with morphine, then asked them to wait in the hallway of the outpatient ward. 'Be seated here, please, until someone can see you. Yes, you'll have to wait a while longer.' Wait for what? To die. And it worked. Just a while ago, as I was finally leaving the hospital, I forced myself to look into that hallway. There was no one left."

Our house was quiet for a long moment, then my mother murmured something I couldn't hear. I saw my father stand next to Dr. McLain and refill his empty glass with Scotch. When my father sat down, Dr. McLain went on.

"On my way over here," he said, "I was thinking about medical school, about a lecture on amputations, and how I thought, *I'll never do this, what a waste of time. I could be studying.*" He took a long drink. "I have no idea how many arms and legs and hands and feet I amputated today. It was like a factory: remove an arm on this girl, a leg on this young man, another arm on the old woman in the corner, the right foot of the baby against the wall. There was no end to it."

I suddenly felt sick and afraid, and I tried to take a breath, but I ended up choking. My mother heard and called my name, and I hurried to the safety of my room, my curiosity overpowered by fear of getting caught. My mother called my name again and I said nothing, and they left me alone.

I lay in my bed, my heart pounding, and my room seemed alive. Outside, a sudden gust of wind whooshed the trees into the window hard, as though something much stronger than I was trying to get inside. I tried to think of good things, which was what my mother told me to do when I was afraid. I thought of Mass, a place that made me feel safe. I tried to imagine being in the Cathedral, but the images of church mixed with those of the hospital, and the people in the pews were missing arms and legs and hands and feet. Dr. McLain was picking up pieces of people and trying to stitch them back together with twine.

I tried to think of other things. I practiced my times tables, something I hadn't been taught yet but knew I would be eventually. I did the answers in my head, counting on fingers under the sheets. Four times four was sixteen. Five times five was twenty-five. Six times six was thirty-six. It was the highest I'd gone, and I kept going up to eight times eight, then started again. Finally I heard Dr. McLain leaving. I listened to the murmur of my parents' voices downstairs, and then I heard their steps on the stairs. They stood at my doorway for a moment as I pretended to sleep. Then they turned and walked down the hall together in silence.

Still I stayed awake, still the wind blew at the trees outside, still I was terrified if I closed my eyes. When I could stand it no more, I took the extra blanket from the foot of my bed and crept down the stairs and through the house to the kitchen. Standing at the door to Chu Shih's room, I knocked softly and heard a rustling. Chu Shih muttered something, and finally the door opened.

I whispered, "I'm afraid."

He did not hesitate but simply took my hand and led me into the dim softness of his room, where he wrapped the blanket around me and picked me up and laid me on his bed. He spoke to me in a Mandarin whose gentle tone I understood, if not its words. And then he lay on the floor next to the bed, and I fell asleep to the solid, even sound of his breath.

:: :: ::

My father predicted that the whole thing would be over in a week or so, and he said that despite the horror of Bloody Saturday, the battle really didn't concern us. The borders of the International Settlement and the French Concession were guarded by American and British soldiers and by the Shanghai Volunteers, and the fighting was restricted to Greater Shanghai, Chapei, which was the Chinese section of Shanghai, and Hongkew, the Japanese section of the

International Settlement, on the north side of Soochow Creek. While he admitted that the battle was cause for some concern and the source of some inconvenience, he said he could not imagine it becoming more than that.

It was, he said, a spectator's war, and at the start, despite my mother's objections, he liked to join the journalists who watched the battle from the roofs of the city's skyscrapers. The dining room on the roof of the Park Hotel and the Tower, a small nightclub on the top of the Cathay, were his favorites. From those vantage points, drinks in hand, he and the others could see the shooting and street fighting around the city while Japanese shells made graceful arcs overhead as they traveled southward from Chapei to Nantao. My father was transfixed. Buildings glowed, the sky filled with dark smoke, and the roofs nearby were crowded with people like him, foreigners who were far too fascinated with the fighting below to pay any attention to the Municipal Council's warnings about the danger of flying shrapnel.

Despite my father's frequent assurance that everything was all right, I worried. I had come to understand that adults could be wrong. I saw, when my parents and I drove through the city, that everything looked different. The streets were always packed with refugees trying to reach the Settlement or the Concession on foot or rickshaw or bicycle. The pavement was still stained with blood, even after the repeated use of disinfectant and sand. The smell was horrible, especially when the sun came out. One day in the car my father muttered that the city smelled like a charnel house, a word I didn't know. I asked what it meant, something he usually encouraged, but he snapped at me. "More questions?" he said. "You don't see that you're not part of this conversation?" I was stung. At home I went straight to his huge *Webster's Unabridged Dictionary* in the den. I had no idea how to spell the word I hadn't known, so I just stood glaring at words I couldn't read, my face hot with anger and hurt and tears.

The Battle of Shanghai was not over in a week. There were more bombs, the fighting grew more intense, the shelling constant, all of which my father seemed to take as a personal affront. He complained about the Chinese military's lack of training, and about Chiang's lack of resolve, and about the downturn in his business, thanks to the battle. He complained about the barbed-wire fences that he said were growing like weeds, and about the rigid security at the boundaries of the Settlement and Concession that made getting around the city take twice as long. The gates to the Settlement and Concession closed at night, and the Municipal Council imposed a 10 P.M. curfew, which put a damper on his social life. Though my parents still went out at night, to parties or dinner or the movies, their evenings became less predictable. On a Friday night late in September my father insisted on attending a dinner he and my mother had been invited to weeks ago. But when they got there, they found they were the only guests. The others, their hostess explained matter-of-factly, had been wounded on Nanking Road.

Each night at dinner my father listed his latest grievances. The banks moved from the Bund and the middle of town to the less central, less convenient French Concession. Some of the big shops closed, and the Country Club and some of the nightclubs were transformed into makeshift hospital wards where the Chinese wounded were cared for. He complained about evacuation. More and more of his friends were sending their wives and children home. He considered them alarmists.

And then, gradually, the complaining stopped and my father himself seemed to almost come to a halt during that fall. When the battle didn't end quickly, when friends packed up and left, when the city he loved became transformed, he, too, was changed. The violation of the safety of the International Settlement and what had seemed like the guarantee of extrality—events that were unthinkable to my father—left him at sea. Other fathers appeared businesslike and even prepared for what was happening. They matter-of-factly set about the business of repatriation, making certain their passports were in order, asking their wives to see that the family's trunks were packed, booking passages for their families to Hong Kong or Manila or Singapore, or even home, and planning to follow as soon as their businesses were in order. They paid the servants, saw to it that their houses would be closed tight, and arranged to stay at apartments on the Bund.

Not my father. He seemed numb. Each morning he came downstairs dressed as though he were going to his office, but when he opened the morning's *North China Daily News*, he headed to the den instead of the car, and passed the morning and sometimes most of the day listening to the news from the radio. Eventually he might have Mei Wah drive him to his office, but he was never gone for long.

My mother's response was exactly the opposite. She became busy, far busier than I'd ever seen her. Until then, she'd led a life of leisure, and it was something she did well. She might eat breakfast at the Del Monte, then lunch at the Cathay, with drinks first in the lounge. She went to the tea dances at the Palace Hotel and met my father for cocktails at the Cercle Sportif Français or St. Anne's Ballroom, then cutlets à la Kiev and tea sweetened with strawberry jam at D.D.'s. Her evenings were filled with dancing at the Casanova or the Ambassador or the Tower to the music of Artie Shaw, or to the Filipino orchestra at the Venus Cafe, or in the clover-shaped ballroom of the Majestic Hotel. Bridge parties, garden parties, dinner parties. Summer evenings spent listening to the Municipal Orchestra at concerts in the Public Gardens on the Bund.

But now she was always occupied and usually distracted. She sat at the mahogany dining room table and polished the ornate silver tea service, a wedding gift from her parents, until its brightness startled me when I passed through the room. She took the drapes down and handed them to Chu Shih to take outside for airing, then she put them back up herself. She ironed our clothes, something I'd never seen her do, had not even known she could do. The first time I saw her doing it, I just stared.

"I'm not sure what you're looking at," she said evenly. "My mother taught me to iron, and it's something I enjoy." She sprinkled the white sailor collar of my dress with water, then pressed hard on it with the iron, making the collar hiss. "It calms me," she added, and I knew enough not to ask more.

But after the first few startling days, my mother's cleaning and polishing and ironing calmed me as well. I liked seeing her occupied, and as the city outside us grew more chaotic, the inside of our home grew more orderly by the day. I tried to believe my father's regular dinner-table reassurance that everything was all right. It would all end soon, and life would be as it was.

In September, I started school at the Convent of the Sacred Heart in the French Concession. The children of most of my parents' friends went to the Shànghǎi American School, also in the French Concession on Avenue Pétain, but my mother had insisted on Sacred Heart. And so, on the ninth of September, I put on my new white blouse and blue tie, the navy blue skirt and blazer, the skirt four inches from the floor when I knelt. I stood very still as my mother brushed and combed and braided my long hair, asking me questions all the while. Had I brushed my teeth? Did I remember Sister's name, the one we'd met? Was I excited? Wouldn't school be wonderful? I nodded when I could, and gave the briefest answers possible when I had to speak for fear that my voice would crack and my mother—or worse, my father—might see my terror. And then, finally, after throwing away my scone and American apple when my mother stood to get her jacket, I followed Mei Wah to the car.

There were many things to be afraid of at school; this was one of the few things of which I was certain. There were other children, for one. Our house was so quiet, I wasn't used to being around children calling jokes and yelling to one another and laughing and running. I was also afraid of schoolwork. I'd heard stories about difficult endeavors like printing and cursive and subtraction, all of which seemed too much to master in only a few hours every day.

My nervousness did not prove unwarranted. School was a trial and a constant challenge in those first months. Maybe I was distracted and could have done better without the backdrop of a battle. As it was, I struggled in every subject, and I was always anxious at my desk. Each time Sister Terèse entered our classroom and whispered to Sister Matthia, I stared hopelessly at my lap, sure that I had done something wrong, that I had failed so miserably on some test or at some assignment that they weren't even going to bother to return it to me, just show me out, and that would be that.

:: :: ::

October brought more sandbags, more barbed wire, more Volunteers patrolling the streets, more Japanese troops. The whole city was dusty and grimy from the constant shelling, and it looked as though it were being carelessly dismantled, just knocked down with great blows. At home our meals changed. Chu Shih was a good enough cook that they were still substantial, but a meal with meat became an occasion, and fresh fruits and vegetables were rare. Foreigners continued to leave Shanghai. Again and again my parents said good-bye to American and British and French families who lived nearby, and the Settlement and Hungjao began to feel empty. We, apparently, weren't going anywhere.

On a cold, still night in the middle of November, I woke to find my father in my room. He was standing at my window, looking out toward the city. There was something about the way he stood that alarmed me. I got out of bed and went to him, and when I took his hand and he looked down at me, I became afraid and said, "Are you sad?"

He smiled, barely. "Yes," he whispered.

"Why?" I asked, also whispering.

He sighed and looked out the window again. "Something's happened that I didn't expect," he said. "Shanghai has fallen to the Japanese. The Chinese general has ordered his soldiers to leave the city. Which means Shanghai is now controlled by the Japanese." He looked down at me. "Do you understand any of that?"

I shook my head. I understood that my father had been wrong. More than that I wasn't sure.

He did not speak for a moment. I knew he was still sad, and I wanted to stay there with him and keep him company, because I knew that being sad alone was worse than being sad with someone else. But I was so tired that I began to lean against him, almost falling asleep, and after a few minutes, he picked me up and carried me to my bed.

after the fall

A STRANGE THING HAPPENED after the fall of Shanghai. Despite the visible reminders of the battle—the city blocks of barbed wire, the sandbags and barricades, the patched-over, repaved streets and filled-in craters in front of the Great World and Wing On Department Store and the Palace Hotel—the Settlement and the Concession resurrected themselves almost immediately, and for foreigners, my parents included, life was once again good. Friends of my parents who had left Shanghai because of the battle, going to summer resorts like Peitaiho and Wei Hai Wei in the north, or to even further places like Manila and Hong Kong, decided the city was safe again, and began to return.

My father acted as though nothing had happened. He and my mother resumed their social life, dancing at the Cathay and the Ambassador, going to the Capitol Theatre to see Charlie Chaplin or Humphrey Bogart or Charles Laughton. He said the only thing that was different was the curfew, which meant that they had to be off the streets by 10 P.M. The Japanese gendarmes and sentries who enforced the curfew were not to be fooled with. They stood guard at the exits from the Concession and the Settlement, and passersby were required to show their respect by bowing. I had seen those sentries, and the sight of their dark uniforms and antiseptic masks frightened me. Chu Shih reinforced that fear by telling me that if you failed to show sufficient respect—especially if you were Chinese—you were punished, even bayoneted. And just about anything was reason enough for a beating.

Soon after Japanese occupation, business resurrected itself, too, and before long Shanghai was booming. My father said the Bund was crowded with more trading vessels than he'd ever seen, and at dinner each night, he talked excitedly about new cotton and flour mills, about factories that produced just about anything you could name—hats and glassware, thermos bottles and flashlights, electric fans and cigarettes. He started to deal in raw materials that were brought in from the interior, Japanese-occupied territories, selling iron ore and coal, tungsten and antimony. He went to his office every day, and he received calls constantly at home, but if the dinner conversation ventured anywhere near the details of his business, he became wary, and my mother quickly asked me how school was. My father's business had become a subject she didn't enjoy.

I found my father's excitement and optimism contagious, and when he said that things couldn't be better, I believed him. So I was surprised and confused when my mother and I went into the city the first time after the Japanese had taken control. The city streets were not the same, and everything looked far from all right. Japanese sentries were everywhere, and people dressed in not much more than rags crowded into doorways, streets, sidewalks, even window ledges.

Things didn't feel the same at all. I was more closely watched and Chu Shih was more insistent about locking the doors and windows at night. Hungjao, the area we lived in, became a no-man's-land. Though officially outside the boundaries of the International Settlement, for all practical purposes Hungjao was part of it, except that the question of who had jurisdiction over it—the Chinese municipal authorities or the International Settlement—had never really been answered. But once the Chinese officials began leaving the city, the Japanese Military Police simply took charge, and their attitude toward Hungjao residents was an uneasy mix of resentment and admiration. There were frequent complaints of brutality at the hands of the Japanese, and residents were careful not to aggravate them. One evening I heard my father telling my mother a story he'd heard from Dr. McLain. That afternoon, he said, something in the hedge near Dr. McLain's driveway had caught Mac's eye. He'd thought it was some kind of animal, but when he went to investigate, he discovered the head of a Japanese soldier. He wasted no time in wrapping the head in a burlap sack and taking it to the Hungjao aerodrome, more neutral territory than his own backyard, he reasoned. He left it there behind the acacia bushes along the road. He had no idea how the head had gotten to his property. What he did know was that if the Japanese found it, there would be serious consequences for him.

When my father finished the story, my mother's response was curt. "How much more proof do you need, Joe? This place is changed."

My father ignored her. He refused to dwell on the darker side of Shanghai, and if my mother commented on any of it, he encouraged her to look the other way. He seemed to see plenty of reasons for optimism. Each evening when he came in from his office with news of someone else who'd come back, he told us with a smug, I-told-you-so edge to his voice.

"You see?" he said at dinner one night. It was November and I could hear the distant sound of foghorns on the Bund, a sound that always made me feel lonely. My father pointed his fork at me as though I'd invented evacuation. "We just had to wait it out, was all."

My mother glanced at him, her eyes the deep rich brown color of the French coffee she drank every morning. You could stare at my mother's eyes without meaning to. I saw people do it all the time. Then she lowered her gaze to the gardenias and pink roses that I had helped Chu Shih arrange in the center of the table that afternoon. She reached for her water glass, her silver bracelets clicking together as she moved, and though she said nothing, there was disagreement in the air.

In addition to the import-export business, my father started up in the insurance business again, adjusting claims for American Asiatic Underwriters. And he pursued a third line of work, smuggler. He had started smuggling tungsten in the early 1930s, buying it in the Chinese interior and selling it in Shanghai to businessmen from Hong Kong, the United States, Britain, and Japan. After tungsten, he smuggled in tires and newsprint and scrap metal. The scrap metal was easy, as it tied in with his insurance business. When he learned of a piece of machinery or a truck that had been destroyed, he simply offered to buy it for scrap from the owner. Selling it was easy. The Japanese were maintaining an army out of scrap metal, and had been doing so for years, buying it from the United States government, which shipped it on the American President lines right to Kobe Harbor. My father, on his trips to Japan, had seen whole shiploads unloaded, and talked of storage yards for scrap iron that covered square miles of land. And he had joined in, selling every bit of scrap metal he could get his hands on.

He was also smuggling yen. Although the Japanese government tried to prevent its currency from being taken out of the country, the foreign black market for yen was thriving. Before the occupation, my father had bought cheap yen in Shanghai or Peking, then traveled to Japan, where he could turn it back into U.S. dollars for a good profit. Traveling to Japan was no longer possible, but, more important, it wasn't necessary. There were plenty of Japanese businessmen right in Shanghai looking to buy, and my father accommodated them gladly, bringing them one hundred yen notes strapped to his body and exchanging them for U.S. dollars or Shanghai dollars, either one would do. And although *what* he sold might change, *whom* he sold to never did: always the highest bidder, plain and simple, regardless of nationality. My father was not one to play favorites where money was concerned.

In the months after the fall of Shanghai, my father's schedule was chaotic, and the whole house felt busy when he was home. But he was gone more than he was home. He was rarely at breakfast and he frequently missed dinner. If I asked where he was, my mother's answer was vague. I woke in the middle of the night to the sound of the car starting, and when I looked out my window, I would see the Packard pulling out into the street, the only car around. There were phone calls at all hours, and he canceled plans at the last minute. On those nights, Will Marsh came to the rescue and escorted my mother to whatever dinner or dance she'd agreed to attend. Like many of my father's friends, he had sent his wife and children home as soon as the city fell.

I knew one thing my father was doing. He was shopping. When he came home late in the day or early evening, he carried in package after package. There was a random, frantic quality to his buying, and his purchases were completely unpredictable, sometimes practical, sometimes pure extravagance. Either way, he was gleeful as a child, his eyes too bright as he unwrapped what he'd bought. There was a new toaster set, and a waffle iron. He said he hadn't had homemade waffles in years, and couldn't we teach Chu Shih? A few days later he arrived flushed and excited and showed us a new camera and a Cine Kodak 8 for home movies. My mother seemed shocked; my father had never really seemed the snapshot or home movie type. Other nights brought Arrow ties, a Remington Rand portable typewriter, which would come in handy, he said, if he ever needed to do some work from home. There was a Speed Sled Snow Racer for me, though we rarely saw snow in Shanghai. And the Taylor Auto

Altimeter would tell us how high we were as we drove, he said, a gadget that made no sense whatsoever in the flat landscape that was Shanghai. The Grosvenor Stormoguide had an automatic signal device that sounded when the barometer rose or fell, warning of us a coming storm.

And then he presented my mother with boxes from Prosperity and Good Fortune, a jewelry store on Hardoon Road, and Chine Tai & Company on Yates Road, a lingerie shop. My mother accepted the boxes nervously and opened the jewelry box, where she found three carved jade bracelets, which she slid over her hand and onto her wrist as smoothly as though they'd been made for her. She moved her wrist so that the bracelets made a quick clicking sound. "They're beautiful, Joe," she said, and although she smiled, she still looked apprehensive.

My father beamed and looked as though the best was yet to come. "Open the other one."

My mother did, and inside she found a chiffon negligee. "It's the Circe model," my father said proudly, as though he were describing some sort of machine. "That color's called crushed rose, and it's the latest." He held it up to my mother and appraised her. My mother was unable to hide her confusion, and when she saw that the midriff of the gown was embroidered with the words *Bonne nuit*, she looked as though she might cry.

He seemed drunk on his new acquisitions, a feeling that I understood, for I was giddy with anticipation every time he came home. Even Chu Shih peered out the window eagerly when he heard the Packard drive up, and all of us thought the same thing: *What has he bought now?* When he wasn't purchasing, he talked about what he might buy next. There was a new set of the complete works of Shakespeare he was interested in, and he said it was time for me to have a bicycle, and it would have to be a Schwinn. General Electric had a new automatic glass coffeemaker he said looked very handy. And then there was the car.

It was at dinner one night in December. He was quiet for most of the meal, and finally he mentioned that he was thinking of a new car, a Bugati. He held up an ad he'd torn out of *Life* magazine. "Ostrich skin interior," he said, "a rosewood dashboard." He looked at my mother, then at me. "Well, what do you think?"

My mother did not meet his eyes. "It's a bit much, don't you think, Joseph?" She carefully cut a carrot into thirds, as though the act required great precision. "And we don't really need it," she continued. "We don't even know how much longer we'll be here. It's hardly the time for a new car."

My father laughed. He looked at me and winked as though we understood something my mother hadn't grasped. "It may be exactly the time for a new car," he said. And then he added that he had a phone call to make, and he excused himself from the table.

:: :: ::

The next morning, the first Saturday in December, he woke me early and told me to get up and get dressed.

"Where are we going?" I guessed the answer could be just about anywhere. Maybe we were leaving for Los Angeles. Maybe we were buying a new car. Maybe we were just going downstairs.

"Out," he said simply, as though that said it all, and although I nodded, I was confused. My mother had said that he wasn't supposed to take me on what he called "outings." It was a point of disagreement between them, one of a growing list. He said it was good for me to get out, and that there was no reason for any American to be afraid. She said it was dangerous; anything could happen these days. As I pulled on thick black tights and a tartan skirt and wool sweater over long underwear, I wondered how he had changed her mind, and I marveled at his abilities.

He was waiting for me when I came into the kitchen. He wore his heaviest overcoat, the dark tweed one with the shiny black leather buttons that looked like chocolate mints. He had on a brown felt hat, and his breath puffed in the cold kitchen, where it was too early for Chu Shih to have lit the fire. Shanghai winters were harshly cold, and we were having what Chu Shih called a "four-coat winter"—days the color of slate, where you could hardly remember the sun. My father held my wool coat for me, then leaned close and buttoned every button, even the top one, which made the coat feel scratchy against my neck. Then he took my wool hat from the counter and pulled it on too low, so that I felt as though I were looking out from underneath something, but I said nothing. He was all business.

Mei Wah was waiting in the car, and as my father and I got into the backseat, he glanced back at us angrily, why I didn't know. If my father noticed, he didn't let on. He gave me a slice of French bread and a thermos of Hershey's cocoa he'd made, and he explained that we were going to Hongkew to look at a piece of machinery that the owner of a printing shop was claiming had been destroyed. On the seat next to him was what he called his grip, a battered leather brief-case that he would never replace because it had been a gift from his father. It was open, and I saw his new camera inside.

He tapped it lightly. "We're going to take a picture, you and I, so that the insurance company doesn't pay for something they shouldn't. If the machinery's ruined, they'll pay. If not, they won't. You see, Anna?"

I nodded.

He laughed. "You'll be some businesswoman someday," and I made a face, certain that I would not like business, nor it me. "Not just anybody can do this, you know," he added, and there was pride in his voice.

I thought of my mother's instructions that he not take me out, and I misunderstood his meaning. "Can we?" I asked.

He nodded. "You bet. We've got a pass from the Japanese authori-ties." He held out a piece of paper that was stamped several times in an angry and authoritative red. And then he said, "And after that, we'll go to Liu and Company."

I forgot my mother instantly. "The paper store?"

He nodded. "Sure thing. Soon as we've got our pictures."

I sat back in the seat, sure that it was going to be a good day. The paper store was a favorite of mine, and I had not been there in months.

At the Garden Bridge, the Japanese sentry motioned for us to stop. No foreigners were allowed in Hongkew without a pass, and no Chinese were allowed, period. The sentry ordered us out of the car, then searched my father, Mei Wah, and the car. My father held out his pass. The sentry stared at it disdainfully, then threw it back at my father and motioned for us to be off.

We crossed the bridge and entered Hongkew, which had been taken over by the Japanese Imperial Army and Navy as the site of their barracks and naval headquarters, in part because it had been the Japanese section of the International Settlement, nicknamed "Little Tokyo," but more importantly because it was the location of most of the city's industry and utilities—the waterworks, the power station, the jail, the larger warehouses and go-downs. Japanese flags were everywhere: on buildings and wrecks of buildings, on boats and sampans, on factories and apartments and offices. As we drove up Broadway, past the brick Astor House Hotel and the Russian, German, and Japanese Consulates, I spotted Broadway Mansions—our lookout in the past—and I asked my father if we were going to stop. He grumbled, "Not anymore," and when I asked what he meant, he explained. The Foreign Correspondents Club on the top of Broadway Mansions was now the officers club for the Japanese generals.

Broadway, Hongkew's main street, used to be lined with cabarets and theaters and cafés, then small redbrick terraced houses. But now we passed block after block of ruins with only chimney foundations and a few telegraph poles left. Wires hung over the wreckage as if in mourning, and a Sikh wearing one rag of a coat on top of another searched through the rubble, for what I couldn't imagine. A red scarf was tied around his neck, the only color in this world of gray.

We drove further, down narrow streets that had turned to slushy mud. We turned northeast, following the curve of the Whangpoo to the warehouses and factories, and my father pointed out wharves that were piled high with scrapped machinery that he said would be shipped to Japan. I could see Japanese freighters moored along the river, but almost no junks. I missed their bows, painted with eyes that always seemed friendly. When I asked my father, he said that the Japanese took care of fishing now. The junks had become practice targets for the Imperial Navy's gunboats and destroyers.

Finally we reached an industrial area that housed warehouses and factories and cotton mills, all of them flying Japanese flags. My father leaned forward and pointed to a low building at the end of a dismal street. "There," he said, "Hsin Hung Chong. That's their warehouse. Stop here."

Mei Wah parked the car and my father opened his door and got out of the car, then waited for me to follow, which I did with reluctance. We were close to the Whangpoo, and the wind was freezing, the sky dark gray. My father took my hand and led us to the building's entrance. He tried the metal door and found it locked, and he rapped on it loudly. When nothing happened, he knocked again, and this time we heard steps, and when the door was pushed open, a Sikh guard glared at us. My father spoke to him in sharp Mandarin, asking for someone, and the guard finally held the door open for us.

Inside there was almost no light, and the vast place smelled damp and cold and uninhabited. When my eyes adjusted to the grayness, I saw that the warehouse was filled with boxes and crates, stacked next to each other, on top of each other, every which way. My father said something else to the guard, and he led us to the back corner, where a machine the size of a small car was pushed against the wall.

My father said something else, and I heard the same name as before, Matsumoto. The Sikh told us to wait, and he left us.

"Who do we have to see?" I asked.

"The guy in charge," my father said vaguely, then he looked at the machinery in front of us, and he laughed softly. "So here it is, you see? Not destroyed at all." He set his bag on the concrete floor and took out his camera and snapped a few pictures.

And then there was a banging at the door and shouting and the place grew less gray from the doors being opened. There was more shouting, and then footsteps coming close. When we turned to see who it was, we faced four Japanese gendarmes.

My father's expression told me that this was not at all what he'd expected, and I was immediately terrified. I'd heard too many whispered stories not to be, and a part of me expected to be bayoneted on the spot. For a long moment, they simply stared at us. Then the one who seemed to be in charge said something and my father shook his head; he didn't understand. The man repeated himself, and when my father shook his head and shrugged, he made a sudden movement toward my father as though he might strike him. But he stopped a foot away.

The superior spoke to one of the others, who walked to the door of the warehouse and leaned out and yelled something. A minute passed, and he returned with a fifth gendarme. The superior spoke to him, and he nodded. In Mandarin, he said to my father, "*Ni tso shenme shêngyi?*" What is your business?

My father answered, "*Wo tso ch'u-ju-kou shang-i,*" I am in the import-export business, but the gendarme waved frantically. "*Mann mhan,*" slowly, and my father repeated his answer.

And then the gendarme began asking questions in a broken, uneducated Mandarin that was worse than mine—what was he doing, where was he going, what was his business, where did he live? My father answered each question slowly, then he gestured to his grip.

The gendarme shook his head and barked an answer, and my father tried again, more slowly. I understood the words *maimai* and *baohsien*, business and insurance. Then he smoothed my hair and added, "*nüerh*," daughter.

The translator nodded and spoke to his superior, who stared hard at my father. Then he nodded, and my father opened his grip and took out a huge black book that he always carried with him on business, the *Directory of Businessmen in the Orient*. He held the directory out to the translator, who handed it to his superior. My father's hand tightened around mine.

Finally the superior said something that caused the soldiers to laugh. My father's hand relaxed slightly, and for a moment, I thought I must have misunderstood, because everything suddenly seemed all right. The gendarme reached down and picked up my father's grip and held it out to him as though returning it, and my father moved to take it. But before he could, the gendarme turned it upside down, emptying it and letting my father's possessions clatter to the concrete floor. The camera hit with a sharp crack, and the Japanese laughed harder and stared at us as though we were in on the joke.

My father stood rigidly next to me and held my hand so tightly that it hurt, but I was too afraid to tell him. The Japanese laughed for another moment, and the superior said something to the translator, who laughed, then looked at my father and said, "*Shihku*," accident, and shrugged in mock apology. They turned as though ready to leave, but then the superior turned back and said something and pointed to the camera. The translator picked it up and handed it to him, and he laughed again.

And then they were gone.

My father remained silent, not moving for perhaps a minute. I was freezing. My teeth chattered and I could feel the flat coldness of the concrete floor through my shoes. My thick tights seemed no better than thin cotton socks, and my nose was starting to run. Finally my father knelt on the floor and began picking up his things and putting them back into his grip—papers, folders, a monogrammed linen handkerchief, his black leather gloves. And the boar-bristle brush that my mother had given him years ago, which he always kept with him.

When he had finished, he stood and took my hand. I could feel myself shaking, partly from the cold, but more from fear, and though I tried to stop, I couldn't.

He looked down at me, then knelt and smoothed my hair from my forehead. "What's this?" he asked, his voice worried. "Are you cold?"

I nodded and felt my eyes fill with tears.

"And you're afraid?"

I nodded again.

"Now look," he said, and the sudden sternness in his voice frightened me more, but when he continued, his voice was gentle. "You don't have anything to be afraid of," he said. "Don't you know that, Anna? Don't you know you're safe with me? I wouldn't let anything happen to you."

I took a breath and looked at him and was startled at the fierceness in his blue eyes. I nodded and whispered, "I know."

He pulled me to him and carried me toward the door, holding me tightly. Mei Wah was waiting for us outside. My father put me down and said nothing as we walked to the car, but when we were perhaps twenty feet away, he squeezed my hand and glanced at me. Then he stopped. He knelt next to me and said, "Can you keep a secret?"

I nodded.

"Do you know what they were looking for, those gendarmes?"

I shook my head.

"They were looking for yen," he whispered, "but they didn't find it, did they, Anna?"

"No," I whispered, as though I were in on it.

"They thought they had us, but it's right here, you see?" He tapped his chest over his heart, then he took my hand and held it to his chest. "You see?"

I felt the smooth coolness of his pressed shirt. And something sturdier and harder than flesh underneath. I looked at him and he smiled. When he unbuttoned his shirt and held it open, I saw the dark black canvas of the money belt from his office.

"We tricked them, all right. They don't own me. Nobody owns Joseph Schoene." He stood and flung open the car door, whistling again, as though we had reason to be jubilant.

:: :: ::

My father told Mei Wah to let us out on the Bund side of the Garden Bridge and to pick us up in an hour. The walk would do us good, he said, and he added that we could buy something sweet. I was still cold, but I didn't argue. My father stopped at the first street vendor we reached and bought a sack of twenty *li sing dong*, lotus seeds, that were as fat and round as grapes, fried and coated in sugar. They didn't make me warmer, but they made me happy as we walked.

Liu & Company—a stationers that I just called "the paper store"—was near my father's office on Szechuan Road, and it fascinated me. I'd never tried explaining that fascination to my mother; it was far too practical for her. I had told only my father and Chu Shih about it, and from time to time, my father indulged me and let me wander in its small, crowded aisles. As my father and I neared it that day, a new worry presented itself: what if the store wasn't there anymore? Storefront after storefront had simply been boarded up with plywood, and we hadn't been there since before the battle. What if it was gone?

We turned onto Peking Road, and when we turned onto Museum Road a block later, I spotted Liu's crimson banner, the wind making it dance as if in greeting. The door opened as someone entered, reassuring me. I looked up at my father and whispered, "Look. It's still here."

"Of course it is," he said. He looked at me as though I'd been worried for nothing. He held the door for me, and I entered slowly, trying to savor the treat.

The smell was the first thing you noticed, the clean smell of paper and the promising scent of new pencils. Shelves lined every wall, from the counters, which were just about eye-level for me, to the ceiling, and every one was crammed with supplies. Stacks and stacks of exercise books, their pages filled with double lines or single lines, or with small neat squares for arithmetic. Pads in all sizes, with sheets of pale yellow, light blue, soft white. The counter along the back wall was filled with pencils, more pencils and more kinds of pencils than I had ever imagined. Pencils of all colors, in boxes, sharpened if you wanted. Pencils with lead so fine you could barely see the mark they made, and fat pencils with thick lead, the kind I used at school to practice the alphabet. Next to the pencils were pens, some with slots for metal nibs, pointed ones for fine, scratchy writing like my teacher's, stubby ones for thick and bold printing like my father's. The shelf above the pens held bottles of ink, blue and red and green, and thick black India ink for drawing.

My father told me I could choose three things, and I was immediately apprehensive, overwhelmed with the task—there was so much! But soon I saw him standing at the window, gazing out at the street and jingling the change in his pocket. He was growing restless. I took a packet of pale blue letter writing paper with matching envelopes, a dark blue-colored pencil, and an Art Gum eraser, and I felt that the possibilities of what I could do with those things were endless.

Outside the air felt even colder. I told myself that we didn't have far to walk to meet Mei Wah. I held my hands inside my coat sleeves and crossed my arms in front, holding my bag to my chest. My father glanced at his watch, stuffed his hands in his pockets, and began to walk more quickly. The thought that even he was feeling the cold alarmed me; I wondered if people ever just froze on city streets, ending up the way we looked when we played statues in the school yard.

When we turned the corner and the bridge was in sight, he glanced at his watch again and said, "Right on time, you see? Mei Wah will be waiting for us and we'll be home in no time."

As we neared the bridge, there seemed to be some commotion. When we got closer, we found a small crowd had gathered, and we heard sharp Japanese from the sentry. When we reached the edge of the crowd, my father pushed me past English and European men in overcoats and Chinese in long blue gowns lined with red fox. We had no reason to cross the bridge; I guessed he just wanted to see what was going on.

The whole place smelled of Soochow Creek, close and cold and stale, and I started to ask if we couldn't just please find Mei Wah and go home. But then I heard something familiar, and when I heard it again, I realized it was Chu Shih's voice, and I thought how good it would be to see him and show him what I'd bought. I heard his voice again—it was low and very guttural and easy to identify—and I started to call out to him. Then the man in front of me moved away slightly, and what I saw took my words away.

Chu Shih was standing on the bridge. He wore his thick black cotton trousers and a padded blue Chinese jacket with his white apron underneath, as though he'd left home in a hurry. Next to him was a Chinese man I'd never seen before, a refugee. His clothes were rags whose original shape and color you couldn't even guess at, and everything about him seemed lost.

The Japanese sentry faced Chu Shih and the refugee, his legs slightly apart. He was shouting angrily, and gesturing at them to do something. Then he moved toward Chu Shih and slapped him, hard, though he had to reach up to do so. I caught my breath and felt so stunned that it was as though it was my cheek he'd slapped.

The sentry pointed at the refugee and yelled again. His gestures made it clear that he was ordering Chu Shih to slap the refugee. Chu Shih wiped blood from his lip and shook his head firmly. The sentry communicated his order again, but Chu Shih still refused. The sentry began to slap the refugee hard, over and over again, until finally the man cried out in pain, put his hand to his ear, and fell to the ground. The sentry turned back to Chu Shih. He barked something at him and raised his arm as though to strike him. I saw Chu Shih brace himself.

Someone pushed past me, and I saw my father striding toward the sentry. He walked up to Chu Shih and stood next to him. His expression was pained as he looked up at Chu Shih and spoke softly to him. Then he began to speak to the sentry. I heard the word cook, *ch'uishi-hyüen*. The sentry glared at my father as he spoke, but my father just kept talking, although the sentry didn't seem to understand. He only sputtered back, furious. My father ignored him and bowed, a movement so slight it would have been easy to miss. From his pocket, he took the pass he'd shown the guards earlier and handed it to the sentry. The sentry looked at it for a long moment before finally nodding to my father.

My father turned and looked for me in the crowd, and when he saw me, he said, "Come on, Anna," his voice so calm you would have thought he was calling me to lunch. I walked to him and took his hand, and he said only, *"Lai,"* come, and led Chu Shih off the bridge.

The Packard was waiting for us at the street. My father opened the back door and motioned for Chu Shih to get inside. Chu Shih rarely rode in the car, and he hesitated. My father said gently, "Go on, get in, we're all right now," and Chu Shih lowered himself into the car's backseat. My father told me to sit next to Chu Shih, and he got in the front with Mei Wah.

Chu Shih was still breathing hard, the sound like something forced. I did not let myself look at him, not because of the blood and the swelling I knew I would see, but because of his shame, which seemed to emanate from him like heat.

In the car, Mei Wah explained that he had gone home while we were at Liu's, and my mother had sent Chu Shih along with him to watch for us, a request that didn't make sense. My father shook his head and rubbed his chin, a nervous gesture of his. He said to me in a low voice, "She didn't know you were going with me this morning. She must have worried," and Mei Wah shot him that cross look again.

Chu Shih said that the sentry had thought him insolent, that he was mocking the sentry, and that he needed to learn respect. He said he had done nothing to make the sentry think that. The refugee standing next to him had bowed, but apparently not to the sentry's satisfaction. So the sentry had called the two of them over and had ordered Chu Shih to beat the refugee. His refusal had sent the sentry into a rage.

When Chu Shih finished speaking, the car was silent, except for the sound of his labored breathing. I stared hard at my hands. His story didn't make any sense to me, but I said nothing. I wanted only for the ride and the horrible day to be over. I did the only thing that I could think of that would help. I took Chu Shih's huge hand and held it between my small hands. He closed his fingers around my hand and nodded, and our conversation was over.

:: :: ::

I ran a fever that night. I woke often, and each time I did, I felt my father's presence in my darkened room. In the evening, I had heard my parents argue, but the fever stretched out a few minutes of cross words into hours, making it seem as if they argued all night.

When I woke the next morning, my father was sitting on a chair he'd pulled up next to my bed. He still wore his clothes from the day before, and I knew he'd been sitting with me most of the night. He was dozing, but he woke when I sat up, and he put his hands on my shoulders.

"Not so fast there. You're to stay put, Anna."

I lay back down and asked, "Why?"

"Dr. McLain's orders. Said you needed rest after"—my father paused—"yesterday." I nodded and my father just watched me for a moment. Then he sighed and ran his palm over his hair. "I really messed up," he said. "A case of bad judgment. I had no business taking you to Hongkew with me." He paused. "I'm sorry."

"That's all right," I said, a reflex. And then I asked what worried me most: "Is Chu Shih all right?"

My father nodded. "He's fine," he said. "Good as new. But that doesn't make what I did right, and I won't do it again." He turned and looked out the window for a long moment. "I just didn't want you to go around afraid," he said softly. "I wanted you to see that you're still safe here, that things are different, but they're not so bad as everybody says." He looked at me and shrugged. "But apparently I'm in a category of one."

"Category?"

He laughed softly. "I'm the only one like me. Nobody else seems to think like I do."

"But you're always like that," I said. "Aren't you?"

My father laughed again, and his face relaxed. "True enough," he said. "You're wise beyond your years, Anna Schoene." He mussed my hair and laughed again. I laughed, too, hoping it would make me feel better, that it would dissolve the hard knot in my stomach and help me trust my father again.

:: :: ::

In mid-December, the Japanese took the city of Nanking, which they saw as the very heart of China, despite the fact that Chiang Kai-shek had moved the seat of his government from there several weeks earlier. In the days after the fall of Nanking, there were rumors of atrocities that were beyond belief. Some said there were photographs that proved the rumors true. My parents talked about it in urgent hushed tones and changed the subject when they realized I was near, their voices becoming instantly cheery. I made a lot of noise when I was nearby; I didn't *want* to hear what they were saying, not any of it. Early on, I had heard my father use the phrase "burning them alive," and I knew I didn't want to hear any more. It was also the first time I heard the word *rape*, and though I had no idea what the word meant, the fear and pain in my mother's voice told me I didn't want to know more.

On a Sunday evening in January, 1938, Dr. McLain and his wife and Will Marsh came for dinner. Casual Sunday-night gatherings in the Outside Roads were a sort of tradition. Everyone knew everyone out there, and often as not, much of the neighborhood would end up at someone's house for an early dinner. But the neighborhood was dwindling as families moved closer to the safety of town. Some took suites at the Palace Hotel, others rented apartments at the Medhurst on Bubbling Well Road in the Settlement, or the Picardie Mansions in the French Concession. My father viewed these moves as compromise, and not an option. The McLains and Will Marsh didn't seem to be moving either, though Will's family had gone. The McLains were staying only because Mrs. McLain was pregnant, due in three months, and a difficult pregnancy had forced them to stay put until the baby was born, rather than risk the trip home.

That night when I had been excused from the dinner table, I stood at my mother's side and asked if I could go to my room, and when she nodded, I went eagerly upstairs, trying not to run. My birthday was soon, only eight days away, and I had asked for a pair of stilts that I had seen in the Sears Roebuck catalog. I wanted them desperately, so much so that I was worried that if I didn't get them, my disappointment would be too great to hide, and I would ruin my own birthday. My plan was to hunt around and see if I could find the stilts—or another present—and then at least I would know, and things would be better either way. But I had high hopes. Christmas had been a muted time, and though we'd decorated the tree and hung paper loop chains and carved angels from soap and opened each window of the Advent calendar, the season had been more of a somber observance than a celebration. I hoped my birthday would be different.

I stood at the top of the stairs and heard my mother ask Chu Shih to clear the table and serve coffee and dessert, and I smiled. They would be at the table for another hour almost. After coffee and dessert, my father would offer Dr. McLain and Will Marsh cigars, another half hour at least. I'd learned that toward the end, grown-up dinners stretched out longer than you had thought possible. I heard a chair being pushed back, and my father walked to the living room and put on a record. I went to my room and put on my nightgown, then walked barefoot down the hall.

My parents' bedroom had a secrecy and formality to it that gave me a small chill when I opened the door. I was entering forbidden ground, for I wasn't supposed to be in there without them. But I was determined, and I went inside and closed the door after me.

The room's scent told you it was a private place. It was intimate, the sweet musky smell of sandalwood and cassia bark—Chinese cinnamon—that lined the drawers of my mother's dresser. The room *felt* private, with its long velvet drapes of a deep rose the color of flushed cheeks, and the four-poster Ningpo bed made of dark mahogany, its huge headboard carved with roses that looked so real I always expected to find delicate mahogany petals on the pillows. The bedspread was made of a thick brocade of more roses than I could count, and under it was an eiderdown so thick and soft it was like someone holding you. But I never climbed up on the bed without permission. It was the most private part of the room, like a separate place all its own.

There was no sign of my father's presence, and I stood in the center of the room for a moment, confused. The teak valet where he hung his suit coat every night was missing. So was the black lacquer box that he dropped his change and watch into at the end of the day. I went to his closet and found empty spaces among his suits and shirts and trousers, as though things had been taken. And though I found nothing when I checked for the stilts, I was suddenly less concerned about them.

Next to my parents' bedroom was a small sitting room that could be reached through their room, or through a door that opened onto the hallway. Its only furnishings were a daybed and a huge teak wardrobe, where my parents stored their out-of-season clothes. The wardrobe was one of my father's prized possessions, a gift from a wealthy client. It had been carved by hand in the interior of China, and it was immense. It could be moved only after it was dismantled, and even then its three sections were massive. The heavy doors to the main section of the wardrobe held beveled mirrors, and underneath was a drawer that was two feet deep.

I entered the sitting room from my parents' room and found the daybed had been slept in. My father's black silk robe lay across the foot of it, and next to it, pushed against the wall, was his teak valet. I walked to the wardrobe and stood in front of it as though I owned it. I pulled open one of the doors and found what I'd expected to find: my father's clothes, not the summer clothes he didn't need for now, but his overcoat, the black cashmere sweater he'd worn yesterday, the striped tie he'd worn earlier that morning, three pressed shirts. His brown felt hat was set carelessly on the top shelf, as though he'd taken it off in a hurry, and the black lacquer box was next to it.

I heard grown-up laughter from downstairs then, and my eyes burned with hot tears. It was as though they were laughing at me for being a child, for not understanding, and I wondered what else they hadn't told me. I slapped my father's overcoat, just for the momentary pleasure it gave me. But when the coat moved from my slap, I saw something brown toward the back of the wardrobe. I pushed the coat aside and found the package I'd hoped for from Sears Roebuck.

For a moment, everything seemed better. Here was an example of order, of things being as they should, I thought. I told myself that him sleeping in this small room meant nothing; it was because of the odd hours he was keeping, so that he didn't wake my mother. I fluffed up my father's coat so that you couldn't tell it had been moved to the side.

I was about to close the wardrobe door when I saw a large manila envelope on the floor of the wardrobe. I was sure it went with the stilts—maybe it was the directions, maybe there was a picture—and I picked it up and opened it.

But there weren't any directions. Instead I pulled out several eight-by-ten black-and-white photographs, and when I looked at them, I forgot about the stilts and the sitting room and the grown-ups downstairs.

The first one showed a Chinese girl lying in a field. She was naked, and her legs had been spread apart. I knew the girl was dead. Standing on either side of her were two Japanese soldiers, grinning as though they were in the midst of something wonderful. The girl was older than I was, but she was still a girl.

I stared at the photograph angrily, then looked at the next one. A Chinese man knelt in the middle of the street, and at first I thought it was a magic act. But I stared harder and saw that the man really was being decapitated by the Japanese soldier standing over him. A circle of Japanese soldiers surrounded him, clapping and cheering.

There were more, but I stopped. I was afraid. My hands shook as I slipped the photographs carefully back into the envelope and refastened the clasp. Then I placed the envelope on the floor of the wardrobe, where I had found it.

I turned out the light in the sitting room and went back the way I'd come, through my mother's room. At the door, I stood listening and heard only my own heart. I opened the door, closed it, and tiptoed to my room, the parquet floor cold and hard against my bare feet. My room seemed a foreign place, but the only place I wanted to be. I closed my door softly behind me. I turned out the light and got into bed. And then I lay in the dark, holding my stomach, trying to make it stop hurting, trying to understand why I felt so homesick and alone in the only home I'd ever known.

stilts

MY MOTHER WAS NOT CONVINCED by good appearances, neither my father's nor Shanghai's, and although he bragged and cajoled and tried to charm her, she was not won over by his high spirits. Shanghai was suspect, as were his purchases and conspicuous wealth, and she made no secret of her doubt. She began to speak of Los Angeles almost daily, as though the fact that we were going had been decided. The only question was when.

My birthday was on January seventeenth, the feast day of St. Anthony of the Desert, and the day started the way it had every year I could remember. My mother woke me early and dressed me in the still darkness of morning, just a grayer version of night, and then we went together to early Mass at the Cathedral. This was our time; later in the day I would celebrate with my father, in his way.

Everything felt expectant that morning: the darkness, the quiet, the hushed sounds of my mother moving about in my room as she found my clothes, the mysterious quality of the two of us going out alone in the cold morning. I was filled with anticipation of what was to come: being seven.

After Mass we went out for hot cocoa in the French Concession even though it was Monday and I would be late for school. When we had settled in a café, my mother pulled off her gloves and set them on the table next to her. Though it was still early, not even eight, she was very alert. Too alert, I thought. There was an intensity to her that frightened me: the bright sparkle in her brown eyes, her flushed cheeks. She took a cigarette from a pack of Ruby Queens, put the pack on the table, lit her cigarette, and inhaled.

She stared at me for a moment, and I grew nervous, wondering if I passed. She seemed about to say something, and I waited, though I wanted to blurt out, *What is it? What won't you tell me?*

And then she did. She took an ivory envelope from her purse and smiled at me. She put the envelope on the table, and I tried to sound out the name and address printed in clear black ink in the upper-right corner: *Mackinnon, Mackenzie & Co., Agents for Tickets, 17 Canton Road, Shanghai, Phone 11428.*

"What is it?" I asked, thinking it was some kind of present.

"It's a wonderful surprise," and she leaned toward me conspiratorially, then tapped the envelope lightly. Her nails were a glossy deep mauve. "It's three tickets to go to Los Angeles." She smiled again. "We leave in a week, so there's lots to do. But we'll do it. And then we'll be home."

I pointed out what I thought was obvious. "But we are home."

My mother did not hesitate. "No," she said quickly, her voice even and businesslike. "This is a place where we've stayed too long. It is in no way home," and she stubbed her half-smoked Ruby Queen out in a white porcelain ashtray in the center of the table.

I stared hard at a scone I couldn't eat and cocoa I couldn't drink, and I nodded when she asked if I understood, thinking only, *He'll fix it.* I pretended to sip my cocoa until she was ready to go, and I said yes when she asked if I'd had enough. She was too distracted to notice I'd barely touched it.

When my father got home that afternoon, he presented me with the package I'd found in the teak wardrobe, which he had wrapped in the Sunday comics. I pretended surprise, and though I was not much of an actress, my parents did not notice the charade. When I'd unwrapped the box and was taking out the stilts, my mother said quietly, "I told Anna our good news this morning."

I could feel my father watching me intently, and I forced myself to be brave and look up at him.

"That was premature," he said stiffly. "I'll need a few more weeks."

"I've purchased the tickets," my mother said. "Booking passage is no easy feat, Joseph, and there was space on the *President Coolidge*. It sails only once a month. If we don't go now, we can't go until March."

My father didn't miss a beat. "Then you two will go without me," he said simply, "and I'll follow when I can."

That was all of the discussion I heard about our leaving, and about my father staying. But by that evening it was fact. After dinner when Chu Shih gave me a rose-colored tin of rare scented flower tea and said it would keep me well, it was clear that he meant on our trip. He and I sat at the table in the kitchen as he told me how to brew the tea and how to keep it fresh, and I realized, for the first time, that he would not be with us. Wind rattled the wooden shutters and sleet harassed the roof above us while Chu Shih made me some of the tea to warm me before bed. He called late January *ta-han*—great cold—and though it was only the seventeenth, I thought the name fit, for I felt colder inside than I ever had.

:: :: ::

The day before we left, my father came to my room. I was sitting at the window, drawing a picture of the view from my window: the acacias, the willows along the back wall, the iron bench underneath it, the huge magnolia in the center of the lawn. Outside, everything looked cold and gray and still, but I didn't draw it that way. Behind the willows and the stone wall, I drew in the skyline of the Bund, as near as I could remember it. It wasn't visible from my room, but I knew it was there in the distance, and I wanted something to remind me of it when Shanghai was far away.

My father gestured vaguely around my room. "Doesn't look like much is going with you, Anna," he said. I followed his gaze and stared at the dolls and toys and books still crowded on my shelves. His old steamer trunk, which was covered with tin and lined with camphor wood, sat on the floor in the middle of my room. He was letting me pack my things in it, and it was only half full. He tapped it with the toe of his shoe. "This was supposed to be packed by now."

I went back to my picture and shook my head firmly. "Those other things aren't going."

"You're leaving them here?" he asked, and I looked at him quickly to see if it had been hope I'd heard in his voice.

"Yep. I'll be back. You said I would. They can stay here for now."

He was silent for a long moment, then he said, "All right then, might as well. You're right. You'll be back soon enough."

It was exactly what I'd wanted to hear.

He just stood in the room for a long moment then. I finished my picture and put it and the map of China I'd drawn in his office into the trunk, and I closed the lid. Still he didn't say anything, and neither did I. There was something he wanted to tell me, I thought. I wanted to wait him out.

Finally he cleared his throat. "Sometimes things aren't so clear, Anna, you see? We just can't predict things, just can't know how things will turn out all the time."

I nodded matter-of-factly. "You'll miss us," I said, hoping my words would hurt.

He turned and left my room.

:: :: ::

And then, incredibly, it was time to go.

The rush and packing of six days had ended. When I woke on the twenty-fourth of January, the house was eerily quiet. Chu Shih gave us breakfast in the kitchen while Mei Wah loaded our trunks into the car. I could not get food down, but I managed not to cry at the table.

When my father said it was time to go, I followed my parents outside. Chu Shih followed, too, then stood silently by the kitchen door. My father said, "Say your good-byes, Anna. No use stretching it out."

I walked to Chu Shih. His expression was hurt and pained and afraid all at once. I took his hand, then I reached into my coat pocket and took out the possession I loved most, the elephant I'd bought with my father on Nanking Road. I still considered it good luck, despite the bad things that had happened. At least we were all right, and I wanted Chu Shih to be safe.

I put the elephant in Chu Shih's palm and closed his fingers over it. "For you," I said.

He nodded and his expression grew more pained. Then he simply picked me up and held me to him, a first.

I began to cry. I held on to him tightly and I whispered what I had felt but never said: "*Yeh yeh,*" the familiar term for grandfather.

He nodded and held me more tightly. I felt his shoulders shake and I realized he was weeping. When I kissed his cheek, it was wet with tears.

My father pulled me from Chu Shih's arms and carried me to the car and I felt a kind of closing off inside. Leaving was too awful, far more difficult than I'd imagined.

Mei Wah drove us to the Bund through gray streets. I sat between my parents in the backseat, pressing my just-cut nails into my palms to stop crying. None of us spoke, and when we reached the wharves, my father asked Mei Wah to see to the trunks. Then he took the wicker picnic basket from the front seat and said, "Shall we?"

I pointed to the basket, but before I could ask, he said simply, "You'll see." I turned to say good-bye to Mei Wah then, but he had already gotten back into the car and he could only look at me, his eyes intense, before my mother took my hand and led me toward the ship.

As we walked up the gangplank, my father called to friends and waved, and my mother smiled and nodded, and they seemed so normal that I could almost believe what they'd said: that everything would be fine, that my father would be with us before we knew it. Once onboard, we explored the ship for a while, my father making a great show of opening doors for us, leading us down hallways, helping us up and down stairways. We saw the huge dining salon and toured the upper and lower decks, along with passengers and a few crew members in stiff uniforms and authoritative brass buttons. Non-passengers, mostly men like my father in suits and ties, their British or American businessman's manners matter-of-fact, were starting to leave the ship. I tried not to notice as they kissed mothers and children good-bye, then started down the gangplank to the dock, their shoulders straight, their strides purposeful.

My father said he wanted to look over our stateroom, and we went below. When we were in our room, he set the picnic basket on a small table and said, "Go ahead. Look inside."

I opened the basket and found a feast, all of my favorites: French bread and dry sausage, Ritz crackers, a thermos of Hershey's cocoa for me and café au lait for my mother, a box of animal crackers, dried persimmons and melon seeds.

"Thank you," I said, and he winked.

Our stateroom was small and tidy, a place that I would have loved under different circumstances. The teak dresser drawers had shiny brass handles and pulled out with the smoothness of liquid; the bunk beds were so neatly made they looked like dolls' beds. The orderly way that everything fit together calmed me. I could still smell the Whangpoo and it made the room feel almost friendly, or at least familiar.

I watched my parents carefully, not sure what to expect. It was a strange day: they were somber but excited in a way. We were all dressed up, the way we would be for church. My mother kept nervously running her fingers over the strand of pearls around her neck, something I'd seen her do while waiting for dinner guests to arrive. A carved ivory comb held her chignon in place. My father's suit and tie gave him an official air, and he seemed in charge of some ceremony as he paced back and forth on the thick green carpet of our small room.

"This all right?" he asked my mother, motioning around him at the tidy beds, the teak closet, the compact bathroom, the round table and two chairs.

My mother nodded and I could see that she was trying to be cheery. "Yes," she said, "it's lovely, Joe. Anna and I will do fine."

He looked at me as though seeking proof. Wanting to please him, I said, "It's very fancy. I love it." But I somehow failed. His expression was hurt, and I looked at my mother, wondering what I'd done wrong. "Don't I?"

"Of course you do." She smiled. "We'll be fine," she said again. She took my father's large hand and held it between hers. I knew exactly what that felt like. It was what she did to me when I was frightened or nervous, and her hands always felt firm and strong and soft all at the same time. I always felt like things would be all right when she did that.

The three of us stood there awkwardly while my mother tried to make small talk, something she was normally very adept at. But her words fell flat. Nothing she did or said was quite right, and it somehow made her seem like a traitor. I began to watch her with doubt and suspicion, and for the first time since she'd told me we had to leave Shanghai, I thought, *Maybe we don't really have to. Maybe she didn't tell me the truth. Maybe we're leaving because of her.*

We heard the ship's chimes then, and a crisp British voice came over the loudspeakers, the tone cordial and no-nonsense at the same time. "Would all non-passengers kindly disembark as soon as possible."

"Eve," my father started, but he was cut short by the repeated announcement. My mother released his hand. Now she was the one who looked pained.

It was time to say good-bye, and though the moment was expected, it came suddenly. My stomach tightened and I felt panic and dread and I thought, *Please, no.*

"Oh, Joseph," she whispered, and she embraced my father tightly. I watched, horrified, for I understood from the passion I saw—a passion completely uncharacteristic for them—that this was far worse than I'd thought. I saw my father's face pressed in the curve of my mother's neck. And then there was a fierce kiss between the two of them.

When my father turned to me, I saw that he was near tears. "Anna," he whispered, his voice hoarse. He held me so tightly that I was afraid he might crush me, but I said nothing. *Harder*, I thought, *harder. Maybe if you hurt me, we won't have to go.*

"We have to do this now, you see?"

I nodded and clutched at his coat, the serge lapel stiff as cardboard between my fingers. "Anna," he said again, and I held tighter still, not worrying about wrinkling his coat, crying hard, furious at both of them for letting this happen. He took hold of my arms and forced them loose. My mother gripped my shoulders and pulled me from him. He straightened himself, ran his hands over his hair, looked as if he might speak. But he said nothing.

"*Tsaichien*," I whispered. Good-bye.

And then he was gone.

My mother held me, pressing my face to her. She knelt and whispered, "Come. We'll go to the deck and wave to him."

I was still crying. She wiped my face with her handkerchief, which smelled like lavender and had the effect of a whiff of smelling salts. My mother's explanation of our departure came back to me, and I grabbed hold of it, repeating her words to myself: *Shanghai has become too dangerous. We have to leave, but only for a while, only because of the war. While we're gone, he'll close up his business and then he'll come to California, too. And when it's safe to return to Shanghai, we'll come back.*

"The deck," I said. "We can see him? We can wave to him?"

"I hope so. He said he'd be easy to spot."

I took a deep breath, still shaky from crying, and followed my mother out of the stateroom and down narrow corridors that made me think of stories about people who lived under the earth, and then up sets of steep stairs until we were on deck.

Everyone was shouting and crowding to the dockside of the ship, trying to get a last glimpse of some father or husband. My mother guided me through the crowd, asking stranger after stranger to please let us through so that her daughter might wave good-bye to her father. Other mothers were trying to do the same for their children, but somehow my mother succeeded. She parted a sea of mothers and grandmothers and secretaries and children, guiding me to the ship's railing, then stood behind me, her hands firmly on my shoulders.

"Now," she said. "Look."

The gangplanks were just being raised. I searched the crowd below for my father and saw mostly men just like him, men in suits, waving to those they loved, but all of them seeming to stare up at me. I stared back at them stubbornly. *It's only a few months,* I thought. *Don't be a baby. Make him proud of you. You're your father's daughter.* I looked at the Bund and saw the Cathay Hotel, the Palace, Big Ching at the top of the Customs House, then I looked toward the Garden Bridge and started from there: the NYK Line, the Banque de l'Indochine, the Glenn Line, and I knew I could go all the way down the Bund to the Shanghai Club. I had learned what he had taught me.

"Look," my mother said suddenly, "there!" And she laughed and her grip on my shoulders tightened. She pointed down and to the right. "See him?"

And there was my father. He was easy to spot as soon as you looked in his direction. You couldn't *not* see him, for he'd brought my stilts and stood three feet higher than anyone around him. He waved awkwardly, almost falling over, and he grinned. I laughed and waved back. "Be careful!" I called, and he waved again.

There was a loud whistle, and a violent slamming as the gangplank was pulled up. The commotion grew even louder. The crew yelled, the men on the dock called last-minute advice, the women and children around us waved more urgently. I stared at my father harder, willing him to save us. *Don't let this happen; surely you can do something.*

The ship began to move. Another loud whistle, and the ship began to ease away from the dock.

"Let's go below," my mother said, her voice low and flat.

I shook my head. "I want to watch."

She hesitated, but she didn't say no. Only, "I don't think I can. I'll be sitting nearby." She walked over to one of the teak deck chairs set out in rows in the middle of the deck. There was a spent quality to her voice. She suddenly looked exhausted.

I looked back at my father. He was alone. Most of the other men were already heading back to their offices along the Bund. He'd gotten off the stilts and stood holding them. I wondered if he would take them all the way back home to Hungjao, or just leave them in his office for now. I wondered what he would do tonight for dinner. Jimmy's, I thought, or maybe Sun Ya's, for long-life noodles.

I waved once, a small wave, more a signal than a good-bye. He waved back, and I saw him smile. And then, as the ship slid from the wharf and was pulled by tugs into the Whangpoo, we simply stood staring at each other from a greater and greater distance, until

I couldn't be sure it was really him that I saw, and until I couldn't be sure there was anyone there at all. But he was there. I knew him. He would not leave until I was out of sight.

the city of angles

ON THE FIFTEENTH OF FEBRUARY, 1938, after traveling 5,673 miles, my mother and I arrived at San Pedro Harbor in Los Angeles. My grandmother met us at the ship. She was not at all what I expected. She was taller than my mother, nearly five feet nine, and although she wasn't overweight, she was a large woman. She was attractive, but not nearly as feminine as my mother, and I saw right away that she was a no-nonsense sort of person. She walked with her back straight and her head high, and when she hugged me and kissed my cheek, I smelled Pep-o-mint Life Savers, which made me think I would like her.

After a porter had loaded our luggage into the trunk of my grand-mother's blue Plymouth, she drove us home, across the vastness of Los Angeles. She and my mother sat in the front seat and talked about how the city had changed. I sat in the backseat, looking out at Spanish homes with red tile roofs and wrought-iron balconies; groves of orange trees that stood like soldiers in rows that seemed to go on forever; spacious streets lined with tall palm trees that swayed softly overhead; and far away, in the background, purplish mountains like something I would draw. Everything was bright: red geraniums, crayon-green lawns, bougainvillea of a deep pink, and above us, the sky a startling blue. There was no garbage in the streets, there were no beggars in the doorways. The air smelled of oranges and jasmine, and it was so clean that I thought it should have a different name from what we breathed in Shanghai. The whole place seemed enchanted. "Is this real?" I whispered once. My mother, sitting in the front seat with my grandmother, only laughed.

My grandmother talked as she drove, telling me things I tried to remember so that I could tell my father when he joined us. We were headed to South Pasadena, she said, about ten miles to the east of downtown Los Angeles. It was where my mother had grown up, where my grandmother still lived, and where we would live now. My grandmother said it was just right: big enough and small enough. None of that mattered much to me, but when we turned off of Monterey Road and onto Chelten, my grandmother's street, I caught my breath, for in the middle of the street grew three huge oak trees, each of their trunks as wide as a door. I felt my grandmother watching me in her rearview mirror, and she smiled and explained that rather than remove the trees, the city had simply paved the street around them.

"Those are *quercus*," she said. "Native oaks. They've been here since this whole place was wild."

I met her eyes in the mirror and nodded, as in awe of her as I was of everything else. She turned into a driveway across from one of the oak trees in the street and said, "Here we are."

My grandmother's home was a two-storey, Spanish-style house with a red tile roof. It was U-shaped, with the patio at its center and all of the rooms opening out onto it. Colored tiles were set around the doors, and bright woven rugs covered the floors. The guest room— "Your room for now," my grandmother said as she led me to it—had doors that opened out onto the garden. My bed was an old oak trundle bed covered with a white comforter embroidered with dragonflies. An antique, the bed had been my mother's when she was small, and before that my grandmother's. It was so low to the ground that when I sat on its edge, my knees came to my chest, as though I were Alice in Wonderland, a fact that I took as an omen: nothing was going to fit here, everything would feel odd. I certainly did, sitting in that small room on that strange bed, still in my navy wool cardigan and tartan skirt and shiny black shoes.

When my grandmother left the room, I just sat there for a while, too nervous to explore the house, too unsure of myself to do anything at all. Finally, shortly before dinner, there was a knock at my door, and when I murmured, "Come in," my grandmother pushed the door open and stood just inside the room. The ceiling was low, and she, too, looked like the wrong size, which was somehow comforting. She wore a dark green suit that set off her blue-green eyes, and her brown hair was brushed back, framing her suntanned face. I thought she was beautiful.

"You're wondering what to call me," she said.

I felt found out. I *had* been wondering that, and though it wasn't my major worry, it was on my list.

She smiled easily. "Thought so. How about Gran?"

I nodded stupidly, and wished I could say something to show her how smart I was. I considered blurting out everything I knew about the Bund as an attempt at impressing her, but I dismissed the idea as inappropriate. "Gran sounds nice," I said.

"Then Gran it is," she said. "Though you'll have to help me get used to it. I'm new at grandmothering."

"I'm new at granddaughtering," I said.

She laughed a wonderful laugh, deep and easy, one that didn't make me feel laughed at. "You'll learn," she said. "We both will." And then she turned to leave, waving good-bye absently. "Wash your hands and come down to dinner, Anna. We don't want you starving yourself up here."

I did as I was told and went downstairs to find my mother and grandmother—*Gran*, I practiced under my breath—at the large oak dining-room table, my grandmother looking stately and official at the head of the table, my mother a little disheveled. She'd loosened the top buttons of her blouse and her hair was mussed from traveling, but she looked happy and relaxed, and the sight of her gave me hope. We were served hamburgers and fresh fruit by my grandmother's cook and housekeeper, a woman named Ella. But although I was starved, I didn't touch my food. I had been taught since I was small not to eat until I'd been given permission, and I knew that fresh fruit had to be boiled before you ate it. My mother had started eating without hesitating, and it was only after she'd taken several bites that I was able to catch her eye and communicate my question to her: Was the food safe?

She did the worst thing she could have done; she laughed. "Oh, Anna, it's all right. Eat everything, eat all you want. Everything's safe and wonderful and good here. You don't have to worry about food anymore." She stared at me for a moment, then added, "Actually, you don't have to worry about anything."

I looked at my grandmother, expecting to see more amusement. Instead I found her gazing at me somberly. "The girl is conscientious," she said matter-of-factly. "Quite admirable." She nodded and I began to eat.

That night when I got into my funny bed and slipped between pale blue cotton sheets, I could hear my mother and my grandmother talking downstairs. The radio was on, and they were listening to the *Palmolive Beauty Box Theater* with Jessica Dragonette and Benny Fields, one of my grandmother's favorite shows, she'd said. It sounded like home: grown-ups talking into the night, the radio on in the background, and outside, the breeze ruffling the leaves of the plane trees— no, I thought, they were called sycamores here.

I got out of bed and went to the window and pushed it open a few inches. It was just starting to sprinkle, and the air smelled of eucalyptus and rainwater and earth, almost like Shanghai. I breathed in the scent to make things better. I could see the oak trees in the road, tall and stately in the nighttime shadows, and they somehow reminded me of my father, maybe because they looked so strong, or maybe because they seemed far away, though they were only in the middle of the street. I hadn't thought of him very much that day, a first since we'd left Shanghai; there had been too many new things to think about. But in that instant I could see him and hear his voice, and I was stricken with guilt. On the voyage over, I'd planned on missing him constantly. I'd imagined myself as long-suffering and noble, similar to the characters in some of the soap operas I'd heard on the radio, a somber girl who never stopped thinking of her beloved father.

But already I'd betrayed him. I'd forgotten him on my very first day here, and I saw that I was a traitor, the most disloyal daughter a person could imagine.

:: :: ::

A few days after our arrival, my grandmother woke me early in the morning and told me to get up, that my mother and I were moving into our house. I sat up in bed and watched as she gathered the few things my mother had unpacked for me—shoes, a few dresses, a sweater, toothbrush, hairbrush, underwear, pajamas. Then she told me to get dressed and come downstairs.

When I came into the kitchen, I saw my mother in the driveway, loading our things into the trunk of my grandmother's Plymouth.

"She's in a hurry," my grandmother said.

I turned and found my grandmother standing behind me, and I looked up at her.

"But she'll calm down. Don't worry. She's just a little unsure of things for the moment."

She took my hand and squeezed it once, and I smiled gratefully. Her hand around mine was warm and strong and soft. I hadn't realized that I was anxious about my mother, but I was.

We joined her outside then, and my grandmother drove us to our new home, a California bungalow that my grandfather had bought as an investment shortly before his death. We didn't have far to go. Our house was only a few blocks away, on Bucknell. My grandmother had had the place cleaned and repainted, and she'd furnished it with odds and ends she'd had in storage.

"You can walk to my house any time you like, Anna." As she pulled into the driveway of our house, she pointed to a huge old oak tree on the corner. "Kids call that the Tarzan tree," she said. "That's your landmark," and she looked at me in the rearview mirror. I nodded, grateful for any landmark at all.

The house looked as though it had just grown from the lot. Trees surrounded it, eucalyptus and oaks and Chinese junipers, and a broad porch spanned the front of the house. The house's foundation was made of round stones, which, my grandmother said, had been gathered in the Arroyo Seco, a canyon that ran through the northwest part of Pasadena. The stones had been worn smooth by weather and time, and the chimney was made of the same stones. Where they stopped, the house was made of redwood, and the roof was pitched and so shallow that it was almost horizontal. The eaves curved up a bit, making the house appear as if it might fly. Over the gable was a weather vane, topped by a wrought-iron squirrel that stared intently in the direction of the wind.

My grandmother unlocked the front door and pushed it open, and I followed her and my mother inside. The interior of the house was all wood. Redwood bookshelves lined the living-room walls, which were also redwood, as were the exposed ceiling beams overhead. The wall nearest to the front door had a window seat, where the leaded glass window looked out on the small front yard, and covering the

wooden plank floor was an Oriental rug. The room was sparsely furnished, just a pair of Morris chairs and a small table between them.
The fireplace was what I liked most. It was bordered with dark red
tiles, each with a small scene on it, and it reminded me of the scenes
of coolies and sedan chairs on the carved desk in my father's office, a
good sign, I thought. Over the center of the mantel, two larger tiles
portrayed facing peacocks, another piece of luck. Chu Shih had told
me since I was small that birds brought good fortune.

The far end of the living room opened onto the dining room,
where a wrought-iron chandelier whose lamp bulbs were shaped
like candle flames hung above an oval oak table and chairs. A
built-in sideboard and buffet with leaded glass cabinets covered one
wall, and French doors opened out onto a small garden filled with
wisteria and jasmine and climbing roses. The kitchen was next to
the dining room, and there everything seemed to be built in: the
wooden table, which folded up against the wall; bins for flour and
sugar; the bread board, the cupboards, spice racks, even the ironing
board. The kitchen walls were bright white, and the room smelled
of fresh paint.

My grandmother opened windows as she led us from room to
room, and a cool breeze let itself in. From the kitchen, we walked
down a short hallway to the bedrooms, which were painted white. In
my room were a wrought-iron scroll bed, a dresser, and a cheval mirror. White lace curtains framed my window, and next to the bed was
a small bookcase, already filled with books.

"Those are mine," my mother said when she saw me eyeing them.
"Or they were. They're yours now."

When we had walked through the small house and stood in
the living room again, I felt my mother and my grandmother watching me.

"Well," my mother said, "what do you think?"

"It's nice," I said, the only thing I could, for it was all too much to take in. I stared hard at my leather Oxfords and remembered my mother buying them for me in Shanghai, and suddenly I just wanted to be away from here, where everything was new. I wanted to go home, to Shanghai, where everything was familiar, even if it was dirty and crowded and freezing right now. I wanted to be where my father was. *Just say something nice*, I thought, but I couldn't, and as my mother and grandmother waited for me to say more, I burst into tears.

:: :: ::

During the next week, my mother worked at getting us settled. She enrolled me in school, she introduced us to the neighbors, she cabled my father's business agent in New York in order to obtain funds, and she relearned her way around the town she'd grown up in. She didn't drive, but there really wasn't much need to. The Big Red Cars were electric streetcars that ran right along Huntington Drive only two blocks south of our house. From the Oneonta Park station, we could go just about anywhere in Los Angeles, from Santa Monica beach to downtown, to Colorado Street and Fair Oaks Avenue in Pasadena.

I started school at Oneonta Grammar School, where I was stared at for a week by the children in my first-grade class—California kids, my grandmother called them, who were rough-and-tumble and adept at things like the Pledge of Allegiance and roller skating. On my first day, the teacher, Miss McGrath, explained to everyone that they were very lucky to have me in Room 3, because I had lived far, far away, and could tell them firsthand what China was like. I froze inside as twenty-three strange children stared hard and evaluated me from head to toe. Word spread quickly. At recess, a boy named Tom Crosby asked me what language they spoke in Africa, and on my way home from school, a girl whose name I didn't know because she wasn't even in my class asked me if it was always hot in India. She spoke slowly, with exaggerated enunciation, and it was clear that she did not think I spoke English. I was tired and unhappy and I snapped, "How would *I* know?," then walked quickly ahead of her, my nose in the air.

But within a few weeks, I was more or less forgotten, which was fine by me. I felt as though I'd come from a secret land, and when Miss McGrath took the globe from the highest shelf and showed me that Los Angeles was on the same parallel as Shanghai, I stared in disbelief. It was not possible, I thought; the places were too different to have anything in common.

In the afternoons, if my mother was going to be busy, I was told to walk to my grandmother's house after school, rather than home. On those days, my grandmother always greeted me in the same way—"*There* she is!"—and seemed so genuinely glad to see me that I felt better as soon as I saw her open the front door. As I ate a snack, she would ask me about my day, and if I was making friends, and whether I liked school. Because I didn't want to hurt her feelings, I said as little as I could and didn't tell her the truth, which was that I wasn't making friends, that no one talked to me, that school was the loneliest place in the world. She only nodded, but the way that she looked at me made me think she knew how unhappy I was. "Things will get better," she said when I'd finished, and she squeezed my hand across the kitchen table. "Just give it time, Anna. All will be well." I nodded, and although I wasn't completely convinced, her words made me feel hopeful, and the next day wouldn't seem so bad. And I did know that things would get better eventually. Everything would be fine once my father arrived. It was only a matter of time.

My grandmother had not known much about me when we lived in Shanghai. My mother was a faithful correspondent but not a frequent one, and my grandmother heard news of me only a few times a year at best, especially since the Japanese occupation, when the mail to and from Shanghai had slowed to a near halt. At the start, I could see from her expression when she looked at me that I was not what she had expected. Maybe she'd wanted someone taller, or prettier, or smarter. But before long, she seemed to decide that I was all right, and she set out to claim me as her own.

I liked her immediately. She was the most down-to-earth, matter-of-fact person I'd ever been around, but she was also elegant, even formal. She was never in a hurry, never raised her voice, never short with anyone. She always looked me in the eye, and she wore practical clothes and comfortable shoes made of soft leather or even suede. She smelled of peppermint and Yardley English Lavender, which she had worn all of her married and widowed life.

She rose at six each morning and walked from her house on Chelten to early Mass at Holy Family Church a mile away. She came home and ate fresh fruit for breakfast—half a grapefruit sprinkled with brown sugar and put under the broiler for half a minute, sliced peaches or berries in cream, oranges in sections, whatever was in season. During the morning she answered letters. She maintained a huge correspondence with old friends and business associates of my grandfather's, and was always prompt in her replies.

In the afternoon she worked. After my grandfather's death, she had taken a correspondence course in bookkeeping, and now she kept the books for two small businesses in downtown Los Angeles, the Typewriter Shop and Foreman & Clark Men's Store. When she finished work, she gardened, and at five o'clock, she sat in an old wicker chair under the eaves on her patio, rain or shine, warm weather or cold, and watched the light begin to fade. A sky-blue tile set into the outside stucco wall of her patio said, *The lands of the sun expand the soul.* It was an old Spanish proverb, she told me, and she added that it was true, and that this place would do me good. If there was a chill in the air, she draped a red wool Pendleton shirt over her shoulders. It had been my grandfather's, one of the few articles of his clothing she hadn't given to the poor, because, she said, it still harbored his scent of Blackstone cigars, and she could not part with that remnant of him.

It hung by the door to the patio. The only other obvious trace of him was his Gruen watch, which she was never without.

Each night with dinner she drank one glass of red wine, and after dinner she listened to opera or to one of the musical variety radio shows she liked, usually *The Bob Hope Show* or *The Chase and Sanborn Hour*, hosted by Edgar Bergen. Before she went to sleep, she read. Her favorite magazines were *Westways* and *Sunset* and *Life*. As for books, she read everything: biographies, novels, gardening books, the lives of the saints and the early fathers of the Church. By the end of each week, she always finished her book, and the pine bookshelves that lined the walls of her house were filled. On her bedside table were her missal, whatever book she was reading that week, and books that dealt with the soul, she said. Her favorites were *Revelation of Love* by Julian of Norwich and *Introduction to the Devout Life* by Francis de Sales. When she went to bed, usually around ten, she read until she was certain she could sleep, and then put out the light. She hated lying awake in the dark. She said it prompted bad thoughts.

On the afternoons I spent with her, she simply went about her business with me in tow, happy to tag along. Much of our time was spent in her car. As we drove, she would rattle off statistics about Los Angeles, which she always pronounced with a hard G—*Los AHN-gay-les*. It was the largest city in California, she said, home to all kinds of people, from all kinds of places. There were eighty-six Indian tribes here. It was the largest Japanese city except Tokyo, the largest Mexican city outside of Mexico City. No place outside China had more Buddhist temples, and no place outside the old Portuguese empire had more Portuguese.

We went downtown, and she taught me the names of the streets. Those running east-west were numbered, from First Street up. For the north-south streets, she taught me the mnemonic my grandfather had made up: From *Main* I *Spring* to *Broadway*, then climb the *Hill* to *Olive*. Wouldn't it be *Grand* if I could *Hope* to pick a *Flower* on

Figueroa? She took me to the building where his office had been. He had died of a heart attack ten years earlier; until then, he'd been a lawyer for the oil companies, with an office on the sixth floor of the Bradbury Building on South Broadway. When my grandmother and I went inside, she leaned close to me and whispered, "Look up," and I caught my breath as I gazed up at the skylight and the ornate iron staircase and the open-air elevator above us. We rode the elevator to the top of the building, and as we descended, I looked down at a white marble floor that looked like ice.

She took me to Olvera Street, the oldest street in the city, and we ate taquitos and held Mexican jumping beans in our palms. We shopped at Woolworth's and at the Broadway department store, where she bought me Bass Weejun loafers and Keds sneakers. We walked through Pershing Square and listened to soapbox preachers and browsed through the books at the Parasol Library. We bought strawberries and watermelon and just-baked peach pie at Grand Central Market, then rode Angels Flight, a small funicular railway that went up and down Bunker Hill. We went to Germain's Nursery on Hill Street and bought packets of California poppy seeds that Gran said we would plant in the back corner of her yard. We stopped at Van de Kamp's Holland Dutch Bakers and bought Dutch Girl cookies and coconut macaroons and Saratoga potato chips that tumbled out of a metal shoot as they were cooked. We ate lunch at Clifton's Cafeteria, or went to Philippe's for French dips and lemonade, where I drew patterns in the sawdust on the floor with the toe of my shoe. And then, if it was Friday, we stopped in at the Typewriter Shop and Foreman & Clark's, where everyone knew my grandmother. Before long, they knew me, too.

When we'd finished downtown, she headed back to Pasadena, which she said was eminently civilized. In a study of 295 American cities, she said proudly, Pasadena had been ranked as America's most desirable city, based on its high ratio of radios, telephones, bathtubs, and dentists to residents. She believed it to be the most beautiful, healthful, cultured, and intelligent community in the West. "There are certain types of pneumonia so rare as to be almost nonexistent in Southern California," she said. I nodded, pretending I understood. We drove down Colorado Street, the street of a thousand palms, where she said I would see the Rose Parade on January first, maybe even wave to the Rose Queen. She drove across the Colorado Street Bridge, a beautiful curved structure that spanned the Arroyo Seco, and then up the canyon to Brookside Park. And she took me to Mass at Holy Family Church, where I knelt next to her and prayed for my father to come soon.

But my favorite stop was Vroman's Bookstore on Colorado Street, for I was finally starting to read, and books were something I could not have enough of. We stopped there once a week, and I was always allowed to choose a book, with the understanding that I promised to finish it within a week, and that I could not choose another book unless I did. It was a promise I never broke, and soon the small bookcase in my room was filled not only with my mother's copies of Louisa May Alcott and Robert Louis Stevenson and Mark Twain, but with my purchases as well, some of which I could read myself: *Millions of Cats*, *The Story About Ping*, *The Velveteen Rabbit*.

On an afternoon in the spring, my grandmother was acting strangely at Vroman's. She seemed to be hiding something, and although she frowned at me when I came near, telling me quite clearly that there was something she didn't want me to see, I was more curious than afraid, and I stayed close. When we reached the cashier, my spirits fell. She had not asked me to choose a book, my punishment for being nosy, I thought. She was buying two books, and I hung back, hoping to redeem myself at the last minute. But it was too late; she paid for her books and took my hand and we left the store.

When we were in the car, she handed me her package. "These will get you started," she said. "Go ahead. Open it, Anna."

I unwrapped the brown paper and let my breath out slowly. And then I sounded out the titles: *The Clue in the Diary* and *The Secret of Red Gate Farm*. I looked to her for explanation.

"They're about Nancy Drew," my grandmother said. "I think you'll like them. Your mother and I will read them to you at the start, but I have a feeling you'll be sailing through them all by yourself before we know it."

I only nodded and stared hopefully at the illustrations on the book covers. Each pictured the same young woman in the midst of some dangerous-looking situation. In *The Clue in the Diary*, she leaned over to pick up a diary from the grass; behind her, several firemen moved toward a huge white house in flames. I was fascinated, and I opened the cover and found another illustration. In this one, a man sitting forlornly in an armchair faced that same brave girl, while a woman leaned over him, speaking. That illustration had a caption below it, and I held it eagerly out to my grandmother, far too impatient to be bothered with sounding out the words.

"What does it say?" I asked urgently.

She smiled and took the book from me, then held it out in front of her, her trombone stance, she called it, because she wasn't wearing her glasses. And then she read, "'Don't give in to Nancy Drew!' his wife screamed." My grandmother closed the book and handed it back to me. "Well, what do you think?"

I took the book and held it close. "Thank you," I whispered, feeling as though I'd been given treasure.

I fell in love with Nancy Drew. Each afternoon and evening I pestered my mother and grandmother until they read to me, and when they tired of it, I pored over the book myself, though my progress was slow. The more I learned of Nancy Drew, the more I liked her, and I resolved to be like her, capable, confident, cheerful, loyal, never afraid, always on the alert. We even had something in common, a fact that I took as a good sign: we lived with only one parent. Her mother had died—I hadn't yet learned how—and her lawyer father was raising her. I did not dwell on the differences in our circumstances. We were similar, I told myself, because we also shared this: we loved our fathers dearly.

Only hers was present, and mine wasn't. I was certain he would come soon, but when? At first I'd expected him to appear any minute, and for a while, I asked my mother constantly when he would arrive. Again and again she answered that she didn't know. She was sure he hadn't been able to close down his business yet, she said, so it would be a while. "But soon?" I pressed. "Soon," she said, and the edge in her voice told me not to ask more.

So we waited. My mother enrolled in the same type of accounting correspondence course my grandmother had taken a decade before, and she began to study, "just for something to do," she said, insisting that it wasn't for the money, since my father had provided for us well. I went to school and spent afternoons with my grandmother and rode the Big Red Cars with my mother to the movies and to Santa Monica beach and downtown. I even made a friend, and after that a few more, and when their mothers asked where my father was, I learned to say that he was away on business but would be here soon.

:: :: ::

On the last day of school, I brought home all of my schoolwork in a big folder I'd made the day before, and my mother oohed and ahhed at how much I'd done, and how much I'd learned. I, too, was surprised when I saw it all in front of me. I had learned to print the alphabet and how to use periods, commas, question marks, and exclamation points. I had learned to carry when I added, and to borrow if I needed to subtract. I had learned that I lived in the city of South Pasadena, in San Gabriel County, and I had learned about the first Californians. I knew how they used what grew around them to survive. I learned about the yucca plant, and how the Indians made rope and sandals and mats

and baskets, even soap from it, and how they boiled its buds and flowers and fruits to eat. I learned about manzanita and piñon nuts and
mesquite beans, and how to crush dried acorns in a mortar, then bake
them in unleavened cakes. I had even tasted the stuff and wished
I hadn't. I learned about Cortes, Cabrillo, and Sir Francis Drake, and
about Father Junipero Serra and his twenty-one missions. And
against my desperate protests that went unheeded, I had played a
silent Indian girl in the school play, *Discovering California*, and I had
learned how stage fright felt.

At home I had learned to do things that others had done for us in
Shanghai: to clear the table and wash the dishes, to sort laundry into
lights and darks before filling our Maytag washer, to answer the
phone politely and ask who was calling, please. I had learned never to
think about Chu Shih because it was too painful, because although
I was sure I'd see my father soon, I had come to think that I might not
ever see Chu Shih again. My mother talked often about my father
coming here, but she never mentioned us returning to Shanghai.

I had also learned about my mother. During that year, I watched
her so closely that I annoyed her at times, but I didn't care; I wanted
to understand why she was so different here from the way she'd been
in Shanghai. She looked different, to start. She had cut her beautiful
hair, and wore it just above her shoulders, and it was as soft and
bouncy as the Breck advertisements she loved to show me in magazines. All of her elegant Shanghai clothes were zipped in garment
bags in the back of her closet. No more cheongsams and tight, fitted
dresses. Now she wore dirndls with wide, high waistbands, colorful
Mexican cotton skirts trimmed with ruffles and embroidery, white
cotton peasant blouses, and flat sandals. She painted her toenails the
same deep pink as her fingernails and the new lipstick she wore—
"Rose Doré by Max Factor," she'd told me proudly—and she had
freckles on her face and arms and legs from the sun. She didn't carry
a purse unless she had to. When she went out, she carried only a

Lady Buxton wallet, with her keys attached to a key chain inside the billfold. She was so completely different from the way she presented herself in Shanghai that I felt embarrassed for her when we walked outside, as though she were walking around naked.

At the start, I thought that the person she was here was a mask, a sort of disguise she was wearing until she returned to Shanghai. My real mother—my Shanghai mother, with her beautiful, mysterious chignon and silk dresses and reserved composure—was there, somewhere. She was just hidden away from the chaos of this city of angles. I understood that, because that was exactly what I was doing at school, pretending I was perfectly at home in this brand-new place, just holding out until my father finally joined us.

But after a while I changed my mind. I decided that as far as she was concerned, we were home. While she mentioned my father often and wrote to him regularly and spoke about him with a certain fierceness, I mistook her steeliness for lack of caring, and I decided she didn't really miss him.

At least not like I did. I didn't just miss my father. I lacked him, and without him, I didn't feel like myself. I was afraid that his absence showed on me somehow, and I thought of Shanghai's beggars. My father had told me once about pain from phantom limbs, and I understood, for I, too, was a beggar now, missing not a limb or an eye or an ear, but a father, and here in this land that was supposed to expand my soul, I no longer felt whole.

lost horizon

ON A QUIET NIGHT in January of 1940, my father ate dinner with Will Marsh at the Holland, a small Dutch restaurant in the French Concession. The night was very cold, and after dinner they walked quickly toward the Nanking Theater to see *Beau Geste*, their hands stuffed into their coat pockets. But as they turned down Avenue Edouard VII, they came upon a crowd gathered around a streetlight. It was just before nine, and they stopped to see what the matter was. It had to be something extraordinary for people to stand in the cold. When they managed to get close, they, too, stared hard. On the sidewalk, propped against the streetlight, was the decapitated head of a young Chinese man. The neck was still bleeding and there were drops of sweat on his brow. His eyes were open, his lips parted. A note in Chinese was tacked to the streetlight: *Take notice: here is what happens to journalists who write articles against the Japanese and Wang Ching Wei government. Stop your attacks, or you will suffer a similar fate.*

Will Marsh recognized the victim and told my father that he had disappeared several weeks earlier, and that he had been the assistant editor at *Shên Pao*, Shanghai's largest Chinese daily, a newspaper that was critical of the Japanese.

My father and Will went into the first bar they came to. They didn't talk about what they'd seen. It was well known that Chinese journalists who dared to speak out against the Japanese or the puppet government headed by Wang Ching Wei were in danger. They both knew of the most recent examples: A bomb thrown into the offices of a Chinese newspaper had killed newsboys and office coolies. Six hand grenades thrown into another window had destroyed a printing press. Severed heads and fingers were anonymously delivered to offices or homes, and only a few weeks earlier, the editor of the Chinese version of the American *Evening Post* had been shot in the back while having lunch at his regular spot, a German restaurant on Nanking Road.

Journalists weren't the only victims of the city's violence. In a part of the city called the Badlands, an area that was made up of the western residential section outside of the Settlement but north of Hungjao, assassinations had become common. Number 76 Jessfield Road, an old Tudor home with a high wall and heavy iron gate, was the residence of Tiny Du, Shanghai's ruling gangster. Wealthy Chinese were brought there and forced to watch the torture of other prisoners until they agreed to buy their freedom, either by joining the puppet government or by giving the government money. Under the protection of the puppet administration, the Badlands' brothels and gambling houses and drug dens thrived. Most of them were residences that had been owned by foreigners who'd left Shanghai; now they had names like the Peach Blossom Palace, Hollywood, Good Friend, and though seemingly established by Chinese gangsters, the places really belonged to the Japanese. Downstairs there was gambling. Upstairs were girls and opium pipes and Shanghai's specialty, a pink opium pill that melted in your mouth like an after-dinner mint.

As the city changed, foreigners fell into two groups: those like my father, who were determined to stay, and those who were eager to evacuate. The U.S. State Department urged all Americans whose work in Shanghai was not essential to return to the United States, and even made passage available. Many of the foreign firms encouraged evacuation as well, cabling regularly from their head offices overseas, warning Shanghai residents of impending danger. Will Marsh was in a third category. He was more than ready to leave, but he worked at the American Consulate and said he could not leave in good conscience.

My father didn't completely rule out leaving. He just kept putting it off. Shanghai was booming, and business was great. There was too much money to be made, too much opportunity, to just walk away. When would he find a situation like this again? So he figured he'd stay a little longer. In the summer of 1941, he closed up the house and moved into town, where he took a room at the American Club, on Foochow Road a couple of blocks from the Bund and his office. And although he felt safer there, he really didn't think he was in any danger personally. His dealings with the Japanese would work in his favor. He was still selling them oil and gas, whatever they needed. As long as he was within American regulations, he saw no reason not to.

:: :: ::

In November of 1941, the last American troops in Shanghai vacated their barracks on Haiphong Road and left for Manila. They were Marines, and my father was one of the spectators who lined the streets to watch the troops march to the Bund. Afterward he walked along the Whangpoo. By that time, only one American and one British ship were left, both of them, Will Marsh had said, small river gunboats formerly used to patrol the Yangtze, now there only to provide direct radio communication between their consulates and their home governments. The HMS *Peterel* had a crew of twenty-seven reporting to an officer who was sixty-three years old. Its only weapons were a couple of machine guns. The USS *Wake* had a crew of twenty-five. That November morning as my father walked along the river, the *Peterel* and the *Wake* were surrounded by Japanese cruisers, destroyers, gunboats, and the *Idzumo*, the Japanese Imperial Navy's flagship.

A few days after the Marines left, my father marked another departure. On the first of December, Dr. McLain and his wife and son left Shanghai on the Dutch ship *Tjisdane*, which sailed for Java. My father saw them off, but he said almost nothing. It was yet another in a long series of good-byes, and he was beginning to wonder if the time had finally come to leave.

:: :: ::

Shanghai is to the west of the international dateline, so for those living there the Japanese attack on Pearl Harbor took place on Monday, December 8. Sunday, the seventh, was a quiet winter's day. That morning my father drove out to the country. He couldn't go far; foreigners were no longer allowed to venture beyond the city limits. He stopped at the Hungjao aerodrome for the Japanese guards, and after showing them his papers, he parked the car at the gate as required, then walked into the country. The gardens were beautiful and calm, a respite from the grim and crowded closeness of the gray Shanghai winter, and nothing had seemed out of the ordinary. It was on his return that he saw something odd: a thin line of lime drawn at the junction of Tsinpu and Hungjao Roads, as though a boundary were being set.

That evening he met friends for dinner at D.D.'s in the Little Russia section of the French Concession. He mentioned the chalk line he'd seen in Hungjao, and how odd it seemed, but his comment was dismissed as inconsequential and of no pressing interest. After dinner he went alone to see *Lost Horizon* at the Lyceum. He'd seen it before, but he went again because my mother had loved the book. After the movie he went home. Tomorrow was a business day.

And then the world changed. At around four o'clock Monday morning, he was awakened by several huge explosions, with flashes of light that lit up the sky. The noise was terrific, like firecrackers just outside the window. He'd brought Jeannie, his German shepherd, with him and she huddled under his bed, trembling and whining softly.

When those first bangs were followed by several more, my father decided there must be some kind of Chinese celebration that included fireworks, and he got dressed and went out to see what was what. Outside, it was still dark and just starting to rain. There were no firecrackers or celebrating Chinese in the streets, so my father headed toward the Bund. But when he reached the end of Foochow Road where it met the Bund, he found the intersection blocked by a Japanese sailor dressed for war, his rifle and bayonet ready. My father strained to see the other intersections in both directions. Every street he could see was barred by armed Japanese soldiers.

Suddenly the entire Bund was lit up by fire. My father followed others as they hurried to the roof of the Palace Hotel, and from there they saw that the fire came from the HMS *Peterel*, which was anchored directly across the Whangpoo. Two smaller fires burned nearby, the launches alongside the *Peterel*.

And then someone had the news, which spread instantly: Japan had attacked Pearl Harbor, sinking the American battleships *Arizona*, *California*, *Oklahoma*, and *Utah*, and damaging others. Thousands of Americans had been killed, and it was rumored that the Philippines, Wake Island, and Guam had been attacked as well. Japan had declared war on the United States and Britain, and was now in the process of occupying the International Settlement, starting with the takeover of the *Peterel* and the *Wake*. The *Peterel*'s crew had scuttled their ship rather than surrender to the Japanese. The *Wake*'s crew had wanted to do likewise, but had not had time before the Japanese demanded surrender.

My father was stunned. He stayed at the Palace waiting for more news. An hour later when he walked back to the American Club, the sky was filled with leaflets falling from a plane. He watched them float gently toward him and reached out and caught one in the air. He unfolded it and read an announcement of a Declaration of War by His Imperial Japanese Majesty on the United States of America and Great Britain. For the residents' protection, the leaflet said, the Japanese military would enter the International Settlement at 10 A.M. Residents were to pursue their "normal avocations" and should not cause any kind of disorder. They should remain calm and trust in the benevolence of the Imperial Japanese forces.

At the American Club, my father found most of the club's residents in the lobby, some in bathrobes pulled on over pajamas, others, like him, in wrinkled trousers and sweaters and coats grabbed hurriedly in the dark when the explosions had started. My father listened to the others' frantic talk and to a British announcer on the radio in the corner. He understood that he had hugely misjudged his situation. He understood that his life might now never be the same, that staying in Shanghai had probably altered his future forever. And he understood that this day was only the start of bad fortune, and that he had to act.

He went upstairs and put Jeannie on her leash, then went back outside with her and hurried to his office on Yuen Ming Yuen Road. The streets were frantic. The air on and near the Bund was thick with smoke, the ground covered with a thin layer of ash from businessmen and government officials burning whatever documents they thought necessary before the Japanese could get them. Japanese sentries were everywhere, but my father had at least some good luck that morning, for when he reached his office, he found it unguarded. The building had not yet been sealed off.

In his office, he settled Jeannie in the corner and filled a bowl with water. In his safe, he had eight hundred dollars in U.S. currency that he'd put aside as emergency cash. He wrapped the bills in newspaper, and loosened a section of one of the wooden floorboards. In a small compartment there, he placed it with the other things he wanted to protect: his chop, and an ivory comb that my mother used to wear in her hair. Then he replaced the floorboard and nailed it down.

In the sink in the men's washroom, he burned every receipt from Nationalist supporters, figuring those could get him into trouble with the Japanese. On his desk, he left out receipts from the Japanese military. He stroked Jeannie's fur and told her that he would return for her soon; he was sure she was safer here until he knew more about what he would do next. The dog whined once and put her large head on her paws. My father locked the door behind him and went back to the lobby of the American Club.

At a few minutes after ten, Japanese Naval Party soldiers arrived and announced that the American Club was now Japanese Naval Headquarters. Residents were required to leave within two hours; they were allowed to take only what they could carry. My father was lucky. He'd moved to the club only a few months earlier, and for him packing would be straightforward. Many of the residents had lived there for years, and would have to choose what few belongings to take.

My father went upstairs immediately to pack. Shortly after noon, two Japanese sailors, armed with rifles and bayonets and loaded down with bottles of Chefoo beer from the bar downstairs, knocked at my father's door. They were drunk. They let themselves in and made themselves comfortable, laughing and joking, looking through my father's things and keeping what they wanted as he packed.

When he'd finished, he was escorted out of the club with the rest of the residents. He caught a tram to the Medhurst, a twelve-storey hotel and apartment building on Bubbling Well Road near the Race

Course, where he and my mother had stayed in their early days in Shanghai. He took a room there, but he didn't bother to settle in. The next problem was money. Apart from the cash he'd hidden in his office, he didn't have much, so he figured the first stop was the bank. But when he reached the Shanghai office of the National City Bank of New York, a line of foreigners and Chinese wound around the block and overlapped itself. He was told that the Japanese had taken control of the Allied banks, and that funds belonging to Allied nationals were now frozen.

It was nearly one o'clock in the afternoon, and the air was freezing. My father got in line and tried to ignore the cold, which seemed to grow worse by the hour. Four hours passed before he reached the front of the line, where armed Japanese guards admitted people in groups of five. But he was lucky; the bank closed at five, and he was one of the last to be admitted. Those who didn't make it were told to return the next day, with no guarantee of their place in line.

Inside, two Japanese officials stood with the bank's books open before them and explained how things were. First, Allied currencies were now outlawed, so you could not withdraw funds in U.S. dollars or British pounds. Second, the amount of money you could withdraw was limited to five hundred Chinese dollars a week. My father nodded to all the explanations, then withdrew his five hundred Chinese dollars, the equivalent of fifty U.S. dollars and not nearly enough to live on.

At a street vendor on Nanking Road, he bought a plate of shrimp and sausage with noodles, coolie food, then headed back to the Medhurst. It was six o'clock in the evening, fourteen hours after those early-morning explosions, and as my father walked through the city, he was amazed how much had changed in those few hours. The winter air was thick with paper ash, and huge signboards repeating the information in the morning's pamphlets were posted all over the city. Japanese soldiers were everywhere. They patrolled the streets and stopped passersby, demanding to see their passports. They stood guard at the Allied Consulates and the Municipal Building, at the largest banks and trading firms, at Shanghai's top hotels and clubs. And above doorway after doorway hung the Rising Sun—the "poached egg" was the term foreigners used—to which all were required to bow as they passed.

That night and the next few days, my father and other foreigners talked in hushed voices about what had gone on, pooling what they knew. The Shanghai Club had been taken over by the Japanese navy, and the British Country Club and Race Course on Bubbling Well Road by the Japanese army. Allied officials had been sent to the Cathay Mansions, an apartment building on Rue Cardinal Mercier, across from the French Club in the Concession. The German Consulate advocated the immediate internment of all Allied nationals, and even offered to take charge of the camps, an offer that the Japanese declined. The Japanese had taken control of the cable and radio offices, the telephone exchanges, and the newspapers. No messages of any kind were allowed to be sent, and the *North China Daily News* was closed and sealed. Communication with the outside world had stopped. The *Peterel* lay at the bottom of the Whangpoo, despite efforts of the Japanese to save it. The Japanese were able to get the *Wake*'s radio equipment, as well as the ship itself, a feat they considered a triumph. They renamed it the *Tatara Maru* and immediately made it part of the Japanese Imperial Navy.

On December 10, notices appeared all over the city informing "enemy nationals"—British, American, Belgian, and Dutch citizens— that they were required to register within three days. They were to do this by presenting themselves at Hamilton House, a modern building near the Bund, on the corner of Kiangsi and Foochow Roads. My father went as soon as the notices appeared, knowing that another long line awaited him. He was right. The line went on for blocks. As people waited in the cold, a Japanese soldier with a movie camera walked up and down the pavement and motioned for them to smile.

The process lasted most of the day. The registration office was small, the Japanese staff inadequate. Inside, my father presented his passport and a photograph, filled out various forms with long lists of questions about himself, his family, his income. When he had finished with the forms, he was given a registration card and told to carry it with him at all times. He was also informed that he was no longer allowed to change his place of residence without a permit. Watching over the process were several Japanese officials eating delicate cakes and sipping jasmine tea.

Afterward my father walked through a city he didn't know. Enlarged photographs of the American ships sunk at Pearl Harbor and military installations ablaze were displayed on walls around the city. Confiscation notices were everywhere, posted by the Japanese army and navy, informing the public that this land, this building, the contents of this house or apartment, were now under Japanese control and belonged to the Japanese government. Even the sidewalks of Japanese-claimed buildings were Japanese territory; to pass, you had to walk in the street or cross to the other side. Either way you had to raise your hat and bow to the Rising Sun that hung in the doorway. Like many, my father quickly stopped wearing a hat so that he wouldn't have one to tip to the Japanese flag.

Two weeks after Pearl Harbor came the most ominous development yet: in the middle of the night, the Japanese Gendarmerie appeared at the homes of some twenty Allied nationals and arrested them on the spot. No one knew why they were taken, no one knew where they went, and for several weeks, no one heard a thing. They had simply disappeared. Then Will Marsh told my father that he'd heard they'd been taken for questioning to a place called Bridge House, Gendarmerie Headquarters now, an old apartment building on the north side of Soochow Creek. More arrests followed, and soon it was

rumored that Bridge House was filled with both Chinese and foreigners, some of whom had been there for many months. There were
Chinese boys who couldn't be over fifteen years old, American missionaries, well-known British and American journalists and businessmen. The head of the China agency for Dodge cars and trucks,
the president of the Shanghai Stock Exchange, the managers of the
National City Bank, the Socony Vacuum Oil Company, the Singer
Sewing Machine Company. Those who were taken were often not
seen again. And if they were, they were not the same, and they never
spoke of what had happened to them during their imprisonment.

:: :: ::

My father responded to the changes around him in kind. Before reg-
istering at Hamilton House, knowing that afterward would be too
late, he had left the Medhurst and rented a room over a rice and grain
shop near the intersection of Hardoon and Avenue Roads in the
western part of the International Settlement, about a mile from
the center of the city. The apartment was in a residential section on
the corner of a busy street, with a main streetcar line passing the
door. Rent was cheap, though for good reason: during every heavy
rain, that whole section of Avenue Road and Hardoon Road flooded
until it became a lake. The shopkeeper was honest, and warned my
father that at times there would be more than a foot of water in his
shop. No matter, my father said, the place was perfect, first because it
was practical—the grain and rice shop below would come in handy
should leaner days come—and second because it was unremarkable.
He had decided that his best strategy was a low profile.

Once he and Jeannie were settled in his small room, he took stock
of what he had. He was poor, but so was everyone else, and a new
black market was thriving. People sold china and silver, glassware
and jewelry, Chesterfield overcoats and cloche hats, silver hand mirrors and silk scarves. My father sold his Norfolk jacket and his radio.

With the cash, he bought as much nonperishable food as he could, tins of fruit and meat and crackers. He'd decided that canned goods were an investment as well as a staple. The price of food had doubled after Pearl Harbor, but at least it was available, a situation he suspected was temporary.

He traded his homburg hat for two white pigeons. In a small corner of the cramped yard behind the grain shop, he built a chicken house on stilts, fenced the coop with split bamboo, and locked it with a padlock he got for a pair of leather shoes. The peddler who bartered with him for the padlock said it had come from a German submarine.

The pigeons proved to be a good business venture. They began to lay eggs within a few weeks, and my father talked the owner of the rice and grain shop downstairs into giving him the shop's sweepings at the end of the day for a few eggs, so the birds didn't cost much to keep. My father was vigilant about their care, always feeding and watering them on schedule, gathering eggs as though they were treasure. In heavy rains, fearing the fowl might get out and drown, he rolled up his trousers and went out into the night after them, then brought them in and dried them next to the small stove.

:: :: ::

Early in 1942, in yet another proclamation, the Japanese ordered all Allied nationals to turn in any motor vehicles they owned at a place and time specified in the *Shanghai Times*, which had become the Japanese mouthpiece. The proclamation didn't affect most people's transportation. The Japanese had taken over all gas stations, and gas had become a rare commodity. My father hadn't driven his Packard in months. He'd talked a German veterinarian friend of his, Dr. Adler, into letting him store it in his garage in the French Concession. Every few weeks, my father went by to start it up. When he sat at the wheel, he closed his eyes and breathed in the car's familiar smell of soft leather and patchouli, and he imagined that nothing had changed, that he was headed toward Hungjao, and that my mother and I would be waiting for him, her with a tumbler of Scotch, me with narcissus from the garden and tales of my day at school.

But keeping the car was no longer a choice. He didn't have enough gas to drive the car to the Race Course, where he was to turn it in, so he hired coolies to push it. A few days later he traded his gold watch for a bicycle, gritting his teeth so as not to spoil the deal, amazed at what he was doing. The watch had been a gift from his father, but he saw no other choice. The buses no longer ran, the streetcars couldn't begin to handle the city's needs, and rickshaws and pedicabs were ridiculously expensive. A bike was the only way to get around, and soon there wouldn't be any to buy. The thing was to keep going, to do whatever needed to be done next, and not to step out of line.

Spring and summer brought temperatures that were warm, then hot. The city was more and more crowded, with refugee camps of straw huts covering every bit of vacant land. Street-cleaning was a thing of the past. The streets and pavement were filthy, and beggars were everywhere. The currency depreciated, prices rose, and my father kept looking for ways to cut back. He changed the electric bulbs in his room to two- or three-watt bulbs and got rid of the bulbs altogether where he could. He ate only what was native: fresh produce, rice, grains, nothing imported. Eventually he narrowed his diet down to cornmeal, which was cheap and easy to get. He baked it, boiled it, fried it, whatever he could think of, never mind the twenty pounds he'd lost since occupation. Even Jeannie's ribs showed.

The only cause for hope, the thing he thought of at night as he waited for sleep, was the possibility of repatriation. It seemed impossible that the home governments wouldn't send ships to take their citizens home. There were far more Japanese in Canada, the United States, and around the world than there were Allied nationals in Shanghai. Surely an exchange was bound to be arranged.

And then he heard from Will Marsh that negotiations were progressing. News spread that the date had been set, and people were elated. Then came the news that the numbers had been fixed, and everything seemed far less certain. Repatriation ships would stop first at ports in Japan, then in Hong Kong, then at other ports in China. There were only so many spaces for British, Dutch, Belgian, and American nationals, and most of those would go to embassy and consular staffs. When Will Marsh told my father the number of passengers from China that would be allowed, my father nodded grimly. The number was low. And then another blow: the Japanese would have some say in who left and who remained.

Fewer than two hundred spots were reserved for Shanghai residents, grossly out of proportion to the enemy nationals in Shanghai versus those in other ports. The names of embassy and consular officials were followed by inmates at Bridge House, employees of the Chinese government, semi-officials like members of Customs and the Municipal Council, those deemed valuable to the war effort, doctors, the sick and aged. My father was none of those.

The repatriation ship was the *Kamakura Maru*, but my father and others soon called it the *Wangle Maru*. The stories of bargaining and favoritism were appalling. The embassy and consular list included temporary and part-time employees, which meant that a secretary who worked perhaps fifteen or twenty hours a week was guaranteed a spot. There were rumors of out-and-out bargaining, the most blatant of which concerned a rich and socially well-connected woman who was given passage as the nurse to the children of the British Consul General.

The list-making went on for weeks. Finally on Friday, August 14, passengers were called and told they would be allowed to sail the following Tuesday.

That Tuesday was a sweltering summer day, even for Shanghai. At the wharf at Pootung, repatriates were checked through. The process took five hours. As officials stood under corrugated iron roofs, passengers lined up, handing over their papers to be checked and rechecked, carrying their baggage, saying good-bye to friends. My father said yet another good-bye. Will Marsh was on the list.

Within a few weeks of the *Kamakura Maru*'s departure, all talk of repatriation stopped. Soon there was another proclamation: Allied civilians were required to wear armbands. Once again my father stood in line, this time at the Japanese Consulate, where he was given a red armband with an *A* for American and the number 27. He was required to wear it on his left arm at all times, so that he could be distinguished from non-enemy nationals—the Germans and Italians and Vichy French. The penalty for not wearing the armband was significant: a stay at Ward Road Jail, a possibility more ominous than ever since the repatriation of embassy and consular officials. It was common knowledge that questioning now included torture.

Enemy nationals were next denied entrance to all forms of amusement—the cinemas, the theaters and clubs, the public rooms in hotels—but no one had much money anyway. Then British and American films were banned. The Chinese went to what had been the British theaters in large numbers, where they saw old German and French films as well as Chinese and Japanese productions, after which they watched footage of Pearl Harbor and other Japanese fronts in Asia and elsewhere, and were encouraged to applaud Japan's victories.

:: :: ::

In late October of 1942, my father found the completely unexpected in his postbox: an uncensored letter from California with a draft for fifty American dollars. It was from my mother and somehow, for no reason my father could explain, had found its way to him. Letters and Red Cross forms came through only rarely, although he occasionally heard news of us through friends. The fifty U.S. dollars were worth ten times as much as they would have been a few months earlier. My mother had sent it on impulse, reasoning that it couldn't hurt. My father paced in his room for almost an hour, trying to decide where to hide it, and finally settled on the place behind the loose brick near the door of his room.

He was at a low point. He was thin and worn down, his nerves were shot, he startled easily. Stealing was the latest problem, and by then many of his belongings, practical and otherwise, had disappeared: his overcoat hanging on a peg near the front door, a sack of walnuts he'd bought from a street vendor, his aluminum pots and pans from the kitchen shelf, except for one small pot that had been filled with hot soup on the stove. Thieves took the brass pendulum from a small clock near his bed, which they apparently realized was not solid brass, but hollow, for my father found it later in the mud by the side of the road. He periodically found that clothes, boots, socks, even undergarments had been taken. The split bamboo fence he'd put in around the pigeon coop was stolen. He eventually took to sleeping with anything he cared about or couldn't imagine losing: the drawer holding his knives and forks, his last aluminum pot, all of it stuffed under the bed except for the bicycle, which he padlocked to the headboard with a heavy chain and padlock. But then, finally, the pigeons were stolen.

Even dogs were stolen, often by the Japanese, who valued trained guard dogs, and my father worried about Jeannie. Though she clearly had arthritis and was getting old—she would be eleven in a few months—she was intelligent and well trained, and the idea of her being taken tormented him, causing him to check on her constantly. She had become far more than a companion. Thieves had taken just about everything else, but they hadn't touched her, a fact that, at moments, made my father think of himself as a lucky man.

On November 4, an unusually mild morning, my father was surprised to find Jeannie huddled in the corner when he woke. Her arthritis seemed to flare up far more often in cold weather, but she was whimpering and could not stand, and when my father examined her, he found that her back legs had gone out.

The vet my father had gone to for years, an Englishman named Dr. Stewart, had been arrested, no one knew why, so my father took Jeannie to Dr. Adler, his German friend, paying a fortune for a rickshaw to carry the dog. On the way, they passed corpses in the street. It was not an unusual sight. No one bothered to pick them up anymore. Chances were they would still be there the next morning and the night afterward.

At the vet's office, he had to wait two hours to be seen, and when he was shown in and carried Jeannie to the metal table, he saw that Dr. Adler had aged years in a period of six months. His reddish hair was mussed, his face was pale, his eyes were bloodshot.

Dr. Adler shook my father's hand, then motioned to Jeannie. "You want her put down?" he asked. His German accent, still so strong after years in Shanghai, startled my father.

"No," he said. "Something's wrong with her back legs is all. Maybe a nerve, maybe a muscle. Can you give her something?"

Dr. Adler placed a large freckled hand on Jeannie's head and gently stroked her ears. "She's a good dog, Joseph. A beautiful animal. You have to think about her."

My father tried to check the impatience in his voice. "Which is why I've brought her to you."

The vet sighed and rested his hand on Jeannie's flank, and my father watched her labored breathing. "She should be put down. You don't want her stolen. I'll do it for you, but you shouldn't wait." He rubbed his eyes then, and he seemed exhausted. "Do you know how many dogs I've put down in these last months?" he asked. "Nearly a thousand, I think. Every day I watch dogs die. I can't do it much longer. I have no . . ." He paused, searching for a word. "*Geist*," he said finally, and he looked at my father. "You know it? *Geist?*" My father shook his head, and Dr. Adler closed his eyes for a moment, then said softly, "Ahh, spirit, that's what it is. What I am lacking."

My father stared at Jeannie for a long moment. Her breathing was quick, too quick, he knew, and her brown eyes were dull. He knew she was in pain. As he watched, a shudder moved through her body, and he saw her wince.

"If it is her back," Dr. Adler said, "there isn't much to do anyway."

My father stared at the dog for another long moment. Then he said, "All right."

Dr. Adler turned toward the counter and prepared the shot. He looked once again at my father, who nodded, then held Jeannie's head in his hands as Dr. Adler gave her the injection. It was so simple as to be startling. "That's a good dog," my father said softly. He stroked the soft fur of her neck. "My good girl. Good dog, Jeannie, good dog."

Jeannie blinked at him, her eyes dark and knowing. Then she closed her eyes. Her paws and eyelids twitched, and her breathing quickened, then stopped.

Dr. Adler was careful not to look at my father's face. "She's gone," he said. "It's a good decision, Joseph. You didn't want to risk her, eh?"

My father coughed, trying to clear his throat. He nodded and paid the vet, then he turned to leave, wanting only to be away from this office.

"It's a terrible place we've become here," Dr. Adler said suddenly. "Yes?"

"Yes," my father said. "Exactly. We have become a terrible place."

:: :: ::

That night he lay awake well into the night. His room still smelled of the dog, and he did not have the heart to air it out. Even without Jeannie near, her scent was comforting. He lay in bed wishing things were other than they were, listening, wondering, worrying, trying to pinpoint just when he should have left. Six months before Pearl

Harbor? A year? Two? He could find no good answer, and his thoughts kept straying to something he'd heard a few weeks earlier, a hard-to-believe story about two Americans who'd made it through the western part of the city and on to Free China, where they had eventually traveled all the way to the Siberian Railway, and then to Russia. What happened to them once they reached Russia was anyone's guess. Very possibly it was worse than being in Shanghai, but the story had a strong appeal: maybe it was possible to get out. He was trying to work out how to go about it. The fifty dollars from my mother would be a start. For something had happened he'd never expected: the one thing he wanted was to leave the place he'd loved most.

:: :: ::

When he was awakened at five the next morning, he knew immediately what it was. The sounds the gendarmes made had grown familiar from my father's constant imagining of them: the smooth swoosh of tires on wet pavement, the sudden dull silence of a car's engine being cut, the sound of car doors being shut, the crunch of boots on gravel. And then the sharp knocking on his door and the carefully worded English: "You will come with us, please."

He did not argue or resist or try to flee. It was all as he had expected, almost. Only the hugeness of his fear and the bitterness of his regret surprised him.

haiphong road

NAME: *Joseph Schoene*

By the request of Japanese Military Authorities you are to be interned from today in the barracks formerly occupied by the Second Battalion of the U.S. Marines Corps on Haiphong Road.

You are to come at once with the Gendarmes who hand this to you. You are permitted to take along your bedding (blankets, night clothes), toilet articles and some foodstuffs.

Protection of your life and properties and your family will be assured.

November 4, 1942

THE SHANGHAI JAPANESE GENDARMERIE

The four gendarmes at my father's door handed him a mimeographed sheet that told him what to do. He filled his grip with the clothes and old shoes he'd set aside for a morning like this, then stuffed blankets and whatever other necessities he could think of into a black canvas duffle bag. When he was ready, the gendarmes led him outside into the darkness, where he was ordered to join some twenty other men in the back of an old army truck.

It was drizzling. The truck eased down the street, then headed west along Bubbling Well Road toward the Western District of the Settlement. It made several stops, including one at St. Luke's Hospital, where the gendarmes strode inside and came out a few minutes later with a man who was clearly ill. He was ordered into the back of the truck.

They crossed Soochow Creek and turned onto Haiphong Road and then into the yard of a sprawling old Chinese structure with a tiled roof and a redbrick exterior. Surrounding the place was a brick wall, ten feet high, two feet thick, topped with barbed wire. The truck parked in what my father guessed had been the Marines' parade grounds. The men were herded into a long wooden shed, its tile floor covered with a thick layer of mud. The room was already crowded. Although it wasn't yet eight in the morning, my father guessed there were a hundred men inside, sitting on their bags, leaning against the walls, their bodies slack, their faces tense. My father found a spot along the far wall, where he dropped his duffle bag on the floor and sat down on it, his back against a door that said VD CLINIC.

For a while he looked around and tried to gauge the situation in terms of good and bad signs. Were so many men a good sign, or more reason for fear? What about the fact that the Japanese didn't seem to have the place ready for them? But his arguments only went round and round, and he gave up and just waited for whatever was next.

He spent most of that day waiting. More men were brought in throughout the morning and afternoon. No one was given food or drink. Finally, at dusk, a Japanese colonel stood on a table in the middle of the room and addressed the internees for the first time. Colonel Odera was a small man with a handlebar mustache who wore an immense greatcoat and sword. He was the descendant of Samurais, he said, and the grandson of a Japanese soldier who had fought the British in 1860. He then talked about the present war. It had been forced on Japan, he said, and now they, these enemy nationals, had been brought here for their own safety. They were under the jurisdiction of the Japanese Gendarmerie, and each of them was here because he had in some way been disrespectful of the Son of Heaven, Emperor Hirohito. If they obeyed the rules and looked after themselves, all would go well. If not, they would be brought up and tried on charges. If they attempted to escape, they would be severely punished.

The colonel's words were badly translated by his lieutenant, a man named Honda, who had a youngish face and a wary expression. When the colonel finished, Honda counted the men off into some thirty rooms. As my father followed others to his room, he became certain that the Japanese had made almost no preparations. Whatever had not been taken by the Marines had been looted since their departure. There was no furniture, no food. The place was filthy, but the men couldn't even clean it; there were no cleaning supplies. Word of mouth was that the whole camp had been set up at the last minute, that the gendarmes had compiled the list of who they wanted only two nights before. It was said that Lieutenant Honda had until quite recently been just another civilian exporting cheap toys and pottery from Japan, and that the colonel had learned that he was to be in charge of the camp only the day before.

An hour after they were given room assignments, a soldier handed out rice bowls and forks, and at eight o'clock that night, my father and the others stood in line for their first and only meal of the day, a cup of smoky tea and a small bowl of congealed stew that had been brought from Bakerite, a restaurant in town, and was carelessly ladled out from Maxwell House coffee tins. When the internees were called to the main hall one last time that night for roll call, they were told to sleep on the floor, despite the fact that it was wet from the rain.

The next day the colonel appointed two men to be in charge, a Briton and an American, who would, to a large extent, take charge of his prisoners. The Briton, Hugh Kelley, had been chairman of the British Residents' Association. He would be in charge of all British internees, which were the vast majority. The American, a tall, lanky man named John Barrows, had been head of the American Association in Shanghai. He would be responsible for everyone else. Kelley and Barrows in turn each chose an assistant. Kelley chose another Briton he knew, and Barrows chose my father. "I happen to know that you can get things done," Barrows said, and my father winced at his reputation.

The four of them settled into what was called the office, a largish room on the first floor of the main building, slightly better quarters than the rest of the camp, and they set about trying to organize the 343 men in the camp. My father found an old Royal typewriter in the office, and he began a record of the internment. Barrows instructed them to get a count of who was there by nationality and age, which my father carefully recorded:

NOV. 6	MEN IN CAMP
Britons	242
Americans	63
Dutch	23
Greeks	14
Norwegians	1
TOTAL:	343

YOUNGEST MAN:	20
OLDEST MAN:	72
AVERAGE AGE:	44.83

It seemed that most of the men had been taken from their homes, but some had been picked up off the street, and a few had just been yanked out of hospital beds. They were told they were "prominent persons and dangerous criminals," but no one was certain what that meant, or what they had in common. There were bankers, business-men, journalists, carpenters, engineers, perhaps forty ex-police, and a few seamen. There were two bishops (one a Methodist and the other an Irish Anglican) and two doctors (an Englishman named Andrew White and an American named Robert Anderson). There were a few known collaborators, presumably there to spy. At roll call and meals and command performances for Colonel Odera, my father kept looking for the connection, staring at the men around him as though they were a puzzle to be solved, asking himself the same question over and over again: *What did we do?*

Barrows was a practical man, and he decided the first thing to do was to ask the colonel if he could telephone the American Associ-ation and arrange for food and supplies to be brought in for the camp until they were able to set up a kitchen. The colonel said yes, Barrows made the call, and the next day a lunch of sausage sandwiches was brought in. When the first delivery of supplies came two days later—a truckload of mattresses sent by the British Residents' Association and on loan from the Shanghai Volunteer Corps—Barrows told Lieu-tenant Honda that it was both customary and necessary to give the driver a receipt for goods received. When Honda said that would be permitted, Barrows quietly wrote on the back of the receipt a list of what was needed next: blankets, pots and pans, toilet paper, soap. It was the first of many lists.

Barrows and Kelley then set about organizing the camp. They instructed each room to elect a room captain, who would attend weekly captains' meetings with Barrows and Kelley, then report back to the men, so that they would be able to communicate quickly and efficiently. My father knew an American who had been a bugler in the Marine band, and he was quickly drafted into signaling meals, wake-up, and lights out. Morning roll call was at seven, followed by breakfast, which, for the first few days, was dry bread with glycine powder and weak tea. Later it was rice or a porridge made from cracked wheat, which Barrows managed to get for the camp through the Red Cross. The porridge had a nutty flavor that somehow wasn't bad day after day after day, and my father was glad to get it. Lunch was stew or rice, dinner more of the same, or sometimes fish or fried eel, though the fish was often inedible. The only meat was slaughter-house scraps that had been frozen in cubes and sent to the camp. It soon became apparent that the quality of the meat had an inverse relationship to the amount of garlic used in its preparation: the worse the meat, the heavier the garlic. And there was always weak tea, sometimes steeped from nothing more than garden lettuce.

Once food and supplies were on the way, Barrows and Kelley assigned jobs to everyone in camp. The jobs were classified as special-ist and nonspecialist jobs. Specialist jobs included tasks like carpentry, electrical repair, plumbing, medical and sickroom duty, and cooking. Nonspecialist jobs were the everyday, not-an-option chores like kitchen detail, which involved cleaning and picking the worms out of the uncooked cracked wheat that had been left to stand too long.

The internees were fingerprinted repeatedly, and they were required to fill out form after form giving personal information and history, all of it on Municipal Council forms, as though these had been legitimate arrests. Photographs were taken for propaganda pur-poses, my father guessed, and the camp was often inspected by high-Gendarmerie officials. Internees were forced to bow to all Japanese officers and sentries, and to Colonel Odera when he arrived at the camp each morning. When, after one of the camp's first attempts at bowing, the colonel was displeased with the result, Lieutenant Honda began conducting bowing practice just after roll call, forcing the men to bow a dozen times or more before they were permitted to line up for breakfast.

During the first week of December, the colonel said it was reason-able for the internees to expect visits from their families eventually. In addition, each internee would be allowed one parcel and one letter a month from families in Shanghai. This was good news until Lieutenant Honda set out the specifics. Visits would be limited to one ten-minute visit per year, with the supervision of the guards. Letters were limited to two twenty-five-word letters per year to families residing outside of China, and one letter per month to families still in Shanghai. All correspondence would have to be approved by the camp censor. My father was pessimistic about a letter actually finding its way to South Pasadena. Besides, what was there to say? What good news could he pass on? And so he didn't write.

The only news the camp received was from the Japanese-controlled *Shanghai Times* and a shortwave radio that got scratchy reception of the Russian station in Shanghai. Those two sources kept the camp vaguely informed concerning the war in Europe, but they knew very little about things closer to home. Only news of Japanese victories was let through; any Allied progress against the Son of Heaven was censored both in print and on the air. In early December, the camp was barred and blockaded for air raid warnings, and Barrows and Kelley were informed that the camp was to be blacked out. Barrows protested strongly and explained to Honda that the blackout of an internment camp was absolutely contrary to international law, especially since the Swiss Consulate had not even been informed of the existence of the camp. Honda replied that two lighted Japanese hospital ships had been sunk by Allied planes and that it was the colonel's solemn intent to protect the camp to the last man against the angry Chinese mob.

But the most galling of the colonel's edicts had to do with money. Lieutenant Honda informed Barrows and Kelley that the internees' home governments would be billed for all supplies that were brought into camp, including coal, wood, and food. My father and others were appalled. It was unthinkable that Japan would not provide for its prisoners, and the idea of home governments being forced to repay

Japan for their internment was deeply upsetting. But the colonel was determined. Home governments would even be billed for heat, he said, and a portion of the amount billed would go toward heating the Japanese administration building at the camp. Many men said they would far rather be cold than do anything to provide heat for the Japanese.

:: :: ::

At the start, there seemed to be only three circumstances in which a man would be permitted to leave camp: if his wife was critically ill and death seemed imminent; if his wife died, in which case he would be allowed to attend the funeral; or if the man himself was so ill that he required medical care beyond what the camp doctors could provide, a matter that the colonel and Lieutenant Honda would decide. An American banker suffered a heart attack, a Greek seaman contracted meningitis, and one of the bishops developed what the camp doctors were certain was a malignant growth. Each of those men was taken to an outside hospital, and each time it was a long job to convince the Japanese that he was truly ill, and that an ambulance was needed. And each time the man died soon after he reached the hospital.

But in early December, when they had been at Haiphong Road for a month, they learned that there was a fourth reason to leave camp. Early in the day on December 5, Lieutenant Honda sent for Barrows and my father and asked them to bring an American journalist named Peter Young to him. Young should bring his overcoat, the lieutenant added. When Barrows asked why Young was wanted, Honda replied only that he was being taken out for questioning by the gendarmes. Barrows then asked if Young was being taken to Bridge House, and Honda's scowl told him he was correct.

Young was returned from Bridge House sixteen days later. The gendarmes said he was only submitted to gentle questioning, but when my father opened the door of the gendarmes' car, the sight of Peter Young was terrifying. He was emaciated and could not walk. He was filthy, his hair and unshaved beard as matted as dead weeds. My father carried him directly to the internees' clinic and the camp doctors.

My father had known Young before they were interned, and so the two camp doctors, Anderson and White, asked him to help with Young's care. My father observed a changed man. He bathed and shaved Young, then fed him warm rice and gave him hot drinks, and although Young was incoherent for most of that first night, he did seem to know that he was being helped and was grateful. In the morning, after his clothes had hung on the line overnight, they were covered with hundreds of dead lice.

Young was at first hesitant to speak. The gendarmes had made it clear that he was not to talk about what had been done to him. But his silence was so anxious, and the look in his dark eyes so wild and panicked, that my father thought talking about it was the only way to calm him down. What happened in Bridge House had been a mystery for years, and it was with dread that my father listened to Peter Young for two days, gritting his teeth during the worst of it, trying not to react, giving Young fluids and trying to get some food in him, and to make him believe the lie that he was safe now.

And as he listened, he developed a new theory about why they were here. Maybe Young was not an isolated case. Maybe he wasn't the only one who was wanted for questioning—he was just the first. Because perhaps that was what all these men had in common: they were all wanted for questioning by the Gendarmerie, and it was just a matter of time before each man's turn came.

:: :: ::

That winter was particularly cold. In a pile of trash in one of the rooms, my father found a thermometer, which he hung outside the office window. When he checked it each morning, he found the outside temperature was often below twenty degrees. For the first month there was almost no heat, but even when there was, it was inadequate, and a cold winter's afternoon might find as many men as would fit sitting close together in the old greenhouse, where it was a few degrees warmer than the barracks. Many of the internees had chilblains, their hands and feet raw and red and inflamed from the cold and wet. But despite that and the freezing temperatures, the whole camp was often made to stand outside for half an hour or more for roll call, the quartermaster insisting that they remove their hats as a sign of respect as the Rising Sun was raised on the flagpole left by the U.S. Marines.

By January, when a man was told that he was to be taken to Bridge House, my father and others lost no time in filling his coat pockets with whatever they could imagine might help: biscuits, cigarettes, toilet paper, coins. Those who were returned were always in the same condition, emaciated and weak, with haunted expressions that made my father want to look away. Each of them was cared for in the same way that Young had been: a bath, a haircut and shave, something to eat, lots to drink, and the chance to tell someone who could be trusted about what he had been through. It all became routine, even in February, when nine men were brought at the same time.

:: :: ::

Once again, my father worked at adapting. He learned to think about other things when Colonel Odera talked about the internees' wives being able to visit soon, and he learned to smile and clap his friends on the back when they cheered at the possibility. He learned to eat fish he wouldn't have touched a few months earlier, to force himself to choke it down no matter how it looked or smelled or tasted. At least it was food—protein at that, hard to come by. And he learned to make believe, for just a moment when he needed it, that my mother and I were close. In the pocket of one of the pairs of trousers he had packed on that hurried November morning, he had placed a photograph of us, one he had taken years earlier at the beach at Tsingtao. I was a toddler, gleeful and triumphant as I stood on sturdy legs on the sand next to my mother, her arm supporting me. I grinned wildly at the camera, and at my father holding it. My mother knelt on the sand next to me, giving me balance. Her wavy hair touched her shoulders, and she wore a tight long-sleeved sweater and a long full skirt that was tucked around her legs, except that the curve of one of her calves showed, lovely and graceful. The fitted sweater revealed the round fullness of her breasts, and the expression on her face as she stared hard at that camera, laughing and trying to hold me still, was all confidence. My father had carried the photograph in his wallet for as long as I could remember, and though as a child I did not know the words to describe my mother's look, I knew it when I remembered it: she was sexy and young and beguiling in that photo, a woman any man would find appealing.

On winter afternoons at Haiphong Road, my father stared hard at that photo, and he learned a trick to bring us closer: if he rolled up a piece of paper and used it like a telescope to stare at the picture, we seemed very near, and he could, for a moment, imagine himself on that beach with us, the reason for our smiles.

:: :: ::

In June an American engineer died of a heart attack, and my father and three other Americans were permitted to leave camp to attend the funeral. The summer of 1943 was the wettest and coldest one that my father could remember in Shanghai, and when he returned to camp two hours after the funeral, he was soaked through and as chilled as if it were winter. But he didn't care. When he hurried into the office to find Barrows, he was elated. At the funeral, he had been able to talk with an acquaintance who worked for the American Association, who whispered good news when the gendarmes weren't looking: there was pretty sure talk of American repatriation, and it was rumored that British negotiations were in the works as well. He said some even thought repatriation was possible before year's end.

Barrows stared hard at my father and finally allowed himself to smile. He slapped my father on the back and laughed, and told my father to tell him the whole thing again.

By the first of August, repatriation seemed imminent. Several of the men wrote letters to their wives and made bets with themselves: they wanted to see if they could beat their letters home. Rather than trusting the Japanese for delivery, they tried to smuggle their letters out of camp by addressing the letters to contacts in Chungking, the seat of Free China. Then they bribed one of the truck drivers or cooks to mail the letter to Chungking, where a contact would re-address the letter to its real recipient. Rumor was that a letter sent like that had a good chance of making it.

Richard Fletcher was one of those men. Shortly before dinner on an evening in early August, Fletcher and another American, Edward Martin, were talking with a Sikh guard named Amar. My father was in the office, and he glanced out of the window at the three men talking and thought it strange that Amar, a man who kept to himself, would be even civil to Martin and Fletcher. Martin walked away after a moment, and as he passed my father's window, he nodded to my father, and they exchanged a thumbs-up. They were of the same build and both had very short blond hair and they were often mistaken for each other.

And then there was shouting, and my father looked back at Fletcher and Amar. Amar was yelling at Fletcher, who shook his head and tried to walk away. But when he turned, Amar grabbed his shoulder and spun him around, then pushed him roughly toward the Japanese administration building.

An hour later, my father was in line for dinner when he saw Barrows heading toward him, his expression pained, his jaw tight. When Barrows reached my father, he said, "Honda wants to see you. You're to bring your coat."

It didn't register, and when my father didn't react, Barrows shook his head and seemed impatient. "Get your coat, Joe, and we'll get over to Honda and we'll see what's what. Standing here won't help you out."

My father nodded without speaking, then followed Barrows to the office, where he grabbed his coat. Barrows dropped a hard roll into the pocket, then led my father to Honda's office.

Fletcher was there, sitting in a chair in front of Honda, whose sword lay across the desk. The lieutenant sometimes used its flat edge as a club, and it was clear from the lump on the side of Fletcher's head that he had just done that.

Amar stared hard at my father. "This man was a witness," he said. Then he looked at Honda. "He must be punished for not volunteering this information."

My father felt Honda watching him, and for a moment, no one spoke. Then Amar began to speak furiously, telling of the wrong that had been done, and how it must be righted, and how these prisoners seemed to do as they pleased, was there no justice? This man Fletcher had asked him to disobey the colonel by smuggling a letter out of camp, and this other man, this Schoene, had been witness to the wrongdoing and had said nothing.

And then my father understood: Amar had confused him with Edward Martin, and at first he felt a wave of relief. This would be cleared up. Honda was focused on Amar, and my father saw Barrows look hard at Fletcher and asked his question by nodding toward my father. *Was it him?* Barrows's look said. Fletcher shook his head.

"Lieutenant," Barrows said evenly, "it is possible that there has been a misunderstanding here. With your permission, I will question one of the other internees."

Honda regarded Barrows skeptically. "I will question *this* one," he said, and he pointed to my father.

And then Honda turned to my father. "You," he said. "You witnessed this betrayal?"

My father hesitated. He was about to explain what he'd seen, and that he and Martin were often mistaken for each other, but something stopped him. Suddenly it didn't make any sense. It didn't do any good for someone else to go instead of him. Martin had done nothing wrong—he'd only been standing in the wrong place at the wrong time. He'd sent his wife and three small children home early on, and he'd had every intention of following soon. Why should he be punished?

Everything seemed clear, and my father nodded at Honda. "I was there when they were talking, and what Fletcher was doing wasn't so bad. He only wanted a letter to go to his wife, was all. It's all your regulations that are the problem here, not us."

Honda looked stricken, and my father braced himself for whatever was next. Honda took a large volume from the corner of his desk and began to leaf through it. "'For disobedience to an officer, ten to twenty-five years' imprisonment,'" he read. He flipped forward. "'For disrespect to an officer, ten years' imprisonment or death. For incitement to mutiny, twenty-five years' imprisonment or death.'" He slammed the book shut and stared hard at my father. "Do you understand?"

My father nodded silently. Barrows started to speak, and my father turned to him. "For God's sake, shut up," he said. Barrows looked as though he'd been hit. He looked at my father for a long moment, stunned. My father nodded and Barrows said nothing more.

Fletcher and my father were led outside, where the black Chevrolet used by the gendarmes sat waiting in front of Honda's office. First Fletcher was shoved roughly into the backseat, then my father.

And then the car pulled away from the building and through the main gates.

:: :: ::

When they arrived at Bridge House, my father and Richard Fletcher were immediately separated. My father was led to a large wooden desk, where the gendarme behind it handed him a printed form and told him to fill it in completely. My father did, writing in his nationality, his place and date of birth, and details of his personal history, including education and the names and addresses of family and friends. He signed the form, and he was fingerprinted, then stripped, searched, and given a cotton coat and trousers to wear. A guard led him downstairs to the ground floor, which had been designed for shops; Bridge House had originally been a modern apartment building. But the shops were cells now, and he followed the guard down a long dark hallway to the chief jailer, who sat at a desk at the end of the corridor. On the wall next to him were rows of metal pegs, and on the pegs were small wooden tags, each with a prisoner's name on it in Chinese characters on one side and in English on the other. There was also a heavy metal ring with a number of keys, everything from small Yale keys that anybody could have, to huge, cumbersome things that were six or even eight inches long.

He was put in a room that was perhaps eighteen feet by twelve. It was very crowded, and the stench made him gag. Once his eyes had adjusted to the dim light, my father counted and found that twenty-five people, mostly men but a few women and one child, sat cross-legged in rows on the concrete floor. A box in the corner was the toilet. There was no room to lie down, no faucet to wash with, no heat. They had been given a bundle of blankets to share, and when the lights went out an hour later, my father watched as the prisoners formed groups of two to six and huddled close together, sharing a blanket. He felt the vermin and lice under his clothes. He heard the rats moving around the cell.

In the morning, he was given a bowl of boiled rice. Next to him was a Korean man who whispered stories to him: he himself had been jabbed in the leg with a bayonet, he said. My father guessed he was dying of blood poisoning. The Chinese woman weeping in the corner had been taken from her professor husband, the Korean said; now she had no idea where he was. A White Russian woman held her three-year-old son in her arms, awake or asleep. Several of the inmates had typhus, but the Korean told him that the only medical care consisted of visits by a female Japanese nurse accompanied by two petty officers. The nurse handed out aspirin for a fever or any other ailment, including boils, swelling, or VD.

My father remembered someone who'd been in Bridge House saying that you had to keep track of the days and hours in there, that doing so helped keep you sane. But by the time he remembered that advice, it was too late. The days had already run together.

He was given a bowl of rice in the morning and evening, sometimes with pickled vegetables or a dried herring head. Some of the Chinese boys would pick lice off him if he gave them some of his food. He was interrogated frequently, always at night. A gendarme would come to the cell and call his name, the door would be unlocked, and he would be led upstairs and told to write the approximate dates of the history of his life. When he had done this, he was told to do it again, and again after that, so that he wrote out his personal history perhaps a dozen times. Each time, it was translated into Japanese. Then the gendarme read it over and questioned him. His answers were written down in Japanese on large sheets of ruled paper, which, when complete, were folded into a sort of book that my father was forced to sign and fingerprint on the last page. Most of the prisoners' statements filled half a dozen books. Some men had been questioned for a month, some for two or more. The intent of most of the questioning seemed to be to link the prisoner with British or American intelligence.

Interrogations were helped along with various kinds of torture. Some of these my father experienced, some he only witnessed. The gendarmes might beat a man with rubber truncheons, or they might force him to sit in a bright light for twenty hours or more. They used the water cure, letting one drop of water at a time fall on a man's head for hours. They would force a prisoner to sit up or stand until he or she collapsed. There was also a way in which a man could be made to sit on a bench, his legs straight out in front of him and tied to the bench just below the knees. Then a brick would be placed under the heel, and the guard would hit the man's heel with a small billy club. They might insert a bristle into the tip of a man's penis, or place delicate bamboo pipes into a man's nostrils and pour water into those pipes until the man almost drowned. This was what they did to my father. Within days, the pressure from the water had been so great that it burst both eardrums, and soon they were infected.

And then, as suddenly as he was taken out, he was returned to camp. His eardrums had started to heal by then, and though his hearing was compromised, it was improving. He had no idea why they were letting him go back to camp. He had not, as far as he knew, answered any of their questions satisfactorily. The questions always centered on American intelligence, a subject about which my father knew little, which was no accident. He had long been certain that no good could come of that type of knowledge, and he'd been careful not to pick it up.

He was driven back to camp in the same black Chevrolet, where he sat slumped in the backseat, not completely certain of what was happening. But then the car pulled into the main gate at Haiphong Road and he knew where he was.

The car stopped, and after a pause, the door opened, and John Barrows peered in at my father. "My God," he whispered. He heard Barrows call for the camp doctors. Then he passed out.

His condition, though horrible, was no worse than that of anyone who'd been brought from Bridge House. In fact, Dr. Anderson told him that evening, he had actually fared better than most. My father asked how long he had been gone; he guessed a month. "Eleven days," Anderson said grimly. "It just seemed longer."

When he had been back for a few days, and had had food and liquids and a bath and a shave and sleep, he learned that Fletcher had not returned. Barrows asked if he knew anything about what had been done to Fletcher, and my father groaned, for he had forgotten what he'd heard: that Fletcher had been taken to the roof, where he was bound and left there, exposed to the elements.

Five days after my father's return, he was up and around. He wrote down as much as he could about his treatment in Bridge House, and he kept to himself, though he knew many of the internees made an effort to welcome him back. Martin tried; he approached my father and met his eyes and my father nodded, but Martin couldn't speak, and that was all the conversation they had. It was enough for my father. After that he worked at putting Bridge House out of his mind. He concentrated on the future, not the past, and told himself that repatriation, not interrogation, was what should fill his thoughts.

∷ ∷ ∷

The weather in Shanghai had been unusual all that summer, but in the days following my father's return from Bridge House, it turned even stranger. What started as a steady rain became a downpour. A typhoon warning was issued, and wet gusts of wind tore at the huge plane tree by the main entrance. By the next afternoon the camp was flooded inside and out, and at dusk the plane tree blew over and fell to the ground, blocking the entrance to the camp.

The wind and rain eased the next day, and in the days after that, the flooding subsided. Lieutenant Honda called Barrows and my father in and instructed them to have the camp begin cleaning up. The first order of business was the plane tree. Barrows nodded; he had assumed they would be cutting it up and hauling it away.

"Colonel Odera orders that the tree is to be put back," Honda said casually. "It is very beautiful and very old, and he does not want to lose it."

Barrows and my father looked at each other and laughed, then stopped. Honda was serious. They tried to explain to him that a tree as big as that could not simply be "put back," but Honda would hear no arguments.

"The colonel's wish," he said again, and he sent Barrows and my father on their way, giving them orders to have a crew of men working on the tree the next day, no matter what.

The next morning a crew of fifty men got to work, tying the tree with ropes and using two-by-fours for leverage to help them lift the tree and get it back into the ground. After lunch a new crew relieved them, and it was sometime after that that the gendarmes' Chevrolet entered the main gate. The work crew was getting close to the point where they could begin to raise the tree, but everyone froze when the car drove into the camp.

The car stopped in front of the administration building. The gendarmes in the front seat didn't move. No one did. Not my father, who had been near the tree, but had followed the car when it entered the yard. Not Barrows, or any of the other men near the car. Everyone waited, watching the gendarmes, who just sat in the front seat, staring hard at the internees as if daring them, waiting for them to do or say something.

My father was closest to the car. The gendarme at the wheel recognized him and nodded as though they were old friends. "You," he said. "Open the door." My father walked to the car and carefully opened the door.

At first he thought it was a prank; there seemed to be no one inside, not on the seat anyway. He thought perhaps it was some sort of delivery, because he saw something on the floor. And then he realized that it was a man. He glanced behind him, suddenly afraid, and met Barrows's eyes. Barrows called for the camp doctors, and my father leaned into the backseat to help the man out. He thought about trying to lift him, but he knew he had no strength. Finally he stood back from the car and let Barrows climb into the backseat, where he sat for a moment, his expression stunned. When the doctors had carried out a stretcher, Barrows and the two of them lifted the man out of the car and onto the stretcher, then carried him into the camp's makeshift clinic. It was Fletcher.

Honda had come out of his office by then. He called for work on the tree to resume, but no one obeyed. The men dropped whatever tools they had, they let the ropes and two-by-fours fall to the ground, and they walked toward the clinic.

By that time, Anderson and White had seen some twenty-five former guests of Bridge House, men they could barely recognize when they were brought in for care. But Fletcher's condition was beyond the pale. He looked more dead than alive. He was naked and far too weak to stand, but that didn't matter yet, as he was unconscious when Barrows and the doctors carried him into the clinic. In fifteen days, he had become a skeleton. Not only was he starved; he was so dehydrated that his internal organs were failing. The skin on his wrists and ankles had been cut to the bone, as though he'd been bound with wire.

My father watched as Anderson examined him, and he heard Anderson murmuring something. He was unconsciously reciting the names of the bones he saw protruding from the skin, as though he were teaching anatomy: *tibia, femur, ilium, sternum, clavicle.*

It was after Fletcher had been bathed that they found some kind of message, letters scratched into the skin on the insides of his thighs. The word *murdered* was visible on the inside of one thigh; on the other was the word *roof.* There were scratches on his wrists as well, but no one could read them.

"Do you think he did it with a stick?" Anderson said softly, for it was clear that Fletcher was trying to tell whoever found him what had been done.

The camp doctors were certain that there was nothing they could do for Fletcher. He was too far gone, and although they doubted that he would survive for long anywhere, they insisted that he be taken to a hospital for more care. Barrows went to the colonel, and the next morning Fletcher was transferred. My father and a few other Americans watched him being taken out, a barely living corpse.

That afternoon Barrows talked the men into resuming work on the plane tree, which was already called Fletcher's Tree. The colonel had given a direct order that they were to complete the work, and it was pointless to risk his anger, no matter how upset they were. By dusk, the tree was back up.

The next morning, Honda sent for Barrows and informed him that Fletcher had died at nine o'clock the previous evening. "He did not receive adequate care in that clinic of yours," Honda said flatly. "We see now that your American and British medicine has its limits, do we not?"

:: :: ::

At the beginning of September, 1943, the colonel announced that Americans and Canadians would be leaving camp in the middle of the month on the Swedish exchange ship *Gripsholm*, which had carried the first group of repatriates out of China a few months earlier.

Negotiations were still in the works for other Allied nationals, so they would stay, for now. On August 14, an announcement in the *Shanghai Times* had said that the *Gripsholm* was leaving New York for Shanghai the next day, and that it would be carrying fifteen hundred Japanese, who would be exchanged for the same number of Americans and Canadians.

That afternoon, my father went to the carpentry shop the prisoners had set up. Martin, the man who resembled my father, was working there that day. Carpentry was a hobby of his, and he'd made a couple of small tables for the camp. He and my father talked for a few minutes about the exchange and about going home, and then my father asked his favor: Could Martin make him a small folding chair for the trip home aboard the ship? He didn't want one of those big deck chairs, just a small chair he could keep with him.

Martin looked confused, but he didn't ask questions. He just said he'd do what he could.

Two days later, Martin found my father in his room. He'd finished the chair, he said, and he set it up on the floor. My father was impressed; it was perfect. To brace the chair, Martin had used a hollow crossbar from a piece of brass curtain rod he'd found. The wooden slats were from a vegetable crate he'd found near the kitchen garbage. My father thanked Martin, they shook hands, and that was that.

When Martin had left the room, my father took from the large inside pocket of his overcoat the journal he'd been keeping. A week earlier he'd taken to rolling it up and keeping it in his coat, thinking that it was the safest place. It was sixteen typed pages on thin white paper. My father rolled it up again, as tightly as he could, then looked from it to the curtain rod that braced the chair. It looked possible. He knelt next to the chair and fitted the rolled-up diary into one end of the curtain rod and slid the journal all the way inside, and out of sight.

Finally the date for the exchange was set: the fifteenth of September. Early that morning, Barrows asked my father to be in charge of the baggage that was to be taken from the camp to the ship, a job my father was more than happy to do. When everything was ready, the Japanese searched every bag and suitcase and box. My father had strapped his chair to his suitcase, and the Japanese guard ordered him to undo it. My father did, and the guard searched his suitcase, then nudged the chair with the toe of his boot and told my father to put it all back together again. An hour later, my father and fifty-four other Americans were taken in army trucks from Haiphong Road to the docks at the Whangpoo, luggage in hand, where they boarded the *Gripsholm*. Because the ship would be stopping in other ports for prisoner exchanges, the trip would take much longer than usual, three months instead of one. My father didn't care. All that mattered was that he was leaving.

Though he knew it would be hard on his heart and his legs, he stayed on deck for the ship's departure, a gesture of respect for what he was leaving. He could not stand for very long. He was thin and weak, his feet and legs and joints ached, and his right hand trembled crazily when he waved to the few onlookers on the dock. He looked years older than he had ten months earlier; he knew that. He knew, too, that as a result of extreme vitamin deficiencies his complexion was sallow, and that the whites of his eyes were a dirty yellow hue.

As the *Gripsholm* began to travel up the Whangpoo, the skyline of the Bund grew small in the distance, and my father strained to keep it in sight. He grieved for the city Shanghai had become, and for what he had lost in the course of that transformation. But when the ship reached the Yangtze and later the Pacific, he ceased dwelling on those things. He was going to a place he would learn to call home, a place where he was loved.

waiting

ON A TUESDAY in May of 1942, five months after Pearl Harbor, my mother had received a letter from my father, the first in a year. She came into the kitchen holding it in the air as though it were good news. I looked up from a page of long division I didn't want to do. "It's postmarked 'Java,'" she said, her voice tight, and for the seconds that it took her shaking hands to tear open the thin envelope, I made a wish. *Maybe he's on his way here.*

And then my mother began to read: "'The McLains are leaving today. They're sailing on the *Tjisdane* for Java, and I'm hoping Mac will take this with him and post it there so you'll know how things are. Shanghai is changed more than you can imagine, Eve. Spirits are low, there's a closed-in feeling that brings on regret, and every week I tell more friends good-bye. Those of us who've stayed don't talk about where it will end. I don't know when I'll be able to get another letter out, so this will have to do for a while, I expect.'"

The letter went on to detail some of Shanghai's changes more specifically, much of which I didn't fully understand. And then there was something I did understand: "'Two months ago, I closed up the house and moved into town and took a room at the American Club, a few blocks from the Bund and my office. It's easier to keep a low profile here, and I feel safer. It was the prudent thing to do, though not the easy one. I know that for many foreigners in China, servants are servants. But Chu Shih and Mei Wah had become friends to me, always had been really, but even more so since you left. Saying good-bye to them was harder than I care to admit. The only good thing I can say is that I was able to pay them well. Tell Anna that they will be all right, especially Chu Shih. He planned to go further south, to Canton, where he has relatives. As for our home, it is one of many beautiful residences that have been boarded up and deserted for now. I saw no other choice, as it is more and more dangerous in the Western Roads District.'"

My mother turned to the last page of the letter. "'I have tried not to say too much,'" she began, and then she stopped and read the rest of the page to herself.

"What?" I asked.

She was still reading and didn't answer at first. Then she glanced at me and said, "It's just more about Shanghai." She refolded the letter and slipped it into the pocket of her skirt.

"Is he all right?" I asked.

My mother didn't answer for a moment. "I don't know," she said finally, "but I'm going to believe that he is. I'm not sure how I would function if I considered the alternative."

I nodded, stunned by her lack of reassurance, a first. For four years, she had told me over and over again that he would be all right, that he would be here soon.

Now she sank into one of the kitchen chairs and leaned forward, her forehead resting on her palm. "I never imagined he wouldn't come," she said softly. She sounded truly confused, and she shook her head and laughed sadly. "I thought I was saving him, by leaving.

I knew he'd never leave on his own, no matter how bad things got. I just thought that if we left, he'd come, too." She looked at me and her expression was pained. "What did I do?"

I took a deep breath. "It wasn't you," I said. "I think it was me."

She looked at me quickly. "What do you mean?"

"I think he didn't come because of something I did. Maybe he's mad at me."

My mother looked puzzled. "I don't understand."

I shrugged slightly, feeling some relief at telling her the secret I'd held for so long. "I don't know what I did, but I think he must be angry with me over something. Why else hasn't he come?" I'd rarely seen him angry with my mother, so it had to be me. I looked to her for an answer yet again.

My mother's face softened. "Oh, Anna, it has nothing to do with you. He loves you, he's crazy about you." She smoothed my hair. "How long have you thought that?"

I shrugged again, trying to seem as though it weren't important. "A few years," I said, and I looked down. "Since second grade, I think."

My mother was shaking her head, and the expression on her face was pained. "I should have figured that out. Or you should have told me. That's not it at all. You're just about the main attraction as far as your father's concerned."

And then I told her the same thing she'd told me a thousand times. "It will be all right," I said.

My mother sighed. "Yep," she said. "That's sort of our party line, I guess."

That evening she fixed creamed chipped beef on toast, which she barely touched. While she watched me eat, she asked about my math homework and the fifth-grade picnic, which was only a few weeks away. When we'd finished dinner, she excused herself to go and freshen up for her bridge group that night. As I was clearing the table and rinsing our dishes, she came in and asked me if I was sure I would be all right by myself. It was only recently that she had started to let me stay at home alone, instead of dropping me off at my grandmother's, and I told her I was fine. She wrote Mrs. McCubbin's phone number, which I'd known by heart for months, on the pad by the phone, and she left.

I locked the front door behind her and waited five minutes to be sure she wasn't coming back for something. And then I went to her room.

The letter was on her dresser. I unfolded it and turned to the last page and found the place where my mother had stopped reading: "I have tried not to say too much, Eve, so that you can read all of the above to Anna. The truth is that I am a changed man, and I suspect I would be unrecognizable to her. I have lost weight; my nerves are worn thin; I am always anxious. Regret is a backdrop to all my thoughts, and it isn't just staying that I regret. It's not that specific. Rather, it's a feeling of general sadness that I suppose comes from a series of bad decisions, things I wish I could change, one after the other. My chances of changing those things are slim, I'll wager. I don't find myself good company, and I am less than proud of the man I have become."

I let my breath out and just stood there for a few minutes, holding my father's letter as I tried to remember the details of his face. *It shouldn't be hard*, I thought. *He's your father; surely you know what he looks like.* But I couldn't; I couldn't even remember his voice. And although I stared hard at his neat black cursive and tried to conjure him up from the words on the page, all I could see was his short blond hair and his eyes, bright blue and intense.

:: :: ::

My father was right: that unlikely letter was the last we heard for many months. Everything stopped after Pearl Harbor—postcards, letters, wires—and we heard nothing, an ominous silence worse than the sporadic bursts of news that had preceded it. Although he was imprisoned by the Japanese in November of 1942, it was not until March of 1943 that my mother received official word of it from the International Red Cross. This was, she said, the bad news she'd been expecting. She said there was some good news: the camp seemed to be for political prisoners, and perhaps my father would not be held for long. For the first time, I didn't ask any questions. I finally understood that there was much my mother didn't know, and that asking only made things worse.

By summer my mother had heard that there was talk of repatriation. Again, I didn't ask questions, not even what "repatriation" meant. Instead I just went to my grandmother's huge dictionary the next time I was at her house, where the closest word I could find was *repatriate*, which meant "to bring or send back (a person, esp. a prisoner of war, a refugee, etc.) to his country or the land of his citizenship." I wrote the definition down on a piece of notebook paper and kept it in my binder. It was the exact word I'd been looking for; it was what I'd wanted all along.

Over that summer, as my mother began to believe that my father might soon be released, she acted as though the news was something fragile. She told almost no one, as though speaking of my father's return might jinx it. In the first week of September, she was notified by the U.S. State Department that my father would be boarding the Swedish exchange ship *Gripsholm* on the fifteenth of September as part of an exchange of American and Japanese civilians, and that he would arrive in New York in mid-December. Even then she remained cautious. I began to think that she wouldn't really believe it until he was standing in front of her.

I understood her caution. I felt like even saying the words might do something bad, but it wasn't only the idea of jinxes and bad luck that made me cautious. I was nervous about seeing him, even though that was what I'd wanted for years. But by then we had been separated from him for five years, nearly half my life. Fathers in general were unknowns to me. I didn't know how to act around them, I was always nervous around my friends' fathers. Now I saw that even my own father was an unknown, and I found myself wondering what he was like. I could describe him on cue—how he looked, things he said, what he liked to eat, the qualities he valued in a polo pony. But the man I knew was a thirty-one-year-old businessman in Shanghai, a millionaire who had everything he wanted. A man in a white dinner jacket, standing in the kitchen with a tumbler of Scotch in his hand, about to go out for the evening; a businessman sitting at a carved blackwood desk, a Philippine cigar in his mouth, a green fountain pen in his hand as he scratched away on a yellow legal pad; a polo player in jodhpurs and riding boots, pacing in a gravel driveway as he held forth on ponies and automobiles and Chiang Kai-shek, while his chauffeur polished the chrome on the Packard. But the man who was joining us was a thirty-six-year-old ex-prisoner who was being sent home with only what he could carry, a man who had not lived in or even visited the United States in fourteen years. I thought it was possible that my father was someone I didn't know.

I guessed that he was faced with the same problem, for my mother and I were changed as well. My mother was thirty-three, but when I looked at photographs of her from Shanghai, I sensed a trick, a sort of optical illusion. She somehow looked younger now than she had in Shanghai. On the weekends she went out with friends, and though she wasn't flirtatious, I could see she liked being around the husbands of her friends, and that she enjoyed the looks she got when we were at the beach or the movies. She seemed to get prettier as she got older, and her prettiness bothered me. I would watch her smiling and laughing at a party or barbecue or just talking to the box boy while we waited in line at the Market Basket on Huntington Drive, and I'd think, *Can't you just look like the other moms?*

I noticed those things. I was almost thirteen. I was just under five feet tall and weighed ninety-five pounds. I had wavy brown hair that just touched my shoulders and bangs that I pulled at when I was nervous. In the middle of September of 1943, a week after we heard that my father would soon be released, I started seventh grade at South Pasadena Junior High, where I would go through the ninth grade. It was a sprawling tiled-roof structure on Fair Oaks between Oak and Rollin, with a clock tower and an inscription over the entrance that read: *Along the cloistered arcade of the junior high school, youth treads its happy way toward the fullness of life.* I wasn't so sure about what I was treading toward, or just what "the fullness of life" meant, but I liked the sound of it, and I liked where we lived. With my blue eyes and freckles and hair bleached a little lighter by the sun, I even looked like a native, a California kid, my grandmother said. I considered that a compliment, though what my coloring really meant was that I took after my father. I saw that as a compliment, too, and a good sign: maybe we would have other things in common as well. Maybe he would like it here, too, maybe he would love the things I loved: the beach, the warm days, the orange groves, the dark purple mountains against the pale blue sky.

I hoped he would, for I thought this place might feel strange to him. My mother warned me that he would need time to adjust. He was returning not to home, but to a country he'd left almost fifteen years earlier, a country that, by the time of his return, had been at war for two years. Newsreels and air raid warnings, rationing and blackout curtains and windows stripped with tape to prevent shattering during a bombing had become everyday things for us. As we grew more certain of his return, I tried to see our lives through his eyes. But I couldn't imagine what that view was like, and I took up wishing again: *Make him like it here,* I thought. *Let this feel like home.*

:: :: ::

On December 13, my mother and grandmother and I went to early Mass at Holy Family. It was the Feast of Saint Lucy, a fourth-century martyr and virgin who refused suitor after suitor and for her obstinacy was condemned to live in a brothel. But when the time came for her to be taken, she could not be moved from her room. Her frustrated accusers then tried to burn her at the stake, but she wouldn't burn, and she was finally beheaded. And now her feast day was the festival of light, held on one of the shortest and darkest days of the year.

My grandmother told me about Saint Lucy over breakfast. She saw to it that I knew many of the saints, and feast days and memorials and solemnities were all occasions for me, days to honor some person who had loved God and pleased Him in always amazing ways. My mother was quieter than my grandmother in her admiration, and though she listened, she rarely commented on what my grandmother said.

That day she was making hot cross buns for breakfast, and when the buns were ready, the three of us ate breakfast in the kitchen. The steady sound of the rain and the warmth of the kitchen and the smell of dough and cinnamon made the rest of the world seem far away, so when there was a knock at the door at a little after nine, I was startled.

My mother went to see who it was, and when she came back, she held a telegram, which she opened and read without speaking. Finally she looked first at my grandmother, then at me.

"He's coming," she said simply, though she didn't really seem to understand what she was saying. "He'll be here on the seventeenth."

"Who?" I said. I just wanted to hear her say it.

The look she gave me bordered on rebuke. "Your father," she said, but she too sounded amazed.

And then she explained: the *Gripsholm*, my father's exchange ship, had docked in New York four days earlier, and my father had booked railway passage almost the second he had disembarked. He would travel on the Union Pacific to San Francisco, then the Southern Pacific to Los Angeles, and he would arrive at Union Station in downtown Los Angeles on Friday, the seventeenth, at nine-thirty in the morning.

I sat stupidly listening to words I couldn't quite take in. My grandmother said, "Well. Answered prayer. You'll be a family again," and although she leaned close to me and held me tight, I sensed a warning in her embrace. But that was not unusual. My father was not high up on her list. My mother had told me he never had been, really, not since he'd whisked her off to Shanghai so long ago.

I tried not to think of him that week. My mother did a few things to make the house ready, cleaning and walking through the living room over and over again, smoothing her skirt, fretting about whether or not he would like our home. I said, "He'll like it, I know he will," as often as I could without sounding mechanical, but I, too, was nervous, and I doubted that my reassurance helped. She only glanced at me and stared hard as if adjusting some internal focus, and then she said, "Of course," as though I had been the one who was worried, and needlessly so. Then she would dust again and straighten the few magazines on the table next to the Morris chair.

That Saturday morning we were up early. My mother had made it clear that this was an occasion and that we should dress up, and by the time my grandmother pulled into the driveway, we'd been ready for half an hour. My grandmother drove, and as we headed west on the Arroyo Seco Freeway, my mother offered unsolicited driving advice, a first, and particularly remarkable since she herself had never learned to drive. The car smelled strongly of mints and perfume, usually good smells, but too strong that morning. I cracked a window in the backseat, craving fresh air.

At Union Station, we parked and went inside. In the huge waiting area, I stared at the high ceiling and wrought-iron hanging lights that seemed as wide as our kitchen table. My mother's heels clicked loudly on the shiny tile floor, and I wanted to ask her to walk more quietly. People stared at us as if we'd been announced, and I wanted camouflage, some kind of cover. But there was no hiding us. My mother wore a magenta suit and she looked beautiful, like royalty. I wanted to tell her that we were too conspicuous, and that we should meet him in private and in comfortable clothes. But I, too, was dressed up in this very public place. Only my grandmother was in her everyday clothes, and it was the sight of her that told me that maybe everything would be all right.

My grandmother led us across the room to the Arrivals board, where we found that my father's train would arrive on Track 8, through Gate D. We were early, and followed my grandmother to three empty seats in the waiting room. My mother wouldn't sit down; she said it would wrinkle her skirt. She paced while my grandmother and I sat in the huge leather seats and played Paper Scissors Rock. My grandmother talked softly as we played, keeping my thoughts occupied, and I was so focused on her voice that I was startled to hear the announcer's formal baritone over the immense speakers on the wall. The Southern Pacific Express from San Francisco had arrived. My mother smoothed her skirt for the twentieth time, then eyed me carefully. She nodded approval, and the three of us walked to Gate D.

As passengers began heading toward us down the long tunnel, I stood close to my mother, my grandmother a few feet behind us. I pulled hard at my bangs and looked carefully at everyone I saw. What if I didn't recognize him? Passenger after passenger passed us: an old man in a homburg hat, a woman holding a sleeping baby, two soldiers in uniform, an elderly man and his wife speaking a language I didn't know, all of them welcomed by others around us. *Not him, not him, not him,* I thought, and a new fear took shape: What if it wasn't true? Maybe he wasn't coming after all. I realized that I hadn't really believed he was coming all week, and I felt ashamed.

And then I saw him. It was his walk that gave him away, a sort of let's-get-down-to-business stride, and I was flooded with recognition and affection and relief. "It's him," I heard myself say, and my mother nodded without looking at me. When he was perhaps twenty feet from us, she dropped my hand and ran to him and threw herself into his arms, and I heard her sob and I saw her shoulders tremble.

I caught my breath at her unprecedented display, and at the strange sight of her in a man's arms. I didn't know what to do, but my grandmother rescued me. I felt her hand on my shoulder and she held me there for a moment and she leaned close to me and whispered, "Just wait a minute—it's your turn next."

I did wait and then it was my turn. My father released my mother from his embrace and looked straight at me so hard that I couldn't have looked away if I'd wanted to. He squinted slightly as though sizing me up, an expression I'd known but forgotten, and I returned his stare and somehow faked calmness. I was, after all, still my father's daughter, even in this faraway land of orange groves and jasmine. I smiled and said, "Welcome home."

He smiled back and it was as though a conversation had taken place, and all my worrying about why he had taken so long to join us went away. I hurried to him and he held me close, and I tried not to notice how unfamiliar we were with each other. I remembered him lifting me up, holding me high above him, and while I knew that I was way too big for that now—I came not to his waist but to his chest—I was still surprised that he wasn't doing it. I pressed my face to his dark suit and breathed in the smell of the train, leather and newspapers and cigarette smoke. And a scent that I knew was my father.

My arms circled him almost as easily as they circled my mother. The sensation startled me, and when he released me, I said, "You're so thin," then regretted it instantly as I saw embarrassment cross his face. I hadn't meant to say it—his thinness was just so striking. His blue serge suit hung on him like drapery. I took in his gaunt face and tired eyes and pale complexion, and the fact that he appeared closer to my grandmother's age than my mother's, and I realized that commenting on his thinness was the kindest thing I could say.

He laughed. Barely, but it was a laugh, and his expression became more amused than embarrassed. "You're right," he said. "It just so happens I've dropped a few pounds." He roughed my hair, then awkwardly tried to smooth it back into place. "Now look what the big oaf has done," he said. "You're too old for that now, aren't you?" He glanced down at himself and shrugged, then he spoke to me in Mandarin. "*Wanshih tachi*," he said, watching me closely to see if I remembered.

I did, surprising myself. "*Wanshih tachi*," I said softly. It was a phrase my father had used all the time. "'Ten thousand things will be all right,'" I said, and he grinned and squeezed my hand.

He turned to my grandmother then, and I felt my stomach tighten. She rarely spoke ill of my father, but she never spoke fondly of him either. But that morning even she softened at the sight of him. He looked as though he was about to say something, and he held out his hand to shake hands. My grandmother pulled him to her and held him for a moment.

"It's nice to have you back," she whispered.

"Not as nice as it is to be back," he said.

We waited for his luggage, and when it came, we watched a porter load it into the trunk of my grandmother's Plymouth, my father talking about his train trip. He had come from New York by way of Chicago, then in Denver had boarded the Rio Grande of the Western Pacific Railroad, which took him on what was called the scenic route, over the Rocky Mountains, through Salt Lake City, and finally over Donner Summit and into California. The trains needed some upkeep, he said. The coaches were run down, the cooling system hadn't kept him cool. He was casual as breakfast, as though this morning were nothing more than a return from a business trip. My mother and grandmother seemed somehow in on the deal. They listened and agreed and laughed gently at his amazement over things we took for granted.

I listened impatiently to their small talk and waited for someone to say something interesting, something real about what had happened, and was happening now: that my father had come home. I had to bite my tongue to keep from blurting out questions—*What took you so long? What happened over there? Did they torture you? Are you all right?*—but the few times I came close to giving in, my mother seemed to read my thoughts and she silenced me with a look. And so I just stared at him when I could, and told myself that he would be healthy soon.

My grandmother drove us home and pulled into our narrow driveway, and my father carried his bags inside. As soon as my father entered, our house felt as though it had shrunk, and I finally understood my mother's nervousness. Now she began to chatter, something she did only when anxious. "There's my bedroom—I mean, *our* bedroom," she said, and motioned down the hallway. I thought I saw her blush. "Anna's room is next to the bath, and through here is the kitchen, and, oh, Joseph, the garden is beautiful, though a little on the unruly side, but soon—"

"Eve," my father said suddenly, and she turned from the kitchen doorway to find him standing at the edge of the living room, where he'd stopped barely six feet from the front door. They stared at each other for a moment. My grandmother and I exchanged a look.

"Slow down," he said to my mother. "I'm here to stay. Just let me get my bearings." And then the most unlikely thing happened: my mother burst into tears and closed the door into the kitchen behind her.

My grandmother and I exchanged another look and I tried to will her to get me out of the room. She opened her mouth as if to speak, and something else unlikely happened: my father laughed, not in a mean way, just a sort of relaxed amusement and relief. "Well, what did we expect?" he said to us. "She's got this strange man called her husband moving in with her. She has a right to be a little nervous. Don't you see?"

My grandmother looked at me. "I'll check on your mother," she said. "Why don't you show your father around if he's ready?" And she walked toward the kitchen.

I faced my father and attempted casualness. "What would you like to see?" I asked. But before he could answer, I blurted out my real question. "Do you like the house?"

He had walked to the fireplace and was running his fingers over the peacock tiles set above the hearth. He turned to me. "Do I like it?"

I nodded and felt an anxious what-have-you-done? tightness in my throat. What if his answer was no?

"You're darned right I like it. They'll have to carry me out of here in a pine box."

"Good," I said, "that's good," and I shrugged, trying to pretend that the question wasn't all that important. "Then maybe you should see the rest of the house?"

My father laughed and said, "I probably better if I'm going to find my way around." And I led him through our home.

:: :: ::

Within days, there was evidence of him everywhere. My mother had kept our house very spare—"No use cluttering things up," she said— and only books and a few photographs took up space on the built-in shelves in the living room. She kept little more than was needed to cook for two, and she was a perfect match for wartime, the expert at salvage. Scrap metal, tin cans, cooking fat, rubber, paper, her old silk stockings—everything had another use when we were finished with it. My mother passed everything along with an efficiency that made me nervous. She read magazines the day they arrived in the mail, then packed them up for the Boy Scouts. The morning paper wasn't in our kitchen long enough to get rumpled, and she regularly went through my closet as well as her own, pulling out pleated skirts and cotton blouses and dresses and shoes that she no longer wore or that I'd outgrown, tossing them all into the center of the room for me to fold and pack into boxes for St. Vincent de Paul's poor. She did it so often that I commented once that I figured my job was simply to break the clothes in and make sure they were comfortable for the poor, a remark she did not appreciate.

With my father's arrival, it was the sparseness that disappeared. He was a reader, but it was never just one book. Whatever he was reading was left wherever he'd been sitting when he got up to do something else. In the living room was *Guadalcanal Diary*, in the kitchen *Thirty Seconds Over Tokyo*, in the bedroom *See Here, Private Hargrove*. Copies of *Life* lay on the kitchen table, and sections of the *Los Angeles Times* drifted into every room. My mother's reminders that the Boy Scouts were due went unheeded by my father. "I'm not finished," he'd say calmly. "It takes a while to catch up on the world."

True enough. Most afternoons, he rode the Red Car up the Oak Knoll Line to the Pasadena Main Library, a place he said he loved for its huge wooden tables and chairs and the strong scent of books, where he read newspapers and magazines for hours. When he finished, or when the library closed, he checked out still more books and lugged them home to our now-crowded bungalow.

Only he never seemed to finish any of them, and his lack of attention worried me. I considered myself an expert on it, and on him, for I watched him every chance I got, staring so hard that I could feel the discomfort my scrutiny caused. But I couldn't make myself stop. I wanted to know him, and because I somehow felt that my surveillance might help keep him here, the second half of my seventh grade was dominated by keeping watch on him. More than boys or clothes or girlfriends or parties or school, he was what occupied my thoughts. In the morning, I watched him shave, then pat Old Spice onto his wet skin, as though he were slapping himself awake. I watched him comb Vitalis into his short hair and brush his teeth with Pepsodent, and in the kitchen I watched him eat Shredded Wheat with enriched milk from the Adohr Dairy while he read every page of the *Los Angeles Times*. When he finished, he gulped juice and washed down three Benefax vitamins. If I thought he'd forgotten them, I reminded him. Then I had to hurry to school, for I always waited till the last minute possible to leave, frustrated that I had to be away for a few hours and afraid that I might miss some key gesture, some important fact that would explain my father to me.

What I saw was a restless man. He couldn't sit still anywhere for long, a condition he attributed to bad circulation, but I had my doubts. It seemed more than physical. At the movies, he'd have to get up at least twice. During Christmas vacation, just a week after his return, we went to the Rialto to see Olivia de Haviland in *Government Girl*, and later that week Gene Kelly and Mickey Rooney and Judy Garland and Red Skelton in *Thousands Cheer*, and while I sat in my seat and stared hard at the screen, my father went to the lobby, supposedly to buy more popcorn. Baseball games were the same. That spring he took me to see a few Pacific Coast League games—the ones that weren't blacked out—and each time, I found myself alone for at least a few plays, watching the Los Angeles Angels at Wrigley Field, or the Hollywood Stars at Gilmore Field, waiting for my father to return to our seats.

At home he wandered through the rooms as though in search of something important, and it seemed as though he paced constantly. Sometimes in the late afternoon or early evening, he and my mother sat outside, sipping drinks and talking about the men of the day— Roosevelt and Eisenhower, MacArthur and Stilwell—but my father seemed unable to speak if he was sitting still, and he usually ended up touring the garden as he talked. Later in the evening, when he and I played Rook or Monopoly or hearts or Spite and Malice, he circled the card table between turns, chewing Black Jack gum and drinking a bottle of Pabst Blue Ribbon, and I was always calling him back—*Your turn, it's your turn!*—so that every game took twice as long as it should have. After dinner when my mother and I listened to *Burns and Allen* or the *G.E. All Girl Orchestra*, my father would burst in with some question about rationing or library hours or how to catch the Red Car downtown. When my mother looked at him as though he were crazy and asked him calmly if she could answer his question later, he looked as confused as if she had answered in a foreign tongue.

I knew part of the reason for his restlessness: money. Upon his release from Shanghai, he'd learned that all of his assets in United States banks—the bulk of his estate at that time—had been frozen by the U.S. Office of Price Administration, which had concluded that my father's money was tainted with foreign control. "Much of it was money paid to him by the Japanese before the war," my mother had explained to me quickly, letting me know she didn't want questions, "and they won't release it as long as we're at war with Japan." My father had provided my mother with enough to live on for several years when we left Shanghai, so we were far from destitute, but the fact that he couldn't get at the money—*my own money*, he said over and over again—irritated him immensely. If money was mentioned, he began his pacing all over again.

But I thought it must be more than money. Late in the night, long after I'd gotten in bed and turned out the light and slid whatever book I was reading under my bed and fallen asleep, I woke to the sounds of my father's midnight wanderings. Water running in the kitchen, the clink of ice in a glass. A bottle set on the tile counter. Muffled footsteps on the wooden floor, the creak of the Morris chair by the hearth as it took his weight. A few coughs, then the creak of the chair again, releasing him, and more footsteps, the compact *whap* of a book being shut. Then an encore, the whole sequence again. Each night that I heard him, I wondered if I should—if I could—get up and keep him company, for his sleeplessness worried me. Maybe he didn't like it here. Maybe he was unhappy. Maybe I could help. But there was too much I didn't know, and I never went to him, partly because I knew that he was a private man, but also because I had no faith that it was company that he hunted. And though I couldn't imagine what else it could be, I sensed his aloneness was not the same as loneliness, and out of a mixture of caution and respect, I stayed in my bed and let him pass those nights unwatched.

:: :: ::

All that spring was a waiting time. My mother waited for my father's health to improve and for him to become stronger. My father waited for Shanghai to be safe again and for his funds to be made available to him. And I waited for our house to feel normal, for my father to seem like the fathers of my friends: gregarious and confident and at ease. Making us into a normal family was something I'd taken on as a kind of project. I was sure we would get there; it was just going to take time.

On a Saturday morning in April, I found my parents sitting at the kitchen table, reading the paper. I'd begun sleeping late and I had just wandered in, still in my pajamas. The sun came in through the open window and the air seemed golden, our first really warm spring day. I liked the sight of the two of them sitting there together. My mother was in a skirt and blouse, dressy clothes for a Saturday morning. My father wore what he often did: a pair of khaki trousers and a clean white shirt. He was barefoot.

It was clear that they were engrossed in their reading, so I opened the refrigerator and took the carton of orange juice and drank from it quickly, a stolen pleasure, then put the carton back and closed the door.

"Get a glass, please." My mother had not looked up.

"How do you do that?"

She glanced at me and seemed to have no idea what I meant.

"See me all the time? Notice everything?"

She smiled, taking my question as a compliment. "I just do," she said simply. "It's a bad habit, drinking from the carton," she added, and stood from the table and took her plate to the sink. "Wonder where you picked it up?"

My father and I exchanged a look as she rinsed toast crumbs from her plate, then shut off the faucet and dried her hands on a dish towel. "The two of you are on your own today," she said. "I'm off to help Gran with some books. She's taken on a couple of new accounts and has asked me to go along."

My father was instantly displeased. "On Saturday now? What's next? Weeknights? A lunch box and uniform? A name tag and a paper hat?" He closed his paper and looked at my mother. "We're not working class, you know."

My mother leaned over and stared at her reflection in the toaster, then put lipstick on and blotted her lips on a paper napkin. "You're right about that," she said. "We don't work enough to be working class."

I looked at my father, expecting a laugh line next, which was the way he often defused my mother's seriousness, but my mother went on before he could say anything. "You know how I feel about this. As far as the money's concerned, we just don't know what's going to happen, Joe. Some income couldn't hurt. And as far as *you're* concerned, a job might be just the thing for you. I see you dragging around here, and dragging yourself up to the library, and dragging yourself home, and that's it. Look where you are! *Los Angeles*. People come from all over the country for the jobs here. I think that some sort of employment would be in your best interest."

"It would do me good," my father said dryly.

"Exactly," my mother said.

"Cure what ails me."

She gave him a look. "I don't know that I'd go *that* far." Then she picked up her purse and looked me up and down, while I wondered what self-improvement program she had in mind for me. "You're sleeping too late, Anna, it isn't good for you. The morning's half gone, and you're barely awake. The Boy Scouts will be by today, so you'll need to gather up the magazines and newspapers for them. Everything can go," and she paused. "Got it?"

"Yep," I said. "Everything goes."

Then she looked at the two of us once more—I had the feeling we did not pass muster—and she left.

My father was silent for a while, staring at the crossword but not writing anything in. I poured myself a bowl of Rice Krispies and filled it with milk, then sat across from him at the table. Finally he said, "What is it you've got planned for today?"

I shrugged and said, "Nothing," through a full mouth.

He laughed. "I've got a project for us," he said. "We'll surprise your mother. Not exactly paid labor, but something to keep us off the streets." He nodded toward the garden. "How about if we tackle that wilderness you two call a backyard?"

I followed his gaze outside. "Maybe," I said. And then, worried that my hesitation might hurt his feelings, I said, "Okay."

We were quiet for a moment, both of us staring outside. I was trying to figure out the right answer, for it was a tricky proposition. My mother was defensive about almost anything negative my father said about our house, and I'd come to understand that he had not been as impressed with our efforts at relocation—my mother's word—as she had wanted him to be. There were only casual comments from him—*Boy, this is cozy, all right. Wonder why the guy built this place so small?*—but my mother took them all personally.

The garden was even trickier. My grandmother made a point of referring to it as "charmingly untamed," her quiet way of reminding us that everything out there had been allowed to grow wild. Her comment was meant to inspire my mother to gain control of all those vines and blossoms and growth, but it never did. My mother loved the garden the way it was. Often when I came home from school I found her outside, standing among wild blackberries and unpruned peach trees and tangled wisteria and jasmine that went everywhere. The blackberry bushes grew along the back fence, and a small patch of romaine lettuce grew in the back corner, the result of some past resident's labor. The ground was a crazy quilt of star jasmine, Job's tears, and St. Augustine grass—at least those were the ones my grandmother could name, but there were patches of other vines and shrubs as well, things she'd never seen before.

That April morning the whole place was green from winter rains, and I loved the way it looked. But when I'd finished my cereal, my father told me to get dressed and meet him outside and we'd see what we could do.

I put on shorts and sneakers and a cotton shirt and found him outside pacing. Though it wasn't hot out, his face was flushed. He looked at me and said, "It's a mess out here. Nobody's done anything for years. This could be a nice little place out here, but it's just gone to pot."

I shrugged. "We've been sort of busy."

"I don't mean you two," he said generously. "You've got plenty to do. I mean that nobody's looked at it for a long time. It's been neglected."

"Well," I said, and I heard my mother's defensive tone in my voice, "there just hasn't been time," as though he hadn't heard me the first time. "But we were going to get to it eventually," I added. I looked at him and knew my expression was blank, but I nodded for emphasis.

"That's the first I've heard of it," he said.

He began to tell me what we would do. We'd cut back the jasmine and blackberries, he said, and get some trellises so we could train them, and the blackberries would bear more berries eventually. We'd prune the peach and plum trees, we'd plant tomatoes and strawberries—we must be the only ones around without a proper Victory

Garden, he said—and maybe a few herbs for my mother, and some lavender. And flowers, he said, sweet peas and stock for scent, and roses, with bougainvillea and wisteria to add a little color.

He walked all around as he talked, and finally he faced me, his eyes alert. "You see, Anna? We can really make something out here. The two of us." He paused for a moment and looked down. "My father taught me about growing things when I was a boy. It's only right that I should pass on what I learned."

"All right," I said nervously, for my father rarely mentioned his father. I heard the tentativeness in my voice and tried to remedy it. "It sounds great. I think it will be beautiful."

He laughed and leaned down to pull a weed. "Oh, it'll be beautiful, all right. Just you wait. You'll have the prettiest place on the block."

:: :: ::

The transformation of our garden was already well under way by the time my mother got home that afternoon. I was pulling up grass in the back corner when I heard the back door open and close. I looked up in time to see the surprise on her face, and I saw the dismay as well. If my father saw it, he gave no notice. He called to her that we'd found something to do with ourselves and that we were doing it for her, so she'd have beauty just outside her window. Then he went back to work, and that was that. My mother stood watching him for a moment, and when I met her eyes, I saw an expression that had become familiar since my father's return, a mixture of resignation and affection and worry.

At the start, the afternoons I spent out there were for him, so that I wouldn't hurt his feelings. When I got home from school I found him watching for me, eager to show me what he'd done that morning, or what he planned to do next, and I said how different it looked already, then I changed out of my school clothes and into old jeans and went to work with him. But soon I began to look forward to being out there with him, not just for him, but for myself. The place really did begin to change, and my father began to change as well. He filled out and looked more his age, and, for the first time since his return, he seemed content.

My grandmother drove us to the nursery, my father with his gardening books in hand, and he would ask what might work where. Strangely enough, many of the plants that had thrived in Shanghai would grow well here, despite the fact that we were half a world and an ocean away, and we started with those: wisteria and camellias, bougainvillea, gardenias. My father added red geraniums, which I wasn't crazy about, but which he loved because of their brightness—and which I grew to love because of him. We planted small Chinese blue column junipers along the back fence for privacy. My father said that they'd come in handy at Christmastime because we could make wreaths from the cuttings.

Along the side were the roses. Everything else he let me work on, but the roses were his, and he attended to them as though they were his life. "To grow roses isn't difficult, Anna," he told me. "But you have to follow some rules. You have to buy varieties for your climate. You have to buy the best plants available, number one grade. You have to locate and plant them properly. And you have to attend to their needs: water, nutrients, pest and disease control, pruning." He taught me how to plant a bare-root rose, and I watched as he soaked it and dug the hole with a cone of soil in the middle, and then how he spread the roots over the cone so that they would fit it without bending, and how he placed the plant so that the bud onion was just above the soil level. He was protective of the roses in the extreme, and if I wanted to so much as cut a few buds for the table, he supervised, showing me exactly where to cut. When he pruned them back and I argued—rare— he reassured me that they would grow all the better because of it.

By late summer our garden was filled with roses. Pink and red China roses grew along the back, the flowers huge and heavy, and

their old rose fragrance so strong that I smelled them as soon as
I stepped outside. Climbing roses and miniature ones grew along the
fence, and across from them were white damask rose shrubs. Light
pink sweetheart roses grew next to the patio, for me, he said, so that
I'd always see them first thing. And in the corner was a small shrub
called Father Hugo's rose, the golden rose of China, my father's
favorite. There were always roses on our kitchen table, and I often
found a rose in a juice glass on the desk in my room. I came to think
of that summer as a whole summer of roses, like a summer of gifts,
one after the other, with my father at the center.

:: :: ::

That fall I started eighth grade, my second year at the junior high.
In those last weeks of summer, I came to believe that eighth grade
was going to be a good year. We weren't the youngest kids at school
anymore, we knew our way around, and the older boys—the ninth
graders—now and then took an interest in the eighth-grade girls.
I looked forward to it as a year of increased independence and possibility, and as my first whole year in school with my father home.
I planned on showing him off whenever I could, at school plays and
Back to School Night and PTA meetings, whatever I could get him
to attend.

   In those first weeks of school, my father's garden had a lot of competition for my time and attention, and I often begged off from working outside. My father waved away my reasons and went out by
himself, and I felt like a traitor, but I did what I wanted anyway. I went
to junior-varsity cheerleading tryouts and to the Rialto with girlfriends and met groups of kids at Fosselman's after school, especially
if I thought a boy named Skip Mitchell would be there. I had told no
one of my interest in him, not even my best friend, Heather, because
I was certain that I was in love with him, and I was worried about
finding my true love at such a young age. He sat across from me in

math, and my heart beat faster when he asked to borrow my eraser, a ruse, I hoped, to talk to me.

On a Tuesday afternoon in late September, I found my father sitting in the shade of the pepper tree outside, sipping a glass of water. He smiled when he saw me, and he motioned to the back corner of the yard, where a hole had been dug. Next to it stood a small eucalyptus tree in a nursery container. I looked at it, then at my father, and waited for him to explain.

"I thought we'd try a eucalyptus back there," he said. "What do you think?"

I put my books on the patio chair and went and stood next to him. "You said eucalyptus was too temperamental."

He shook his head. "You have to plant them right, is all. How they're planted affects their growth for their whole lives. They have to be in good condition and you have to start with a vigorous plant. You don't want any can-bound roots. But I think we can manage those things, no?"

I nodded.

"And if I'm not mistaken, you like eucalyptus. In Shanghai, when you were little, you liked the way they smelled after the rain. And you liked the color of their leaves, and the smoothness of their bark."

"I love them," I said, surprised that he remembered things I had nearly forgotten, and even more surprised that he was mentioning Shanghai. He had never talked about what had happened to him there, or even what our lives had been like before the war, and the few times I had dared to ask, he had waved my questions away.

"Well, this is a good one. It's *Eucalyptus nicholli*, a Nichol's willow-leafed peppermint gum, a perfect garden tree." He stood then, and I followed him to the small tree. It *did* remind me of Shanghai: its narrow leaves were a light green, barely tinged with purple. There were a few small white flowers, and its bark was light brown.

I touched the slender trunk and said, "It's so soft."

My father nodded. Then he plucked a leaf and rubbed it between his fingers and held it to me. "Smell," he said.

I breathed in. "Peppermint," I said.

"You like it?"

"I love it."

He smiled, pleased, and then he stared at me for a moment in a way that looked so serious that I wondered if I'd done something wrong. But all he said was, "I'm taking a picture of you up here," and he tapped his head. "You're getting prettier all the time. Did you know that?" I felt myself blush and he laughed, and I wondered if I had imagined the sadness in his voice. And then he said something in Chinese, "*His hua hua chiehkuo, ai liu liu ch'êngyin,*" and although I didn't remember the meaning, the sound of the words was familiar. My father looked at me carefully. "Do you remember?"

I hesitated, willing myself to remember. "Almost. I think Chu Shih said it when he pruned the roses."

My father nodded and smoothed my hair. "That's right. Seems like a hundred years ago."

"What does it mean?"

"'Love and attention make all things grow,'" he said, and I nodded, for I did remember once he said it.

We took turns digging. After nearly an hour, he finally said he thought the hole was deep enough. "Hold the can, Anna, and I'll take the tree out."

I knelt and held the edges of the can as my father jostled and pulled and finally slid the base of the tree and then its roots from the can. Then he set the tree on the ground and knelt next to it. "A little root-bound," he said under his breath, "but we can fix that." He told me to turn on the hose a little and bring it over, and when I did, he gently rinsed the soil from the tree's exposed roots. Then he told me to shut off the hose and he said, "Do what I do, like so," and he began to spread the roots out, gently untangling them the way you would wire, and arranging them in a sort of fan shape coming out from the tree's center. "This will help," he said.

We worked at the roots like that for perhaps ten minutes, both of us on our hands and knees. He was humming something, and I smelled sweat and Vitalis and Black Jack gum. Finally he sat back on his heels and looked at the roots. "Looks about right," he said, and he stood and brushed his dirty hands on his already dirty khakis. "I think we're ready," and he picked up the tree near the base of its trunk and lowered it carefully into the hole. "Fill her in," he said. We knelt again and gently pushed moistened soil into the hole, surrounding the roots, pushing in more soil, gently packing it down.

"Now we'll water," my father said finally, "and she's on her way."

He turned on the hose and handed it to me, and I stood next to the tree, moving the hose around the trunk, trying to make sure that water soaked in evenly. He watched for a moment, then nodded his approval. "Little by little, you see, Anna? This will be a good tree for you. Vigorous, durable. Your own peppermint tree. It can remind you of Shanghai, of the good parts." And then he said he was going inside for a drink of water.

"I'll come in a minute," I said, "I just want to look for a while."

He nodded and looked around the garden. "I know what you mean," he said. Then he went inside.

When I'd soaked the base of the tree, I turned off the water and coiled the hose next to the house the way my father had taught me. Then I sat down on the step and took a deep breath. My hands and knees were caked with dirt, and it felt good somehow, not like dirt but like earth, even under my fingernails.

Sitting there alone, my father inside, the sounds of my mother moving around in the kitchen, all of a sudden I felt content. Not just happy, but something deeper, quieter, as though the three of us had finally landed. For the first time in a long time—maybe since I was a little girl in Shanghai—everything seemed truly all right. Maybe we, too, had been successfully transplanted; maybe that long move from Hungjao to South Pasadena had worked, and maybe we really could adapt. My father had been home for nearly ten months, and I had started to believe that what I had wished for had come true: he seemed to consider this home.

I looked at the roses along the side fence, still blooming though October was only a week away; the junipers along the back, already starting to grow and spread out a little; the bougainvillea and wisteria along the other side, romantic and a little wild, a concession to my mother. In three rectangular beds to my left were tomatoes and lettuce and strawberries, and in the narrow bed closest to the kitchen, a few herbs, parsley and thyme, rosemary and chives. "You see," my father had said, "you'll have a whole salad here, everything you'll need."

I breathed in and smelled eucalyptus and roses. I looked around once more for anything amiss. But there was nothing. It was perfect.

I went in to wash my hands and found my mother and father in the kitchen. My father had brought the mail in and was standing at the sink, gazing out at the garden. He had opened a quart bottle of East Side beer and poured himself some in a juice glass. My mother was sitting at the table, her hands spread out in front of her, a gesture I knew well, one that meant she was trying to stay calm.

"What?" I said.

My mother did not hesitate. "Your father received a letter," she said simply. Her tone was one of forced evenness. "A letter from an old friend from Shanghai, Shang Chen. In China he was governor of the Hove province. Maybe you remember him, Anna. Your father's polo team used to play his. He was quite good, your father says."

I nodded stupidly, with no recollection of the man she had named. It was as though she were asking me to recall some other child's life.

"Well," my mother continued, stretching her hands out further on the table, "Shang Chen is now *General* Shang Chen, and he is the Chinese military attaché in Washington. It seems he can do something to help your father. He has a position for your father in Chungking, as a liaison between the American and Chinese troops. It sounds very interesting, doesn't it?"

I wanted to ask her to speak English, please, as I had when I was small and Chu Shih asked me something in Mandarin. My mother's words felt like some kind of code.

"Chungking," I said, a guess of a response.

"Yes," my mother said. "Chungking."

My father faced us then. At least he faced my mother, and I saw that I'd walked into something that I shouldn't be in on. "You have to see this, Eve," he said. "There's a war on, and they'll send me someplace if I don't go first. In my experience, the military sends you exactly where you don't want to go, simple as that. Where would that be? Where would they send me? To Europe, where things are a mess."

My mother said nothing.

I went to the counter to read the letter, which said just what my mother had said: that General Shang Chen was requesting that my father act as a liaison between American and Chinese troops in Chungking, the seat of the Nationalist government. He asked that my father travel to Chungking as soon as possible.

I looked at my father. He had turned on the water and was washing two beefsteak tomatoes my mother had set out for dinner. He set them on the cutting board and began slicing them into fat round slices that we would salt and eat cold. He put the slices on a plate and tossed the ends into the grocery bag under the sink. He rinsed our small wooden cutting board—my mother and I had bought it at Woolworth's, one of our first purchases, and one my mother had let me pick out—and I watched the red watercolor juice from the tomatoes run into the sink. He dried the board, put it back in its place against the drain board, and wiped the counter, the picture of calm. Then he turned to leave the room. This was my father: no fuss, no muss.

At the door, he turned to us. "I'm going to clean up," he said.

"What letter?" I said.

He didn't answer.

"What letter?" I said again. "He says he was surprised to receive your letter." I held the general's letter out to my father, not worrying about my dirty hands.

My father shook his head as though I were asking the obvious. "A letter I wrote to him a while back," he said. "To find out about things."

"When did you write to him?" I said.

Now he looked me in the eye. "It's not a daughter's place to cross-examine her father."

I looked outside at the garden and saw holly seedlings and junipers and I remembered his encouragements. *You'll have pumpkins at Halloween, and your mother can bake the seeds for you. You can cut branches from the junipers for a Christmas wreath, and you can decorate the table with holly cuttings. You'll have lilies just in time for Easter, and strawberries all summer long.* Only he always said *you,* never *we.*

I said, "You knew," and it made such sense. It made everything fit together so neatly that it almost didn't hurt. "You knew all along. That's why you've been so happy lately. Because you were leaving."

My mother looked up, and I addressed her, as if explaining things she didn't know. "He never planned on staying with us. That's why he didn't argue about this house, it's why he didn't move us to some-place bigger. He knew this was just a visit." I looked at him then. "That's right, isn't it?"

It was the first time in my life that I had spoken angrily to my father, and he looked stunned. He said nothing. It was my mother who spoke.

"I know that, Anna."

My father was looking at me as though appraising me. "Why don't you get cleaned up for dinner? This conversation's gone far enough."

"But how can you leave us? You don't know—"

"I know exactly as much as I need to know," he said. "I already explained. This is my only decent choice here. So we might as well not dwell on it."

I said nothing.

"Don't cloud up on me, Anna. No melodrama. It's how things are."

I nodded, stung. It was the first fight we'd had like that, where it seemed there was no allowance made for my age. I felt not rebuked so much, which I often had, but more pushed away, and it hurt.

"Are we clear?" he asked.

"Yes," I said softly.

"That's my girl," he said, and he walked out of the room.

My mother didn't wait for me to say anything. She came and stood next to me and held me to her as I began to cry. "I'm sorry," she whispered, "I'm so sorry."

:: :: ::

That was a Tuesday. My father made arrangements to leave ten days later, on a military transport that would depart from Los Angeles on the first Friday morning of October.

Over those ten days, I worked hard at convincing myself that his leaving would be a relief. It hadn't been that bad without him, I thought. In a way it was simpler. Without him, I had spent more time with my grandmother. My mother and I had eaten out more. We'd done what we'd wanted, and we hadn't had to worry about those quiet moods of his. We were both so good at catering to him, at revolving around him, and we'd picked it up again so thoroughly and so immediately when he'd come home—home?—that the mood and feeling of our lives had changed a lot after he joined us. So, I thought, back to what we were, which hadn't been so bad after all. Be grateful, I thought, and I worked at keeping my mother's words in my mind: *we'll be fine, we'll be fine, we'll be fine.*

All that effort paid off, to a point. It must have because I got through those awful days that precede separation. Things were almost festive that week, on the surface at least. I helped my father pack, and I laid out his new and laundered and patched clothes in the living room until he packed them the night before he left. We put a good face on it all, and the only time I let myself feel the huge sadness that I carried around was in my bed, once the lights were out and the house had been still for a long enough time to make me think my parents had fallen asleep. That was when I knew I would miss him the most. I loved that time of night, when I knew my parents were both asleep in their bed in the very next room.

And then it was his last night.

Dinner was an occasion—steaks and baked potatoes, ambrosia and angel food cake with strawberries—and after dinner, my father and I stood in our garden for a long time, sipping our drinks, his a glass of Scotch, mine a juice glass of Pabst Blue Ribbon, which he was allowing me this once. I didn't like the taste much, but I liked the way the cold beer felt in my stomach and the way it made my head feel a little blurry. Inside I could hear the sounds of my mother and grand-mother talking in low voices as they did the dishes and made coffee, while outside in the garden, my father reminded me about all the care it would need. When he started sentences with phrases like, "And then, in three or four months, Anna," I didn't, as he would say, cloud up, something I considered an accomplishment, one I was proud of. But when we came inside, my mother and grandmother had only to look at my face to know how much it hurt.

Even the next morning, I was calm, at the start. His flight wouldn't leave until noon, but he had been instructed to be at the airport two hours early. We'd been up since six, though I thought I'd heard my father up even earlier than that, pacing.

When it was almost time to leave, I stood in the bedroom doorway, watching him finish packing. He wore suit pants and a white shirt and a red tie. He hadn't put his coat on yet. I thought he looked very handsome. He placed his shaving kit in his suitcase and let the lid fall, then he stood and looked around him, checking the room. But he'd been thorough. The suitcase was the only thing left.

"Looks like that's about it, huh?" He smiled at me.

"Yep," I said. *Don't cry.*

"So," he said, and he ran his hand across his cropped blond hair, a gesture so familiar that it hurt to watch. His suit coat was folded on the bed, and he put it on and straightened it, giving each white shirt cuff a quick yank. He was exact about his appearance. An inch of cuff, no more, no less, should show beneath your coat, he said. Then he leaned over to close his suitcase.

It was that sound that did it to me: those two neat clicks of the metal latches, *snap, snap.* All of my hard work at mimicking my mother's composure over the last few days unraveled. I stared at those shiny silver latches as if I could pull my composure back from them, and I felt my father watching me. I knew that he moved toward me, that he put his arms around me and held my face against the cool whiteness of the shirt my mother had ironed last night.

"Anna," he said quietly, "don't do this now, all right? It's not so bad, you see? It's not so bad, Anna, just a little while again."

I nodded stupidly, but I knew it *was* so bad. And as I finally cried in his arms, I felt a fierceness in his embrace and a sigh go through his chest that told me I was right.

a happy man

MY FATHER'S STAY IN CHUNGKING lasted barely longer than his stay in South Pasadena. He was there for only eleven months, from October of 1944 until September of 1945. But that had been his plan. It was just a place to be until the war was over. When Japan surrendered in August, my father lost no time in trying to get back to Shanghai, which was all but impossible unless you were Allied or Chinese Nationalist military or government. As liaison between the American and Chinese troops in Chungking, my father qualified.

The second he left Chungking, he stopped considering himself an official. The war was over and he was in business, simple as that, though he knew business would be different now. The Treaty of 1943, signed by Britain, the United States, and the Nationalist Government of China, had abolished extraterritoriality, and for the first time in one hundred years, Shanghai belonged not to foreigners, but to China. The Nationalist government controlled business now. Even so, my father was certain there was a place for him.

He arrived by train at Shanghai's North Station on the last day of September, just a month and a half after the end of the war. He carried two suitcases and he had made sure to have plenty of U.S. currency on him before he'd left Chungking. Nobody trusted the Chinese currency. The value of the Chinese dollar was decreasing, and the rate of exchange fluctuated from hour to hour and place to place. He'd heard the whole city was chaotic. It had taken weeks after Japan's surrender for the Chinese to reclaim control, and American GIs and Chinese Nationalist soldiers and officials had not arrived until the third week of September. Everything was in a state of flux. Chinese authorities had begun taking control of businesses that the Japanese had controlled during the war, and many of those who'd left during the war were returning—American and British journalists, employees sent by foreign firms, fortune seekers and entrepreneurs like my father.

At the train station, he hired a pedicab and gave the address of his office on Yuen Ming Yuen Road. Once there, he paid the coolie and carried his suitcases to the doorstep and fit the key in the lock. When he pushed open the door, he felt as though he'd simply stepped back three years, to that limbo year that followed Pearl Harbor. Papers were scattered about, and a pile of newspapers in the corner looked as though it had been flattened into a bed, which was fine by him. He saw no reason to pay for a hotel.

Everything was still there: his carved desk, his chair, the watercolor of the Public Gardens over the desk. And underneath a loose floorboard near the back wall were the things he'd wanted to save: his chop; the account ledger he'd been using as a journal, which he'd placed there only a few days before his arrest by the Japanese; eight hundred dollars in U.S. currency, plenty to get started, he thought; and my mother's ivory comb.

From there he walked toward the Whangpoo, and when he first set foot on the Bund again and gazed around him and breathed in the sharp scent of the muddy river, he laughed out loud, for he knew one thing: that he would stay in Shanghai, no matter what. He was home—his real home this time, no bungalow, no city of angels. It was home now more than ever, because he'd tried someplace else and he'd found it wouldn't work. He had been foolish to think he could have been happy anywhere else, he saw that now. How could a man like him live in a place like Pasadena? Too many rules, too much order, not enough to do, and what would he possibly have done for work? Taken up accounting? Imported Japanese tea sets? As for my mother and me, he didn't know when he could arrange for us to join him, but he'd worry about that later. First things first.

He walked along the Bund for a while, getting his bearings. For the first time in years, there were American and British warships on the Whangpoo. The White Sun flag of the Kuomintang flew from the tops of government buildings, and pictures of Chiang Kai-shek decorated with paper flower garlands were everywhere. The bronze lions in front of the Hongkong and Shanghai Bank were back after having been hidden during the war, and when he stopped in at the Shanghai Club's Long Bar, behind the bar he saw more brands of Scotch than he could count. Even the billiards tables had been repaired. The Japanese had lowered them by sawing off the legs, but here they were, good as new, remounted on wooden platforms and back in use.

After a glass of Dewar's, he walked back up the Bund and turned down Nanking Road. Hawkers had set up rickety stalls over every inch of the sidewalk and my father saw things he hadn't seen in Shanghai for years: toasters, cameras, typewriters, radios. Butter and powdered milk, canned meat and Spam, cigarettes and coffee. The streets were jammed, the shops crowded and noisy, their windows filled. He passed GIs buying things to send home to their wives, silk stockings and lingerie, embroidered slips and negligees and Chinese slippers. The big department stores were busy, too, and my father saw that once again, you could buy anything from the latest American lipsticks to rich Swiss chocolates at Sincere's. There were also things he didn't want to dwell on. Medical supplies and blood plasma were for sale because Chiang's government had turned relief parcels from the American Red Cross into cash instead of distributing them by selling the goods to middlemen, who then resold them to anyone who could pay.

After an hour of walking, he suddenly wanted coolie food. He stopped at a stall on Foochow Road and bought noodles and cabbage. Next he was going to buy copies of the *Shanghai Evening Post and Mercury* and the *North China Daily News* and head back to his office and read every inch to find out what was what, and who was here, and where the opportunities were. But as he started walking back, he forgot about the papers, and for a moment it was as though he'd dreamed the last four years. Parked on Foochow Road just a few doors down was his Packard, he was sure, the same car he'd turned in to the Japanese in 1942. It was dinged up and filthy and the left rear fender had been lopped off somehow, but he was certain it was the same car. He'd known the dealer who sold him the car in 1936, and he knew for a fact that his was the only Packard of that model and color brought into Shanghai that year.

He just stood for a moment, watching and waiting to see what was next. A Chinese man sat at the wheel, smoking a cigarette. As my father watched, he got out of the car and slammed the door. Before he headed off, he spat on the hood of the car.

My father hurried after him. He called out in Mandarin for the man to stop, but the stranger kept walking. My father ran to catch up with him. He put his hand on the man's shoulder and turned him so that they faced each other. Then, as though it were the most natural thing in the world, my father explained in perfect Mandarin that the man had no right to this car.

"It is a government car," my father said, "Chiang's car," and he showed the stunned man his identification papers from Chungking, which bore the bright red seals of the Nationalist government. The man hesitated. People had stopped to listen, and an old woman clucked at what she saw. My father heard someone say, "Thief!" and for a moment he was outraged. Then he realized they were referring to the man in front of him. My father waited another instant, and then he held out his hand.

"Give me the key," he said in Mandarin. "Do not shame our Generalissimo. No good can come of such a thing."

For a moment, the man looked indecisive, even afraid. Then he dug into the pocket of his grimy coat, dropped the key into my father's palm, and walked away.

My father nodded to the onlookers as though dismissing them, then walked to the car and got inside. It smelled strongly of garlic and cigarettes and grime, but he didn't care. He started it up and listened carefully to the engine. Not perfect, but it would hold out for a while. He drove to his office and picked up his suitcases, then he started down Nanking Road toward Hungjao, as though this were just any day. As though he'd never left.

:: :: ::

He found the house ransacked and dirty but uninhabited. By noon the next day he had hired a Chinese man and his wife to care for him and the house. A woman house servant was something new— before the war, women were hired only as amahs, to care for children—but he had no quarrel with having her around. He gave the two of them instructions and money to cover their first week's wages and food for the three of them, then went back into town to buy what he needed, for starters—some new clothes and shoes, a box of cigars, new sheets and towels, dishware, flatware, a bottle of good Scotch.

He had planned his next step for days. He went to the Chinese Consulate and showed his papers from Chungking around again, and within a week he was given the necessary and hard-to-come-by import license. With that in hand, he made contact with vehicle dealers in the United States, some of whom were the same men he'd dealt with before the war. Two months later he brought in and sold at a healthy profit his first few Dodge trucks and cars. They cost him twelve hundred dollars, and he sold them for six to eight thousand dollars. After that, he started in with newsprint, another badly needed commodity, buying it for one hundred twenty dollars a ton, then selling it for over six hundred.

The household purchases he made the day he returned to Hungjao were his first and last; everything else he left to the servant couple he had hired. The only problem was that they were far too timid and cautious to buy anything more than what was required for meals. So, except for a crude table in the kitchen that the housekeepers had found stuffed in a corner of the attic, and cots that my father had had delivered, the house remained unfurnished. It was as though the three of them were camping out, just using the house until they moved on. My father seemed not to notice. He returned mainly to sleep and bathe. Other than that, he stayed in town, and his servants were left to themselves.

Even so, his life was familiar again. The restaurants and bars had come back to life, and my father was at his old haunts, restaurants like Jimmy's and Kafka's and St. Petersburg, nightclubs like the Argentina and the Metropole, Ciro's and Caliente, the Lido. American films were brought in from Chungking: *Naughty Marietta* with Jeannette MacDonald and Nelson Eddy played at the Roxy, and *Aloma of the South Seas* with Dorothy Lamour was at the Nanking. Many of the country clubs around the city had been turned into internment camps during the war, but they reopened, too, and my father drank and talked while the bands played "Sentimental Journey" and "Accentuate the Positive" in the same places that had housed internees only a few months earlier.

On New Year's Eve, my father toasted 1946 with friends in the Horse and Hounds Bar at the Cathay Hotel, and they all agreed it was going to be a good year. My father insisted on buying the champagne because, as he explained to anyone who would listen, he'd had a good week. He'd just learned that thanks to the help of a U.S. senator who'd been a classmate of his at Vanderbilt, the U.S. government had released his assets frozen in the Bank of New York nearly three years earlier by the Office of Price Administration, around four hundred thousand dollars. It was more than enough to take care of my mother and me and to get him started, and he saw it as an omen. Business would be good; life would be good. He was back in the city he loved, and for the first time since before the war, he was a happy man.

tickets

IN MAY OF 1945 when the war in Europe ended, my mother grew more hopeful that my father would return, despite the fact that we'd heard nothing from him since he'd left seven months earlier. On the afternoon of Tuesday, August 14, when Japan surrendered and the war was officially over, the siren on top of the Los Angeles Times building blared the news and everyone celebrated, including my mother, who began to act as though my father would show up any day. When August became September she said less, but her expression remained determined as she doled out made-up reasons for his silence. I didn't question her certainty out loud, but I was more and more skeptical. He had been gone for a year, and I had learned firsthand that if you were without someone you loved for a year, it got easier. You didn't miss them as much, you didn't even think of them as much. But I kept my thoughts to myself. In the second week of September I started ninth grade, my last at South Pasadena Junior High.

Finally, on the last day of September, we heard from him again. The Santa Anas had kicked up that week, which meant the wind was blowing the wrong way, bringing us hot air from the desert instead of cool air from the Pacific. The temperature was nearly one hundred degrees, and everything felt wrong.

I had dragged myself home from school and was lying on the living-room floor where it was cool, listening to Frank Sinatra and wondering what I would be like when I was twenty-five, the age I considered adulthood. I was picturing the kind of house I would have. It would be more spacious than our bungalow, and lighter and cooler, maybe on a hill, with lots of windows. I pictured what I could remember of our house in Shanghai, and I thought I'd like something like that—verandahs, a staircase, lots of room, only here, not in China—and I wondered if it had bothered my mother to live in such a small house after such a large one. I was sure it had bothered my father.

I started to think about Mark Young, a handsome boy in my social studies class whom my friends had labeled as too quiet. I liked his quiet. I considered him a find, and I was wondering whether or not he was going to pay any attention to me at the dance the next night, and what I would do to encourage him if he didn't. I had decided that I would choose the boys I dated with great care. I wanted someone who would never leave me, and I knew that it might take time to find someone like that.

The doorbell rang, and I heard my mother walk to the front door, her bare feet patting the wood floor. She had just taken a bath and was wearing a cotton robe, and the scent of lilac drifted into the living room as she passed. Hot weather didn't agree with her. It never had, not even in Shanghai, and I always associated her bad moods with the heat.

I heard her open the door and say hello. She said something else, and then the door shut and I heard paper tearing. Then silence.

"What is it?" I said.

She cleared her throat, and then she read aloud: "'Am in Shanghai, all is well. Recovered house, hired cook. Business opportunities

unbelievable. Hope you are well. Date of return to States indefi-
nite. Joseph.'"

It was as breezy as an I'll-be-late-for-dinner phone call. I tried to
understand what it meant, why he wasn't coming home, but I came
up empty. "I don't understand," I said.

My mother stood in the doorway. Her face was drawn. "Well,"
she said, "it appears that your father has not seen fit to come home
just yet."

I nodded stupidly. "He can, but he won't?" I asked, more an accusation than a question.

"If you have to put it like that, yes," she said. And then she walked
to her bedroom and closed her door softly behind her, and I knew
that she was upset and wanted to be alone. I turned up the record so
I wouldn't hear her.

That night I called my four closest friends, one at a time, and
casually mentioned that we'd heard from my father and that he wasn't
coming back for a while, taking back all my mother's he'll-be-back-
when-the-war-is-over predictions I'd been quoting so confidently.
"Oh, it's all right," I said in answer to their surprise. "It's just how
he is. We're used to it now." And then I moved on to topics more
interesting: the dance on the following night, and how tall some of
the boys were getting, and how broad their shoulders were, and how
far we thought a girl named Valerie Rutherford was going with
the high-school boy she was seeing. When I hung up, I felt cold
inside. I hoped those phone calls had done what I'd wanted them to,
which was to make my father go away, so that I wouldn't have
to talk about him in school. I doubted I could act so casually about
him face-to-face.

It was only when I went to bed that night, when my door was shut
and I was sure that my mother was asleep, that I let myself cry.

A few days after the telegram I was at my grandmother's house
after school. The heat wave had retreated as abruptly as it had arrived,

leaving the weather cool and rainy. We sat at her kitchen table and played Scrabble. I wanted to talk to her about my father. I wanted comfort, and some reason to hope, and a reminder that he was a good man, if an unusual one.

"My father's in Shanghai," I said casually.

My grandmother nodded without looking up from the board. "So I hear."

"It's probably for the best," I prompted. *Say something good.*

She said nothing.

"There's some sort of reason," I added, hoping she would explain it.

She placed a G on the board and said, "Grommet. That's twelve points." Then she took a breath as though she were trying to be patient. "Anna, I'm going to tell you something, and I'm telling your mother, too," she said. "Your father is a difficult man. I'm sure he has his good side, and I suspect his heart is sometimes in the right place. But his good intentions never become actions, and you'll only be hurt if you allow yourself to depend on him. It's not a question of love. It's a question of who he is, and what he wants."

I nodded, stung. The sound of the rain made what she was saying more difficult to hear, as though the weather were in agreement.

"Your father is a troubled man. He has no vision, can't see what's right in front of him. He is, was, and always will be an opportunist who watches out solely for himself. He will be affectionate with you when it serves his purpose. You will not be part of his life when it doesn't. And the sooner you accept who he is and distance yourself from his influence, the better off you'll be." She paused and took a breath. "I'm being harsh, you think. But it's true, and I don't want you hurt. You and your mother have done nothing wrong. Your father is a risky person to love." I fought tears. She nodded at a bottle of Hires root beer that I'd opened and forgotten. "Take a sip of something and get back to the game. I've said all I can say, and all you can hear."

I was silent for perhaps a minute. Listening to her made me feel disloyal, and I hated hearing it. "You're very wrong," I said softly. "You've no idea what kind of person my father is." And then, before she could answer and in an effort to appear casual, I added a Y to the board and said, "Cyclops. Fourteen points."

For the rest of the afternoon, I was diligent about not recalling what my grandmother had said. If I didn't remember her words, then maybe I wouldn't believe them. And maybe they wouldn't seem so true.

:: :: ::

The rest of that fall brought us two more telegrams that gave us no reasons for my father's stay in Shanghai, and no reason to hope he would return any time soon. My mother said she didn't like it, but she didn't know that she had many choices. Mostly she just stayed busy. She'd always had a full social life, but it got even busier after that telegram. She said yes to bridge parties, cocktail parties, dinner parties. She got more invitations than she could accept, but although she went out night after night, she didn't seem happy. She didn't seem exactly unhappy, either. She just seemed neutral, as though she was going through the motions.

I, on the other hand, was on a roller coaster that fall. I felt different every day, as though I were controlled by some force outside myself. One morning I woke up happy and couldn't wait to get to school. Three hours later I'd be despondent and discouraged, almost in tears over a bad grade on a quiz or my friends not waiting for me for lunch. I cried when I got home from school, and I couldn't have said why. I didn't like how I looked: my hair was too thick, my face too round, I wished my eyes were brown. I knew only extremes: I had no energy or too much, I was starved or couldn't even think of food, I slept for hours or couldn't fall asleep till late at night. I thought maybe I missed my father so much that I was going a little crazy, and I worried that people could tell.

Two months of that up-and-downness passed, and one evening my mother found me in my room, the lights off, the shutters closed, the air still. It was the week before Christmas, and almost time for dinner. She'd knocked lightly, thinking I was napping. I was awake, but I didn't answer because I'd been crying and didn't want her to know. But when she opened the door a crack, she felt how stuffy the room was and she came in to open a window and saw that I was awake.

She opened the shutters and cracked a window, then sat down on the edge of my bed. I looked up at her and thought how beautiful she was and how unbeautiful I was. She smoothed my hair from my face and I saw the worry in her expression and felt worse than ever.

"What is it, Anna?"

I shook my head. "I'm just tired."

"Then you've been tired for a long time. I can see how unhappy you are."

I turned away from her. "I'm all right," I said.

She waited, rubbing my back lightly. I tried to think what to tell her, how to explain what was wrong, what was bothering me without alarming her. I tried to think logically, to be calm. But finally I just blurted everything out.

"I cry all the time and some days I hate school and some days I love it and my friends are nice but they hurt my feelings and I don't like the way I look and I feel so lonely sometimes and it's not your fault and I don't know what I'm doing wrong—" I stopped for a moment and looked at her to see if she was alarmed or frightened or disgusted. But she just looked worried and like she loved me, so I gave in and told her what I was afraid of. "I think something's wrong with me." And I began to sob.

My mother smiled, but in a way that was so gentle that it gave me hope. "Oh, Anna," she said, in the same way she'd said it since I was little, and she just held me for a few minutes, rocking me. When my crying had slowed, she said, "Nothing's wrong with you. You're not crazy, you're not sick. You're just . . ." She paused. "You're just fourteen," she said finally. "This is what it's like. And having a missing father doesn't help. But you've got a mother who's not going anywhere. Who'll be right here as long as you need her. And it will get better. I promise."

I took a few breaths, trying to be calm. "Are you sure?" I asked, because my mother was always polite. If I was crazy or disturbed, she might not tell me.

"I'm positive," she said firmly. "I felt exactly like you do when I was fourteen." She smiled again. "Only I don't think I could have explained it as well. Fourteen is just like that. You feel a little crazy, but after a while, things start to make sense again. You'll see."

I nodded again, still not completely convinced. My mother smoothed my hair, and then she was still, gazing out the window. "Your father is making a terrible mistake by not returning," she said. "And there's nothing I can do about it. I can tell you that he'll regret it for the rest of his life. He's missing out on the best thing in the world." She looked at me. "And that's you."

I smiled finally and felt so grateful to her that I almost started to cry again.

"Don't forget that: this is his mistake. The fact that he hasn't come home is no reflection on you. It's just evidence of his bad judgment." She looked at me evenly. "Which, unfortunately, is something that we can't control."

:: :: ::

In the middle of June, I graduated from ninth grade at South Pasadena Junior High School. The next night my mother and grandmother and I celebrated by going to dinner at Musso's on Hollywood Boulevard, the oldest restaurant in Hollywood. My grandmother had told me stories about the bar and its past patrons, Charlie Chaplin and Orson Welles, Hemingway and Faulkner and Fitzgerald, and I felt famous by association as soon as we sat down in one of the red leather booths.

We ordered New York strip steaks and onion rings from Glen, a handsome blond waiter-but-hoped-to-be-actor whom my grandmother had known for years. As he tossed our salad at our table, he smiled at me and I smiled right back, for I considered myself eligible for flirtation. I was fifteen and a half, and at the graduating dance at the Women's Club the night before, Mark Young had kissed me good night and told me he'd call me soon, and could I go to Santa Monica beach on the Red Car with him? I was giddy with excitement and giddy at the prospects of romance.

After dinner, when Glen had cleared our places and brought us glass dishes of vanilla ice cream, my grandmother presented me with a small box from D & G Jewelers. I clumsily tore off pink flow-ered wrapping paper and opened the box, and I found inside a Lady Elgin watch, similar to one my mother wore, only smaller. It was, I thought, the most elegant watch I'd ever seen, and I was amazed that it was mine.

I looked at my grandmother across the table and held the watch out to her. "Can you put it on me?"

She nodded and looked pleased, and she took the watch from its small box and undid the clasp. I held my arm across the table while she fastened it around my wrist. "There," she said, "it's perfect. And it's something you'll wear for a long, long time, Anna, in the best of health and with much happiness, I hope."

It was something in her voice, a catch or a seriousness, that alarmed me, and I tried to ask her my question with a look: *What's wrong?*

My mother answered before my grandmother could by taking an envelope from her purse and holding it out to me. "And I have something for you, too, Anna." She patted my arm lightly with the envelope.

I took the envelope and opened it carefully. Inside was a thick packet of paper, and I looked at my mother for explanation. It looked very official, and it made me nervous.

"It's all right," she said. "You don't have to take everything out." She took a deep breath. "It's tickets, Anna, to Shanghai. We're going to see your father."

All I could do was nod. My mother had been in a strange mood all that week, and suddenly everything fit, and I felt a sense of dread. I held the envelope in front of me, remembering my seventh birthday, hot chocolate on a cold winter's morning after Mass in Shanghai.

My mother took the envelope from me and slipped it back into her purse. "I know you're surprised. But I've thought about this for a long time. We leave in a month, and I don't know when we'll come back. But it's time to be a family again."

I stared at the tablecloth, trying to figure things out. Seeing my father was exactly what I'd wanted for a long time, but that desire had waned, and the thought of going to Shanghai and of leaving my grandmother and my friends made me sink into our booth. The whole thing felt like a punishment. And I was wary. What evidence was there that my father wanted to see us?

"Couldn't we just wait for him to come back?" I asked, and I looked across the table at my grandmother, as if the decision were hers.

She met my eyes for a moment and I saw anger in her expression. "It's no use asking for help from over here," she said. "Your mother knows what I think of her plan, but she's determined."

My mother was shaking her head. "I can't live like this anymore," she said softly. "It's not right to be separated. If he's chosen not to return to us, then we'll just go to him."

"It doesn't seem to bother him," I said. "You even said that this separation is his fault."

My mother let her breath out. "Yes, it is," she said. "Nonetheless, we are the ones who are going to remedy it." She took a sip of water. "Families don't live like this. I'm his wife, you're his daughter, and I'm all out of excuses as to why I don't live with my husband. It's time to join him."

I nodded. I couldn't look at my grandmother—I knew I'd cry if I did. I was already dreading saying good-bye.

:: :: ::

My mother had booked passage for us on the Danish freighter *Laura Maersk*, which would arrive in San Pedro Harbor from New York via the Panama Canal on the fifteenth of July, then depart for Shanghai the following day. Two days before that, Heather, who listened to my nearly endless complaints and tears and anger and woe, had a good-bye party for me at her house. Toward the end of the evening, Mark Young asked me if he could talk to me alone, and when I said yes, he took my hand and led me behind a lattice gate just outside Heather's backyard. He kissed me there, a real kiss this time. Then someone called my name and he stopped, and he looked at me and told me he would miss me and that I was the prettiest girl he knew. I wanted to say, *Kiss me again!*, but all I could do was nod and tell him I liked him a lot, giving myself plenty of reason to think up all the things I could have said in the days that followed.

I hardly saw my grandmother that last week, and when I did she was almost stony, as though this departure had been my idea. But I understood the feeling of being mad at the one who was leaving, no matter what their reason, no matter whether they deserved your anger or not, and her mood didn't bother me. Apart from a quick hug when she was leaving our house the night before we sailed, she did not say good-bye.

Which was all right, because the day we left was bad enough as it was. Our belongings were packed in boxes and ready to be put into storage, which my grandmother would arrange for once we were gone, and our bungalow itself had become an empty box. Heather lingered in the house until she started to cry, and my mother gently suggested that she go home, that I would write to her soon.

:: :: ::

My mother was in good spirits when we boarded the ship, and with the good-byes over with, I began to cheer up, too. My mother suggested that we stay on the deck to bid farewell to California's coast, and we found two chairs and faced them toward the rear of the ship. The *Laura Maersk* was guided by tugboats from the harbor to the sea, first through San Pedro Harbor's Turning Basin, then the Y-shaped Inner Harbor, then the channel and into the Outer Harbor, and finally past the breakwater. But as Cabrillo Beach Park faded in our wake, my mother's good spirits seemed to as well. She grew quiet, and when we could no longer make out a single thing on shore, she said she was going below to rest, and that I should not wake her for dinner.

It was the start of what turned out to be a pattern. For most of that journey, my mother was fatigued and out of sorts, and I was left to my own devices. Her inattention and bad humor made me cross at the start, because I saw no reason for them. We were doing what she wanted, weren't we? *She* was the one who'd dreamed this whole thing up; *I* was the one who had reason to be unhappy, because I was the one who hadn't wanted to go. But somehow we'd traded places. She had slipped into the role of the morose captive, and I had become the carefree adventurer. I'd decided that going to Shanghai at the age of fifteen was a very glamorous and exotic thing to do, and that there was no reason not to enjoy it.

No one bothered me on the ship, about what to do or where to go, about the dishes or the trash or homework, and I did what I wanted. I sat in the afternoon sun and played shuffleboard with anybody I could find—old men, middle-aged women, young married couples who seemed not that much older than I was. I read shadowy mysteries and risqué romance novels that my mother wouldn't have approved of had she noticed, and I sat on a deck chair and pretended to doze near a couple I was sure were newlyweds so that I could eavesdrop on their romantic talk. I wrote letters to Mark Young that I planned on mailing from Shanghai, letters in which I tried to sound worldly and independent: *Miss you dreadfully—I ache for your smile!— but life is very full here in exotic Shanghai, and there is so much to take in!*

And I spent hours imagining our arrival and our reunion with my father. In my mind, he would be waiting on the dock as the *Laura Maersk* approached. He would shield his eyes against the sun as he looked up at the ship and anxiously scanned the deck for us. Because of his eagerness, he would spot us long before we found him, and he would call out and wave his arms. When we came off the ship, he would say, "What took you so long?" Then he would wink at me and boast about how much I'd grown. He'd ask me if I had boyfriends, and he'd say they must be lining up for miles, and I would blush. I imagined the scene several times a day, refining it and adding to it each time, and soon the whole thing felt real, far more remembered than imagined.

On August 7, we reached the estuary of the Yangtze River. We'd seen the coast of China for several days. When the blue of the ocean turned muddy, my mother smiled and said we were getting close.

And then we were there, traveling up the Whangpoo toward the Bund. My mother and I stood on the deck and she pointed out Woosung, and then, on the east bank of the Whangpoo, Pootung with its docks and oil yards, its fish canneries and factories. I nodded vaguely as she talked quietly about the geography of this foreign place I once knew, but my thoughts were not on what she said. I was thinking about the only thing I could just then: the heat.

It was impossible to ignore. I felt captured, bound, and gagged, and though I had thought I remembered the heat and had told my mother I did when she tried to prepare me for it, I was certain I'd never known anything like it. There was no breeze, nothing to even push the hot air around. Heat clung to us, a suffocating feeling, and I looked frantically at my mother and thought, *What have we done?* It was as though we'd traveled to hell, by choice.

My mother wiped her face with a lace-trimmed linen handkerchief that looked as limp as wet tissue, then glanced at me. "You see?" she said. "*This* is what I was talking about."

The ship docked at the Bund, and I stared hard at the famous skyline. I had hoped that the names would come back to me at the sight of those buildings, but not many did. The Hongkong and Shanghai Bank, I thought, and I remembered rubbing the lions' noses. Jardine Matheson, and the Customs House, with Big Ching—words I hadn't thought of in years surfaced in my mind like bits of wreckage from a sunken ship. I couldn't remember any of the others, but I told myself I would relearn them, and my spirits rose as I looked below and saw a small crowd on the dock. I scanned the crowd quickly for my father, half hoping he'd be on stilts again. But there were no stilts, and no one who resembled him, at least from that distance.

My mother turned from the deck railing. "Shall we?"

"I'm looking for him," I said.

She sighed and smoothed my hair gently. "Oh, Anna, I'm sorry. I should have explained. I knew he wouldn't be here yet. We have to go through Chinese customs and immigration, and he knows how long that takes. But he'll find us."

I swallowed hard, surprised by my disappointment, then followed my mother off the ship. *Don't argue*, I thought. *At least you'll see him soon.*

Two hours later, my mother and I were still waiting in line on the customs jetty on the Bund, and three hours after that we were nearing the front of the queue at immigration. We had had no food since toast and juice that morning, we were filthy from the grime and film of travel, and the heat had become like a nagging illness, something you just couldn't shake.

When we finally emerged from the Customs House, it was nearly six o'clock in the evening, and I looked around me in shock, for I found myself in the dirtiest and shabbiest place I'd ever been. I'd expected someplace glamorous, like Paris maybe, and although the buildings that faced us on the Bund were beau.iful—stately and majestic—the street itself was crowded and chaotic, packed with cars and people and pedicabs, all competing for far too little space, a crazy version of musical chairs. Everything was filthy, the odor nearly overpowering, the sidewalk lined with garbage and rickety, makeshift stalls where hawkers held out all kinds of things—watches and shirts, electric razors and cartons of cigarettes, canned goods and jewelry—all the while yelling things I didn't understand. There were beggars everywhere—lying on the sidewalk, propped against buildings, huddled in entries as though they had been deposited there. With their diseases and open wounds and missing limbs, they hardly looked alive.

I looked around for something good and did not find it. And I thought, *This? This is the place he couldn't leave, the place he had to come back to?* Just standing on the street was a sentence I didn't think we deserved.

My mother glanced about nervously, and I was startled at her expression. I saw that she was afraid, and for the first time in my life, I had the urge to take care of her.

"What is it?" I asked.

She attempted a smile. "I'm just not sure what to do next."

I thought the heat must be getting to her. My mother was never uncertain, and what we should do seemed obvious to me. "We just wait for him, don't we? You said yourself."

"That's what I'd thought, but it's getting so late that I . . ." Her voice trailed off and I wanted to reassure her, but didn't know what to say.

We waited for another minute, and I was about to take my mother's arm and try to lead her across the street through the anarchy of the traffic and trash when a car pulled up perhaps twenty feet away. It was a Packard, and though it was beat up and matched no memory of mine, I knew, without knowing how, that its owner was my father. As if to answer my thoughts, the car stopped, the back door opened, and he got out.

I caught my breath at the sight of him: he was so *clean*, so pressed and spotless and handsome in his white linen suit that he seemed to have materialized more than arrived, and I wondered for a moment if I'd made him up. I was immediately embarrassed for my mother and me. I tugged on her sleeve like a child—his appearance had reduced me to one—and my mother nodded and stared at him without speaking, just as I did. She smoothed her rumpled skirt, a sad gesture because it didn't help. I saw how difficult it was for her to be seen like this, so grimy and traveled.

He stood by the car for a moment and scanned his surroundings, and when he saw us, he leaned into the car and said something to the driver, then walked purposefully toward us. I held back, expecting my mother to run to him the way she had at Union Station, but she didn't. She waited next to me, and as my father neared us, she took my hand and squeezed it twice, her signal for *Be brave*. I squeezed back, glad for her encouragement, for I was afraid.

"So *here* they are," he called jubilantly as he approached us. His voice was so loud that I looked around to see who else he was talking to, but I found no one. He went on. "Here are my girls, and none the worse for wear," and he laughed. I winced and tried to hide it with a smile, for I couldn't tell whether or not he was teasing. We were most definitely the worse for wear, as anyone could see. He leaned toward my mother and kissed her cheek, then put his hands firmly on my shoulders and kissed my forehead, his hands keeping me at arm's length so that I wouldn't muss him, I guessed. But when he met my eyes, though it was only for a moment, I saw the reason for his formality: he was nervous. He looked us over, and he laughed loudly and somehow strangely, especially because there wasn't anything funny that I could see.

"Come on now, let's get your things and be off to dinner. We've got a full schedule this evening. Lots to do around here, *plenty* to do," and he turned toward the car and whistled for his driver. I knew it wouldn't be Mei Wah, but I was still surprised to see the burly Chinese strongman who got out of the front seat, and another word surfaced from my childhood in Shanghai: *bodyguard*. He wore a dark suit and looked like my father's opposite. My father called something to him and motioned to our luggage, which the driver began to carry to the car as effortlessly as if all we'd packed was air.

My mother and I watched in silence, as though the loading of the luggage were a ceremony with great meaning. I found the silence awkward, but I could think of nothing to say, though I'd pictured my father and me talking up a storm as soon as we saw each other. When the car was loaded, my father turned to us. "Off we go," he said, as though he were our tour guide.

My mother coughed slightly, a sound I knew as a signal that she disagreed. Apparently my father had forgotten her language. "Joseph," she said, "we're really not presentable. We should at least change and—"

"Nonsense. You've just arrived in Shanghai—the Paris of the Orient!—and we're not going to waste your first night here. You've come all this way, there's no use sitting at home." He gave her a long look and he seemed to soften for a moment. "You look as lovely as ever," he said simply. Then he looked at me and winked in a stagy way. "I'm showing you off, is what I'm doing, to the whole town."

I smiled weakly. My mother and I followed him to the car.

All that night he was cheerful as Christmas morning, laughing and making toasts, waving and calling out to acquaintances across the restaurant. "We're celebrating," he kept saying, and he'd clink glasses yet again, and say how good it was to have us here. But there was an almost manic quality to him, and with each dinner course, with each toast and new introduction, I wanted to say, *What's wrong? It's just us.*

At last, after dessert and coffee and cordials, he asked my mother if she was ready to go, and when she nodded wearily, my father smiled gently and looked like himself for the first time that night. "Then we're off," he said, and he rose and led us to the entrance and to the Packard outside, where he got into the front seat with the driver.

I slumped against my mother in the backseat. I thought I had never been so tired. My whole body felt worn down. I started to fall asleep, but my mother's voice woke me when we were only a few blocks from the restaurant.

"Where are we going?" she asked. I felt her shift on the seat next to me.

My father didn't answer.

"Joseph?" she said.

"Not to worry," he said, his voice low. "Hungjao isn't ship-shape yet, is all. So I've arranged for an apartment in the Concession for now. You two will be comfortable there. And I'll go out to Hungjao and have it ready in a day or two."

My mother fell back against the seat. I could feel her disappointment and fatigue. "Oh," she said dully. "I'm sure we'll be fine."

:: :: ::

The apartment my father had arranged for us was on Rue Ratard in the French Concession, and you could tell it had once been someone's nice home. The Copen blue drapes that hung from floor to ceiling had not always been faded. The wainscoting on the walls had not always been chipped. The Oriental rugs had not always been thread-bare, and the parquet floors hadn't always been warped. I was certain that the windows overlooking the street had once been clean, the mahogany furniture new, the wallpaper bright, the rooms elegant. You could tell. But I guessed that it had been neglected for years, and I wondered just when it had changed.

I wondered the same thing about my father: When had *he* changed? Just after he'd left us, or just before we'd arrived in Shang-hai? During our first few days there, I thought he was just nervous around us, and that the newness of a wife and daughter were what made him so unpredictable. But when he was still that way the sec-ond week and then the third and after that the fourth, I realized that this was who he was now, and that the impulsive man who'd taken us to dinner that first night was the real thing, and not an act.

"Impulsive" was a compliment; "completely unreliable" was more accurate. We never knew when we would see him, and we rarely saw him two days in a row. He would say he'd come for dinner, then call an hour after he was to pick us up to cancel. One night he would be dressed immaculately—pressed shirt, silk tie, linen suit—and two nights later he'd show up in the same clothes, only by then they'd be rumpled and stained, and it was clear he had not changed since he'd seen us last. When he did keep his promise for dinner, he might take us to one of the nicest restaurants in town—Senet and St. Petersburg were his favorites—but it was just as possible that we'd end up eating noodles on Foochow Road, elbow to elbow with shopkeepers and clerks. Whatever the mishap, change of plans, or faux pas, his one-word explanation was always the same: business. Business was what made him late, kept him away, and delayed the work on the house at Hungjao.

The one thing my father did do, the one thing we could depend on, was financial support. There was always money. He passed a handful of bills to my mother each time he saw her, he offered a few to me when we said good night, and he had cash delivered to our apartment on Rue Ratard several days a week, a gesture that seemed crazy at first, but which soon seemed as necessary as providing running water. Shanghai's economy was in chaos. Rumors of civil war between the Communists and the Nationalists in northern China made people distrust China's paper currency, and it was worth less every day. By that fall of 1946, you needed a suitcase of cash to shop for the day.

During our first week in Shanghai, my mother accepted unconditionally my father's constant use of business as an excuse. She began making up some of her own, to boot. She said his undependability was a phase, that he just hadn't been ready for us, that he was embarrassed because the house was not prepared. He had always been a good provider, she said. Now he was afraid that he had lost face in our eyes, and he was frantically trying to make up for it. She was gracious without fail. Every time he canceled or showed up late, she made excuses for him and told me not to hold it against him.

I nodded silently and tried, for her sake, to hide my anger, not always with success. "Don't hold it against him, Anna," she said. "Resentment does not become you." I turned from her and said I was hoping to grow into it, because it probably wasn't going to go away soon. In fact, resentment was something I clung to. I resented our apartment, I resented Shanghai, its dirtiness, its beggars, its crowdedness. And I resented everything about my father: his lateness, his cancellations, his inattention, his general disregard of us. Most of all, I resented the way he treated my mother, as though she were an acquaintance, nothing more. But resenting him, I knew, was a good thing. It meant that things didn't hurt so much.

:: :: ::

On a Thursday morning in September, my mother and I celebrated the Feast of the Nativity of Mary at the early Mass at the Cathedral in

Ziccawei. We had been in Shanghai for a month and a day, though it felt more like a year to me. All I wanted was to go home, but if I so much as mentioned the idea, my mother was short with me. We hadn't seen my father in six days, a record. When she'd asked him about when we might be able to move to Hungjao, he had only shrugged, then changed the subject.

After Mass, we took a pedicab back to the Concession. We'd almost reached our apartment—our cell, was what I had begun to call it— when my mother said suddenly, as if in answer to some question I'd just asked, "We're going to move to Hungjao tomorrow. This is crazy."

I could only stare at her.

"It's ridiculous," she went on. "We came here to be a family. There's no reason that we shouldn't join him. The house can't be that bad, and it's not as though we're accustomed to luxury. We'll pack up this afternoon. I'll ask him to stop by this evening, and we'll tell him. And all this foolishness will be over." She looked at me, her expression hopeful and calm, so that it almost seemed like things had already changed. "Don't you think?"

I nodded, and did not tell her how wrong her plan seemed.

We packed that afternoon. I felt like a child pretending to get ready for a trip. I couldn't believe that he would come, that we would go. If my mother was uncertain in any way, she did not show it. She was all efficiency, packing as though our move had been planned for weeks, sorting the things we'd bought since our arrival in Shanghai into various boxes and crates. At seven o'clock she hadn't mentioned dinner, and although I was starved, I knew she was hoping that my father would appear. Finally, at almost eight, she sat down and smiled, and although she looked tired, she also looked happy.

"I know what we can do," she said. "We'll go to Jimmy's. Do you remember it? We haven't been there in all this time, because I was saving it for a celebration. But I think we've earned that today."

I was too exhausted and too confused to say anything but yes. My mother told me to hurry and clean up, and half an hour later, we were on our way.

In that month, there had been much about Shanghai that I had not remembered, but when my mother and I walked into Jimmy's that night, I remembered the Saturday my father took me there immediately. I remembered his suave assurance and his attention to me. I remembered his argument with Will Marsh, and the stolen yen in my shoe, and the shock of the kidnapping, which I hadn't thought about in a long time. And I remembered how much I'd loved him then, and how he could do no wrong.

And so when my mother and I walked inside, I just stood in the doorway for a moment, a little stunned by the presence of so much past. I breathed in that same American smell from years before—barbecued chicken and hamburgers—and I smiled and looked at my mother.

At first I thought she must be ill. She looked stricken, as though she might faint, and I was afraid all the packing had made her sick. And then I followed her gaze and saw a familiar face.

My father was there, and I felt a wave of relief and gratitude. I started to wave to him and to call out, but my mother grabbed hold of my wrist so hard that I tried to pull away, more out of anger than hurt.

"*Don't,*" she said firmly. "Just leave."

But it was too late, for I saw that he was with a Chinese woman I'd never seen before. She was leaning against him familiarly, and just as I looked, she said something and my father laughed and kissed her cheek. I was stunned at first. And then I had a worse feeling, for I realized I'd been expecting her all along. Things had been too strange; of course there was some explanation beyond business. As I stared hard and tried to see her more clearly, I was even more surprised; she wasn't even pretty, really. When she laughed, there was something coarsely appealing about her, but she was no match for my mother. Which for reasons I couldn't explain made everything seem worse.

My father said something to her and looked around the restaurant. And then he saw us.

For a moment, he just stared. Then he said something to the woman. I wanted to see her reaction, but I saw no more. My mother took my arm and guided me out of the restaurant and into Shanghai's streets of beggars and hawkers and who knew what else, and she said that we were going home to our flat.

There she gave me a glass of sherry, a first, which I drank as an act of trust, despite the horrible taste. She put me to bed as though I were a child, soothing me, talking in a low voice. She was gentle and seemed inexplicably calm, and I thought she must know more than I did, but I had no interest in knowing what that was. She told me to sleep and that we would talk in the morning. I shut my eyes gratefully. I felt sick and tired and sad.

It was after midnight when I heard someone knocking on the door to our flat. It was quiet at first, then more forceful. I heard my mother's steps moving toward the door, and I heard the door open and close, then my father's heavier footsteps over my mother's muffled ones.

My room was on the second floor of the apartment, and my mother had closed the doors between us—my bedroom door, the door to the hallway, and the door to the living room—so there was no way to make out my father's words. All I heard was the rise and fall of his voice, the tones going up and down, louder and softer, as he spoke to my mother. I did not hear my mother's answers. Her voice was too hushed.

For a long time, I stayed in bed. When I finally got up, I walked down the stairs and toward the double doors that led into the living room. I guessed my mother had meant to close them, but she'd left a crack, and I stood behind it, not really caring if they saw me. I was suddenly tired of both of them, and impatient. I just wanted whatever was going to happen to have happened. I wanted to go home, either to the one in Hungjao or the one in South Pasadena. Just not this sad apartment anymore.

They were sitting on a worn chintz loveseat, like some old prop from a second-rate play. Both of them looked exhausted. My father's linen suit was rumpled, his tie loosened. My mother was next to him, her back straight, and she seemed to be staring at the floor.

Neither of them spoke for a moment. Finally my father faced my mother and looked at her carefully. "Could you *possibly* have thought that I wanted the two of you here? Could you *possibly* have thought that I wanted a family again?"

My mother did not move. "I wanted to believe you did," she said softly. "And Anna–" she started, but she did not finish.

My father nodded. He took her hand and held it between his own, but said nothing.

:: :: ::

Later, I remembered going upstairs and getting back into bed, but I did not remember falling asleep. When I opened my eyes and saw my father sitting on the edge of my bed, I thought only moments had passed.

"I'd forgotten you did that," I said.

He shook his head, not understanding. "What?"

"You used to watch me sleep when I was little," I said. "I'd forgotten that till now."

He nodded and smiled slightly, and the conversation I'd overheard came back to me. I glanced at the window and saw that it was morning.

My father was quiet for a few minutes. He looked even more tired than he had in the night. Finally he said, "Do you know what I do every day?"

I shook my head and thought that he was the most unpredictable person I knew.

"The way I look at it, I fix things," he said. "Every day, I get out of bed and people come to me and tell me what they need. They need tires or newsprint or a truck chassis. They need a generator or a radiator or scrap metal by the pound. So I get it for them: I know where to buy just about anything anybody can think of, and I deliver it back to the guy who asked. All day, all week, I get things no one else in this city can. I'm the guy who can make it work."

He looked at me to see if I was listening. I nodded.

"But you," he said softly. His voiced cracked, and he cleared his throat and looked toward the window. "You're a problem I can't fix, Anna, the first one in a long time. And now I'm stuck." He tried a casual smile and failed. "I can't have you and your mother here. It's not safe. Shanghai's not a city for a young girl."

I nodded, suddenly wanting the conversation to be over with. "You don't love my mother," I said matter-of-factly. I was so tired of not knowing, of my mother's weak excuses for him, of telegrams that said nothing and evenings where he barely noticed us. I just wanted to understand.

"No, I—" he started, but he stopped and let his silence be his agreement.

I went on without hesitating, as though I were the one in charge. "So we're going home, and we won't see you again."

He nodded and I watched him for a moment. I decided I wanted to see what he knew. So I said, "How old am I?"

He laughed. "Fifteen. You'll be sweet sixteen on the seventeenth of January."

"What's my favorite color?"

"Blue. Always has been. Especially blue-green, like the ocean."

"Why do I love elephants?"

"Because Chu Shih told you they brought good luck. You believed everything he told you, because you loved him, too. Which made him a lucky man."

I nodded, remembering Chu Shih and how good I felt when I was with him.

My father was waiting. "That's it?" he said. "Did I pass?"

I looked at him evenly and asked the real question. "After we leave Shanghai, will I ever see you again?"

He winced and looked as though he were experiencing physical pain. "Yes," he said. "Don't ask more than that. But yes." Then he stood and left the room. A minute later, I heard him leave our flat.

:: :: ::

The day before we sailed, he took us to lunch, a grim and nearly silent meal at the Cathay Hotel. When he brought us back to our flat on Rue Ratard, he said he'd be by in the morning, but even I saw that he had no intention of doing that. At the chipped door to our flat, he embraced my mother and kissed her cheek. He hugged me and held me to him for a moment. Then he was gone. He did not say good-bye.

My mother closed the door and leaned against it heavily. I was trying to take everything in, and to choose one question out of the many that I had. Finally I asked, "Do you know who she was?"

My mother looked down and smoothed her skirt. "Her name is Leung Mancheung. Your father has known her for years, through business."

"She's not pretty," I said flatly.

My mother laughed at first, and I looked at her, startled. Then, in the space of a minute, she began to cry. "Your father loves beautiful women. The fact that she's not a beauty tells me he must truly care about her."

I blurted out what I really wanted to know, what I couldn't figure out. "Do you still love him?"

She looked away from me. "Yes," she said. "But it doesn't matter."

We left Shanghai the next day, October 8, 1946, just two months after we'd arrived, and almost nine years since we'd left the first time. But this time I understood that our departure was permanent. There was no tearful good-bye with my father at the ship this time, no waving, no stilts. Only my mother and me boarding the *President Cleveland* for the second half of its maiden voyage.

For me, the trip home felt endless, but for my mother it was worse. For the first time in my life—and maybe in hers, I thought—she was not beautiful. Her color was bad, and she had aged several years during our two months in Shanghai. The change had probably been gradual, but I hadn't noticed. It wasn't until we were surrounded by the blue of the Pacific, with China's vast coastline no longer visible behind us—it wasn't until we were away from my father—that I realized that she was ill.

I felt foolish and ashamed for not seeing it earlier, because when I looked at her on the ship, it was so obvious. Her skin had a yellowish tint to it, as did the whites of her eyes. She had lost weight, and the beautiful suits and afternoon dresses she'd bought for our trip hung on her. I saw how fragile she was, how carefully she negotiated stairs, how slowly she walked down the hallways. The sight of her was painful, and I considered my father to be the cause of her condition. And as we traveled further and further from him, I grew angrier with him by the day, and my anger led to a resolution: I would not allow him into my life again.

graduations

MY FATHER WAS A MAN who, over the years, developed a frequent and strong association with the word *debt*. Early in his career in Shanghai, he borrowed regularly and shamelessly from almost anyone he could talk out of their money. He was also well known for his attempts to pass bad checks. He seemed to believe that a dollar borrowed was a dollar earned, and his use of the phrase "urgent need" .came to mean nothing more than plain old broke.

As an adult, still years before I encountered all of his final debts, I became aware of a debt of my own. I owed him much, I saw. My stability, for example. My good taste in boyfriends, and later in choosing my down-to-earth husband. My cautious nature in just about everything. My dislike of drama and deceit, and my wariness of a quick profit, extravagant spending, and out-of-whack ambition. I owed all of my honest and conservative qualities to my father, for from the moment my mother and I left Shanghai that second time, I became determined never to be like him, and never to be involved with anyone who was. My father, I decided, was the embodiment of what not to do, and by extension I came to believe that anyone who was unlike him was safe, and dependable, and worthy of my affection. It was all a matter of common sense.

When my mother and I returned to Southern California in November of 1946, our days had a quality of déjà vu to them. Once again, my grandmother met us at San Pedro Harbor and drove us to her home. Once again, I was awed by the startling beauty of Southern California—the brilliant flowers, the soft light, the spread-out feeling of the place—even though we'd been away for only a few months. And once again, I spent my first few nights in the small guest room in my grandmother's house. The old trundle bed was still there, the dragonfly comforter freshly cleaned, the sheets stiff from being dried outside in the sun, and I slept so long and hard that when I woke I had to think for a moment to remember what day it was.

But not everything was the same. We were no longer waiting for my father. And when my grandmother met us on that first day, I saw her sadness and surprise, the reactions she could not mask as she took in my mother's thinness, her wanness, her tentative smile. She was a fraction of herself.

At dinner that first night, the three of us sat as we had nearly nine years earlier at my grandmother's old oak dining table, my grandmother at the head, my mother and me on either side of her. My grandmother made spaghetti, and after she served us, she poured Chianti for herself and my mother, then looked at me and took a third crystal wineglass from the sideboard behind the table.

"I think you're entitled after what you've been through," she said. She poured half a glass, then glanced at my mother, who winced. My grandmother put her hand on my mother's shoulder as she passed behind her chair. "All shall be well, Genevieve. All shall be well, and all shall be well, and all manner of things shall be well." She seated herself at the head of the table and I looked at her gratefully, for I found I could believe her. For the first time since last summer when my mother had presented me with our tickets at Musso's, I felt hopeful.

My grandmother lifted her glass and held it in the air for a moment. "To my girls," she said, "and to home," and my mother and I raised our glasses and clinked.

When my mother clinked her glass with my grandmother's, her hand shook and she quickly put her glass down. Then she smiled tentatively and said, "Be careful, Mother. You don't want us getting too comfortable here or we'll never move out. We'll be here long enough as it is."

My grandmother laughed. "The longer you're here, the better I like it."

My mother shrugged. "Good thing," she said. I was cheered by the seriousness with which she was eating her spaghetti, and by the roses in her cheeks, even if they were from the Chianti, and even if her cheeks were a little sunken. "We're going to be here for a while, you know. It's going to take some time to get everything out of storage and get the house livable again. At least a few weeks."

My grandmother shook her head. "Not that long," she said, and she set her fork down. "Confession is good for the soul, Genevieve, and to forgive is divine, as I hope you'll recall. I didn't have your things stored. They're all in the house, packed up and sitting in all those boxes, just as you left them."

My mother's expression relaxed. "But that's wonderful. Things will be far easier than I'd thought." She turned to me. "Do you see what a charmed life your grandmother leads? She's so rarely forgetful that even when she is, things work out."

When my grandmother answered, her voice was matter-of-fact. "I didn't forget. I was never convinced that you'd be gone for very long. I know the man, Genevieve."

My mother pursed her lips as though keeping words captive. She nodded, but said nothing. As far as I know, they said no more about our early return.

In our bungalow the following week, my mother and I pushed open the windows and French doors to air everything out as we unpacked and put things in order. I stacked blue willow plates in the kitchen cupboards and forced myself not to think about the Bridge of Nine Turnings that led to the teahouse in Yu Gardens in Shanghai's Old City, the model for the teahouse in the blue willow pattern. I polished our copper pots and pans till they gleamed and caught the sun, then hung them from the wrought-iron rack over the stove. I unpacked the linens and stacked them neatly in the small closet in the hallway, and I breathed in their strong scent of cedar as though it had been prescribed. I told myself that the hard part was over, and as I worked in our house, I worked at putting things in order inside of me as well. My mother had told me in Shanghai, *No more waiting*, and I believed her; she was different now. And I thought I knew what to do. I could, I thought, pack up my feelings for my father as well, and haul them up to the attic of my heart, where I would not trip on them, or come upon them unexpectedly, or hurt myself on their sharp edges. No more wondering when he was coming or wishing he were here or feeling like our lives were always on hold. When that felt harsh, I reminded myself of what hurt the most: that this had been his choice.

:: :: ::

A week after our arrival, I started tenth grade at South Pasadena High School and tried to pick up where I'd left off, despite the fact that I'd missed the first two months. But soon I was seeing the same friends, and we talked about the same boys, and I was invited to parties and dances, which I went to as dutifully as if they'd been acts of charity, gritting my teeth and thinking, *I can do this*, for everything had an unreal quality to it for that first month. At the start, friends asked about my father and about the trip and about what Shanghai had been like. But my answers were less than enthusiastic, and they heard what I didn't say: that I didn't want to talk about it. Mostly they left me alone, no questions asked. Then they just acted like nothing had happened, like I'd never even been away, and I was grateful for their casual disregard of the disaster of our trip to Shanghai. Only Heather sensed how bad things had been. "You look so sad," she said over and over again. "Are you sure you're all right?" I only nodded. Talking about it only made things worse.

My mother was more direct on the subject of my father. "He is no longer part of our lives," she said simply, and she gave me a look that told me the matter was settled. Over the next months, she worked hard at making certain her statement was true. His name was not mentioned; there was no sign of him in our home; if she was questioned about him by some well-meaning soul, she simply said they'd separated, and left it at that. She even went on a couple of dates with the brothers of friends or the bachelor acquaintances of neighbors, though she never saw the same man twice. The evenings she went out left me pacing around the house with an argument going on in my head. I was mad that she'd gone, but I understood her reasons. In the end, I just ended up even angrier with my father. All of this was his fault.

We heard nothing from Shanghai. We heard nothing that fall, nothing in January of 1947 when I turned sixteen and got my driver's license. Nothing that spring, nothing in June, when I finished my sophomore year. By then I'd become pretty good at not thinking about him. My mother had removed the photographs of him from the bookshelves and table in the living room, and the only one that remained was in her bedroom. I made sure I didn't do more than glance at it. Schoolwork had helped, too. When my mother and I had first returned from Shanghai, I'd found that studying like crazy helped me not to think about things, and I'd gotten straight A's ever since. I especially loved history, where you could get some perspective on things, and where the past made sense.

When a small package arrived in February of 1948, the middle of my junior year, the familiar handwriting and Shanghai postmark and foreign stamps that nearly covered the box all seemed like a trick. My first thought was that it must have been sent years ago. Why would he send anything now? Did he even remember us?

But when I ripped open the brown paper, my hands shaking, I found a small card inside that wished me a happy seventeenth birthday. *To my dearest Anna*, it read. *With love from your Dad.*

My mother wasn't home—a blessing, I thought—and I opened the box quickly and found a pair of pearl earrings. I liked them as soon as I saw them; they were sophisticated and looked like jewelry that a college girl would wear. But it didn't matter, and I didn't waste time. I left the house and walked quickly to Monterey Road, then to Fair Oaks and then to Mission Avenue, straight to D & G Jewelers, where Mr. Vagnino, who had made my mother's wedding ring and the gold locket that held my baby picture, looked at the earrings for a moment and sighed.

"They're basically on the order of costume jewelry," he said with a shrug. "No gold, fake pearls. But they look all right, don't you think?"

I didn't, and I happily sold the earrings to him for fifty cents. I told him they were a gift from a relative I didn't like, and I begged him to promise not to tell my mother about our transaction. When he reluctantly agreed, I thanked him and hurried to Holy Family Church, where I gladly dropped my two quarters into the St. Vincent de Paul box by the door, happy to be rid of any trace of my father.

I didn't tell my mother about the earrings or what I'd done with them, and although the guilt made me feel grimy and suspect, my stubbornness won out. A few weeks later when we were on our way to afternoon Mass, she pulled over several blocks before we'd reached the church. My stomach tightened. It was the middle of March, the third week of Lent, and as I prepared myself for the coming accusation, I told myself it was for the best. I'd confess to my mother and confess to Father Locatelli, and the matter would be closed.

"I have something to tell you," my mother said, "and I might as well tell you now even though it won't be final for another year." She took a folded sheet of paper from her purse and held it out to me. "This is a conversation I never intended to have, Anna, and I'm sorry for my part in this. But it's all I can do, after everything that's happened."

She was confessing, not accusing. Although what she said wasn't what I had expected, I nodded as I unfolded the sheet of paper, for I already knew what it was. I'd heard bits and pieces of my mother's conversation over the past month, and I'd taken several phone messages from Andrew Martin, my grandmother's attorney. I was actually almost proud of myself for knowing, before I was told, that my mother was filing for divorce.

But I still wanted to see it in black and white. I looked carefully at the paper I held, at its formality and officialness and fact. It was dated that day, which explained my mother's nicer-than-usual appearance—the midnight-blue suit, the cream-colored blouse, the white gloves, the hat—and her vagueness about her plans earlier that day.

Book 2783, I read, *Page 335*. And then:

Genevieve Schoene, Plaintiff, vs. Joseph Schoene, Defendant.
Interlocutory Judgment of Divorce
(Default)
It is adjudged that plaintiff is entitled to a divorce from
defendant; that when one year shall have expired after the entry
of this interlocutory judgment a final judgment dissolving the
marriage between plaintiff and defendant be entered, and at that
time the Court shall grant such other and further relief as may
be necessary to complete disposition of this action. That plaintiff

is awarded custody of the minor child with rights of reasonable visitation reserved to the defendant.

I refolded it and handed it to my mother. "Neat," I said. "Congratulations."

She started the car and said, "There's no need for sarcasm."

I stared out the window. "It's not sarcasm," I said. "I just have no idea what to say."

"In a hundred years, I wouldn't have dreamed that I'd be apart from your father."

I nodded. "I just try not to think about him," I said matter-of-factly. "There are lots of better things to pay attention to."

:: :: ::

In March of the next year, my senior year in high school, my mother requested that a final judgment be entered, which it was. The Final Judgment of Divorce arrived at our house by messenger. It was a strange day, for an hour after that news arrived, decidedly good news came in the mail: I'd been accepted as an entering freshman to the University of California at Los Angeles, my first choice, for the upcoming fall.

We celebrated that night with my grandmother, in the same way we'd celebrated all of our collective birthdays and special occasions: with a nice dinner out. That night we went to a new Italian restaurant in Hollywood, Miceli's, where we sat upstairs at a carved wooden booth, the table covered with a red-and-white checked tablecloth. Bottles of Chianti and fake grapevines hung from the ceiling, and the walls were covered with painted murals of busty girls in off-the-shoulder blouses and full skirts frolicking in the Italian countryside. The whole place smelled like warm bread.

By the end of dinner, my mother's food was almost untouched. She had been quiet, almost morose, and more worried than she had been in months. While I often found her behavior perplexing, this time it made no sense at all. I was growing annoyed with her. She should be happy, shouldn't she? Or at least relieved? *Au contraire*, as my French teacher would say.

"Genevieve," my grandmother finally said, "what is it that's bothering you? Is this regret or worry or the flu or some combination?"

My mother's cheeks flushed and she looked down at her uneaten meal. "There's something else besides the divorce," she said. "I don't want to talk about it more than we have to. It may not get the popular vote," she added dryly, and glanced at me. I shrugged, my teenage shorthand for, *So what am I supposed to do?*

My mother took a breath and said, "I've changed our name, Anna's and mine. The spelling of it, I mean. I've thought about it for a long time. There's no telling what he's doing in Shanghai, what sort of trouble he might get into. I want to be apart from that. From who he is now. And so I've changed the legal spelling of our last name. It's Shoen now, S-H-O-E-N. So it sounds the same, but we won't be associated with him."

I stared at her hard, not understanding what she said. "You changed my *name*? How can you change my name?"

"With a court order," she answered easily, and she suddenly seemed relieved. "It's quite simple actually. This was the right time to do it. You're coming up on a new start, Anna, where no one will know you. So you won't have to go around explaining to everyone. You're still Anna Shoen. It's only the spelling, and it's only for practical reasons." She took a long drink of water. She looked at my grandmother and me in turn, and she seemed more confident and sure of herself than she had in months. "In any case, it's done." She turned to me. "And you'll just have to trust my judgment on this one. It's for the best, I assure you."

My grandmother shook her head. "Well, it sounds as though the matter's settled, Anna. I'd suggest you learn to live with it." Though her words were neutral enough, the flatness of her tone made it clear that my mother's action had taken her by surprise, and that she was not impressed.

:: :: ::

I graduated from South Pasadena High School in June of 1949, and in September, just before I started at UCLA, my mother received a hefty check from my father's agent in New York, a man named James Rankin, whose name and handwriting I was to see for years, and whom I never met. I often tried to picture him, and usually came up with someone tall and thin, which was the way his name sounded to me. In his letter, Mr. Rankin explained that my father had asked him to express his sorrow in what had come to pass, but that he had also seen it as inevitable. My father fully understood my mother's decision, Mr. Rankin said, and he would not shirk his financial responsibility. The substantial check that was enclosed would be the first of many.

That check seemed to represent some kind of permission for my mother, something to do with finality, and she reinvented herself yet again. The first thing she did was to buy our bungalow from my grandmother, a gesture that my grandmother insisted was completely unnecessary. But my mother would not be dissuaded. "I want to be able to call it my own," she said. "I know it doesn't make sense to you, and I know it seems unnecessary. But it's important to me. I want to own this house." My grandmother acquiesced. My mother's only compromise was in the below-market price she paid for the house.

The second thing my mother did was to go shopping, and although the sight of her coming home every day with more and more packages was startling, I was glad to see it. In the three years since our trip to Shanghai, she had spent almost nothing on herself. Fashion had changed dramatically after the war, and my mother loved the new styles—tight waists and bodices, rounded hips, longer skirts. She bought afternoon dresses, and wool slacks, and cashmere sweaters, high heels and T-straps that made her look like a movie star. And a dinner dress with a tight bodice and long full skirt—the New Look, she explained proudly.

She was, once again, a master at adaptability. She cut her hair, a feather cut this time, a shorter style that framed her face. She began to spend more time dressing before she went out, even if she was just going to the market or shopping or on other errands. She always had to be prettier, with higher heels, more stylish hair, more beautifully manicured nails. I watched her transformation with equal parts admiration and awe.

When she helped me move into my small dormitory room, she was the one who turned heads, which was fine by me. The limelight was not something I sought. A colorful father and elegant mother had made me only too glad to be part of the background in public, a desire my mother didn't understand. At the end of summer when she urged me to shop for new college clothes, my response was a disappointment to her, for the most she could talk me into was a plaid street dress, two pairs of shoes—loafers and saddle oxfords—a Pendleton fisherman's knit sweater, and some gray flannel slacks that I loved and wore so much that she finally bought me a second pair, saying that at least this way I could get them cleaned. I did, however, agree to a trip to the beauty salon, where I had my shoulder-length hair cut in a chin-length bob, a style I liked for its practicality, its straightforwardness, and its simplicity.

The fact was that I couldn't imagine I'd have time for fashion and elaborate hairstyles at college, for I planned to be disciplined and study hard. I would major in history, I thought, and I would take advantage of cultural opportunities and become sophisticated in the arts, like my grandmother. I would get a part-time job, so that I wouldn't have to depend so much on my mother's financial support. I would take care of myself.

But my program was short-lived, for in the fall of my freshman year I fell reluctantly in love with a boy named Jack Bradley. He ran on the cross-country team and on Saturdays he worked at Bullock's Wilshire, where he sold women's shoes and where I went every chance I got with no good reason other than the fact that I wanted to be near him. I would stand behind leather purses and handbags so that I could watch him unobserved. It seemed I couldn't stay away from him, and my heart beat faster when he was near. He had a crooked smile and clear blue eyes that I was sure could never lie and that at times could focus on me so intently that I felt undone inside, or unlaced, as though just by looking at me he were gently taking me apart to see how I worked. He was dependable but not predictable, honest but also guarded. He was competitive in the extreme. When he was with friends, he was only too glad to turn everything into a contest: at the pool, who could hold their breath underwater the longest; at the beach, who could swim the furthest out. Who could name the song playing on the radio, who could rattle off state capitals, who knew the population of Los Angeles? He thrived on winning, and although track was his sport of choice, he was good at just about anything he tried—golf, tennis, baseball, even basketball, though he was only five-foot-nine. He was forthright and thorough and the most earnest person I had ever met. He was also orderly in the extreme, always on time, always organized. Even the way he ate was orderly, one thing at a time—salad, then potatoes, then meat, no mixing things up—and at the end of a meal his plate was always clean.

He was, in every way that I could judge, the exact opposite of my father, and as far as I could figure out, he was a safe person to love. Nevertheless, for the first few months, I fought my feelings for him. It was too early, I thought, I didn't know him well enough. I was afraid that once I loved him, he would leave. And I didn't want to make the mistake my parents had made, though I wasn't even sure what that was. But I lost my fight. He was a sport I could not help but watch, and in the fall of 1949, I finally gave in and admitted that I was thoroughly in love with him.

I even knew when and how it happened: from ten o'clock to ten-fifty on Monday, Wednesday, and Friday mornings in Josiah Royce Hall, where the two of us sat with some twenty-one other freshmen who'd also registered for English 51, American Literature—Realism to the Present. Jack Bradley sat in front of me during those first few weeks as we listened to passages from Walt Whitman and Emily Dickinson, Mark Twain and Henry James, all read to us and patiently expanded upon by Professor Edward Daniels, a man who clearly loved literature so passionately that at the start, I wanted to do well in the class only for him, because I could see how much he wanted us to love what we read. I listened hard and tried to take in all that Professor Daniels said, but I also took in Jack Bradley: the way the back of his chestnut hair was so neatly cut, and the one-of-a-kind graceful curve of his hairline at his neck, the solidness of his back and shoulders. As the days grew shorter and the semester wore on, Professor Daniels's love for great writing got mixed up with my feelings for Jack Bradley. By the end, I loved them both, the words and the boy, and for the very first time since my childhood in Shanghai, a small hard knot inside of me began to dissolve—and I was happy.

the poor in spirit

ON A COOL NIGHT in the third week of April of 1949, my father went for a walk along the Bund. It was sometime after three, and he'd been asleep in his office since midnight. He'd started sleeping there now and then, on a flimsy camp bed he'd set up near the window overlooking Yuen Ming Yuen Road. That small room had come to feel more like home than home did. The air smelled of cigar smoke and stale newspapers, comforting smells, and there were no reminders of the past there, nothing to make him think of my mother, or of me, or of Shanghai as it used to be.

When he woke that night, he found himself restless and unable to return to sleep, something that happened often. It was the silence that bothered him. He was used to noise in that part of the city—traffic and shouting, the sound of people talking and laughing and arguing—and the stillness made him anxious. He was stiff and groggy, and he decided to do what he had done most nights for the last month: take a walk while the city was quiet, for the hours before dawn were the only time when Shanghai felt familiar anymore. In the smoky night, he could walk along the Bund, still his favorite part of the city, and it was easy to remember why he had loved this place. He even liked the pungent, smoke-and-fish smell of the Whangpoo. It was one of the few things about the city that had not changed.

From his office, he followed his usual route, walking first to Peking Road, where he turned left, toward the Bund, intending to turn right at the corner and walk the length of the waterfront down to the Shanghai Club at Number 3. But for the first time in a month, he found that his familiar walk was not possible, for when he turned the corner, he faced half a dozen Nationalist soldiers who stood guard in a line across the Bund as matter-of-factly as if they did this every night. Their faces were expressionless, their stance no-nonsense. My father was curtly told that he could not pass, and that he was to leave the vicinity immediately.

My father faked nonchalance, nodding grimly as though he'd expected as much. He turned from the soldiers and walked purposefully away from them and toward the Garden Bridge, his head down, his hands jammed in the pockets of his worn herringbone coat, all the while wondering what in the world was going on. When he had gone two hundred feet, he glanced back and saw the sentries pointing toward the water, at what he didn't care, as long as they weren't watching him. When he reached the Public Garden, he stepped carefully onto dark wet grass and ducked under a cypress tree, then stood there for a moment, listening and waiting. But nothing happened. There was no yelling, no pounding of soldiers' feet, so he decided to cut through the garden to the Whangpoo so that he could see what was up.

He headed toward the giant magnolia tree and the bandstand, eerie in the stillness of night. When he reached the riverfront, he faced south and stared toward the Bund, looking for what he didn't know. Then he stared harder, trying to interpret what he saw: a line of coolies walking evenly from the Bank of China to an ordinary-looking freighter tied up across from the Cathay Hotel. Electric lanterns hung from the freighter's masts, and in that wide golden circle of light he could see the coolies' dark blue tunics, and the way they stooped from the weight of whatever was in the packages hanging from the bamboo poles they bore on their shoulders. As each coolie crossed the gangplank and reached the freighter's deck, he was relieved of his load, and he methodically turned back toward the Bund.

The scene appeared at once both ordinary and bizarre. The coolies shuffled between the Bank of China and the freighter and back again, and the crew, too, seemed to be following a routine, moving around on the decks of the ship as though departure was imminent. There was no commotion, no shouting or hurrying, nothing but the fact of the middle-of-the-night darkness to signify the unusual. My father wondered if he'd overlooked some obvious explanation for this strange nighttime activity. Perhaps there'd been something in the paper. He glanced around him as though expecting a fellow bystander to explain, but he found only acacias and willows and white poplars leaning toward him, pushed by a woozy breeze from the Whangpoo.

He looked back at the coolies and the freighter, determined to make sense of what he saw, and as he stood motionless next to a monarch birch, he heard the strange rhythmic chant that coolies sing-songed as they worked. He'd heard the sound a thousand times, maybe ten times that. But never at this hour, never after dark, and the sound made the skin on the back of his neck prickle with apprehension.

Somehow the sound made things clear. Suddenly he knew; it was crazy, but here it was, right in front of him, and he let his breath out as he realized what he was seeing. *Chiang's stealing the gold*, he thought, and he shook his head in amazement at the idea and that he had happened to be an eyewitness.

It was a few days before my father's journalist friends could confirm his theory, but they did confirm it: Chiang Kai-shek had robbed the vaults of the Bank of China, taking the gold that belonged to China's citizens, many of them his last Nationalist supporters, to help finance his retirement years in Taiwan. The seemingly ordinary freighter that my father watched that night was crewed by members of the Nationalist navy, men Chiang had carefully chosen. Also aboard were a handful of officials of the Bank of China, who had been bribed with the guarantee of safe passage in return for opening the bank's vaults.

My father was amazed. Even though he'd felt that Chiang had at times acted brazenly since the civil war that had begun only days after Japan's surrender in 1945, this was by far the most appalling of Chiang's actions.

Chiang had lost much in those years. Thousands of Nationalist soldiers had defected to Mao's People's Liberation Army as it moved southward toward the Yangtze River. Chiang had fled first to Fenghwa, the coastal town to the south of Shanghai where he had grown up, and later across the China Sea to the safety of Taiwan. In January of 1949, Peking and Tientsin had fallen to the Communists without a fight, and in that same month Chiang retired. To my father, it seemed that the Communists took control of the country so quickly and easily that it was as though he had glanced up from his desk one day and found China permanently changed.

Although nearly four years had passed since the end of Japanese occupation, life was worse in Shanghai. Once again, it was a dangerous place. The Nationalist government, already corrupt, had become desperate, and a reign of terror had begun as the government tried to retain control of the city. An arrested man was guilty until he could prove his innocence; anyone accused of collaborating with the

Japanese was taken to Bridge House for questioning, which usually lasted until money changed hands.

The city became a place of extremes. The shops on Nanking Road were busy, nightclubs filled. But so were the streets—with garbage, and refugees fleeing the civil war in the north. Most of the trams and buses had long ago broken down, and the ones that did run were packed with people. Traffic was backed up in the streets for blocks, but the police only stood on the corners and talked. Each night hundreds of people died on the streets from cold and starvation. Each morning municipal trucks made their rounds, gathering the bodies.

There was guerrilla activity in Hungjao, and my father found himself anxious and jumpy. Wanting at least the trappings of safety, he began to buy guns, at first a couple of .45's and .38's, and then a few carbines, and finally a small water-cooled machine gun that was a rarity. He had seen only one like it in the city.

By the winter of 1948 another exodus had begun, and my father once again found himself saying good-bye to friends. Foreign firms began closing their offices and either leaving altogether or moving to the safety of Hong Kong, and even foreigners who'd been determined to stay made plans to leave. Some went to Bangkok and Manila and Hong Kong to wait things out; others left with no intention of ever returning, selling the belongings they couldn't take with them to the secondhand dealers on Peking Road.

While those around him packed and booked passage and said their good-byes, my father remained, believing again that the whole thing would blow over. He had guessed wrong with the Japanese, but the idea of China becoming Communist was too far-fetched. The United States would come through, he thought, or Chiang would regain his political strength, and even if those things didn't happen, he couldn't imagine the Chinese people truly embracing communism, a system that seemed to go against their whole way of family-centered life. So he figured he'd wait. He'd keep a low profile—a talent he'd developed to a science—and he'd keep making money. Shanghai was the only place he *could* make money anymore. He'd lost thousands thanks to the Japanese, and now he was making it back, and more. He'd even follow the rules, and in that vein, he got rid of his .45's, his .38's, his carbines, and his water-cooled machine gun, for the government had recently said that citizens had to turn in their guns. He didn't want trouble, but he also didn't want to give those guns to the Nationalists, so he took all of them except a .38, which he thought he could get a license for, put them into a gunnysack, and went out to the small pond in the back corner of the garden. It was late at night and the servants had gone to bed and the grounds were still as he took each gun from the gunnysack and dropped it gently into the water, making certain that it landed where the mud was deep. As he walked back to the house, he felt he'd made a good decision. He'd gotten rid of the guns, for now. He could retrieve them when all this blew over.

While he told friends that he had no desire to leave Shanghai, there was another part to it. Even if he'd wanted to leave, what would be the point? Where would he go? Who would welcome him? Everything he had was in Shanghai now. He'd exiled himself, and there was no going back.

:: :: ::

My father would remember the spring of 1949 as a time of noise. On a cool day in February, he was startled by a disorganized racket of sound that included trumpets and cymbals and drums, and when he went outside, he found some thirty young men in the street, all playing their instruments at the same time, but all seeming to play different songs. The sound was horrible. When he asked the young bandleader who they were and what they were doing, the young man confidently gestured to his band with his baton and replied that they were from the Evening Star High School, and that they were practicing so that they would be able to give the People's Liberation Army a proper welcome when it entered the city. My father suggested they practice elsewhere, but he was told that was not possible, and the noise started up again. And from that night on for the next three months, the band practiced in the street from eight to nine every night. My father routinely closed all the doors and windows of the house, stuffed cotton in his ears, turned the radio on as loud as it would go, trying to ignore the noise outside.

The People's Liberation Army entered Shanghai on the night of May twenty-fourth. On the morning of the twenty-fifth, my father found long lines of People's Liberation Army soldiers in blue-gray uniforms sitting on the curbs. They rested their rifles across their knees as though awaiting instructions and they remained that way until evening, when they retired to camps set up around the city. They refused all offers of food. They were clean and disciplined and in no way threatening. Nationalist troops had surrendered without a struggle, and my father watched from his window as Chiang's troops left the city. The retreat seemed as though it would never end; for two days and one night, soldiers passed in rows of four, row after row after row, leaving the city as fast as they could, seeming to simply disappear.

Two days later, two Communist soldiers knocked on my father's door. They were, the shorter of the two calmly explained, representatives of the People's Liberation Army, and they were speaking with everyone in the neighborhood. If residents were dishonest, the young soldier said, or if they refused to cooperate, there would be trouble. If residents cooperated, all would be well.

"There is no cause for worry," he said carefully. "We are here to protect you. To protect everyone, foreigners and Chinese alike, we're all the same. No need to worry."

My father nodded as he listened, and then he smiled at the boy, for the soldier couldn't have been more than seventeen years old, and the northern dialect he spoke was familiar. "Shantung province?" my father asked in Mandarin.

The soldier looked surprised for a moment, and then he grinned. "Tsingtao," he answered eagerly. Then he asked, "Why do you speak so well?"

My father tapped his chest. "I am China-born, also from Shantung province."

Confusion played over the boy's face and my father laughed. "Not to worry," he said, and he gestured between himself and the two teenagers. "We're neighbors now."

The soldier nodded, apparently relieved. "We will take care of you," he said.

"Then I'm in good hands," my father said, and the two soldiers left. My father squinted against the afternoon sun as he watched them walk down the street toward the next house. These were good boys, he thought, just country boys, clean-cut, orderly. Maybe this would all be all right. There were bound to be changes. His business would no doubt be affected. But if worse came to worse, he'd just shut down his import operation for a while and live out here in Hungjao like a country gentleman, cows and chicks and dogs and all, until Shanghai came to its senses.

:: :: ::

The boy soldier from Shantung was right: there was no need to worry, at the start. The Communist troops were well disciplined, there was no looting, there was no interference with foreigners. Within days, the city looked better. The street cleaners and garbage trucks and traffic policemen came back. Almost overnight, there seemed to be fewer refugees. People's Liberation Army sentries stood at their new posts in the streets, armed but not with bayonets, their bodies relaxed as they calmly regarded the city around them.

The changes, when they came, were gradual. The first had to do with the money changers; the second, with spies.

Because of his currency smuggling, my father had always watched the value of the Chinese yuan closely. In 1949 he watched without much surprise as the yuan fell in value from four dollars to one American dollar, but over that year, it eventually fell to an unprecedented fourteen *million* to one, a plummet that startled even him. U.S. currency was accepted everywhere, and in response to the continuing devaluation, money changers were soon found on every street corner. My father watched with fascination as the value of the yuan changed from hour to hour, and the money changers did a healthy business. In true Shanghai fashion, difficulty gave way to opportunity.

In May, when Shanghai fell to the Communists, the money changers and their constant crowds disappeared. But after a while, when nothing seemed to have changed dramatically, the money changers cautiously reappeared, first one, then a few more as they came out from hiding. Soon they were all back, doing as healthy a business as ever. My father saw this as a good sign: those stories about the ruthlessness of Communist rule seemed untrue. No one bothered the money changers on their street corners. People's Liberation Army sentries watched them calmly and said nothing. Within several weeks, the money changers were thriving, a stall on every corner.

Then, overnight, they all vanished. Even their stalls were gone. The government had simply waited until all of them could be arrested at once, then eliminated the whole business overnight.

Weeks later, my father saw another change, a sign on the front of the Central Police Station on Foochow Road: SPIES REGISTER HERE, it read, in characters three feet high. My father didn't know what it meant. No one did, and soon the message was appearing all over the city, on police stations, on walls, and in the press as well, where citizens were urged to rid the city of its spies.

My father watched warily as the government's control of daily life spread. Private schools were taken over, businesses were investigated, their assets appropriated. Foreign firms were given the choice of leaving or being taken over by the government. Communist officials began to take a closer look at the businesses of foreigners like my father. *What had he been trading?* they wanted to know. *What had he been selling?* What he'd been doing was buying goods from elsewhere for as little as possible and selling them for a profit. The Communists said he was exploiting the Chinese people, but for reasons he did not question, they left him alone. But he did not count on more good luck. The next week he locked up the house in Hungjao, stored the few valuables he cared about in his office, and moved to a small apartment in town.

The city began to change dramatically. Communist propaganda was posted everywhere, and in every school and factory, in every office and business, daily meetings were held so that Shanghai's citizens could publicly confess and renounce their sins—and inform on those who were in any way antagonistic to the state. Brothers informed on brothers, fathers on sons, and anyone suspected of being a capitalist was arrested. A man could be arrested, charged, and imprisoned or executed all on the basis of his neighbor's word. Mass trials were held at the former Race Course. Huge crowds turned out, tens of thousands of people all facing a makeshift stage. The trial was broadcast over loudspeakers to those present, and over the radio as well, and work stopped all over the city as citizens were compelled to listen. Accused criminals were paraded through the city wearing dunce caps, then led to the stage where witnesses could testify to the crimes committed. When the evidence had been presented, the crowd was asked what should be done. *He is guilty,* came the expected response. *Kill him!* And the accused was "liquidated" with a bullet to the back of his head.

My father watched as the city turned into a place of fear. There were so many suicides from tall buildings that the government posted anti-suicide guards, for the bodies falling from the tops of buildings had become a public menace. Hospitals were filled with people who'd been hit by those plummeting to their deaths from above.

The *President Jackson* arrived and departed and after that there were no more official passenger ships. My father found that his life had changed again. There wasn't much of a social life for foreign residents. There were fewer and fewer left, for one thing, and second, many of his clubs and favorite haunts had closed. The Shanghai Club was turned into a seamen's restaurant and hostel, with pictures of Mao Tse-tung and Chou En-lai covering the walls. The Country Club became a government school. Names that hinted at foreign rule were changed: Avenue Edouard VII in the former French Concession became Yenan Road, and Broadway Mansions, where my father and I had looked out at the Bund so long ago, became Shanghai Mansions.

:: :: ::

On April 27, 1951, the government made its most dramatic move yet: twenty thousand people were rounded up and arrested overnight, among them my father. At two o'clock in the morning, he woke to the sound of car doors closing outside of his apartment. When he walked to the window and looked out, he saw two Jeeps parked in the street.

He opened the door before they knocked, and he faced four armed police from the Public Security Bureau. They wore padded blue uniforms and carried Luger pistols, which they used to prod and threaten him as they told him that he was accused of being a spy and that he was to come with them.

My father was tense but managed to stay calm. People were being "taken in" all the time, in such great numbers and with such frequency that it was possible to think it would not amount to much. Maybe it was a formality.

He was told he could get dressed, and that he could bring some clothes and a blanket—not a good sign, he thought. He packed four

shirts and a pair of trousers and as many socks and as much underwear as he could find, and he pulled on khaki pants and a blue Oxford
cloth button-down shirt that he'd recently bought for good luck.

When he was ready, one of the guards put some ancient handcuffs
on him and they led him outside, where he was shoved into the backseat of an American car. They drove to Foochow Road and stopped
at the Central Police Station, only a few blocks from his office. There
he was strip-searched and his belongings—including his belt and
shoelaces, lest he consider suicide—were taken from him and put in
an envelope with a number on it in thick black letters. When he had
dressed again, he was taken upstairs and locked inside a small room
with a guard just outside the door. As he walked, he had to hold up his
pants, and his shoes flapped with his steps. Once in his cell, he did not
allow himself to consider his situation very thoroughly. There were
too many grim possibilities, so he just paced for a while, expecting
he'd shortly be taken someplace else for questioning. *And then everything will be cleared up*, he thought. *I've done nothing wrong.*

But the night wore on, and the day after that and after that and
after that. Two weeks passed, almost three, and he was simply kept
in that room. He was never questioned, he was never charged with
any crime. He was just kept there and watched, as he grew more and
more nervous. He was fed rice every day, either in soup or in a solid
form that was like a salty doughnut, and he tried to act calm, knowing that he was in a waiting game, and that his jailers were watching
his reaction. Although his outward appearance did not communicate
his nervousness, his body did. His bowels stopped functioning, and to
the amusement and amazement of the guards, he did not eliminate
in all those days. The guards laughed and shook their heads at first,
but their amusement grew to suspicion. *What's the matter with this
guy?* he heard them say. *What's going on?* Then he heard the reason
for their interest: the week before, a teenage boy had refused to go to
the bathroom for a week. The boy finally became ill, and when he

was taken to the hospital, the examining doctor found a ten-ounce gold bar concealed in his rectum. My father shook his head when the guard told him the story. "No gold," my father said grimly. "Just fear."

At the end of three weeks, my father was taken downstairs into what seemed to be a holding area, a room twenty feet long and fifteen feet wide. When he'd gotten his bearings, he counted and found that, including him, the room held forty-three people. As in Bridge House eight years earlier, the stench in the place was horrible, and fleas and lice covered everything. A bucket in the corner served as the toilet. When night came, he found that he could not lie on his back, but was forced to lie on his side, fitted against other prisoners like spoons. If one person needed to turn over, the whole row had to do likewise. When five days had passed and yet another man was brought in, my father saw that those on the floor were the lucky ones, for the new prisoner was forced to sit on the waste bucket all night, sleeping if he could.

My father was held in that room for sixty-one days; he kept track by making tiny marks on the wall behind him, close to the floor so that the guards wouldn't see. He guessed it was around June thirtieth when a guard called the name Joseph Schoene and told him to come. He wasn't allowed to gather his few belongings, a fact he chose to view as a sign that he was being released. As he stood and followed the guard, he was relieved that at least something was finally happening.

That relief was short-lived. A guard pulled a gunnysack over my father's head, then led him outside and pushed him into a Jeep. They took the sack off. He was told to keep his head down during the ride, and as he stared at the Jeep's dirty floor, his head pushed down between his knees by the guard's rifle across the back of his neck, he tried to picture Shanghai's streets and where he might be. But he couldn't; all he could do was try to stay calm.

The car jerked to a stop, and when he was pulled out of the back-seat, he knew immediately where he was because of the trees. He was in the French Concession, on what had been known as Route Joseph Frelupt, and he was being pushed toward the entrance of Loukawei Jail.

Inside he was handed an armband, which he was told never to remove. It was, the guard said, his new identity: #744. He was then led to a block of twelve cells, each of them no larger than twelve feet by six. He was pushed into the last one and told that talking was not allowed, and that other rules for criminals were posted on the wall. Criminals were to spend all of their waking hours, five in the morning until nine at night, meditating on their crimes, it said. They were not to sleep during that time. They were to sit where the guard told them to, on the floor with their backs to the wall, and they were not to move from that position. There would be no reading, and there was no smoking. They would stand at attention for their guards.

The guard left and slammed the wooden door and my father sank to the floor as he was told, his back against the wall. The smell of filth and human waste in the room was overpowering, and he forced himself to think about other things so that he would not vomit. He had taught himself the art of intellectual diversion during those two months at Foochow Road, and he had convinced himself that that one skill would help him survive.

The trick was to think about places other than where he was, and so he thought of the beaches of Tsingtao, and of my mother swimming in the bay. He thought of a polo game in which he'd played particularly well. He thought of the Bund, and he forced himself to name each building from the British Consulate down to the Shanghai Club. He pictured the beautiful tree-lined boulevards of the French Concession, which, though they were just outside the window, seemed like streets from a distant land, and he tried to remember the taste of blini with caviar at the St. Petersburg restaurant on Avenue Haig.

Replace this stench with the scent of eucalyptus after the rain, he thought. Replace the coldness of sitting on this floor with the solid grace of riding a polo pony. Replace the sight of men dying in front of him with the view of a bungalow's small garden in Southern California: wisteria, jasmine, honeysuckle, junipers, and a fourteen-year-old daughter cutting roses.

Those substitutions he could do. The difficult part was the feeling at his very center: a tight knot of fear that he did not know how to dispel.

:: :: ::

My father was a prisoner of the Communists from that April night of 1951 until January of 1954. During those three years, he was moved three times, from Foochow Road to Loukawei in the French Concession, and then to Chopay, a prison constructed recently though poorly by the Communists. The ventilation was poor, and the door had a small peephole so that the guards could watch prisoners constantly. And finally he was taken to the northeast of the city, across Soochow Creek to Ward Road Jail, the same jail in which hundreds had been tortured and killed by the Japanese ten years earlier.

Ward Road Jail had been built by the British and was said to be the largest prison in the world outside of Russia. Its walls were six inches thick, and it included eight buildings that held some four thousand cells, and at its height, the jail held fifteen thousand people. Each cell had a leader, a prisoner who was well versed in Communist doctrine and whose responsibility it was to discuss the failings of other governments. Prisoners could ask questions, but most refrained, for it was obvious that anything remotely anticommunist would lead to trouble. In addition to the leader, there were always spies, prisoners who had agreed to tell the guards of anyone who seemed antagonistic toward Mao. They were usually fairly outspoken in support of the government, and though my father guessed that he could usually tell who they were, he never knew for sure. And so he kept quiet, and mostly listened, nodding silently as though he agreed with whatever was being said.

My father thought of his cell as "the international quarter." There were eighteen men, and he was the only American—the guards made a point of keeping the Americans apart. Among those in his cell was an Irish priest, Father Aidan McKenna, a small, fierce man with close-cropped reddish-brown hair and intense blue eyes who had worn out more than a dozen interrogators because he refused to say or sign anything. He had worked with the Legion of Mary, a Catholic lay group that the Communists insisted was an American spy organization financed by the United States government, and he was accused of being a false priest and a spy with the rank of colonel in the American army. The priest denied the charges but said he was complimented by his imaginary high rank. Although his obstinance made him a frequent target of the guards' anger, they could not wear him down. He told my father he'd only denied his charges more resolutely, and prayed his matchstick rosary more fervently, and kept track more carefully of the number of days since he'd received the Body and Blood of Christ in the Eucharist.

There was Martin, a withdrawn Frenchman who had been a bookkeeper at Jardine Matheson, and Senna, an earnest Portuguese man who had tuberculosis that eventually killed him, and whom the guards forced to sit on the waste bucket in the corner. There was Muto, a Gypsy, small and thin and dark-complexioned, with bright eyes and a quick mind, who said his mother taught him to steal a chicken, his father a horse. He shared his bread with my father on the night my father was brought to Ward Road. It was a risk: giving anything to another prisoner, whether it was soap or food or clothing, was forbidden. Iritz was Hungarian and married to Muto's sister, which was a puzzle: she wasn't over twenty, and he was fifty-five, divorced a couple of times, short and bald with thick glasses. He received money from his family each month which he could use for toilet articles and vitamins, and he arrived with a large bundle of clean clothes—quite a status symbol at Ward Road. He was later allowed a cell to himself, all of which told the others that he was an informer. He was a con man known for double-crossing on the outside, and in Ward Road Jail, prisoners kept their distance.

There were two Russians, brothers, one married to a Russian, the other to a Chinese woman, both of them well known for crooked business in Shanghai. They'd worked with the Japanese during the occupation, and now they were gangster types. They did a lot of strong-arm stuff, holding people up and threatening them if they didn't pay protection money. The Chinese wife committed suicide while they were in prison. The older brother went blind from illness and malnutrition, with the Communists all the while telling him he was faking it.

The others my father didn't know as much about. They kept to themselves, and no one bothered them. The eighteen of them slept close together, lying alternately head to foot in order to keep warm. They didn't talk much until Iritz had been moved out and they were certain they could trust each other. Sometimes they were allowed to shower and wash their clothes once a month, but there was no guarantee; they could go for as long as four months without bathing. They killed the lice with their teeth as dogs do, and they mashed stink bugs and bedbugs with their fists. When there were too many blood marks on the walls, the guards gave them small pieces of glass to scrape the walls with, and told them there was to be no more mashing of bedbugs. The cockroaches were less of a problem. The Chinese prisoners killed them and ate them for nourishment.

They ate what they were given—potatoes, or pickled cabbage, once some seaweed, occasionally a soup made from a cow's head, with eyes floating in the broth and with spices added so that at least it had some taste to it. There was *ta t'ou ts'ai*—nobody knew the English name—a kind of bamboo shoot but with the taste of chopped-up wood. Father McKenna let it be known that he hated the stuff, and for that he was given it and nothing else two times a day for six weeks straight. For the rest of them, there was always rice in one form or another, though they had to be careful of the small white rocks that were added and that could break your teeth because you were ordered to eat as fast as you could. There was congee, which was rice in hot water, maybe with a few limp string beans, or hard rice, which had been steamed at some point but was cold by the time they got it, or thin rice, which was soup, and which was what my father always chose because sometimes it was warm. Iritz often got *mant'ou*, Chinese steamed bread, heavier and more nourishing than regular bread. And there was always garlic, which they were given as a preventative for stomach worms.

They were fed twice a day, and between meals they sat cross-legged and immobile on the concrete floor. Scabies were common, and some rear ends were just raw flesh. Sometimes a man would get down on his knees and beg the guards to let him change positions—*Just don't make me sit down*—but their requests were always refused. There was nothing to read except for a couple of Communist magazines and an old *Reader's Digest*—nobody knew how it got there, but most of them knew it almost by heart. If they didn't make too much noise, they could talk.

There was almost no news of the outside world. Father McKenna knew a little because the Catholic priests scratched Latin phrases to each other on the lacquer-painted waste buckets, which were collected and washed out and redistributed every day. The guards didn't recognize the Latin as anything meaningful. There were no calendars, there were no clocks, but prisoners learned other ways to keep track of time. A crack of dim sunlight traveling across the floor and ceiling told the time of day. The summer heat brought prickly heat and boils; in the winter, hundreds died from the cold.

Firecrackers in winter meant Chinese New Year, and that meant late January.

On a warm April morning as they ate cold rice, Father McKenna leaned close to my father. "Joseph," he whispered, "today is the first Sunday after the first full moon following the vernal equinox."

My father regarded the priest carefully, wondering if he was beginning to lose his wits.

Father McKenna grinned at his confusion. "Joseph, give thanks," he whispered, and there was urgency in his voice.

"Give thanks for what?"

The priest looked genuinely surprised, as though the answer to the question were obvious. "Why, it's Easter, Joseph. The Lord is risen. And we're alive. That's a start."

My father nodded and then was quiet for a moment, and he did give thanks, for in those months at Ward Road, he had experienced the beginning of change. There was no wife and daughter waiting for his release this time; there was only an ex-wife and an estranged daughter, they were an ocean away, and chances were they didn't even know of his imprisonment. He'd lost everything, he figured, and he'd finally started to try to find something inside, something to hold on to.

He gazed at the priest for a long moment and saw strength and affection in the older man's eyes. And then he joked, "What did you give up for Lent?"

For a moment, Father McKenna looked stunned—what was there to give up? He shook his head and the two of them laughed out loud for the first time in months.

A guard looked in and yelled to be quiet, and Father McKenna seemed to catch his attention.

"You," the guard said, "where does that food you are eating come from?"

The priest did not look up. "It comes from God," he said simply.

The guard's face turned red and he glared down at Father McKenna. "Your food," he said, "is from the blood and sweat of the Chinese people," and he bullied and harangued the priest for more than an hour as the others in the cell sat silently. But when he'd finished yelling, he still wasn't satisfied, and he bound the priest's arms with tourniquets and forced him to kneel. "Your God got you into this, now let Him get you out of it," he said.

Father McKenna was undaunted. "To be a priest is to suffer," he said evenly, "for a priest is an *alter Christus*."

The guard left him like that, bound and kneeling, for the rest of the day. When Father McKenna was released that evening, he nodded at the guard. "Thank you," he said, "for allowing me to kneel before my Lord for a while."

The guard stared at Father McKenna for a long minute. Then he whispered, *"Súti"*—We are enemies until death—and he left the cell. They did not see him again.

:: :: ::

The sounds of the place were eerie, too strange to ever become routine. Because of the way the buildings were built, the acoustics were like those of a concert hall. There were more than two thousand men in each block, and every one of them could hear everything that went on in the building, even just one man talking in a normal voice. On a winter afternoon when the rain nagged at the windows and ceiling and walls, they were waiting for their second meal, and except for the rain, the whole place was silent. And then they heard the old Buddhist at the other end of the hall say, "Waiter, bring me twenty ravioli, will you?" and the place was filled with the unfamiliar sound of laughter.

At night there were whistles that told them what to do. The first whistle meant get ready for bed, and the prisoners would unroll their blankets or whatever they had. The second whistle meant get in bed, and the third whistle meant lights out. When the place fell into darkness, there was an ocean of voices that heaved one huge sigh, a sound of fatigue and despair and pain. And then the music would start, the guards playing one of the two records they had, either Artie Shaw's "Lady Be Good" or a somber piece by a German orchestra—no one ever knew its name.

Late in the night on the second Christmas Eve, the solid silence of the place was broken by someone's beautiful singing of "O Holy Night," and my father recognized the rich voice and strong New Orleans accent, and he lay in his cell and listened in awe. The man's deep voice echoed through the corridors and cells, and my father thought he even felt its vibration inside of him. *Fall on your knees, oh hear the angels' voices, Oh night divine, oh night when Christ was born.* My father listened as though the sound could save him.

The man singing was Mitch Patten, my father was sure. He'd run the Shanghai office of J. T. Edwards Ltd., cotton controllers of Boston, and my father had known him through business and seen him at parties. Both of them were man-about-town types. Mitch was young, only twenty-eight, and tall and handsome, over six feet, an extrovert who loved a party and a good time. On a warm night some months later, my father heard Mitch's voice again, this time against a backdrop of commotion: the sounds of someone thrashing about, the banging of metal against the walls, the sound of Mitch's voice as he wept and yelled. The place was silent as everyone listened unwillingly to his collapse, and then to the sound of the guards trying to subdue him. But he finally just wore himself out, and my father listened to the sound of Mitch's cell being unlocked as he was taken from it, then the sounds of footsteps as Mitch was led down the hall and finally chained to the bars of my father's cell, where he collapsed on the hallway floor, weeping. "Some American company for you," the guard whispered, and then they'd left Mitch there for the night. As my father listened to him weep, he repeated a Cantonese phrase that Father McKenna used often: *Pu yao pa, pu yao pa.* Do not be afraid.

In the morning Mitch was taken away, and there were only whispered rumors about how everything had been so sudden, and how he'd torn his clothes and thrown his waste bucket and smeared excrement on the wall. My father did not speak for four days afterward.

:: :: ::

Like all prisoners, my father was given paper and pencil and told to think over what he had done with his life, and to then write his confession, which was to include where he had gone wrong. *T'anpai*, the guards said over and over again, *t'anpai!*, confess! He was also to write his complete life history, a detailed account of the events of his life since the age of six. The questions to be answered were extensive and detailed: What is your age, your place of birth? Who are your parents, your siblings? What are their occupations? What schools have you attended, what courses did you take? When did you arrive in China, and what places have you visited? Do you have guns at home? To what political party do you belong? Do you know President Truman? Do you own land? What are your attitudes toward the officials of the People's Republic of China?

When he'd answered all the questions, the completed forms were carefully folded and taken away, and my father never saw them again. And then he was asked to write it all again, and again after that, a total of five times in the course of his imprisonment.

He, like hundreds of others, was accused of being a spy. More than that he didn't know, until late one winter's night in 1953 when a guard called his name and unlocked the heavy steel door, then told him to come along. He led my father down the dimly lit passageway and then downstairs into what felt like a dungeon, further down than he'd ever been before. His legs were stiff and cramped from confinement and inactivity, and he shuffled as he walked.

He was taken to a small room at the end of a corridor. The sign on the door said COMMANDANT. The guard knocked and was told to enter, and when my father followed him into the room, he found the warden of the jail, Colonel Wang. He was sitting at his desk, smoking a long tailored cigarette. Next to him was a simple table covered with a red cloth, where a Chinese girl sat at a typewriter. On his other side was a guard whose eyes were closed, and my father wondered if he was sleeping. *As well he should be*, my father thought, for he guessed it was the middle of the night. The jail was eerily silent.

The guard motioned for my father to be seated on a hard wooden chair that had been placed directly in front of the colonel's desk. He did as he was told, and the guard trained a bright light across his face. And then the colonel began to speak.

He addressed my father by his Chinese name, and he smiled broadly as though they were old friends. My father bowed, as he was required to, and the colonel nodded. "Such good manners! And from an American!"

My father said nothing, waiting.

"We have something to talk about, but first you need food, do you not?" The colonel stared at my father for a moment, and he nodded. "I see that you do," the colonel said, and he motioned to the guard, who handed my father a bowl.

My father stared at the bowl and saw that it held an egg. He had had very little protein for months, and he had to resist the urge to crack the egg and wolf it down on the spot. But he didn't want the colonel to have that pleasure, so he said casually, "Thank you."

The colonel smiled again. "Go ahead. Eat. You will need your strength. And protein is good for the mind."

My father cracked the egg open and stared for a moment. There was a chick inside, pin feathers and all, and for a moment he thought he might be sick. He glanced at Colonel Wang and saw how carefully his reaction was being watched and enjoyed. It was all a test, or a dare, just a trick to see what he'd do. And so he did the most unpredictable thing he could think of: he ate the chick. At least there would be protein.

Colonel Wang grinned and nodded his approval. "A tough one," he said. "China-born is a tough one all right," he said. "Now, to our business, China-born. We have information that you have firearms at your house. You have refused to confess thus far; now we will make you confess. What about it?"

My father worked to keep his voice calm as he answered. "I have no illegal firearms," he said. "The only firearm I have is a thirty-eight, which you gave me permission to have. I have a license for that, and I was keeping it only to protect myself. You know how the city is these days."

Colonel Wang shook his head. "No," he said, "you have plenty of firearms. You've got guns all over your place, you have ammunition in your house. We have found everything."

My father said, "I don't have guns. If I do, you can shoot me."

Colonel Wang looked up and narrowed his eyes at my father, assessing him. "Do you mean that?"

"Yes."

The colonel smiled and seemed pleased. "You think you can outsmart the people of China. You cannot. We know far too much. Let me illustrate. You are an expert polo player. You know a great deal about gardening. Though you are right-handed, you prefer to deal cards with your left hand. You call your former wife Eve, though she is known to everyone else as Genevieve."

My father blanched at the colonel's accuracy, but the colonel waved his reaction away. "But none of that is important just now. What's important is this," and he motioned to the guard and said, "Bring it in."

The guard left the room for a moment. When he returned, he carried a basket full of firearms. On the top was the water-cooled machine gun.

My father was startled, but he looked at the colonel and said, "Yes, those are my guns. But they weren't in my house. Everybody within five miles of my place knows I threw those guns into the pond."

"No," Colonel Wang said evenly, his tone scolding. "They were all over your house."

"I threw them into the pond when the Nationalists came, long before you were here."

Colonel Wang was still shaking his head. "China-born," he said calmly, "do they look as though they have sat in mud?"

My father took a breath. "It is well known that I destroyed those guns."

Colonel Wang leaned toward my father slightly. "So you think they are destroyed?"

"I'm certain of it."

"You will allow me to fire one at you?"

My father froze as the colonel pulled out a chrome-plated Remington .45. It looked like new. "If this gun has been sitting at the bottom of a pond for years, I am most surprised," he said coyly.

"The only gun I had was a thirty-eight. That's what I have told you. I have nothing to add."

Colonel Wang aimed the gun at my father for a long moment. My father stood motionless, staring at the desk. He thought of Hungjao, and of the huge plane tree he had planted. He thought of the way my mother looked when she was getting ready for bed as she undid her hair and let it fall down her back. He thought of watching me sleep when I was small. And then he closed his eyes.

A minute passed. One of the guards shifted and stifled a yawn. Suddenly the colonel laughed, and he motioned to the guard. "Take him," he said, pointing the gun at my father once more. And he placed the gun back in the basket.

The guard led my father back up the stairs, prodding him with his gun. My father concentrated on not tripping on the stairs—his knees shook, and the sweat that had soaked him had made his thin shirt cold and wet on his back.

"You're pretty lucky guy," the guard said.

"How's that?" my father answered, trying to catch his breath.

The guard laughed. "Looks like no execution for you after all. Not tonight anyway. Lucky, lucky guy."

:: :: ::

His eyesight diminished, his legs weakened, he suffered from dysentery and he lost weight, going from a solid and barrel-chested two hundred pounds to a skeletal one hundred and thirty. Because he always chose thin rice for warmth, he became severely deficient in vitamin B, which led to beriberi, an illness of the nervous system. It started as a strange relaxed feeling in his legs, the sensation almost pleasant, and it grew to numbness and swelling and then to stabbing pain that made him cry out for the guards, annoying them so much that they placed him in solitary confinement, an octagonal cell six feet across and fifteen feet high. There was a small peephole in the door, and no vent or window. The floor was covered with a leather mat, the walls with leather mattresses, and when he entered the place, the crazy scratching on the walls told him that men had lost their minds in that room. He was allowed no change of clothing, no bathing, and given no water to wash his face. There was no waste bucket; he was given ashes to cover his excrement. But, the guards said, he could move and use his legs in there, and maybe that was what he needed.

It wasn't. His condition only grew worse. And now he was alone.

The trustee who brought him his food was a Russian named Nikolai Petrovich, an old man with cataract-blurred eyes who smelled of cigarettes and something more pungent, and who always spoke of himself in the plural. On one of my father's first days in the jail, Nikolai had admired my father's heavy wool sweater. Even the opportunity to bribe a trustee was a godsend, and my father took the hint and handed the sweater over, hoping that it would someday help. It did. Nikolai took a liking to my father—"We think you're not so bad," he confided—and he did small favors for him. A little extra rice, an occasional cup of strong tea, an old pair of socks that Nikolai found in an empty cell, which my father used as mittens. My father viewed him as a future investment, the only one he had.

On a rainy morning when my father had been in solitary for what he guessed was several months, Nikolai was unusually talkative and my father asked the favor he had been pondering.

"You know that priest? Father McKenna?"

Nikolai grunted and regarded my father coolly. "We know him," he said. "*Shēnfu*," he added, spiritual father, Mandarin for priest.

"Will you give him something for me?"

Nikolai hesitated and my father said nothing, waiting. Finally Nikolai shrugged, and my father opened his hand. Nikolai nodded and took the scrap of toilet paper and read my father's message without hesitating: *Father, I am in despair. Can you give me something to fill the black hole of my thoughts?*

Nikolai smirked at first, but then he refolded the paper and nodded. "We'll see what we can do."

A few nights later, my father woke in the middle of the night. At first he thought the cold had woken him. He found the old socks he used as mittens and pulled them over his freezing fingers, then breathed on his hands to try to warm them. And then he heard it, and he knew it was not the cold, but the sound of people that had woken him.

A huge crowd seemed to be leaving a concert hall or theater, and it seemed as though they were just outside in the small courtyard below that was used as an execution ground. The noise was tremendous, hundreds of muffled voices leaving and passing below and then into the night, and my father listened with awe and fear and amazement and even longing at the sound of so many voices, and he covered his mouth with his hands to keep from calling out.

In the morning he chalked it up to a dream. He had dreamed far stranger things; this one had just seemed more real.

But that night he heard the sound of the crowd again. He heard it again the next night, too, and the night after that and after that, for five nights in a row. He had no explanation for what the sound was, but although it frightened him and he wanted a simple answer, he kept his question to himself. The guards were never there to ask anyway; on those nights they seemed to go to the other side of the building.

Then, on the sixth night, the sound was tremendous, like a thousand people passing by. There seemed to be a leader as well, someone wearing wooden clogs whose footsteps clickety-clacked on the brick courtyard below. The leader was shouting some sort of commands that my father did not understand. And then, slowly, the sound died out.

The next morning when Nikolai brought my father's rice, he was agitated and anxious, and as he handed the bowl to my father, he motioned for my father to come closer. The clothes he wore came from other prisoners: my father's sweater, someone else's shoes, Martin's gloves, Muto's wool cap. Nikolai leaned close to my father and his eyes were wild. "Did you hear it?" he whispered.

My father regarded him carefully, wondering how to answer. Nothing was straightforward anymore. He'd already decided that he was probably losing his mind, and because he could see no benefit in making his loss known, he only shrugged.

Nikolai nodded. "You did," he said. "I can see it in your face. You heard it every night, didn't you?"

My father nodded tentatively and Nikolai looked satisfied for a moment. Then fear shaded his face, and he leaned closer. "It is the spirits of the dead, passing through."

My father shook his head.

Nikolai's expression didn't change. "You don't know of the executions? A thousand every day last week."

My father searched his face for contradiction. "Impossible," he said.

Nikolai's eyes filled and he shook his head. "No," he said. "Anything is possible in these times. There is no limit to what is now possible."

My father nodded, and Nikolai whispered, "We're afraid, all of us," and then he stuck his hand out. "Here. From your *shēnfu.*" He handed my father a scrap of folded toilet paper. And then he was gone.

My father walked slowly to the corner of his cell. With effort, he sat down and leaned against the wall and closed his eyes.

He agreed with Nikolai: the limits were gone. A thousand a day executed in Shanghai. *Seven thousand last week.* Impossible to comprehend. Had the Chinese authorities gone mad? Hard to tell in here, because the limits here were gone, too. The limit to how hungry you could be, and how weak, and how discouraged, and how sick. The limit to how hopeless you could feel, and, if you let all of that sink in, there was no limit to your despair. He was forty-seven years old but felt far older. He suspected he'd been at Ward Road for two and a half years, but he'd lost track. He weighed eighty-five pounds and was nearly paralyzed from the waist down. He had not slept through the night since his imprisonment.

He took the scrap of toilet paper that Nikolai had given him and smoothed it across his thigh, which he knew was the size of a healthy man's upper arm. He could see that there were marks on the rough paper, but he couldn't read them, and the fact almost made him weep, for it felt like a great loss. He held the paper up to where the most light made it into his cell, and he tried to read again, and as he peered hard, he made out careful handwriting. And then, with work, he made out Father McKenna's words: *Joseph, Do not be afraid—He will not let your foot slip. Think of the Beatitudes: Blessed are the poor in spirit, for theirs is the kingdom of heaven. Blessed are the meek of heart, for they shall inherit the earth.*

headlines

IN THE SPRING OF 1952, when I was finishing my junior year at UCLA, my mother and I learned of my father's imprisonment. We did so courtesy of *Life* magazine, which, in its issue of May 19, included an article on Americans who were being held captive in Red China. My mother called me to tell me about it, saying that she had feared as much but had kept her worries to herself. When I'd hung up the phone on the second floor of the dormitory, I hurried through campus toward Westwood Boulevard. At Janss Drugstore, I placed the magazine on the counter and handed over my twenty cents, then hurried back to the dorm with the magazine as though it held shameful news, something that no one should see.

In my room, I sat on my bed, the magazine in front of me. On the cover was a photograph of the French-Arabian actress Kerima, the starlet from *Outcast of the Islands*, who said she was "une femme sans homme . . . My heart does not make boom boom for anyone." I turned to the table of contents and found the article I was looking for—"Red China's Captive Americans"—and my hands shook as I turned to page fifty-one, where I found before-and-after photographs of Father Robert W. Greene, a forty-year-old Maryknoll priest who had recently been released from Communist prison. "One betrayed and tortured priest is freed, but many more U.S. citizens remain Communist prisoners," the article said, and on the following page were the photographs of some fourteen Americans listed as dead or under house arrest. I scanned them and did not find my father, and I turned the page again. This time the heading read AMERICANS ACTUALLY IN JAIL, SOME FOR MORE THAN A YEAR. Facing me were the photographs of some thirty-six Americans, almost all men. And there, in the fifth row, second from the left, I found him: *Joseph Schoene, Shanghai businessman, imprisoned April 1951.*

I stared at it hard. It was a photograph I knew, for I had been present when it was taken. It was in September of 1946, during the few weeks that my mother and I were in Shanghai, on one of the only afternoons I had spent alone with my father. We had eaten long-life noodles for lunch—"just like old times," he'd said—then we'd gone to his office, and after that we'd walked along Nanking Road. The afternoon should have been nostalgic and even sentimental, but it was neither. It just felt like my father was killing time for those few hours. He was distracted and I had the feeling I was keeping him from something. He had said he needed a new photograph for business reasons, and our last stop had been at a photographer's studio, where I stood behind the camera and watched as my father posed and talked with the photographer. When they'd finished, he winked at me and awkwardly tweaked my cheek, as though I were much younger than I was. "I'll save one for you if they're any good," he said, and I tried to smile, wanting to ask if we could have a photograph of us together, but not having the nerve.

Here was that same photograph, my father looking young and handsome and distinguished. He was surrounded by thirty-five strangers. Four were businessmen, one an explorer. The rest were clergy, Lutheran and Presbyterian and Church of Christ and Methodist missionaries, a Maryknoll sister, Jesuit and Vincentian and Passionist and Franciscan priests. For a long time, I just sat there, stunned, the magazine spread out in front me. It was one thing to think that my father was in Shanghai living it up; it was quite another to know that he was in prison, that his future was uncertain, and that there was nothing anyone could do about it.

When my roommate finally came in an hour later, I was still sitting there. She glanced at me and then stood still, staring. "What is it?" she said. "You look horrible."

"Nothing," I said, and I closed the magazine and slipped it between my books. "I think I've got the flu." I picked up my books and grabbed my sweater. "I'm going to the library," I said, and when she called after me, I did not answer.

I told no one, but carried my father's imprisonment with me like an awful secret. Every morning when I woke, I remembered it again and had to think through it as though it were new news. It gave me nightmares. It stayed with me wherever I went and forced me to think about him more than I had in years, and I found that all my years of trying to teach myself not to care about him had backfired. Now that I was older, I missed him more than ever. And despite the anger and hurt, I loved him intensely. I read the article in *Life* more times than I could keep track of, never mind the fact that it didn't mention anything remotely specific about my father, and the faces in those photographs grew familiar from my late-night examinations of them. At Mass I prayed that God would be with them.

Not even my mother and I talked about my father's imprisonment. I didn't know what her reasons were; mine were the same as always, that talking about him only made things worse. But that was business as usual between the two of us, for by then we hardly spoke of my father at all. He had become like a distant relative, a man we never mentioned, not on good days or bad, on Christmas or Easter or birthdays, not even when my mother received her quarterly check from my father's agent in New York. My father was not mentioned when Jack and I announced our engagement in February, or when I graduated from college in June of 1953, or two weeks after that, when Jack and I were married at Holy Family Church. My father, I explained matter-of-factly to my future parents-in-law, was no longer part of my life, and no longer the recipient of my affection. On that beautifully still summer morning, it was Jack's father who walked me down the aisle, first past friends and then past my mother and grand-mother, and finally to Jack, standing at the front of the church and looking intense and certain and determined until he saw me, and then he just looked happy. I felt as though I had come home from a long and arduous journey, and although at times I felt suspicious that I'd found someone I loved so early and so easily, in the end, I stopped worrying and let myself do what I really wanted to do: to be with Jack.

:: :: ::

In the fall, Jack would begin teaching history at Flintridge Prepara-tory School for boys, and over the summer he helped coach the Flint-ridge cross-country team in the afternoons, and did odd jobs to pay the bills—he mowed lawns, he painted houses, he trimmed hedges, whatever he could find. I started a part-time job at the Huntington Library in San Marino, where I cataloged manuscripts, a job for which I was well suited and one that probably saved me for a while because it forced me to think of things besides my father. It was the most orderly activity I'd ever imagined. I was given a box of turn-of-the-century letters that described early California and one of the state's first important families, the Arguellos. It was my job to read each let-ter, make a folder for it from light blue, acid-free paper, and then, on the front of the folder and in legible script with a number two pencil, to note the date of the letter, the author, the addressee, and any his-torical details mentioned in the letter. My days were spent in near silence, and by the end of the afternoon, after reading letter after letter, I felt as though I'd been living in Spanish California, and I had to remind myself what day it was when I carefully put everything away at five o'clock.

Jack and I rented a small garage apartment on Monterey Road in South Pasadena, only a few blocks from my grandmother and mother, a fact I later came to appreciate. We furnished it with odds and ends from secondhand stores, an eclectic mix at best, and when we moved in during the second week of July, the apartment was still nearly empty.

The rest of that summer we were like teenagers with no parents, doing whatever we liked. Jack cut his chestnut brown hair very short and he looked like a kid, especially when he was asleep, which was when I liked to watch him and consider my good luck. We played miniature golf at Arroyo Seco and walked to Gus's Barbeque on Fair Oaks and then to the Rialto, where we saw *Casino Royale*, *Roman Holiday*, *Gentlemen Prefer Blondes*. We played bridge with friends and watched TV–*Playhouse 90*, *Your Hit Parade*, *Ed Sullivan's Toast of the Town*. On Friday nights we stayed up late for Steve Allen on the *Tonight Show*. Jack's one indulgence was buying records, which he did every chance he got. A record was barely in the stores before he brought it home. He was a romantic through and through, and all that summer, we listened to Frank Sinatra and Bing Crosby, Perry Como and Rosemary Clooney, and we danced in our stocking feet in our barely furnished home.

In the fall Jack started teaching and my job at the Huntington was extended to full time. The weather finally turned cool in mid-October, the prettiest fall I'd ever seen, with beautiful clear days and nights, and all of Los Angeles was a place I never wanted to leave. We spent our first Thanksgiving alone in a cabin in Lake Arrowhead, and in December, to make up for it, we hosted Christmas Eve dinner for both families, a baker's dozen of guests. Jack wore a chef's hat and apron and cooked a fourteen-pound turkey, and though it was a little dry, nobody really noticed, thanks to the martinis he'd perfected. I made cornbread dressing and green beans and mashed potatoes and gravy that had only a few flour lumps floating on the top, and I didn't burn a thing, a first.

At Midnight Mass, surrounded by both our families, I prayed silently for the one who wasn't there, the one who was always somewhere in my mind, and for a few moments, I let my feelings of love for him win out over the anger and frustration and hurt. *Keep him safe*, I prayed, the same words I'd used in Shanghai so long ago. *Protect him, guard him, keep him safe.*

:: :: ::

In January of 1954, on the first Monday of the new year, the phone rang too early to be anything but news. Jack and I were lying in bed, listening to the sound of the rain. He reached for the phone and said hello, then handed it to me, and I knew from his proper tone it was my mother.

"Good morning," she said quickly. "I know it's early, but I wanted to get you before you left the house. Look at the *Times*, Anna. There's something about your father on page five. He's been released and he's in Hong Kong. You can read the rest."

"Thank you," I said, as though she'd held a door open for me.

"We'll talk later, if you want," she said, and then she hung up.

I pulled on a robe and went outside for the paper, which I spread out on the kitchen table. I turned to page five and found what I was looking for in the top right corner: AMERICAN FREE AFTER 3 YEARS IN SHANGHAI JAIL. "A 47-year-old China-born American businessman, lame and nearsighted from beriberi, arrived in Hong Kong yesterday after spending three years in a Shanghai jail," the article read. "Joseph Schoene told newsmen he was released without explanation last Monday from Shanghai's notorious Ward Road Jail."

The article went on to say that Schoene had been released with five other prisoners, three Russians and two Italians. He said that other Americans were still held in Shanghai, but that he didn't know how many; that death and suffering were rampant in the jail; that new prisoners were being brought in at the rate of six to eight a day; and that firing squads were shooting them.

Mr. Schoene, the article said, had been arrested in April of 1951 on what he said was a trumped-up charge of owning illegal firearms. He had not been tortured, though he had spent most of the past year in solitary confinement, where he had subsisted on a diet of watery rice. His weight had dropped from two hundred to eighty-five, and he had suffered from beriberi, although he had gradually recovered the use of his legs.

He did not know the reason for his sudden release. "I was just rolled out of Red China," he was quoted as saying, "I have no idea why." The day of his release he had been taken from his cell to the warden, who told him that he was to appear in the People's Court at noon that day. At the courthouse, the judge informed Schoene that he had three days to leave China, that he could take only minor personal effects, that any funds he'd had in Chinese banks now belonged to the People's Republic, and that he was expelled from China for the rest of his life. Schoene said he left the jail and walked to the British Consulate, where he was given passage on the SS *Fernside* to Hong Kong. Then he went to what had once been his office, where he gathered the few possessions he still had, several account ledgers from his business and a few personal items. He left Shanghai the next day.

Jack had come in while I was reading. I had finally told him about my father a few months before we were married, and now he stood next to me, looking over my shoulder. When I finished reading I said, "He's all right."

Jack put his arms around me and held me and asked, "Are you?"

I nodded. "Relieved," I said. "I'm glad he's safe, and I'm glad I won't be hearing about him again."

But I was wrong. That article was only the first of many over the next four months. My father apparently caught the interest of the *Los Angeles Times*, which printed the AP accounts of his situation and kept us posted about his life with the regularity of a soap opera serial. All that winter and spring, I opened the morning paper with an unpleasant mix of fear and anticipation—*What has he done now?*—a feeling that was familiar where my father was concerned, as I pieced together what had happened.

When my father was released from prison in Shanghai, the British Consulate there issued him a visa for a seven-day stay in Hong Kong. The authorities in Hong Kong admitted him on human-itarian grounds, and he then applied for and received a six-month restricted passport from the United States Consulate. He intended to stay in Hong Kong for good. Once he regained his health and strength, he borrowed some money and bought the Glenbrook Poultry Farm in Aberdeen, on the south part of Hong Kong Island, a few miles south of Victoria.

But just a few weeks after that, he received unwelcome news: he was ordered to be expelled from the colony and deported for life. The only reason the government would give was that his presence "was not conducive to the public good."

My father was outraged. It was a great injustice against him, he said, as well as an infringement of his human rights as set out in the Charter of the United Nations. He had not violated any of the laws of Hong Kong, he had committed no crimes to warrant deportation, he would be unable to earn a living in the United States. And, he said, why should Hong Kong object to his presence? The U.S. Consulate had no objection to his remaining in Hong Kong. ("I'll *bet* they didn't," my grandmother commented dryly when she read that piece of news. "*They're* in no hurry to get him home.")

When he received no satisfactory answer to his question, he fought the deportation order. He hired a lawyer and contested the validity of the order. He went so far as to petition Queen Elizabeth to stay the deportation order, but, he said, he "had no reason to believe she would help me out." His attempts were unsuccessful, and finally, on March 5, he lost his action before the Supreme Court, and the government ruled that the deportation order was valid and final.

But he wouldn't leave.

His lawyers informed him that everything had been tried and that there was no recourse for objecting, but still he wouldn't leave, and when, by the end of the month, he was still in Hong Kong, he was arrested and taken to the Upper Level Police Station. AMERICAN BUSINESSMAN JAILED IN HONG KONG was the headline this time. The next day there was more: SCHOENE REFUSES TO EAT, it said. The day after his arrest, he had begun a hunger strike. Five days after that, he was taken to Queen Mary Hospital.

There was a photograph this time. There was my father, casual as Saturday morning, wearing a dark-colored sport shirt and light-colored trousers and reclining on a cot. A glass of water and a radio were on the table next to the bed. The caption read, "Schoene is little the worse from 6-day fast." As I stared at the photograph, all I could think was, *He's crazy.* And even though by that time my name had been twice changed—from Schoene to Shoen, and then from Shoen to my married name, Bradley—a part of me still wanted to wear a sandwich board around town, or to publish something in the paper that said, *He's not my father. I don't even know him.*

The government had made arrangements for my father to travel on the same ship that had taken him to Hong Kong, the Norwegian vessel *Fernside*, which was to sail for the U.S. three days later. But luck was with my father: the ship developed engine trouble and had to be taken to the docks for repairs, and when it sailed, my father was still not on board because the government felt he should be on a ship with medical care, and the *Fernside* had none. He would be deported as soon as a proper ship was available.

Then, just as suddenly as he'd begun his fast, he broke it. The paper did not say why, only that there were rumors of a visit from a friend recently arrived from Shanghai, but there was another photograph. This time my father was sitting up and eating congee and chicken soup.

Finally, on April 30, 1954, the last article:

SCHOENE LEAVES QUIETLY, OUSTED BY HONG KONG

An unheralded departure from Hong Kong was made by American Joseph Schoene, 47, aboard the Swedish American Lines vessel Wangaratta, bound for Vancouver, B.C., and Seattle. Schoene boarded the ship at 5:30 P.M. yesterday. "He left quietly and of his own accord," a U.S. Consulate official stated. Schoene said that he had "run out of legal options in trying to offset the Hong Kong government's decision" that he must leave the colony. He called the actions of Hong Kong's government "a shame, a disgrace, and a gross injustice. I tried to pick up the threads of my life, breaking no laws and endeavoring to make a living. But I found out democracy is only preached, not practiced."

Schoene said he will be visiting relatives in the United States. He will not pursue any further legal action. He has left his share of the Glenbrook Poultry Farm in Aberdeen to Miss Leung Mancheung, a longtime friend from Shanghai, who arrived in Hong Kong last week.

I knew from experience that if my father had left Hong Kong on April 29, he would be arriving in Seattle three weeks later, somewhere around May 20. As that day drew closer, I found myself as nervous as if I expected him to show up on my doorstep. Though I knew it was irrational, sharing a continent with him made me anxious, and the only thing I could do was try not to think of him, and, when I did, to change the subject in my mind as easily as I changed it in conversation on those rare occasions when his name was mentioned.

:: :: ::

My mother insisted on having a party for Jack and me for our first wedding anniversary. She said we'd had everyone over to our house far too many times for newlyweds, and that it was only right for someone else to play host once in a while. And so on the eighth of July, Jack and I went to her house for dinner. It was supposed to be a barbecue, and my mother had said to dress casually, but "casual" to my mother usually meant "dressy" to everyone else. Jack wore khaki trousers and a white shirt and plaid bow tie, and looked like he was nineteen. I wore a navy blue sundress that I loved, never mind the fact that it was a little tight in the waist.

We walked from our apartment to my mother's house, Jack carrying half a dozen roses he'd picked from our backyard for my mother. When she met us at the door, I was speechless, for she wore a fitted dress of pink and gold brocade and she looked beautiful. *Cheongsam*, I thought when I saw her, the word a surprise, for I had not thought of it for years. The dress was familiar, though from long ago. When my mother saw my look, she shrugged.

"It's from Shanghai days," she said. "I've lost a little weight, and I was curious about whether or not it still fit." She looked down and smoothed her dress and seemed shy and almost girlish for a moment. "It was my favorite dress, a long time ago. Does it look silly?"

I shook my head. "No, it's beautiful," I said. "*You're* beautiful. You look like a movie star." And I was surprised to see her blush. My mother had never been one to need compliments.

Jack nodded. "That's some dress. You look great, simple as that. And you sure don't look like a mother-in-law."

My mother beamed like a schoolgirl, and I squeezed Jack's hand, grateful that he'd made her smile, for there was a frailty about her that worried me.

When everyone was there, Jack and I were toasted with my grandmother's sangria. Jack's father grilled hamburgers on the patio and there was sweet corn on the cob and more fruit than anyone could eat—watermelon and peaches and Bing cherries and strawberries, all bought from a fruit stand at Farmer's Market that my grandmother insisted had the best fruit in Southern California. It was the kind of party where the guests were like a big family. People wandered in and out of the house the way they wandered in and out of each other's conversations, and the sound of talking and laughter was constant, always to a backdrop of whatever record Jack had put on—"Mr. Sandman" by the Chordettes, "Hey There" by Rosemary Clooney, "That's Amore" by Dean Martin. Everyone knew each other, at least from our wedding if not before, and when Heather, in the middle of conversation with Peter Shelton, a friend of Jack's from UCLA, called to me, "Anna, when did you and your mother move to South Pasadena?" I had to think for a minute, for it seemed I'd been there all of my life. Shanghai was like something imagined.

Late in the party, when only a few friends and Jack and my mother and grandmother and I were left, I went outside. The others were talking in the living room, but I was tired and wanted to just sit for a while, so I went outside to look at the garden I'd worked on so long ago.

I stood on the patio and listened to the crickets. There was a fingernail moon that was just a white scratch against the dark sky, and there were more stars than I'd seen in weeks. I had only stared up at the sky for a minute before I saw a shooting star, and I heard my mother say, "Did you make a wish?"

I turned and found her sitting on the chaise lounge, her back to the house, hiding her from view. The air had grown cool the way it does at night in Los Angeles, and she had wrapped a white shawl around her shoulders. The light was dim, but I saw that she was smiling. "Well, did you? You don't want to waste a wish."

I sighed. "I'm too tired," I said. "And I can't think of anything I want that I don't have."

She nodded and seemed pleased. "That's wonderful. I think that's called happiness." Then she patted the chair next to her and said, "Sit with me for a while?"

"Gladly," I said, and I sat down and pushed off my sandals and tucked my feet up underneath me.

The garden was lovely, overgrown and wild, fragrant with roses and jasmine and eucalyptus. In the light that spilled out on the patio from inside the house, my mother seemed ethereal and lovely and otherworldly in her beautiful cheongsam, so much like she had seemed in Shanghai that I found myself staring, as though she were someone I hadn't seen in a long time. Apparently she could tell, even with her eyes closed. "You're staring, Anna," she said softly. "Have you forgotten your manners?"

I felt my cheeks redden, and I feared I might even cry as though I were a child who'd been reprimanded. "I'm sorry," I mumbled.

She waved my words away and smiled at me. "Don't take everything so seriously," she said, and she looked at me closely. "You *are* tired."

I sighed. "The party. I feel like I could fall asleep right here."

She nodded, and then she was quiet for so long that I was thinking she'd fallen asleep when she cleared her throat and said, "You should probably see this."

She held a folded paper out to me, which I took. "It's a letter from your father," she said, and when I winced, she laughed softly. "Don't worry. You don't have to see him. He's only asking to borrow some money, but you might as well know about it. I wouldn't put it past him to ask you next."

"What happened to *his* money?"

"It's gone," my mother said simply. "I think he spent quite a bit before he was imprisoned. The Communist government kept the rest."

I unfolded the letter and held it up so that the light from inside fell on it. *Eve*, it began, *I'm well and living near Santa Barbara in Carpinteria, a little place not far from the beach. Am raising chickens, something I learned about in the not-so-good days in Shanghai and briefly in Hong Kong. The enterprise will be all right, but getting started is tough. Could you see your way clear to helping me out with a short-term loan? A thousand dollars would turn everything around for me. I've been unable to recoup anything from before the–*

I turned the paper over, looking for the rest of the letter, and I looked at my mother. "Where's the rest?"

She shook her head and waved vaguely toward the house. "It was just talk," she said coolly. "I've misplaced the second page."

"You aren't going to give him any money, are you?"

"Oh, I don't know. He supported us for a long time, and now he doesn't have anything. I don't need much anymore, and it seems only fair to give back some of what was his."

"What possible reason can you have to trust him? Maybe he's bluffing. Maybe he has plenty of money."

She laughed. "I doubt that. He's working as a school janitor until he can get the chicken farm going."

I felt ignorant and in the dark. I asked, "And how would you know that?" and I hated the accusation that I heard in my voice.

"Another letter. He keeps me posted about his goings-on. I don't know why, really. Habit, I guess."

"You shouldn't correspond with him," I said, and then I forced myself not to say more, because I had the oddest feeling. I felt jealous, even betrayed, and I didn't know why.

My mother said, "We've known each other for a long time, Anna. We had a child together. Those are hard ties to break. If your father wants, for reasons of his own, to remain in touch with me, I won't say no."

I considered my options and said nothing for perhaps a minute. I mainly wanted to say, *You can't!*, and stamp my foot and throw a fit, and to get her to promise that she would have nothing to do with this man I considered dangerous.

And then my mother said, "I want to tell you something. I thought for a long time I'd keep this to myself, but apparently my old age is getting the best of me."

"You're forty-four," I said.

"It was a joke," she said dryly, and she glanced at me. "What's happened to your sense of humor?"

I shrugged. "A casualty of my tiredness, I guess."

She nodded. "Fatigue will flatten a sense of humor pretty quickly. Take the air right out of you." And then she took a deep breath and said, "I owe you an apology."

I started to speak, but she held her hand out, silencing me. "Just let me keep going. I haven't rehearsed this speech much. As I said, I didn't really plan on giving it." She turned slightly in the chaise so that she faced me. "I've always felt that apologies don't count unless you look the person in the eye. Don't you agree?"

I nodded stupidly, afraid of what was to come.

"I shouldn't have taken you to Shanghai so long ago. It was selfish and stupid of me, and my only explanation is that I didn't realize just how bad things would be. I'm sorry for putting you through all of it—the trip, the weather, the filth. Your father." She squinted at me, as if trying to understand something in my expression. "I shouldn't have brought you along."

I laughed. "Don't be silly," I said. "You couldn't have known—"

She waved my words away like nuisances. "I did know. That's what I'm saying. When I first thought of us going, I sent your father a telegram, with what I thought was good news. I received his response two weeks later. 'Don't come' was the gist of it, without much more of an explanation than that." She paused and cleared her throat, and I wished I could tell her that was enough, that I didn't need to know more.

"I knew what we'd find. I knew about his feelings toward me and our marriage." She let her breath out softly. "I knew about Leung Mancheung, the woman at Jimmy's on that awful night, and I suspect there were others. But I didn't know what else to do. I knew how hurt you were, how much you missed him. And I missed him. I couldn't imagine giving him up, and I didn't think it possible that he would give you up. So that trip was sort of my last resort—and I thought you were my ace in the hole. That was wrong, and I hope you'll forgive me."

It was the first time in my life I could remember my mother apologizing to me—and the first time I could remember a time she had reason to—and I just sat for a few moments, trying to fit this new square fact into the round hole of memory, waiting for things in my mind to be revised. "Of course I forgive you," I said finally. "But I'm glad we went. Because now I know who he is, and I won't forget, and I won't be fooled by him."

My mother said, "Oh, Anna. There's more to him than that," and it was only then that I heard sadness in her voice. She was staring out at the back of the garden, where the junipers that my father had planted so long ago were twice as high as the fence. "Do you know what I thought when I met Joseph Schoene? I thought, *Here is a man I can watch forever.* He was so driven and ambitious, with this wonderful energy." She laughed grimly. "It never occurred to me that that energy would backfire. Or that *he* would grow tired of watching *me*."

"He didn't grow tired of it," I said. "He just stopped."

She closed her eyes and nodded slightly. "Thank you," she said. "I think that was a compliment." She was quiet for a moment, and then she said, "Do you know what the strange thing is? I still love him.

I'm sure that doesn't make sense to you. It certainly doesn't to me. But it's true." And then she spoke in Mandarin, a first since our return from Shanghai. "*Jênhsin nan mo*," she said softly. "'The human heart is hard to grasp.'"

Neither of us spoke for a few minutes then. I felt so sad inside, and although I wanted to comfort her, I didn't know how. I stared at the night sky and tried to find the few constellations I knew—the Big and Little Dippers, Cassiopeia, Cepheus, Orion—and I thought that what looked like a bright star to the east might be Jupiter, and I tried to think of what to say.

We heard laughter from the house then, Jack's voice the loudest, and my mother smiled. "He seems very happy, Anna. I think you're good for him."

"Hope so," I said. "He is for me." And I couldn't help but smile because he *was* happy, and it was so obvious. He'd been near me all evening, resting his hand on my waist, dancing with me on the patio, telling me I looked pretty so often that I began to feel myself glow. And once, when we found ourselves alone in the kitchen, he took me in his arms and whispered that I was the best thing that had ever happened to him. I had never felt so intensely loved, and the feeling left me in awe.

The laughter from inside quieted, and Jack began telling a story. I could hear the rise and fall of his voice but not the words, the way you hear adults talking when you're a child. Then there was more laughter, and something from my grandmother. Someone opened a bottle of beer and the cap bounced around on the tile floor in the kitchen. I heard Francis Albert Sinatra singing "I Get a Kick out of You" and I knew that Jack had put on *Songs for Young Lovers*, an album he liked so much that he took it with him to friends' houses, just so they could hear it, too.

"He's crazy about that album," I murmured.

"It's lovely," my mother said. "An anniversary present?"

I laughed. "Nope. He didn't give me a chance. He bought it the day it was in the stores."

She nodded. "That sounds like him. Always a little ahead of the game. What *did* you give him?"

"I'm glad you asked," I said, for her question answered one of my own, and I knew how to comfort her. "I gave him a box of twenty-five H. Upmann cigars, Churchills, which are supposed to be cool and mild." And then I thought of my father's cigars when I was a child. "These are Dominican cigars, not Philippine."

"I didn't know Jack liked cigars. And since when are you the aficionada?"

I shrugged, an attempt to fake nonchalance and hide my enjoyment of her confusion. "Since yesterday when I bought them. And no, he's not an avid cigar smoker. He just likes one once in a while."

"Then *why* a whole box of them?" she asked. Her exasperation was obvious.

I was quiet for a moment, letting her question hang in the still night air for dramatic effect. I could almost hear her wondering what kind of a wife *was* I?

"He'll need them seven months from now," I said casually. "To pass out when the baby comes."

She looked at me as though I were crazy, but when I nodded, she shook her head and just looked amazed. And then she smiled.

"We were going to tell everyone tonight," I said. "But the doctor thought it better to wait a little longer, to be sure everything was all right. But I thought you'd want to know, and I figured you could keep a secret."

"Oh, Anna," she said, "a baby," and she shook her head again. "I've been so worried about you."

"Why?"

"You've seemed tired, and not quite yourself. I thought you were sick." She shrugged and seemed a little embarrassed, but then she started to laugh, softly at first, but it kept going, and soon she was laughing hard, the way you do with your best friend when you're fourteen. I watched for a minute, waiting for her to regain her composure. The sound startled me, and I realized I hadn't heard my mother laugh for a long time. But now she laughed and laughed and laughed. Tears ran down her cheeks, and then I started to laugh, too, and each time one of us tried to speak, we only laughed harder.

"Why are we laughing?" I managed to say once, but it only set her off again. All she could do was shake her head.

Finally she was quiet, and when she had wiped her cheeks, she reached over and squeezed my hand. "I'm happy. I thought you were sick, and I'm relieved."

I was still at the end of laughing. "I thought you were sick, too," I said. "You've looked—"

But she waved my words away. "A baby," she whispered, "you're going to have a baby. The whole world feels different now."

a promise

ON A TUESDAY MORNING a few weeks after our anniversary party, my mother and I went to early Mass together and then to breakfast at Fosselman's on Mission Avenue in South Pasadena, for old times more than anything.

My mother and I sat at a booth and I ordered dry toast and a glass of milk, a combination that would have repulsed me at any other time in my life, but I was three months pregnant and never hungry in the morning. I wasn't the only one with a diminished appetite. My mother barely glanced at the menu before closing it, and when the waitress asked for our order, she answered only, "Hot tea." She didn't seem like herself, and I kept trying to figure out what was wrong. Her color wasn't good, and she seemed not just tired but weary, as though something more than lack of sleep had fatigued her. Although it was August and already warm outside at nine in the morning, she said she was cold, and she wore a scarf around her neck because she said she had a sore throat. I asked if she was coming down with the flu and she dismissed my question and said curtly that it was nothing to worry about, then changed the subject before I could ask more, and I knew not to try. But when she reached for the sugar, I saw bruises on her wrist, and I asked what had happened. Again, she was casual. "Oh, I'm always bumping into things," she said, and she sat with her hands in her lap, out of my sight, during the rest of the meal.

That afternoon I called my grandmother with my concerns, mostly for reassurance. My grandmother was the most down-to-earth, unsentimental person I knew. I thought I was getting anxious over nothing, another kind of side effect of pregnancy.

"I know," my grandmother said when I described my mother at breakfast. "I'm worried about her. She doesn't seem well, and I've been nagging her about it. Last week she finally promised she'd see Dr. O'Connor." My grandmother paused, and then she said softly, "I think something's wrong," and for the first time in my life, I heard fear in her voice.

That was how my mother's illness started: so gradually and unobtrusively that it was easy to ignore. She was so casual about the bruises and the fatigue and the sore throat that I shrugged it all off and chalked my uneasiness up to unnecessary worry, so much so that in September, when, after doctor's appointments and tests and consultations and examinations, she was diagnosed with acute lymphocytic leukemia, I was as shocked as if I'd never noticed anything wrong.

I found the name alone terrifying. A few days after her diagnosis, I went to the library to try to learn from medical books what was happening to her body. I had to steel myself to read about the uncontrolled growth of leucocytes, the white blood cells that defend the body against germs and viruses. I read about the damage caused by that frantic growth, the way that white blood cells flood the tissue and blood, and the way in which the bone marrow becomes unable to produce red blood cells, which leads to anemia. And because it was happening to my mother's body, it all seemed unbearably violent.

Easy bleeding, I read, and in my mind I saw my mother's bruised arms, *enlarged spleen and lymph glands, weakness, fever, frequent infection*—the language of cancer.

The illness was classified according to the type of white blood cells it affected, and it was also classified as chronic or acute. Chronic leukemia was the "better" version, developing more slowly. A patient with chronic leukemia could live with the disease for many years. Acute leukemia—my mother's variety—was the more aggressive and dangerous type. Without treatment, it could lead to death within a few months, usually as the result of bleeding or infection. What caused the disease was unknown, as was its cure.

When I'd read all I could, I left the library and went outside into the hot September day. The Santa Anas had kicked up, and the hot desert air had blown every trace of smog to the west, so that the purplish-brown San Gabriel mountains were so beautiful and clear and distinct that they seemed magnified. I blinked in the bright light and sat down on a stone bench just outside of the library and waited to feel like myself. I hadn't eaten breakfast and I was weak, and I thought I should wait a minute before heading for home. It was Saturday and Jack had the car, so I had taken the bus there and would need to take it home.

I closed my eyes and let the sun beat down on me. I felt myself getting hot, and whatever energy I had dissipated. I thought I should get up, but I was too tired, and although a voice inside said, *Get up and walk to the bus,* a louder and seemingly more authoritative one said, *Just stay here,* and then I couldn't and wouldn't and didn't get up, and I thought, *It's all right, you're falling asleep,* and I gave in.

:: :: ::

I woke inside the library, and for a moment, I thought I'd just fallen asleep in there and that I'd only dreamed I'd gone outside. But my head hurt, and when I touched the place that seemed to produce the pain, someone said, "No, no, dear. It's just a cut, but leave it alone," and I looked up to find the librarian staring down at me. She wore a light blue blouse that looked like the sky, and her hair was a beautiful deep chestnut color.

"You fainted," she said, "and you bumped your head on the bench, but it doesn't look like anything to worry about. We've called your husband and he's on his way. In the meantime, just rest." Then she smiled kindly. "When is the baby due?"

I put my hand to my stomach, embarrassed. I'd only started showing a week or so earlier. "February," I said, and a voice inside asked, *Will she still be alive?* "Yes," I said out loud, and the beautiful librarian looked puzzled. "Yes, in February," I said weakly.

When Jack arrived, the panic and alarm in his face were so startling that I thought something else had happened, something besides me. "What is it?"

He looked confused. "I was worried."

I shrugged. "I was reading about"—I couldn't say the word—"her. And then I went outside and got too hot and I hadn't eaten and—" I stopped.

He put his arm around me to help me up. "You have to take better care of yourself," he said gently. "She'll be all right." He wore a UCLA T-shirt that he'd had since he was a freshman, and he smelled of sweat and cut grass, and the sight of him made me feel better. He looked up and saw the librarian watching us, and he said again, "She'll be all right," and I nodded.

I rested that afternoon under Jack's somewhat strict supervision. I ate a turkey sandwich and an orange and felt fine, but getting up was not allowed, and I realized I was under a kind of house arrest. I put up with it, figuring I could do so for an afternoon.

But my little fainting incident wasn't forgotten. It got everyone paying attention to me—Jack, my grandmother, my mother, his parents when we saw them. They were all worried that my worry over my mother would affect my health, and I felt all their anxiety every time they looked at me. And despite the fact that there were pregnant women just about everywhere you looked in that fall of 1954, my family seemed to view my condition as unique and even precarious, and I was as closely watched as my mother. We two worried over each other while everyone around us worried over both of us.

In October, as I entered my sixth month, my obstetrician expressed concern over my blood pressure, which he considered a little high, most likely due to stress, he said, for he knew of my mother's illness. I was told to take it easy, and since I'd planned on leaving my job at the Huntington Library in only two more months anyway, I quit then, which left me with more time than I knew what to do with. My mother was in a similar position, and though her reasons were different, the fact was that we were both tired and unable to do the things we usually did. So we began to spend a lot of time together, as if on a strange sort of vacation. We went to matinees, we played cards and Monopoly and Scrabble, we did puzzles, we read piles of books from the library and exchanged the ones we liked. On warm days, we sat outside in the sun, sometimes in her overgrown garden, other times our postage-stamp backyard. We were like best friends, and we quickly fell into a routine. In the morning she watched *The Today Show*, her one guilty pleasure, she said, and I knew not to call until it was over. Sometime after nine one of us would call the other and ask, "What are your plans for the day?" and be asked in turn, "What have you got in mind?"

During those fall and winter days of 1954, I watched my mother transform herself yet again. Since that first time we'd left Shanghai when I was seven, I'd come to understand that she was someone who changed with her environment and the circumstances of her life, so I shouldn't have been surprised at this latest transformation.

But I was. She grew more open and talkative than I'd ever known her to be. Conversation seemed to soothe and relax her and, later, to make it easier for her to fall asleep. I gave up trying to follow her train of thought. One minute she might be asking what it was like for Jack to teach at a private school, and after I talked a bit about Flintridge and the boys in Jack's classes and the way he met a group of seventh-grade boys every morning to tell them a stupid joke, she'd describe a certain dress shop she'd loved in Shanghai, a place I'd never heard her mention before. In fact, Shanghai was one of her favorite topics. She mentioned my father only in passing, when it was impossible not to, but she talked with obvious affection about our home in Hungjao, and the Bund and the Old City and Chu Shih and Mei Wah and that foreign life we'd lived so long ago.

At the start, her talkativeness confused me; she had never been so forthcoming. But the transformation in her body was far more dramatic than any changes in her personality. She tired after very little exertion, she needed transfusions more and more often, and she appeared more frail each day. I didn't even ask how much weight she'd lost. By Thanksgiving I understood: in those long conversations, in the give-and-take of our thoughts and feelings and pasts, she was telling me good-bye.

:: :: ::

On an unexpectedly warm afternoon during the first week of December, my mother and I sat outside with my grandmother on her patio. It had not changed since I'd seen it when we first arrived from Shanghai. Although it was December, everything was still green, and a few narcissus bloomed near the brick walk. My mother was lying on a chaise lounge in the afternoon sun, a glass of water on the table next to her. She had aged ten years in six months. Her disease was aggressive, to say the least, and it seemed that each day there was less energy, less strength, less *her*.

My grandmother and I were on either side of her. I was just starting *The Morning Watch* by James Agee. My grandmother was reading the afternoon *Pasadena Star News* and commenting on what she read. The day before, the Senate had voted 67 to 22 to condemn Senator Joseph McCarthy on two counts of abusing the Senate, news that pleased my grandmother, but her relief was overshadowed by her concern for Pope Pius XII, who had collapsed and fallen into a coma the night before. He was seventy-eight years old and suffering from a perforated ulcer, and he had been fed artificially for the last four days. His physician had spent the night at his bedside, and the Pope had received the sacrament of Extreme Unction. And although my grandmother did not usually hold him dear, the fact was that he had traveled to the United States and become an acquaintance of President Roosevelt, whom she did hold dear, and so she said diplomatically, "We'll pray for a happy death for our Holy Father."

Illness was not something I wanted to think about, so I said nothing, waiting for a chance to change the subject, which I did by asking my grandmother what she wanted for Christmas.

"A new pair of gardening gloves," she said quickly. "And nothing more. You spend too much as it is. You'll need to save your money this year."

"We are," I said, already tired of such dull advice. "What about you?" I turned to my mother.

She had drifted off during my grandmother's detailing of the Pope's illness, and she stirred slightly. "I want to see the baby," she said softly.

I laughed. "Not till February, with any luck."

"I want to see the baby," she said again, and she looked me in the eye. Her eyes were strangely bright, her face so pale that she looked otherworldly. Her hair was in a chignon, and she looked beautiful and fragile, and I understood that it was not a Christmas wish she was expressing. She was hoping to live until February.

My grandmother and I exchanged looks, and my mood changed in an instant. "You will," I said quickly, my chest tight.

And then she said something I did not understand. "*Yu ping c'ai chih chien shih hsien*," she said softly, and I stared at her for a moment. She smiled and said, "Something Chu Shih used to say. 'Health is not valued until illness comes.'"

I nodded and asked her to repeat it in Mandarin, for it had been familiar, and when she did, I could hear Chu Shih's voice and see his large frame in his small room more distinctly than I had since I was a child.

"Do you remember Chu Shih very well?"

"Yes."

My mother looked pleased. "That's good. He loved you dearly."

We were quiet for a few minutes, and I was thinking about the taste of the tea that Chu Shih made me when I was sick. I remembered its sweetness, and the taste of oranges.

Then my mother said, "I want your promise about something, Anna."

Something tightened inside me, partly in anticipation of what she might ask, and partly because of what her asking meant. "All right."

She took a breath and let it out slowly, and I was sure that she was in pain. "I want you to forgive your father. It's only natural for you to be angry with him, but I want you to forgive him in your heart."

I spoke before I could stop myself. "After everything—"

She cut me off before I could go on. "Yes. After everything. There's goodness in him, Anna. There was a saying in Shanghai: *Hsin chong yu shei, shei chiu p'iaoliang*. 'Whoever is in your heart is beautiful.' If you hold him in your heart, you will be able to forgive him. It won't happen overnight, but it's a grace, and if you ask for it, it will come." She reached for my hand. "Do you promise?"

"Yes," I said, though I did not see how I would keep my word. "I promise."

"Good," she said. "That's one less thing for me to worry about." She turned to my grandmother. "Any chance of a glass of cold beer? I'm desert dry and I can't see that a beer could do any harm."

:: :: ::

At a checkup with my obstetrician during the third week of January, he told me he was concerned about the baby's growth and about my health. My blood pressure was still high, and I'd had the flu a week before and lost a few pounds. And so he suggested that the baby be delivered by cesarean section, and that it should be scheduled for the next week. He smiled. Was there any particular day I preferred? I was, after all, choosing my child's birthday.

I knew immediately, and I asked him to schedule the surgery for the thirty-first, a nice stroke of luck. It was the feast day of St. Francis de Sales, whose *Introduction to the Devout Life* was one of my grandmother's favorite books. But more important, it was my mother's birthday.

And so on Monday morning, Jack and I drove to Huntington Hospital. We parked and walked inside, Jack carrying my small suitcase, the two of us as nervous and afraid and not talking much. Jack was not easily rattled, but even he was anxious. I knew that he'd barely slept the last few nights. I'd heard him in the living room, shuffling cards and dealing, over and over and over again, as he played Solitaire until he thought he could get back to sleep. The dark circles under his eyes reminded me of his worry.

It was early, and I knew that my mother and my grandmother were offering prayers for the baby at Mass just then, and I added some of my own as I undressed and put on a gown and lay on a gurney and held Jack's hand for all I was worth. "You're going to be fine, Anna," he whispered, "both of you," and I nodded, because he sounded so sure. As the anesthesia took effect, I looked into his blue eyes and thought they were the most amazing eyes I'd ever seen, clear and honest and intense, and that if the baby could just have his father's eyes, he would be beautiful, and all would be well.

:: :: ::

I woke to find my mother sitting in the chair next to my bed, and the sight of her made me panic and think that something had gone very wrong. I started to speak, and she looked up and smiled and said, "Jack, she's awake," and I heard footsteps and then Jack was there, too. He was smiling like crazy, and he held the baby toward me and said, "We have a daughter," and I could not imagine that life was so good, that God was so good.

I took her in my arms and looked down at the small sleeping face of an angel. She had eyelashes as pale as down, and a shocking amount of dark brown hair, and hands and fingers so tiny that I could not believe they were real. And then she opened her eyes and looked up at me, and I knew that I would never be the same.

I looked at Jack and his boyish can-you-believe-it? expression. I was woozy and unsure of what was real. "A girl?" I whispered, wanting confirmation, trying to take everything in. He nodded.

I looked at my mother then and was struck by how healthy and how beautiful she looked. Her skin glowed, her cheeks had more color than they had in weeks, her eyes were bright. It was as though we'd found the cure. "Happy Birthday," I said, and she laughed. "Do you want to know her name?"

She looked surprised. "You already have it?"

Jack nodded. "We've known the *girl's* name for months," he said. "It was the boy's name that was tough, but that's a problem we don't have to solve."

"Well?" she said.

Jack looked at me and smiled. "Her name is Eve," I said simply. "Genevieve for the record, but we'll call her Eve."

:: :: ::

February was a golden month. My mother's face lit up every time she saw her namesake, and it was even possible to believe she was getting better. She laughed and joked with us, she talked and sang to Eve, she danced gracefully around our living room as she rocked her to sleep, all of which I watched with joy and desperation. This was fleeting, I knew, and precious, and I wanted to somehow stop everything and somehow capture what I was seeing. The time was going too fast.

At the beginning of March, my mother's health grew suddenly worse, and by the end of the month, she had been hospitalized twice. The hospital stays were not only painful but humiliating. She had always been modest, and to have strangers taking care of her was a great indignity. I saw that a request for a long life was not always the best prayer.

On a Tuesday morning in the middle of April, I went to her house at a little after ten. She'd been in the hospital the week before but had grown strong enough that her doctor thought it safe to send her home, the one thing she wanted. I found her sleeping, so I just sat with her for a while. I usually brought Eve with me, but I'd gotten a sitter that morning, and I wasn't used to the leisure of just sitting quietly with her. My grandmother called and asked how she was and said she'd be by at lunchtime, and my mother woke for a few minutes and asked if the roses were fresh, a nonsense question—there were no roses in the house. A short time later when she woke again, she seemed more alert, and she remembered asking about the roses. She said she'd dreamed she was walking in the rose garden at the Huntington Library. Then she asked about Eve, and whether I was getting enough sleep. She told me what a good baby I'd been, and that

Eve had gotten her good nature from me. I noticed she was flushed, and I asked if she'd like a cool washcloth, and when I brought it to her and put it on her forehead, I found that her skin was so hot that it frightened me, and I started to cry.

"Oh, Anna," she said softly. "You'll be all right. Don't you know that?"

I nodded, embarrassed. "Would you like some water?" I asked, "Or something to eat?" mostly because I wanted to leave the room for a moment.

She tried to clear her throat but ended up coughing a hard, painful-sounding cough that did no good. "I'm so tired," she said, "and hot. What did Chu Shih call hot weather? I think it was *tashu*, for 'great heat.'" She licked her lips and swallowed. "Maybe I'll be better this afternoon."

"You will," I said, and I wished I could hide the fear in my voice. I stood to go get a glass of water from the kitchen, where I rinsed my face and scolded myself for crying in front of her. I put ice in a glass and filled it with water and picked up an apple that was on the counter, an offering. I wanted to give her something—health, love, reassurance, hope, comfort, any of those would have done. The apple was the only tangible thing I could find. I heard the first drops of rain from a sky that had been threatening all morning, and I called, "It's finally started to rain. It sounds lovely. Do you hear it?"

When I came into the room, she was dozing again, but she turned toward me when I sat down, and she held out her hand. I sat on the edge of the bed and held her hand as gently as I could, afraid of its frailty, and I whispered, "You look so beautiful."

She smiled, barely, and she murmured something I couldn't hear. I squeezed her hand lightly, hoping she would repeat it, and she said, "The roses are so beautiful, Anna. Can you smell them?"

"Yes," I whispered, a last try at comfort, and she smiled and her face relaxed. She inhaled as though she were breathing in something wonderful, and a breeze brought the scent of rain into the room, and I breathed in, too. And then she exhaled, her breath making a soft sandpapery sound that made me want to hold on to her, to keep her here, to do anything in the world to keep her here. But she was gone, and I was alone.

:: :: ::

On Wednesday morning, the mortuary called to tell me that my mother's body was ready for viewing. I nursed the baby and dressed quickly, then told Jack that I would be back soon. I wanted to do this alone. He nodded and hugged me before I left. One of his best qualities was his habit of respecting people's privacy. He never asked me to explain.

At the mortuary, I was directed to a small chapel, silent and dimly lit. There were perhaps ten pews on either side of a center aisle, and my mother's open casket was in front. I was alone, and I sat down on a pew halfway from the back, because it felt more private there. I wanted to be close to her, but I didn't want to be too close, in case anyone else came in. I wore a black veil of my grandmother's, and in the interest of anonymity, I had it pulled down over my face, and I didn't feel like myself. It seemed that all I'd done for the last awful day was talk to people—on the phone, at my mother's house, at the mortuary, at the church. Everything felt wrong, and I had no idea how to make it better.

I had been sitting for only a few minutes when I heard the door at the back of the room open and the sound of someone coming in. The door closed softly and a man cleared his throat, and I heard his muffled steps on the thick carpet. He came closer and I braced myself when I felt him near, ready to make conversation if I had to. But I didn't. He made his way slowly toward the casket, and when he was past me and I could see his back, I held my breath. The way he walked, the slant of his shoulders, the close-cropped hair—it was my father.

When he reached the casket, he leaned over and kissed my mother, and I heard him whisper, "Oh, Eve." Then he crossed himself—something I had never seen him do—and he knelt at the casket, his head bowed, one hand on my mother.

He seemed to be praying, and we stayed like that for perhaps ten minutes, my father kneeling at my mother's casket, me watching, unable to move. I saw his shoulders shake and I knew that he was weeping, and when he finally stood, it was with stiffness and difficulty. He took a handkerchief from his back pocket and wiped his eyes. And then he leaned close to kiss her again, and he whispered words I will never know. Then he turned to go.

I stared hard at my hands and pulled my veil further over my face. I could not look at him, and so I sat in silence until I was sure he was gone, knowing that I was a coward and a liar, and certain I could never forgive him.

:: :: ::

To those who attended my mother's Rosary and funeral Mass, I suppose I was my mother's daughter, perfectly composed. But what appeared as composure was simply denial. I floated through it all, through every part of the official observances of my mother's death, telling myself it wasn't real and working hard at not thinking about what was happening. The viewing and Rosary on Wednesday night, the funeral Mass on Thursday morning, and afterward the walk out of the church behind the casket, the drive to the cemetery behind the hearse and the walk through thick grass to the plot, the priest's quiet graveside prayers, the last condolences of friends afterward—all of it was a blur, dreamlike and indistinct.

So that when it was finally time to leave the grave—to really say good-bye—I didn't want to go. *As long as I'm here*, I thought, *she won't be buried, and it won't have really happened.* And so I lingered at the curb near the Cadillac that was to take my grandmother and Jack and me home, perhaps forty feet from the grave, talking with the few friends who remained and working at keeping them there. I held Jack's hand tightly and thanked the priest, I talked with my grand-mother about anything I could think of and ignored the seriousness and exhaustion in her eyes, and I just kept thinking, *Don't go.* When I felt a hand on my shoulder, I turned eagerly, ready for more distrac-tion, and I found myself facing my father.

For a long moment, we just stared at each other. His eyes were even bluer than I had remembered, and his hair was more white than blond. He wore what he'd worn the day before—white shirt and blue tie, navy blue blazer, gray slacks—and I saw that he was heavier, and that he'd aged. But I would have known him a mile away.

It was clear that he was waiting for me to speak, but I couldn't, from stubbornness or anger or awkwardness or grief, or maybe all of them at once. I could only stare, and wait for him to say something.

"Anna," he said finally. "I'm so sorry." The anguish in his face was plain.

I nodded, and fell back on good manners. "Thank you for com-ing," I said, and I hated the falseness in my voice.

He shifted his weight and looked beyond me, clearly uncomfort-able. "Is it all right if I say good-bye?"

I nodded mechanically, and he turned and began walking toward the grave.

I followed him, I don't know why—some sense of propriety, the need to make sure he did nothing wrong, I don't know, but I went with him. When he reached the grave, he stood for a moment and took a deep breath. "I was so foolish," he whispered, and though I wasn't cer-tain he was talking to me, I nodded. It was a sentiment I shared.

The casket had been lowered into the freshly dug grave, and a large sheet of plywood covered the opening. My father leaned down and took a handful of earth, then held the plywood back and dropped the earth on the casket. He whispered, *"Tsaichien"*—good-bye—and then he stood and wiped his hands on his pants, and he turned to leave.

I think it was the sound, the barely heard softness of a handful of dirt falling on the casket lid, that made something come loose inside of me. I caught my breath, and he looked at me anxiously, afraid he'd done something wrong. I shook my head, trying to tell him I was all right, but I started to cry and it was clear that I wasn't all right at all. Without hesitating, he took me in his arms and held me close. A part of me worried that people were watching and that I was causing a scene. But then I breathed in the scent of Old Spice and cigars and something like sandalwood, and as I felt something inside give way, I let myself be comforted by my father.

new moon

IN HER WILL, my mother left me the small bungalow on Bucknell along with most of her estate. While the inheritance didn't make Jack and me rich, it did make us more comfortable, and in May, when we moved into my mother's house, it was as though we let our breath out a little. During our almost two years of marriage, Jack had taken just about every odd job he could find on weekends and after school, anything to bring in some extra cash. After my mother's death, those odd jobs stopped. That was her greatest gift to me: the freedom she gave Jack.

Moving into the bungalow was a bittersweet experience, a homecoming and a good-bye. Those first few evenings, after long days of unpacking boxes and trying to keep Eve entertained in the process, Jack and I would sit on the patio drinking cheap Chianti from juice glasses, holding Eve and listening to the cooing noises she made when she was happy. The garden was wild again and the scent of jasmine and gardenias seemed to almost bring my mother to life.

I missed her more than I could have imagined. During the winter and spring we'd spent together, she'd become my friend and confidante, and we saw each other or talked on the phone every day. Underneath our friendship was the bond of my father, for she alone understood how I felt. He was the secret we rarely spoke of, the fact that was always there.

With her death, a part of my life just disappeared. Many times a day, I picked up the phone and put it down again, remembering too late. Over and over, I thought to tell her something, or ask her something, or see if she'd like to do something, and over and over, I reminded myself that she was gone—a fact that never made any sense—and the dull ache inside me would start up again.

As the days grew longer over that spring and summer, so did my grief. I had expected it to lessen, but instead there was day after day after day where everything just hurt, one thing after another. Opening a closet hurt because of the scent of Chanel No. 5 that lingered there. Glancing out at the garden hurt because of the sight of the wisteria, growing wild and untamed in the back corner of the garden that my mother loved. Coming home hurt because of the memory of her watering the grass in capri pants and a cotton peasant blouse nearly twenty years earlier, when we'd first arrived from Shanghai. And in a strange way the days that didn't hurt were worse, days that were just long and slow and flat with absence.

I came to feel like a spectator. I watched myself hold Eve each night and rock her to sleep. I watched myself make waffles or French toast or Dutch baby for breakfast, and I watched myself set the kitchen table and make dinner and clean up afterward. I watched myself fold laundry, read *Goodnight Moon* to Eve, pay the bills, and make love with my husband, and I watched myself cry when I couldn't hold it in, all the while waiting for my life to feel familiar again.

:: :: ::

When my father and I parted at my mother's graveside, I assumed that it meant what most of my good-byes with him had meant: that I wouldn't see him again for years, if ever. There was no talk of exchanging telephone numbers or addresses, there was no mention of getting together again. There was just an embrace and the feel of his solid chest against me, then a whispered "Good-bye, Anna." And that was that.

So on a warm afternoon in June of 1955, two months after my mother's death, I was caught off-guard at the sight of his handwriting as I leafed through the mail. I was glad Jack wasn't home and that Eve was sleeping. I wanted to read whatever it was unobserved, even by my infant daughter. I put his letter aside until I'd looked at everything else. Then I ripped open the envelope and found a piece of folded-up yellow legal paper. I unfolded it and read what my father had thought important enough to write:

> *My dear Anna,*
> *1. Hope you and yours are thriving. I think of you often.*
> *2. All goes smoothly here. Chickens are laying well. Photo enclosed.*
> *3. Have been drinking V8 juice for breakfast every day for two weeks. Energy is much better. You might try it.*
> *4. The enclosed is for your Eve, with affection.*
> *With love,*
> *your Dad*

My dad, I thought, a phrase I'd never used. Inside the envelope was a black-and-white snapshot of my once-upon-a-time millionaire father surrounded by nine wire baskets of eggs. He wore a light-colored T-shirt and dark trousers, and he held a chicken, and he grinned at the camera as though this were really an occasion. Behind him stretched a long narrow structure that I guessed was a chicken coop. I stared at the picture for several moments, trying to absorb it, wondering who had taken it. And then I laughed. He looked so proud, so pleased with himself, surrounded by those hundreds of eggs. I wondered why he'd sent it. Was he hoping I'd feel sorry for him or proud of him? I couldn't guess.

There was something else in the envelope: a small pink tissue-wrapped square, as hopeful as a promise. When I'd managed to peel off the tape and unfold the tissue paper, I found a small silver heart-shaped locket on a thin chain. It was clear that it was not new; it was worn and slightly tarnished, and the back of the locket was scratched. But it was lovely, delicate and almost lacy. I held it for a moment, then took it and the photo and put them in a Joyce shoe box on the top shelf of the linen closet, where I kept anything to do with my father. It was a meager collection: the few letters and telegrams that my mother had received from Shanghai, which I'd found after her death, newspaper and magazine clippings telling of his imprisonment and release by the Communists, and a birthday card he'd given me when I was a child.

I wrote a hurried postcard, more a reflex than a decision, the result of my grandmother's twenty-year emphasis on the importance of prompt correspondence—that and the fact that I didn't want to feel like I owed him anything. Actually I wrote four quick postcards, but the first three ended up in the trash. The first one sounded too formal. The second one sounded too friendly. The third sounded awkward. The fourth probably wasn't much better, but I'd had enough: *Hi,* I started, because I hadn't called him anything in so many years that nothing felt right. *Got your note and the gift for Eve. Thank you. We're all fine. Glad things are going well for you. Best, Anna.* As I walked quickly to the mailbox on the corner, Eve in my arms and the postcard in the back pocket of my jeans, I wondered how many tries it had taken him to write his letter.

I didn't mention the letter to Jack or my grandmother. It just seemed more trouble than it was worth. And I figured that that letter was a one-time thing, no reason to make a big deal out of it.

But a week later there was another letter, and the week after that there were two, and within a month it was clear that what I'd considered a one-time thing was becoming a regular correspondence, at least on his end. Though my father wasn't a predictable writer, he was a frequent one. His letters came like the wind, in impetuous bursts. There'd be nothing for a week, and then three letters would come in a row, sometimes two in one day.

At the start, they were like the first one, not much more than a few handwritten lines on a legal pad, the items usually numbered. Later they were typewritten, the type uneven, mistakes X'd out, the style formal, even self-conscious, his comments limited to the baby's health and well-being and whatever was in the news—George Meany and the AFL/CIO, President Eisenhower's heart attack, the Warsaw Pact. He often enclosed clippings with his letters, with comments scrawled across the top: *This guy knows what he's talking about*, or *Can you beat that?* But most often he simply said, *Please read*. There were other enclosures besides the clippings—coupons for baby food, advertisements for vitamins. There was only one constant to all of the letters. *My dear Anna* was how they always began. I did not respond.

Then a few days before Christmas a package arrived. I opened it angrily, thinking, *Now what does he want?*, a strange reaction since all he was doing was sending us gifts. Inside the box were a blue-and-red rep tie for Jack, a small stuffed bear for Eve, and a book for me—*Baby and Child Care* by Dr. Benjamin Spock. I stewed around the house for a while, cross with him for upping the ante, and cross with myself for my reaction. I realized I wouldn't rest until I'd sent something to him in return, so the next day I put Eve in her pram and walked to the Fair Oaks Pharmacy, where I asked the clerk for a suggestion and on his recommendation spent two dollars and ten cents plus tax on the

Kings Men Twosome, which contained a bottle of Kings Men After
Shave Lotion and one of Thistle & Plaid Cologne. I went home and
packaged them up and sent them off as fast as I could, my just-get-it-
over-with intentions a far cry from any Christmas spirit. I wasn't
giving anything, really. I was just trying to get him off my mind, and
off my conscience. All I wanted was for him to go away.

But things with him had a boomerang effect. Three weeks after
I sent the package, I heard from him again.

> *My dear Anna,*
>
> *I am an ingrate for waiting so long to write. But notwith-
> standing my sloth in writing, I do appreciate the gifts. You were
> very generous, and I am feeling quite dapper. The aftershave is
> so refreshing that it just about makes shaving worthwhile, and
> the cologne has made me far more pleasant to be around—at least
> I hope so! All thanks to you. Who knows—maybe I'll be a gentle-
> man yet.*
>
> *Thank you, Anna.*
> *With love,*
> *your Dad*

I handed the note to Jack. "Another letter from my pen pal."

Jack read it quickly and laughed. "I'd say his timing is off," he
said mildly.

"Oh?"

He handed the letter back. "When you want him around, he's not.
When you don't, he is."

I laughed. "That's a kind explanation. I, on the other hand, just
keep thinking, *What does he want?*"

Jack smoothed my hair from my forehead. "Looks like the man
wants to get reacquainted with his daughter," he said.

I felt my cheeks darken with embarrassment at my distrust of my father. "Are you suggesting I actually befriend him?"

Jack shrugged. "I don't see what ill can come of corresponding with him. From all I've heard, you're all right as long as you don't get too close."

"Simple as that," I said sarcastically.

He nodded. "Yep. Simple as that."

:: :: ::

I turned twenty-five on the seventeenth of January 1956, and when Jack brought me coffee in bed, I gave him the unbirthday present I'd bought the week before: another box of cigars. He looked startled, then scared, then happy, and he had to ask me over and over again when the baby was due–*August 7*–and how was I feeling–*just tired*–and how long had I known–*two weeks*. We opened a bottle of champagne even though it was seven o'clock in the morning and neither of us would be able to drink much of it. We toasted me, we toasted him, we toasted Eve, and we celebrated the idea of a second child while our first one walked shakily around our bed, grinning with delight with her ability to entertain us.

At seven-thirty, Jack left for Flintridge to teach American history to rowdy eighth-grade boys. I wished him luck, then bundled Eve up and met my grandmother at Mass. When we got home, I gave Eve mashed bananas and warm milk, and she fell asleep at nine o'clock, as exhausted as though a day had passed.

I was determined not to miss my mother too much on this first birthday of my life without her, and I'd come up with a plan for how to do that. I'd stay out of the garden, which never failed to remind me of her. I wouldn't be alone in our bedroom, which now and then still seemed to smell faintly of Cashmere Bouquet soap, though Jack said I imagined it. I would keep busy, I'd decided. I'd finish reading *The*

Quiet American, I'd write a letter, iron shirts, sweep the cobwebs on the broad front porch, clean out closets, work on a crossword, just about anything at all to keep me from dwelling on my mother's absence.

So when the doorbell rang sometime after eleven, I was grateful for the diversion. Eve was still asleep and the house was too quiet. I'd felt as though I were sinking.

And then the day changed, for when I opened the door, I faced my father.

He wore khaki trousers and a pressed white shirt, no tie. He looked healthy—ruddy faced and barrel chested, and he'd put on some weight since my mother's funeral, which somehow made me view him as a traitor. Only his hair was the same: the same short blond hair that was his trademark.

He cleared his throat and held a dozen white roses out to me as tentatively as a shy suitor. "For my girls," he said gruffly, and he took a try at a smile.

I wanted to say that we weren't his girls, but I didn't. I just nodded as I took the flowers. I breathed in their scent and said, "They're beautiful. Thank you."

He nodded. "No trouble," he said, and he stared at me closely. "If I'm not mistaken, you're a year older today."

I smelled the roses again. "I am," I said. "It was sweet of you to remember."

"I always do," he said quickly, and then he laughed grimly. "I just haven't been so great about letting you know."

I nodded but did not meet his eyes.

"And this is for you," he said, and he held out a small package wrapped in white tissue paper. "I'm not much of a gift-wrapper."

"Thank you," I said, and I tore the tissue paper away and found a bottle of perfume: Evening in Paris. I loosened the top and breathed in a strong floral scent that was a little heavy for my taste. "It's lovely," I said.

He nodded. "That actress wears it," he said. "That young French girl, very pretty, with your eyes. Do you know her?"

I shook my head.

He tapped his forehead. "Sometimes things take a while to surface," he said, and then he grinned. "Jeanmarie," he said. "That's all she goes by. The photographs of her remind me of you." He paused. "Wear it in good health, Anna, for a long time to come."

I heard Eve's tentative waking cries then, cries that would quickly grow into full-fledged yowls as she woke and found herself alone. I looked at my father and thought, *You can leave now.*

He nodded as though he'd read my thoughts. "Go ahead, go ahead," he said, and he waved me on, as though he were giving me permission. Then he stepped into our house and closed the front door behind him.

I could only nod, stunned at the ease with which he'd entered my life. As I walked toward Eve's room, he called, "Take your time. I'm in no hurry."

Hardly music to my ears. "All right," I said, my voice tight, and I went into Eve's room and closed the door carefully behind me. As I took my time changing her diaper and dressing her in a turtleneck and a blue corduroy romper, I whispered my complaints to her—"I cannot believe him, just showing up, saying he'll wait, acting as though he owns the place, and what am I supposed to do with him now, just sit and talk and pretend we know each other?" Eve smiled at me and touched my nose and said, "Ohh." And then we heard whistling, and Eve looked surprised and interested. She pointed to the door and said, "Out," and she began to squirm in my arms.

"Here goes," I said, and I smoothed her wispy dark hair away from her face and looked into her brown eyes and thought for the thousandth time how beautiful she was. "You're gorgeous," I whispered, and she grinned as though she knew it.

My father was sitting in the old Morris chair that he'd liked during the months that he'd lived with my mother and me so long ago. He stood up when he heard my steps on the hardwood floor, then he turned to face me and started to speak. But he stopped in the middle of a word and just stared at Eve and me, his expression a mix of affection and wonder and interest—a look I'd known but forgotten.

"This is Eve," I said. She was staring at him and a part of me wanted to warn her about him. *Don't love him*, I thought. *Don't get attached.*

He whistled softly. "Would you look at her," he whispered, and he walked to us tentatively, as though we might startle and bolt if he wasn't careful—which we would have if I'd done what I wanted. "Isn't she the beauty," he said. "A perfect mix of you and your mother."

"With a little of Jack thrown in, I hope."

He laughed. "I'm sure there is. I just don't see it. What I see are your mother's beautiful eyes and that determined expression of yours. You looked so much like that when you were this age," he said. "I'd forgotten how—" he started.

"Yes?" I asked quickly, perfectly willing to play the role of inquisitor.

He shook his head. "I'd forgotten a lot of things," he said. "More than you want to know." Then he gently smoothed Eve's hair and made a soft clucking sound. Eve watched him warily for a moment, then grinned, then hid her face against my chest and clung to me.

"She's a little shy," I said.

He shrugged it off. "No matter. Doesn't even know me, I'm a complete stranger. Which is something I'd like to fix. If you're free for lunch, I thought I'd take you two out. There's a place nearby with *chiaotzû* that are pretty good. New Moon, over on Fair Oaks." He paused and cleared his throat, waiting for my answer and watching me in that sizing-you-up way of his.

I had no intention of going, but as I stood there searching for a good excuse or a plausible lie, good manners won out and I heard myself say, "We'd love to."

He beamed, and I wondered if I was imagining a look of triumph on his face.

"I'll just get changed," I said, for I was wearing an old red pullover and a pair of Wrangler jeans that I'd had since college, clothes that I loved more than ever once I could fit back into them after Eve's birth.

My father shook his head as he looked me over. "No, no, you look just fine. Like a schoolgirl. We're not going anywhere fancy."

:: :: ::

I had not heard my father speak Mandarin for nearly ten years, and I had forgotten both the sound of the language itself and of his voice, speaking it, so that when a young waiter came and handed us menus and my father handed them back and began to speak Chinese, I was almost as stunned as the waiter was. The waiter was almost indignant as he rattled off what I guessed were questions having to do with why my father spoke so well. My father answered his questions at some length, and the waiter's expression relaxed, and I could see that my father had won him over. It was five minutes or more of conversation before the waiter ran out of questions and took our order. The moment was familiar: my father, the hero, the man about town, though we were only in a small Chinese restaurant in South Pasadena, and I was surprised at the pride I felt. I was charmed, even if reluctantly so.

It was clear that he'd charmed our waiter as well. He took our order to the kitchen, then returned with two other waiters so that my father could entertain them as well. Judging from their laughter, I guessed he was quite the raconteur, though I had no idea what he was saying. Finally he turned to me and I heard the first familiar word: "*Nüerh*," he said—daughter—and I smiled as though I'd understood everything else as well. The waiters bowed and smiled and said something about me, I thought, and I, too, was a guest of honor simply by association.

When they had gone and my father faced me again, he was transformed. His eyes were a brighter blue, and he looked younger and happier, more like the man from my childhood. "They're always surprised," he said, and he laughed softly. "They never expect me to know what they're saying." He gestured toward the kitchen, where we could hear strains of Mandarin. "That youngest one—he said you were a real beauty, by the way—he's from Shantung province, where I was raised. His parents are still there, at least he guesses they are. Nobody knows with the Communists in charge."

I nodded, and then we were quiet for a moment, and I thought he was thinking about the past, and I hoped he would talk about it. But then he asked, "Do you still practice?" and he eyed me carefully, as though this were a test.

"Practice?" I asked.

"Your faith," he said. "Do you go to Mass, receive, all that?"

His question surprised me. "Of course," I said, "I never stopped," for it was as though he'd asked if I still breathed.

He nodded. "That's good. And you'll raise Eve in the Church."

"Yes," I said, and I tried to keep the irritation out of my voice. I could remember going to Mass with my father on Christmas Eve, and that was it. Even then, he didn't receive—my mother was the believer. What possible concern was this to him?

"That Pope you've got, Pacelli, he's not so bad as people think."

This comment surprised me. My grandmother was Pope Pius XII's constant albeit respectful critic. "What is it you like?" I asked.

It was his turn to look surprised, and he waved my question away. "Oh, there's plenty. What's not to like? That aloofness that bugs everybody is a small thing, just his manner. He's worked toward good all along. Tried to prevent the war, then tried to stop it. Saved hundreds of thousands of Jews. And he's figured out that communism in Eastern Europe is no small thing." My father shook his head. "He's on the right track, that guy."

I listened with something like amazement, and I had to work to keep from laughing. It was so like my father to speak of the Pope with such familiarity, such casualness, using his family name, talking about him as though he were an old acquaintance and critiquing the Pope's views as though he were the expert. I considered pointing these things out to him, but it seemed futile. "Well, maybe you're right," I said.

He nodded as though I'd stated the obvious. "He knows where he stands," my father said, "and there's no inching him over, left or right. That's a good thing." He took a long drink of tea and refilled his cup and mine, then he leaned toward me. "I'll tell you, Anna, and this is free advice, worth every penny you paid for it, but you have to have something to hold on to. Some sort of center, something you can turn to in a difficult time. My dad raised me with that, and I threw it all away, like it was some old coat that I'd outgrown. That little Eve there, she needs education, and she needs a real grounding in the faith. Don't overlook that."

"I won't," I said evenly, and then I corrected myself: "I'm not." And I tried to figure out how I'd gotten into the position of defending myself to him.

He laughed softly. "Now look, you've got your back up, I've offended you. But I'm right about this one. Promise me you'll raise her with a strong faith, all right?"

"Yes," I said, and I stopped myself from saying what I was thinking: *But not because of you.* "I've never considered doing otherwise," I added.

He nodded and I waited, thinking this was only the start of the advice, but nothing came; he was suddenly quiet. He straightened his chopsticks, then tapped his fingers on the white tablecloth. He moved the bottle of soy sauce closer to the jar of hot oil, and then he looked around the restaurant as though awaiting reinforcements. I could hear him humming softly, and I recognized the awkwardness you see in people who spend most of their time alone.

I finally attempted conversation. "How are the chickens?" I asked, and immediately felt ridiculous at the question.

He shook his head. "Not so good, not so good," he said. "I mean they're fine. They're just not mine anymore. I threw in the towel and sold the place two weeks ago. Enough is enough for that business. I'm moving on to something steadier."

"And what's that?"

"This and that. The details are boring. Suffice it to say I'm in the Bradbury Building. You know it, down on South Broadway? Lot of marble and wrought iron? I think your grandfather officed there a long time ago. It's just to tide me over, until something better comes along."

"In Los Angeles? But you live in Carpinteria."

He shook his head. "*Lived*," he said. "Not anymore. My place up there went with the chicken farm. I'm an Angelino now, I've moved to Bunker Hill, right by Angels Flight. I can walk downtown, argue with the soapbox preachers in Pershing Square, eat lunch at the Yorkshire Grill, be at the Main Library in five minutes flat, and I've got Grand Central Market for my groceries. I've had enough of the sticks. Even the ocean didn't make up for the isolation."

I cleared my throat. "You're living here now?"

He laughed grimly. "Don't worry, Anna. The old man won't be showing up on your doorstep every week. Today's an exception."

I nodded weakly, embarrassed that my panic had shown, but panicked nonetheless at the prospect of having him so close. "It's fine," I said. "It's wonderful that you'll be nearby."

He waved my words away. "We'll see about that," he said, and then his new friend the waiter saved him from having to say more by setting plates of steaming food on our table.

My mother and I had done a pretty good job of avoiding Chinese food since our return from Shanghai in 1946. I don't think she'd ever liked it much in the first place, so it wasn't hard for her. I, on the other hand, loved it, but at the black-and-white age of fifteen, abstaining from it had seemed both a matter of principle and a show of loyalty to my mother. And then it became habit.

And so my mouth watered as soon as I smelled the food: fried noodles with shrimp, steamed dumplings—*chiaotzû*—a plate of steamed vegetables, steamed white rice. I must have stared, for my father leaned forward and touched my hand.

"You wanted something else? It doesn't look good to you?" he asked, worry in his voice and his expression.

I laughed. "No, it looks wonderful. And I'm starved. I haven't had this in a long time," I said.

He smiled and glided easily over the reference to the past. "Dig in," he said. "Eat all you want. We'll keep ordering more until you're full."

I did dig in, and if eating and enjoying Chinese food made me in some way disloyal, I was a traitor on a grand scale. It was heaven: the taste of ginger in the *chiaotzû*, the hot peppers in the noodles, the crispness of the carrots and water chestnuts. Even the taste of steamed rice with soy sauce was a treat. I didn't speak for a full five minutes, just shoveled it in as fast as I could, as though I hadn't eaten for days. I put a few noodles on the tray of Eve's high chair and let her fool with them as I went to work. When I finally came up for air, I found my father grinning at me.

"Food of the gods, eh?" he said.

I nodded and stopped eating for a moment. "It's wonderful," I said. "Thank you."

My father looked pleased. *"Hao sho,"* he said, and he watched to see if I remembered, which I didn't. He shrugged. "Don't mention it," he said. "The pleasure is mine."

:: :: ::

During the second week of August 1956 as I reached and then passed my due date, my father called every day. Finally, on the fifteenth, when he called and got no answer, he figured something was up and took the bus to Huntington Hospital, where he stood at the nursery window and stared intently at the rows of bassinets. He pestered a nurse, telling her he just had to see the Bradley baby, until she held up his second granddaughter for him to see. Then he just stood there, shaking his head, telling those around him that she was his. That was where Jack found him, and he brought my father to my room. I was drowsy, and when he smoothed back my hair and kissed my forehead, it was as though I'd dreamed him, the way I did as a child.

He came to see us two weeks later. It was a gray day, overcast and dark but it wouldn't rain, a muggy Friday morning that had me feeling tired and unpretty. I had the blues, and when Jack left to teach school, I was sure the day would feel endless.

So when my father appeared at our front door a little after ten, I was less than thrilled about having a visitor. I was still in my robe, my hair pulled back in a ponytail, and I hemmed and hawed at the doorstep, but he was insistent and invited himself in. He marveled over the baby I held in my arms—two-week-old Heather, whom we had named for my best friend, past and present. Eve had followed me to the door and was holding on to my robe. Her wavy hair was mussed and she was still in summer pajamas with one sock on, one sock off. My father knelt so that he was her height, and he told her how grown up she was, and Eve nodded knowingly. She was one and a half years old, and pretty sure of herself. Her pediatrician had said she was approaching her first adolescence, and I had winced.

Then my father told her how lucky she was to be a big sister. Eve looked unconvinced. In those two long weeks since Heather's arrival, she had found that having a little sister mostly meant less attention and more competition. My father saw things differently. "You are the eldest daughter," he said urgently. "*Tì i*—that's you, you're 'number one.'" I saw a hint of satisfaction on Eve's face.

I offered him coffee then, which he refused. But he said he'd like to sit down for a minute, and he followed me into the kitchen.

Heather had fallen asleep in my arms, and I laid her gently in a bassinet we'd set up in the corner in the kitchen. I lifted Eve into her high chair and gave her a handful of Cheerios to play with, and my father and I sat at the table.

"I have something for you," he said, and he handed me a parcel the size of a bar of soap wrapped in newspaper.

I unwrapped it and found a small teak box that I recognized immediately. Its corners and top were rounded, and the dark wood was so polished that it gleamed, and if you didn't know what it was, you might not know how to open it, or even that it opened at all. But I did, and I gently slid the cover back the way I'd seen my father do it when I was a child.

The box held my father's chop, a column of pale marble three inches tall, a half inch square. On the bottom was his seal, the name *Schoene* in Chinese characters. Beneath the chop, in a separate compartment, was a square of thick red ink.

It was like handing me a piece of my childhood, something known and loved and forgotten all at once. As a child in Shanghai, I'd seen my father use his chop a hundred times, carefully placing his seal next to his signature on letters and contracts and other legal documents, the red ink as bright as a warning. I had coveted it, and had never been allowed to play with it.

"I loved this," I said.

He nodded. "I had it made just a month after your mother and I arrived in Shanghai, when I got my first job. I felt like it made me a resident, not a visitor. That was important to me." He ran his hand over his hair. "It's one of the few things I have from those days."

"How did you manage to keep it . . ." I paused, searching for a phrase, for there seemed to be an unspoken rule that we never talked of Shanghai. "With everything that happened, how do you still have it?"

He shrugged the question off. "That's a long story," he said, "and one I'm not up to telling. The point is that I want you to have it." He was quiet for a moment, and I waited. A dog barked in the distance, and the wind stirred in the eucalyptus tree outside, the one my father and I had planted years before. He tapped his fingers on the table as though he were impatient. "I know you can't just forget everything I've done, Anna," he said finally. "But I'd like to make amends. I'm hoping you can begin to forgive me."

I stared at the chop and ran my finger over its surface, hard and smooth and cool, and I understood that he was giving me his past. For the first time, my caution toward him began to dissolve, and forgiveness seemed possible.

I took the chop from its case and held it up to the light. The carved end was stained with red ink, as though it had just been used. I pressed it carefully into the small square of red ink in the box. "Is this how you do it?" I asked.

He smiled slightly, watching me. "Yes," he said.

I took the newspaper that the box had been wrapped in, and I pressed the chop down on a smooth corner. When I lifted it, the Chinese character for our name was bright red against the black newsprint, a declaration.

"Welcome home," I said.

He nodded. *"Hsiehhsieh,"* he said. He looked me in the eye, and I remembered: *Thank you.*

:: :: ::

In the years after my mother and I left Shanghai in 1938, I became something of a conjurer, able to imagine my father in any scene I wanted. Thanksgivings and Christmases, Easters and birthdays and summer vacations—after a while, I filled in the father-shaped holes without even trying. I knew how he would act, what he would say, where he'd sit, who he'd talk to, how it would feel to have him there.

And so Thanksgiving Day 1956, when he finally was there after all those years when he wasn't, was a strange day, almost eerie. At long last he'd reappeared, just as I'd wanted him to on that hot July afternoon in Shanghai when he was kidnapped, and just as I'd wanted him to for years after that. It was as though all those years of conjuring had finally paid off.

I'd invited him tentatively, but he'd accepted without hesitating, and he knocked on our door at three o'clock on the dot on that cooler-than-usual November afternoon. He wore a white shirt and a paisley tie, a navy blue blazer and gray flannel slacks, and looked quite dapper, I thought, and I was proud to introduce him to my in-laws. If he was at all uncomfortable, it didn't show, and while I wasn't exactly uncomfortable, I felt a kind of giddy nervousness. It was alarming to see him: I'd be in the kitchen and glance into the living room to see him handing Jack's mother a glass of sherry and talking about President Eisenhower's reelection a few weeks earlier. Or I'd be putting bowls of mashed potatoes and gravy on the dining-room table and catch sight of him in the kitchen with Jack's father as he carved the turkey, my father offering unsolicited but good-natured advice on his every move. The rest of Jack's family, his parents and his brother and his family, seemed to take my cue and to act as though my father had just returned from a long trip. Even my grandmother welcomed him. She sat in what had become "her chair" in the living room, the Morris chair that my father had loved. She liked it because it was easy for her to get up from, which was important because of the arthritis that was becoming more and more noticeable. My father pulled up an ottoman and sat next to her, and when the food had been blessed, I saw her take his hand and I heard her say, "It's good that you're here." And I was amazed.

:: :: ::

Over that next year, he eased himself into our lives. He was with us on Christmas Eve and Christmas morning, on my birthday and Eve's in January, and by spring he was something of a fixture. He watched the girls for me whenever we needed him, day or night, and he called several times a week, often at odd times—early in the morning when I wasn't quite awake, late in the evening when everyone had wound down, at dinnertime, when the girls were tired and cranky and dinner the only important event. He never said hello or identified himself. He just started in with whatever he wanted to talk about. With Jack he talked politics and cars and sports and the economy. With me he just asked how the girls and I were, and he offered health advice. "How is everything over there?" he'd say, as though we lived much further away. When I called him and asked how he was, his answer was always the same: "Better since you called."

After a few months of regular visits, he asked if he could do a little gardening. He didn't have much of a yard at his place, he said, and the exercise would do him good. When I said yes, it became a weekly thing and we settled into a pattern: my father taking the bus from Bunker Hill to Huntington Drive, then walking the few blocks to our house, always appearing on our doorstep at around nine in the morning, an offering in the form of a bag of caramels in one hand, and a duffle bag holding his dirty laundry in the other. He'd work in the garden, Heather and Eve helping or hindering as the spirit moved them, then he'd finally come inside at around four in the afternoon. Once he'd showered, we'd sit at the kitchen table and have a cold beer together and talk.

He had opinions about everything. He worried about the riots in Little Rock, Mao's visit to Moscow and Khrushchev's to East Germany, the Russians' success with Sputnik, and our failure with a satellite of our own. He followed polo, and spent most Sundays in February and March at Will Rogers Memorial Field on Sunset Boulevard, watching matches. He liked the horse races at Santa Anita as well, not for the betting, but for the pleasure of watching the horses, he said. He liked to go early in the morning and watch the horses work out. His favorite cars were Triumphs (for sports cars) and GM (for everything else), and he was not subtle about expressing his concerns over the Studebaker Parkview Wagon that Jack had bought. He tried to talk us into signing up for Encyclopaedia Britannica's Book a Month Payment Plan, which allowed you to buy the entire set over two years at a reasonable monthly cost. "Those girls of yours will be needing it for school before you can blink," he said. "You'd be smart to invest in it now, so you're ready." He got along easily with Jack, and he was careful to the point of vigilance about overstepping his bounds and our privacy. "Don't want to wear out my welcome" was always his good-bye, and once he decided it was time to leave, there was no convincing him to stay.

He was just as careful about his own privacy, so much so that I knew very little about his life apart from us. I never saw where he lived; he said it was a little cramped and that once he'd cleared some things out, he'd have us over, but it never happened. Once he mentioned that he attended the Church of the Open Door, a nonsectarian church that met in the Bible Institute of Los Angeles, on South Hope, next to the library. He didn't speak of friends, or how he managed to live—I knew he'd left Hong Kong with almost nothing. I knew he sold scrap metal only because he asked if he could sell some old pipes that Jack had stacked by the garbage after we'd had some plumbing repairs done. He never said just what he did at the Bradbury Building, either. I found that out myself.

One afternoon when I was downtown I stopped in to say hello, thinking I could surprise him. But when I looked at the building directory, I did not see my father's name, and when I asked the guard in the lobby where his office was, the guard laughed.

"There's no office, Miss," he said. "Joe's the night janitor around here. His shift starts at six P.M." The guard looked at me with curiosity. "Is there a message?"

I opened my mouth to tell him there had been a mistake, and then I stopped because suddenly things made sense: my father's silence about his work, his guardedness in conversation.

"No message," I said, and I hoped the guard would not tell my father that a young woman had asked for him.

I watched my father more carefully after that. I saw that he always wore the same clothes when he gardened, and I saw how gratefully he accepted whatever I'd fixed for lunch. In our conversations, he often mentioned bargains he'd found— "Safeway's got tomatoes on sale," he'd tell me, "you should stock up, Anna." Or potatoes or bananas or cereal or noodles, whatever was reduced. *That's my father*, I'd thought, the eternal businessman, always on the lookout for a good deal. I'd figured that he was just a good shopper, the type whose day was made by saving a few dimes. I understood now: he could afford only what was on sale. But he never talked about needing anything, or money being tight, or not having enough. And I stopped asking.

Nor did he talk about the past. He never mentioned my mother, or Shanghai. If the conversation veered in any of those directions, he curtly changed the subject, making it clear that that was off-limits. I honored that preference, though it apparently didn't apply to the girls. I sometimes overheard him telling them stories and describing places from my childhood.

"You would never have wanted to leave if you'd been in Shanghai then," he told them one rainy afternoon. "You could go anywhere in the world from the Shanghai Harbor, you could start up any business, you could be anybody you wanted to. Nothing was impossible there."

"Shanghai," Eve said softly, and Heather, always the mimic, tried to copy her and managed to make a soft *shhh* sound, which made Eve laugh.

My grandmother said I was doing the right thing but that I should still be careful. I shouldn't loan him money, she said, unless I didn't need it back. I shouldn't depend on him, I shouldn't expect anything from him. I listened to her and hoped she would be wrong but I also braced myself for the awkwardness I would feel the first time he asked to borrow money, or the first time he didn't come when he'd said he would.

Those things never happened. He never asked for money, he never let me down. He was as faithful as anyone I'd ever known, and when my grandmother told me to look carefully at who he was, what I saw was a changed man, a man whose presence calmed and cheered me. And in the end, I abandoned her warnings and let myself be reclaimed.

:: :: ::

On a cool afternoon in March of 1959, I was putting groceries away when my father came into the kitchen. He'd worked outside, then showered, and he smelled of soap and aftershave. After showering he'd watched *Mr. Wizard* with the girls, a show he'd taught them to like, and I'd left them alone in the den, the three of them sitting close together on the sofa, all of them entranced. Eve was four, Heather was two and a half, and they were both crazy about my father. The three of them seemed to have their own little world. When Eve had begun to talk a few months before her second birthday, she shortened Grandpa to just Pop, and that became his name to them.

When he came into the kitchen, my father took two bottles of Schlitz from the refrigerator, opened them, and put one on the counter for me. Then he sat down at the kitchen table and took a long drink. I'd folded his clean laundry and left it on the table for him.

"You do too much for me," he said. "You shouldn't fold all those clothes. That's what I was coming in here for."

I laughed. "I can do laundry in my sleep," I said. "Not to worry." The sound of the girls' laughter floated in from the den, a light, watery sound that I always wanted to capture. "How's Mr. Wizard?" I asked.

My father shook his head. "Those two rascals of yours think he's the real thing, all right."

I nodded. "Did you know they've taken to calling you Mr. Wizard?"

He laughed, but I could see he was pleased. "Not this old know-nothing."

"Yep," I said. "They've told their friends that their Pop can make anything grow. They call you Wizard of the Garden. They think you know magic."

My father took another drink of beer. "They're smart ones, all right. They're good girls, Anna."

I was filling a canister with flour, and there was a seriousness in his voice that made me look at him. When I did, I found him watching me closely. "I have a favor to ask you," he said.

I swallowed. Here it was, I thought, after all these years: the request for money my grandmother had warned me about. I wiped my floury hands on my black slacks and left smudged handprints on my thighs. Then I said, "Of course."

My father laughed. "I know that tone of voice," he said. "You're thinking it's money I want."

"No," I said, my voice high and fake. "Why—" I started, but he waved the rest of my question away.

"Don't worry about it," he said. "What I'm going to ask has nothing to do with money."

He had a habit of leaving the two middle buttons of his shirt undone and using the shirt as a pocket, and he reached into it and took out a packet of papers, which he unfolded and smoothed on the kitchen table.

"It's my will," he said. "I'd like you to be executrix of my estate." He laughed softly. "I use the word *estate* loosely. It just means that I'd like you to handle whatever I leave when I die."

I abandoned the groceries I hadn't gotten to yet and sat down at the table. "All right," I said.

He slid a few stapled pages to me across the table and I began to read.

> I, Joseph Schoene, residing in the County of Los Angeles, State of California, being of sound and disposing mind and memory and not acting under duress, menace, fraud, or undue influence of any person whosoever, do hereby make, publish, and declare this to be my Last Will and Testament, hereby expressly revoking all other and former wills and codicils heretofore made by me. I hereby give, devise, and bequeath all of the rest, residue, and remainder of my estate of every kind or nature and wherever situated, including property over which I have power of appointment, to my only child, Anna Shoen Bradley. I hereby nominate and appoint

her as Executrix of this, my Last Will and Testament, without
bond required.

I tried to read quickly, partly because he was watching me, and
partly because I did not want to dwell on it. But the last paragraph was
hard to skim:

> *I do not want a pagan approach to burial. At long last, I am*
> *a believer. When my body has died, my soul will have left this*
> *earth. I have few friends, and no desire for a service. My per-*
> *sonal preference, unless my daughter has a different notion,*
> *would be cremation with ashes scattered at sea.*

When I looked up, I found him watching me carefully. I nodded,
trying to tell him that I accepted his wishes, and then I took a good
long drink of beer, hoping it would undo the knot in my stomach.

My father tapped the table four times. "Cheery stuff, eh?" He
cleared his throat.

I nodded. Then I asked, "Is there something wrong with you?"

He laughed. "There's plenty wrong with me." I must have looked
shocked, because he quickly said, "No, not like that. There's plenty
wrong up here"—he tapped his head—"but in here"—he tapped his
chest—"I'm healthy as a horse."

We were quiet for a moment. My father looked out the window,
and his expression reminded me of the way he used to gaze at the
skyline of Shanghai from the verandah in Hungjao, as though he
were searching for something. "I've lived longer than I thought
I would, all things considered, and maybe I'll live to a hundred. But at
this late stage of the game, I've learned that you never know. And
I've made so many mistakes, and taken wrong turns just about every
time I could." He shook his head. "These papers aren't about any big
estate, and you won't find yourself an heiress when I die. After all

these years, I just want to do things right." He looked down, and his voice was low. "I guess I'm trying to save face."

I nodded. "You already have, in my eyes," I said.

He looked startled for a moment, then he just looked relieved. He laughed softly and mussed my hair the way he did when I was a child, and I felt my cheeks redden from his affection.

debt

MY FATHER'S ASSURANCES ASIDE, I worried about him after that. I worried when he came inside short of breath, and I worried when I looked outside and saw how much trimming and weeding and raking and pruning he'd done. I worried when his energy seemed low, when he turned down an invitation for lunch at New Moon, when I called him and he wasn't home. I worried late at night when I couldn't get to sleep and early in the morning, when I woke before Jack and the girls.

A few months after our conversation about the will, I took Eve and Heather to the beach. It was a Saturday in June, the first summery day of the year. Jack had made plans to golf at Brookside with his father, so the girls and I took off alone for a day at San Clemente.

When we got home, Jack's car was in the driveway, and the girls climbed out of the station wagon and ran into the house, calling for him, eager to tell him about our day. I followed after them, happy to have him home so early, and the three of us tramped into the kitchen, trailing sand.

Jack was sitting at the kitchen table. The girls ran to him and he hugged them, but he was looking at me over their heads. I thought how handsome he looked, and how beautiful his blue eyes were, and how lucky I was, and then I noticed the serious anxiousness in his expression and I stood still and said, "What is it?" only half-trying to sound casual.

He nodded as though I'd guessed something, and he told the girls they could go outside and rinse the sand off with the hose. Heather stood next to him, and he pulled her T-shirt off, not bothering about the sand, which crumbled around his feet. Eve looked back and forth between us suspiciously; she had caught the tone of my voice and was alert at the unexpected, the way she always was at anything out of the ordinary.

"It's all right," Jack said, and he grinned at her and tickled her belly. "Go squirt your sister with the hose."

She nodded knowingly, as though she were aware of the bribe but accepted it. Then she took Heather's hand and led her outside.

"What is it?" I said.

"He's not feeling well," Jack said. "I think it's his stomach. He wasn't very specific."

My father had called an hour or so earlier, Jack said. He didn't sound good, but when Jack asked what the matter was, my father tried to laugh it off. "Some stomach thing," he said. "You know how it goes. The parts start to give out after a while."

Jack had tried to be casual. "So they say," he'd answered.

And then there was a pause, and my father said, "Is she around?"

It was his voice, Jack said, that worried him. He sounded afraid, a first.

"Well, shoot, she's not," Jack had said, not missing a beat, though he knew something was wrong. This was not my father's usual call. He never talked about his health; he never told you if something was wrong. "She's at the beach with the girls," he told him, and when my father didn't respond, he added, "What can I do?"

Another pause, and then my father said that he'd call back later, and he hung up.

But by the time I called, my father said he was fine—a false alarm, he said, just some indigestion or something. He still sounded odd, but there was no convincing him to come over, or to let me drive over and pick him up, or to see a doctor on Monday.

"Why are you being so stubborn?" I said finally.

He laughed. "Anna, you're about fifty years too late if you want to change me." He paused and said, "I know your intentions are good. But I'm fine. I just wasn't feeling so good and I got a little worried, but it's passed and I'm right as rain. Stop worrying and take care of those girls of yours."

:: :: ::

I took his advice and tried to stop worrying, and for a long time, my father gave me no reason for concern. For the next two years, he continued to come over every Thursday and whenever else I asked him to. The girls were crazy about him, Jack's family entertained and intrigued, and little by little, even my grandmother seemed to lose her reservations. He was something I'd never expected—part of our family—and I came to consider both of us lucky.

On a warm, clear day in May of 1961, he came over a little later than usual, around ten in the morning. Eve was six and a half and lonesome for kindergarten. She'd had chicken pox, and the last few bumps were keeping her home. Heather was almost five and determined to contract the pox, which she seemed to consider a rite of passage, since it had made its way through most of Eve's kindergarten class. Heather hardly let her sister out of her sight. She drank from her cup, snuggled with her in front of the TV, did everything she could to expose herself to germs. So far her efforts hadn't paid off, and both girls were tired of the whole affair.

My father had shown up just in time. When he knocked at the door and said he had something special, all three of us were hopeful.

What he had was ladybugs. He held a small cloth bag, and inside were twenty-five of them, and when he showed it to the girls, they shrieked and called for me. He said they were the best control, live or otherwise, for aphids, which were threatening to harm his beloved roses, and that Eve and Heather—"my beautiful assistants," he called them—could help him scatter the ladybugs.

The three of them tramped outside and I watched from the kitchen window as my father opened the bag. "Now, there's no guarantee that they'll stay put," I heard him say, "but I've just got a feeling that they'll do the trick." From the window, I saw him lean over his roses, the girls mimicking his stance and concern. Eve, always careful, hovered over the roses carefully, as though if she got too close, she might inhibit the ladybugs and even the roses' growth. Not Heather. She seemed to have strong ideas about which ladybugs should be where, and began moving them around, trying to create little families, until my father talked her into just leaving them alone.

The girls stayed close to him for the rest of the morning. I caught glimpses of them from inside as I paid the bills and changed the sheets and folded laundry and picked up toys. I could hear Heather questioning my father about everything he was doing, her voice high and insistent with curiosity: "But why, Pop? *Why?*" And then I'd hear the low tones of my father's voice, explaining, the breeze carrying away most of his words, so that only a few made it inside: *aphids, roses, pests, harm. Vigilance, reward, full bloom.*

At around one, I noticed that things had gotten quiet outside, and I looked out the window to see where everyone had gone. My father was lying on the grass on his back. Heather and Eve stood on either side of him, leaning over him, peering at his face. It was a game they played often: he would lie down on the grass and pretend to fall right to sleep, while the girls whispered over him, trying to decide if he was really awake. But it worried me that day, and I called to them, and when my father stood up, I felt a rush of relief that surprised me.

They came inside for lunch then, and I sent Eve and Heather to the bathroom to wash their hands. I was making tuna sandwiches, and my father leaned against the counter, watching me spread tuna on raisin bread. He was breathing hard, and I said, "Are you all right?"

"I'm fine," he said. "Just a little winded."

And then he collapsed.

He fell first onto one knee, then to the tile floor, his body and then his head hitting with a horrible thump. I screamed and dropped the bowl I was holding, then I knelt next to him and held his face between my hands, and I knew that he was unconscious. I grabbed the phone from the counter and dialed the operator. "My father," I said, "my father," and I didn't know what to say next.

"Do you need an ambulance?" the operator asked, and I nodded, then managed to blurt out our address. She read it back to me and said someone would be there in minutes.

And then I hung up and saw the girls standing in the doorway staring at my father, their eyes wide. Eve's chin was trembling; she looked terrified. Heather looked perplexed, as if she was just waiting for me to explain.

"Pop?" she said softly.

I looked at Eve. "Run to Mrs. Porter's and tell her to come quick. Can you do that?"

Eve stared at me blankly.

"Mrs. Porter," I said. Sally Porter was the neighbor two doors down. I didn't know her well, but I knew she'd been a nurse before her children were born. "Get Mrs. Porter."

Still a blank look. I remembered the oak tree with the knothole in the Porters' front yard. "The house with the tree with the secret hiding place," I said frantically, and she nodded. "Go to the house with the secret hiding place. Take Heather with you. Tell Mrs. Porter to come quickly."

Eve nodded hard, then took Heather's hand and said, "Run!" and the two of them hurried out of the house.

I turned back to my father. His breathing was labored, and his body jerked. I put my hand on his chest and felt a heartbeat. "You're all right," I whispered, "your heart's beating, and you're all right, you're all right." I rested my hand on his chest and felt his body working to breathe. I stroked his hair and I whispered, "It's Anna, Dad. I'm right here with you." I leaned close to him and put my cheek against his, which was too cool.

"Please," I said. "Please don't die yet."

As if on cue, my father stopped breathing.

I looked at the clock, then back at my father. It seemed as though Eve and Heather had been gone for an hour. I had no idea what to do for him. I had never felt so useless.

A minute passed. I kept talking to him and stroking his face and holding his hand. And then, finally, I heard hurried footsteps in the living room, and Sally burst into the kitchen. "Oh, my God," she said. I looked at her, then at the clock. He had not breathed for two minutes.

"Can you do something?" I said. "*Can you please do something?*"

Sally knelt next to him and put her hand on his wrist. "He doesn't have a pulse," she said, "I don't know," and then she placed her hands on my father's sternum and began to press down, counting each push. The scene was nightmarish and grotesque, and I thought of my daughters.

"The girls," I said.

She was pressing and counting. When she reached fifteen, she said, "They're at my house. Doug's home. Don't worry." And then she breathed into my father's mouth, and I thought, *Make this work.*

She was starting to press and count again when we heard the ambulance. There was a lot of noise in the living room, clattering and running and urgent voices, and three men appeared with a stretcher. They asked hurried questions that Sally answered in words I didn't understand. I did understand the grimness in their expressions and in her voice. I leaned against the refrigerator, wanting to give them room, and I saw, on the counter, my father's leather gardening gloves, fresh with dirt. He had taken them off twenty minutes ago.

The men lifted my father onto the stretcher, then said I could ride with them, and I nodded, and asked Sally to call Jack, and said his number was next to the phone. She was crying, and I thought, *Why is she crying?* And I looked at her and knew that my father was gone.

:: :: ::

At the hospital, a nurse told me to wait, and she asked if I needed to call anyone. I said my husband would be here soon, then I sat down on a dark blue scratchy couch. I held my head in my hands and tried to will Jack there.

I didn't wait long. A man who introduced himself as Dr. Pearson came within the half hour and told me what I'd known in my heart: that my father was dead. He had died shortly after reaching the hospital of cardiac arrest, probably caused by ventricular fibrillation, very rapid irregular contractions of the muscle fibers of one of the lower chambers of the heart. He had never regained consciousness.

I listened carefully, wanting to understand what had gone on in his body—what had gone wrong, and why. I found myself repeating some of Dr. Pearson's phrases: *myocardial infarction, ischemia, ventricular fibrillation, cardiac arrest, sudden death.* A part of me wanted to sit down with him and have him explain everything in detail, so thoroughly that it all made sense, moment by moment. I wanted causes and events, reasons why, a sense of order.

But when Dr. Pearson finished his explanation of my father's death, I couldn't say what I wanted. I found him watching me carefully. I was waiting for him to tell me something useful.

And then he said, "Would you like to see your father?"

I felt an odd sort of relief, an almost hopeful feeling— *I can still see him*, I thought, *he's still here*—and I said, "Yes."

Dr. Pearson nodded. "Give me a minute," he said, and he disappeared.

Jack found me while I was waiting. He knew somehow, and he looked at me strangely, as though trying to see how I was. I must have looked odd. I wasn't crying. I might not have even looked upset. Inside I felt something like calm, but not a peaceful calm—just a sort of numbness that made me feel very quiet. Jack sat down next to me and put his arms around me and just held me there, without speaking. It felt as though he was holding me in, containing me, and I think it was the only thing I could have tolerated just then.

When perhaps fifteen minutes had passed, Dr. Pearson came for me. I told Jack I was all right, and that I wanted to go by myself, and I followed the doctor through the double doors.

We walked down a hall to a door that said LOUNGE. Dr. Pearson held the door open for me, and I hesitated at the threshold. Inside was a small sitting room. A green couch was pushed up against one wall, and a gurney was against the opposite wall. On it was my father's body, covered with a white sheet from the neck down. Dr. Pearson stood behind me, and I could feel his worry; I could feel him wondering if he should say or do something.

But I was all right; in some strange way that I didn't understand, I was all right for that moment. Because here, in front of me, just a few feet away, was my father, familiar and solid and real.

I knew what to do then; my father had taught me, just as he'd taught me the names of the buildings along the Bund, how to plant a eucalyptus tree, how to prune China roses. I could hear his words in my mind: *Respect your elders, Anna. Shake hands firmly, as though you mean it. Look people in the eye when you talk to them.* At my mother's funeral, he had taught me how to say good-bye.

And so, almost as though the scene were familiar, I rested my hand on his chest. With my other hand, I traced the features of his face: his broad forehead, his brow, his cheekbones, his jaw, his chin. He was clean-shaven, a detail that for some reason comforted me. His skin was too cool, but I did not dwell on that; what I did dwell on was his hair, recently cut, the shade not all that different from what it had been so long ago in Shanghai. Then it was very light blond; now it was light white. I touched it gently; it was as soft as a child's hair. I thought how handsome he was, and how I loved the way he looked.

I leaned close and pressed my cheek to his and whispered a confession—"I don't know what I will do without you." I said a prayer for him and for my mother, and then the Lord's Prayer. I did not cry. I touched his hair again, and I stroked his cheek. And then I kissed his forehead and I whispered, *"Tsaichien."* Good-bye.

:: :: ::

When Jack and I got home, it wasn't even two o'clock. The house looked the same: The garden was freshly watered. The kitchen table was set for four. It looked like guests were coming, except for the broken bowl and tuna fish on the floor.

The girls were still at the Porters'. Jack called and told Sally what had happened, and she offered to keep them there for the afternoon, but I said no. I suddenly wanted them home. And I wanted my grandmother. I called her and told her, and she stayed on the phone only long enough to understand what had happened, and then she said, "I'm on my way," and she hung up.

I just sat in the kitchen while I waited for her, staring at my father's gardening gloves. When I heard her and the girls in the living room, I got up to meet them, but suddenly my grandmother was there.

It hadn't felt real, until then. I'd been waiting to hear there'd been a mistake of some kind; he couldn't be gone, I thought. But when I saw my grandmother, it all became real. It was as though my life started up again. She was walking slowly toward me, using the cane that she'd finally given in to, and I went to her and let her hold me in her arms, and although I could feel my children watching, their eyes big with disbelief at the sight of their mother falling apart, I didn't care. There was nothing I could do.

"He's gone," I whispered.

"I know," she said, and she held me close. "You'll be all right. But it's going to hurt for a very long time."

:: :: ::

That night after Jack and the girls were asleep, I got up and went into the kitchen. I hadn't tried to fall asleep; I had no intention of sleeping that night. *As long as I'm awake*, I thought, *he was still alive this day*.

For a while, I just wandered through the rooms of our house. I felt as though I was looking for something, I didn't know what. Finally I poured myself a beer and toasted my father, then I went outside to sit in the garden, the one place where I thought I might find comfort. *I can wait out here*, I thought, and I realized a part of me was waiting for him to reappear.

I sat on the brick step and looked out at my father's handiwork. The night was cool, the air fragrant, and I thought how beautiful it all was late at night, and I regretted never sitting out there with him at this hour, when the world was so quiet. The garden felt like someone had just left. He always watered last thing, just before he came inside, and the air felt vaguely misty. And although I knew that the moisture was from the dew, it was easy to imagine that it was a remnant of my father. I looked at the beauty that had been his gift to us: the wisteria, the gardenias, the jasmine and bougainvillea, the roses. I breathed in the scent of the garden and I thought that I should feel comforted in that place that he'd loved.

But I didn't. Everything felt foreign: the air, the stillness of the night, the way Orion shifted overhead, the way the neighbor's cat glided along the back fence, the feel of my cotton nightgown against my skin. Breathing was different, seeing was different, sitting in the garden on the step was different. In twelve hours, everything had changed, and I found myself faced with something I'd never imagined: the world without my father, a far more desolate place than I could have imagined.

I added up the time I'd spent with him. My first seven years. The ten months that he had lived with us in this house, after his release from Haiphong Road. The two months my mother and I spent in Shanghai, which didn't really count, I thought, but I included it. And these last six years.

Fourteen years, if you rounded up. I had turned thirty in January, so for many years we had not shared a home or even a name, all of which had led me to believe that I'd lived without him for most of my life. But I was wrong. He'd been there all along, in the background, just beneath the surface of my life, even when I'd been angriest, most hurt, most distant; even during all those years when we didn't know where he was, even when I'd pretended I didn't care anything about him, he'd been there, and now I was at a loss without him.

:: :: ::

I didn't have a memorial service. I didn't know who to ask, and while I knew that my friends and family would have come, I thought that kind of service would be more for me than for my father, and I didn't want that. I wanted to grieve for him in private, and to keep his passing to myself. It was too hard to talk about, too hard to explain, too painful to bring up. The fact of his absence was too awful. I arranged for a Mass to be offered for his soul, and on that day, I prayed that he was at peace.

:: :: ::

A week after my father's death, I called his landlady and arranged to come by for a key so that I could begin to sort through his things. The landlady, an older woman with a strong German accent, said she was sorry to hear of his passing, that he had been a good tenant, and that his rent was paid through the month, a week away. I'd need to have his room cleared out by then, she said, or she'd have to charge me.

"His room?" I asked. I had pictured an apartment, or the floor of a house.

"Room," she said. "This is just a rooming house. Nothing fancy." Then she gave me directions, and I said I'd be there that afternoon. I called a sitter and said I didn't know how long I'd be, and I set off for my first and only visit to my father's house.

The house was on South Olive on Bunker Hill, an old Victorian that needed work. I parked and sat outside for a moment, just looking at it, trying to take it in. It was a far cry from what I'd expected. It needed painting, the small garden in front was mostly weeds, and on the porch was cast-off furniture that I guessed was supposed to be hauled away.

The landlady, Mrs. Wendt, met me at the front door and handed me a key. "The door's around to the back," she said, and she gestured toward the driveway. I didn't want her to know I'd never been there, so I nodded, and walked down the front steps and toward the side of the house.

"The garage," she called. "The door is on the side."

"Thank you," I called, and I tried to keep my expression calm until I was out of sight. When I reached the door, I unlocked the bolt and pushed the door open and walked inside, then closed the door quickly behind me.

I was met by my father's smell, a mix of aftershave and soap and something else that I could identify only as him, and when I breathed it in, I didn't know if I could stand to stay in the room; it hurt too much. But there didn't seem to be a choice; there was no one else to do what needed to be done, and so I began.

The room was small and cramped and dark, just an old converted garage that held a bed and a rickety dresser, a torn easy chair and a vinyl ottoman patched with duct tape. Bookshelves lined the far wall. The wall facing the backyard had been knocked down and a small alcove added. The plaster walls were painted white, my father's doing, I guessed. He said white was the best color for any room, that it looked clean and made the room appear larger. It did neither of those things here. A hook rug covered the floor, and although the day was warm, there was a chill in the room. A space heater sat in the corner.

I just stared for a moment, trying to take it all in. Once again I thought about leaving; once again I told myself I had to stay.

There was a single bed in the corner, and over it hung a watercolor of the Bund that I remembered from his office in Shanghai. I could not imagine how he had managed to keep it. I went to the dresser and opened the top drawer and found things I knew well: the blue and red bandanas that he always kept in his back pocket, his green fountain pen, an ivory comb, and a strand of pearls that had been my mother's.

The easy chair and ottoman, both of them worn, were at the foot of the bed, facing the opposite wall, which was covered with the kind of bookshelves that you put up yourself. An old black-and-white TV sat on the middle shelf, wedged into the middle of the books. I recognized the set: it had been Jack's and mine, and my father had offered to drop it off at Goodwill two years earlier when we'd gotten a new set. I did not see the new Philco Table TV we'd given him last Christmas.

I sank down onto the patched ottoman. The whole place was smaller than our living room, and though everything was clean, it was also worn. The rug was threadbare, the walls dingy, despite the white paint. The bookshelves that lined the far wall were packed with books, and I stood and scanned the titles. It was an odd collection. There were some classics, Modern Library editions of Austen, Freud, Keats, Shelley, Tolstoy, and some history and current events. There was a handful of health and diet books, and plenty of self-improvement books and pamphlets: *How to Boost Your Brain Power to Enrich Your Life*; *How to Say a Few Words–Effectively*; *The Harry R. Lange Do Sheet System of Personal Efficiency*.

But the majority of the books were religious. I was intrigued; I'd never known my father to be much of a reader of things spiritual. But I ran my fingers across the spines of a whole section of New Testaments and counted fifteen of them, including two in something called Pitman's Shorthand. There were some of the spiritual classics my grandmother loved–Thérèse of Lisieux, Julian of Norwich, John of the Cross, *The Cloud of Unknowing*–but there were also books by Billy Graham and Mary Baker Eddy, *The Sermon on the Mount* by Emmet Fox, *My Utmost for His Highest* by Oswald Chambers, almost as though my father was trying to cover his bets. And there were twenty-nine books by a Christian mystic named Joel Goldsmith, all of them underlined and highlighted. I opened one called *Practicing the Presence* and read an underlined passage: *God is the very strength of my bones; God is the health of my countenance; God is my fortress and my high-tower, my safety and my security . . . God in the midst of me is mighty, and because God is in the midst of me, I need nothing; I lack nothing. Of myself I have no ability; I have no understanding of my own, but God's understanding is infinite.*

At the far end of the room, in the added-on alcove, were a small refrigerator and a miniature gas range and oven. A shelf over the range held a few canned goods: Franco-American spaghetti, a jar of

Ovaltine, Chase & Sanborn instant coffee, Campbell's soup, V8 juice. Taped to the wall nearest the range were two recipes in my father's handwriting. One was for something called "Diet Stew," which included hamburger, cabbage, onions, celery, and tomatoes. The other was for *chiaotzû*, and I pictured Chu Shih as I read the ingredients: *2 lb. pork, 2 lb. cabbage, 3 thumbs ginger, 2 bunch onions, 2 eggs, 2 t. salt, ¼ cup sesame oil, 2 T. soya sauce.*

A large window overlooked a postage-stamp garden, most of which was shabby and neglected—I could see a few heads of lettuce and some scrawny tomato vines—but there was a corner that I was certain had been in my father's care. Four rosebushes were in bloom, plus some gardenias and a small orange tree.

That cramped alcove apparently doubled as an office, for next to the stove and pushed up against the window were an old swivel chair and desk. The desk was nicked and dented and old, the kind of unappealing office desk, huge and metal, found in government offices. I sat down and the swivel chair creaked. The hand-me-down Royal typewriter that Jack had nabbed for my father when the secretaries at Flintridge bought new equipment was in the center of the desk, and next to it was a sheet of paper that said, *Résumé–Joseph Schoene.* I read my father's account of his professional life:

> *January 1955–Present: Building maintenance, Bradbury Building. Seeking to improve position.*
>
> *Proprietor of poultry farm, October–December 1954. Sold farm for profit.*
>
> *School janitor, June–September 1954. Quit to improve position.*
>
> *Owner and manager of Aberdeen Poultry Farm, Hong Kong, 1954.*
>
> *Prisoner of Communists, 1951–1954.*

Claims adjuster and importer-exporter, Hong Kong and
Shanghai, 1931–1951.
Prisoner of Japanese, 1942–1943.

The rest of the desk was covered with papers—medical bills, lab reports, receipts from "Reliable Drug Co., The Rexall Store," a paper bag from another pharmacy with a shopping list—and over-the-counter medicines, not a surprise because of my father's strong belief in self-prescribed drugs, usually taken in double the recommended dosage on the theory that if a little was good, a lot was better. I'd seen him browse in the Fair Oaks Pharmacy the way other people browse in bookstores. On the windowsill behind the desk were what I assumed were his current favorite medications: a bottle of Pepto-Bismol, Tums, Milk of Magnesia.

In the middle desk drawer was a cigar box. I took it out and opened it and found what I supposed were treasures: a list of one hundred of the world's languages, written in pencil on pages ripped from a spiral memo pad—*Afrikaans, Amharic, Apache, Arabic, Arabic Mogrebi, Armenian, Aymara*—pages and pages of languages, with English listed at the end, just after Welsh and Yosuba. I had no idea what it meant. There was an eight-by-ten black-and-white photograph taken in the lobby of the Bradbury Building. My father wore dungarees, a work shirt, and work gloves. He leaned against a dust mop and grinned at the camera. Four sheets from a memo pad were held together with a straight pin. On each one was a Chinese character, and below it, the individual strokes required to make that character, and I understood that he was practicing. I had no idea what the characters meant. There were a few black-and-white snapshots: our house in Hungjao, my father playing polo, Chu Shih standing in front of the house. He stood very formally, and I stood next to him, holding his hand.

In the lower drawer was a thick file labeled *Bills Outstanding*, and in it I found bill after unpaid bill, both new and old, some from just after his return from Hong Kong seven years ago. The bills were mostly medical, but there was a little bit of everything. He owed a whole range of people and companies: the Reliable Drug Co.–The Rexall Store, $33.19; Edward Henderson, M.D., Orthopedic Surgery, $63.45; the Memorial Hearing and Speech Clinic, $32.00; Michael F. Swan, M.D., M.C., Nephrology and Internal Medicine, $170.10; Theodore Aarons, M.D., Dermatology, $37.10; the Los Angeles County General Hospital, which was known among other things for admitting indigents able to meet residence requirements and county jail prisoners, $65.17. There were overdue notices from the Central Public Library, and a letter from his landlord's lawyer, dated four months earlier: *Three Day Notice to pay rent or surrender possession of the premises.*

Some of the bills had messages stamped at the bottom in red or blank ink: *Past Due*, they read, *Please Remit, Second Request, Final Notice, This account has been assigned for immediate collection.* Some included handwritten notes: *Do you want us to take further action on this? We need payment now!* A pharmacy bill from six years ago: *When are you planning to pay this bill?* A vitamin supply company: *We would be happy to fill your order, but a review of our files indicates that a previous order from you remained unpaid. Demand is being made for immediate payment of $38.85, and $9.00 service charge, for a total of $47.85. We can no longer defer to your creditor's faith in you. Payment must be made now.*

He was turned down for magazine subscriptions because he owed them money from past subscriptions, $18.97 to *Popular Mechanics* and $7.93 to *Reader's Digest.*

All of these were neatly filed, stapled to the return envelopes, as though my father had fully intended to pay them eventually. I knew my father; I was certain that he'd been thinking that any day now, things would turn around and he'd be on his feet again, making money. But all you had to do was look around that room and you knew that was a lie. Whoever lived here did so in poverty.

There were odd notes and pictures taped to the walls. Photos of the girls and me were taped to the refrigerator, and pictures that they'd drawn decorated a cupboard by the stove. A fold-out postcard of the Bund was over his bed, and taped to the wall above the phone was a scrap of paper with my telephone number on it. Next to it were two photographs. One was of my mother and me at the beach in Tsingtao. I was around two years old; my mother looked young and beautiful, and I remembered that my father used to keep it in his wallet. The other photograph was of my father and me standing in front of the Hongkong and Shanghai Bank. My father smiled broadly at the camera. I was six; my hand rested on one of the bronze lions that stood guard at the entrance. And stuck in the mirror frame over the dresser was the postcard I'd sent him six years ago, when I had reluctantly answered his first letter. I read it with difficulty: *Hi—Got your note and the gift for Eve. Thank you. We're all fine. Glad things are going well for you. Best, Anna.*

Those were things I understood. There were also handwritten notes taped here and there:

> *Priorities—Start—Persevere—Do!*
> *Love, Lay, Listen, Let, Light.*
> *Keep it simple—Leave it to Emmanuel.*
> *Pray for inspiration and intelligence, claim understanding,*
> *and believe that Divine Love is working through me.*
> *Ever ready—Be prepared—Be ye ready and alert!*

I had been in the room for nearly two hours and nothing made sense. I was tired from sorting through papers and clothes and books, and I was upset by the oddness of the place. If you asked a stranger who lived here, I could imagine the answer: *A man who had next to nothing, whose health was precarious. A man who was in so much debt he could never hope to recover. A man who seemed intensely spiritual, a man who seemed disturbed.* Janitor, debtor, dreamer, schemer; rich man, poor man, beggar man, thief. My father had just about all of it covered.

I had looked at everything in the room, I thought, through all of the desk and dresser drawers, through the papers on the desk. I'd scanned the books, I'd looked at bill after bill, waiting for something to catch my eye. Nothing did.

And then I saw it: a wooden fruit crate on the highest bookshelf, almost touching the ceiling. I pushed the ottoman to the bookshelf and pulled the crate down, not caring about the dust that came with it. Then I put it on the bed and sat down.

In the box, I found a manila envelope with my name in pencil in my father's even handwriting. I pulled out its contents and found his letter to me, the map, and the journals. I read the letter and looked at the map. And then I opened the first journal—an accounting ledger—and I felt a wave of affection. I remembered him buying these ledgers at the paper store I had loved in Shanghai.

The journal, too, was addressed to me:

January 25, 1938

My dear Anna,

I have had the notion of writing some things down for you, some things about Shanghai and about what is happening around me in this amazing place, at this amazing time. I want you to know these things, and writing them down seems to be the only way to tell you. If you were here, I would probably try to explain it all to you, the way I always do. Your mother is often reminding me of your age—She's only a child, Joe, she'll say—because, she says, I often expect too much of you. So it's probably

*better that I write these things down, so that you can read them
when you are older.*

*But I couldn't tell you these things now, even if I wanted to.
You and your mother left Shanghai yesterday, and overnight,
I have become a wanderer. I could not leave yet—there is too
much business to do, too much opportunity—but seeing you off
yesterday was more painful than I care to admit.*

*So I will have to settle for this, for these pages as our conver-
sation. I hope that you will understand it all someday, and that
you will find it at least mildly interesting.*

I flipped through the pages of that first ledger with something
like awe. I lost track of time, and when I finally looked up, it was getting dark in the room. I stood and turned on the overhead light,
which made the room look even dingier than it had in daylight, and
as I looked around me, I imagined my father watching TV here, reading in the easy chair, warming up a can of spaghetti, calling me and
telling me how well he was doing, and I ached with regret.

:: :: ::

I spent the next four nights at home reading my father's journals.
Each night, I read late into the night, until I couldn't stay awake anymore. I couldn't read them during the day—it was too hard to put
them down, and the one time I tried, I was cross with the girls afterward because all I wanted was to be reading again. So after dinner,
once Heather and Eve were asleep, I sat in the living room in the same
Morris chair that my father had loved, and I read. Jack wandered in a
few times, asking when I was coming to bed and pointing out that it
wasn't as though I had a deadline here. Once he stood behind me for
a moment, and I could hear the evenness of his breathing, a sound
I loved.

"I miss you," he said, his voice low.

"I'm right here," I said, and I reached for his hand.

"You're miles away," he said, and he left the room.

I ignored his loneliness. The one thing I wanted was to finish reading, and in as few sittings as possible.

It was Monday night when I started reading. Late, late Thursday night, I finished. It was a little after three o'clock in the morning. The last entry was something my father wrote in February of 1954, after his release from Ward Road, when he was trying to gain permission to stay in Hong Kong. *Hard to say what will happen next*, he wrote. *Once again, my life is unraveling, and I don't see where things will end up. I have no home anymore. I am forbidden from returning to Shanghai, the one place I love. I am forgotten if not despised by my wife and daughter, the only people I truly love, and I am only starting to see what my mistakes will cost me.*

I tried to imagine his voice—the rhythm of it, his inflection, his emphasis—and I closed my eyes, picturing him. A man stands on the verandah of his home, looking out at the city that he loves and calls home, wondering if the talk is true. A year later he carries suitcases to his car, and he tells his wife and daughter good-bye. He tries to imagine joining them, but he knows it will break him. His city changes under the rule of strangers, and he is ordered to leave. He doesn't; he is taken prisoner, and when he is eventually released and returned to his family in their faraway home, he knows he should be glad. He plants things in the hope of soothing his soul and of forgetting what he has seen. He grows gardenias and narcissus for scent, bougainvillea and wisteria for color, roses for love. And eucalyptus for the girl, so that she will remember him. He works silently, and he answers his daughter's questions when he can. But he cannot stay in that distant land, and when he parts from his family a second time, he knows they will never live as a family again.

Christmas, years later. He is imprisoned again. He lies in his cell and listens to the great sigh in the building when the lights go off, a sound he cannot describe, a sound he will never forget. He is sick, he is nearly starved, he spends a year alone. He repeats the priest's words, again and again, his only refuge: *Blessed are the poor in spirit, for theirs is the kingdom of heaven. Blessed are the meek of heart, for they shall inherit the earth.*

The man is exiled from the city he loves, forbidden ever to return. His wife has divorced him. His daughter does not know him. He has lost everything. When his former wife dies, he feels he will never recover. He walks down a short aisle and kneels at a casket, leans forward, kisses, kneels and prays. When he sees his daughter, he sees hope. It is the possibility of winning her back—of her forgiveness—that sustains him.

I put my father's words aside. I had never come close to imagining what had happened to him, and the revelation of it cut through me. I began to weep, and although I had cried every day since his death not even two weeks before, I didn't cry out of grief that night. It was not the huge hole his absence had made in my life. I wept for my father, for his life, and for his loss.

:: :: ::

A month after my father's death, I received in the mail a certificate notifying me of the scattering of his ashes: *I, Patrick Freyne, master of the vessel New Dawn on the date of 8 in the month June of the year 1961 did proceed and engage in the scattering of the cremains of Joseph Schoene in the Pacific Ocean, at latitude North 34:47:86 longitude West 122:36:09. The time being 10:23 A.M., the prevailing weather conditions at the time were clear skies and calm seas.*

At night, when I lay awake and missed my father and regretted things I hadn't said and done, I imagined his ashes drifting closer and closer to China, his home, and I felt a part of myself drifting further and further away from my family.

I had started to sink by then. I felt far away from everyone, and a kind of numbness was the closest thing I felt to peace. I made lists of regrets in my mind, and I blamed myself for not knowing who he was—what he'd been through, and how he was living. *He was your father,* I thought. *How could you have let him live like that? How could you not have known?* In my mind, I apologized to him over and over and over again, but I felt no peace, only a sort of sinking down into loss, like settling at the bottom of the sea.

:: :: ::

That sinking feeling lasted for nearly a year. I was distant with Jack, distracted around my daughters, who had to tell me things several times to get my attention. Jack was, for the most part, patient. Though there were times when I saw anguish in his expression, he mostly tried to let me go, and seemed certain that eventually I would be all right.

Time slowed down, and I felt as though I lived a different kind of existence than everyone else. Nothing seemed real, nothing was important, nothing mattered. Nothing inspired joy in me; there was nothing I looked forward to. And although I could see how much my remoteness hurt my family, there was nothing I could do to change it. All I could do, I thought, was wait.

While I waited, I read about Shanghai. I read and reread the journals, I read the books he'd left me, I read everything about Shanghai that I could find in the Pasadena Library. I dreamed about it, I imagined it, I worked at picturing the things my father had experienced. But it was all so distant, as though I were reading about something I'd made up. Even my father seemed made up at times. I could not remember his voice, or his laugh, and it pulled at me.

:: :: ::

In April, eleven months after my father's death, I began to feel a change. One night I woke at three o'clock in the morning, something I'd done often since my father's death. I no longer tried to fall back asleep. I just got out of bed and went into the kitchen to sit and stare out the window. The world was very beautiful at that hour, and the night usually comforted me. The darkness made things feel less painful, and God felt very near.

I'd been sitting by myself for perhaps half an hour when Heather, round and sturdy and sure of herself at five and a half, wandered into the kitchen as casually as though it were breakfast time. She walked to me and climbed into my lap, then sat back almost luxuriously, so at home and with such a strong and obvious sense of entitlement that I smiled.

"What's the matter?" she said matter-of-factly.

"I miss Pop," I said. "I'm still getting used to him not being here."

She nodded knowingly and I considered again an idea that my daughters made me consider frequently: that we are born with a certain kind of knowingness that diminishes with age. "I know," she said. "It was too soon for him to go."

I nodded, too, for I couldn't speak. Her answer made my throat and chest tight.

We were quiet for a moment, and the solidness of the fifty pounds of her against my body was more comfort than I had expected or hoped for. Suddenly she turned to me and took my face in her hands, which was what she did when she really wanted me to listen. She looked me in the eye and her eyes were of a deep dark blue-green that was like the ocean, darker than my father's but similar in their intensity. The only light was from the streetlight that spilled in through the window, and her eyes were shining in that way that children's eyes do when they know a secret. Then she whispered, "I bought you a present."

I smiled. "Why? It's not my birthday."

"I just did," she said, and she shrugged. "Gran took me shopping, and I saw it, and I wanted to give it to *you*." She touched my chest with her fingers as she said *you*. She paused and seemed to consider me. "Do you want it now?" she asked.

"Do you *want* to give it to me now?"

She nodded. "I think it would cheer you up."

I said, "Maybe it would."

She stood up and walked to the kitchen drawers. She squatted next to them and pulled out the bottom drawer, the junk drawer that I always planned on sorting. Then she reached toward the back, past a hammer and pliers and twine and I didn't know what else, and she took something out. "I knew you wouldn't find it here," she said.

"You were right."

She walked back to me and held out a small cardboard box. I took it and kissed her cheek and whispered, "Thank you."

"Don't say thank you," she said. "You don't even know what it is."

I opened the box.

Inside was a small ivory elephant, so much like the one that I bought with my father when I was a child that I caught my breath, thinking it was the same one. It wasn't; when I held it up to the light, I saw that it was a little larger, and slightly darker, and less intricately carved. But it still felt familiar, and the feeling left me shaken.

Heather was silent as I looked at her gift, and finally she pulled on the sleeve of my robe. "Don't you like it?"

"I love it," I said, and I held her to me. "I love it very much." I looked at her carefully and smoothed her hair from her forehead. "Why did you pick him?"

"Gran said that he was from China and that he was good luck. And I said that *you're* from China and that *you're* good luck. So I thought you went together."

I nodded. "Why am I good luck?"

She looked at me with disbelief. "You don't know?"

I shook my head.

"Because you're here and you make me happy," she said.

She climbed back into my lap and laid her head against my chest, and I felt her breathing, even and deep. The feeling calmed me, and I remembered my father, coming into my room when I was a child, to watch me sleep. The thought that I had in some way comforted him, just as my daughter was comforting me, made me feel peaceful. And I thought to him, *I understand.*

Then, as suddenly as the appearance of an unexpected guest, I felt him near. It was as though he stood perhaps two feet away from me, just to my left. *Old Spice*, I thought. *Four Roses, Philippine cigars.* In my mind, I could see his cropped blond hair, his blue eyes, his bearish stance. He wore the old jeans that he gardened in, and a white T-shirt underneath his maroon corduroy shirt. It had a zipper at the neck, which was always hot when I took it from the dryer when I did his laundry for him.

I had not felt his presence in all those months, not waking or sleeping, and I stayed very still, holding Heather, who had fallen asleep in my lap. He seemed as close as my heartbeat, as near as my breath, and I knew then that I was deeply and passionately and permanently loved by him. That knowledge made something change inside of me. There was an odd shift in the balance of my heart, and on that quiet night, I felt blessed to have been his child.

epilogue

APRIL 1981. On my fiftieth birthday, the seventeenth of January, I received a gift of tickets for the third time in my life. This time it was two tickets to Shanghai, a gift from my husband and my daughters, though only Heather and I will go. Jack is something of a homebody, and leaving Flintridge, where he is head of the history department, is not easy in the middle of the semester. Eve takes after her father—and her namesake—and gets nervous when she is away from home, even at twenty-six. There is an ethereal quality to her that makes her attachment to this earth and its things tenuous at best. She has my mother's deep brown eyes, her even temper, and her love of order, and she can gaze at you in a way that makes you wonder what she knows about you.

Heather is a different story. She is and always has been the adventurer and entrepreneur. As a child she was the lemonade-seller, the scrounger of quarters from underneath the cushions of the living-room sofa, the inventor and doer of endless household chores in the name of earning another dime, which she would spend as fast as she could, as though buying things was a competition. At twenty-four, she is just a year older than my father was when he returned to China in 1930. Sometimes the expression on her face has an intensity that is so like him that I am startled, and I have to stare for a moment to bring her back into focus.

The tickets were Heather's idea. She was the one who did the research and planning, and it will be the two of us really going. The other two have assured us that they will be with us in spirit. We leave in the morning, and I have said my good-byes, which felt important, even though we will be gone for only two weeks. Last night I visited my grandmother. She will be ninety-six next month, and she is the most beautiful person I have ever known. Although her body is weak and she requires live-in care, her mind is sharp, and she, more than anyone, understands what it means for me to return to Shanghai. When I kissed her cheek, she held my face in her hands and looked me in the eye. "Look for the best part of them," she whispered. "Don't dwell on the rest of it. They loved you dearly." I nodded. "I know," I said. For a strange thing has happened as I've aged: I have felt my parents' love more strongly every year, even with them gone.

So now it is Heather and me. She arranged for our visas, and page seven of my passport shows my tourist visa from the Consulate-General of the People's Republic of China. We will fly to Hong Kong on Cathay Pacific Air. From there we will board the passenger ship *Jinjiang* to Shanghai, a journey that will take fifty-eight hours—three days and two nights. She wanted me to approach Shanghai in a familiar way, from the water, not the air. We will disembark at the International Passenger Terminal to the east of what is now the Shanghai Mansions, but what used to be the Broadway Mansions, where my father and I looked down on the city so many years ago. After two weeks, we will leave for Los Angeles from the Shanghai International Terminal, a good decision, I think. It would be difficult to leave by sea a third time, too slow and too painful.

bo caldwell

I have read the guidebooks. I know the city will be much changed from the city of my childhood. The books say that the run-down buildings give the city a feeling of decay and neglect. The city is crowded, and its roads and houses and factories are decades old. I read that tipping is forbidden in China, and I smile as I remember my father's painstaking efforts at cumshaw wherever he went. As a result of Pinyin, the system of romanization introduced by the People's Republic in 1958, even the names are changed. The Whangpoo is the Huangpu, Nanking Road is Nanjing Lu, and Hungjao is Hongqiao, though its villas and estates are still the favored homes of foreigners and diplomats.

A few things are still there. The Old City remains, where Chu Shih bought the ingredients he used to heal us—ginseng, pilose antler, tiger bone wine. The Cathay, where my mother loved the tea dances, is still a hotel, though it is now called the Peace Hotel, and the Park Hotel remains also, on that corner across from the Race Course— the People's Square now, and the seat of city government—where my father was kidnapped.

And there is the Bund. It is there, the books say, that you will find hints at Shanghai's past. Though today it is called Zhongshan Dong Yi Lu, and although the busier wharfs are no longer there, the buildings are much the same, and if you start at Waibaidu Bridge—the Garden Bridge—you can walk along the waterfront past European-style buildings and imagine what the city used to be like. A paragraph describes the former occupants of the Bund, and I can hear my father's voice as I read the list: *the British Consulate, the Russian Consulate, the NYK Line, the Banque de l'Indochine, the Glenn Line, Jardine Matheson, the Cathay Hotel, the Palace Hotel, all the way down the Bund to the Shanghai Club.*

In the old guidebook that my father left me, I find listed the Chinese names that Chu Shih used for the seasons, and I see that early April, when we are traveling, would be called *ch'ingming*, pure brightness. I find the phrase fitting. To be able to return to one's past, to visit a place where much was lost but also gained, is a gift, a gift of pure brightness. And I am ready.